THE PASSENGER

Frank Willard

First published by Dog Ear Publishing
4010 W. 86th Street, Ste H
Indianapolis, IN 46268
www.dogearpublishing.net

dog ear PUBLISHING

ISBN: 978-1-4575-3172-9

Library of Congress Control Number: has been applied for

This book is printed on acid-free paper.

This book is a work of fiction. Places, events, and situations in this book are purely fictional and any resemblance to actual persons, living or dead, is coincidental.

Printed in the United States of America

PEELING PAINT

Diana's anxiety had been growing worse by the month, the week, the day; and now it was growing worse by the hour and minute and second. Things didn't add up, at least they didn't add up to anything good. Her husband's employer was evil; all of them in that garish villa were evil, all of them were rotten to the core. Did they even have a core? Did they even have a real heart beating in their chest? Did real blood flow in their veins and arteries? Or was their blood green-blue, the color of antifreeze? Did they even have veins and arteries? Did they have a soul? Did they have a spirit? And if they did have a spirit what kind of spirit was it? Evil! All of them! All of them were evil, evil, evil! And dangerous.

Diana's husband Max had taken the job as Pontius' chauffeur in good faith, first because he'd very much needed a job and second because the job had looked so good, so very good—-the schedule was easy, and the salary and benefits were fabulous. They'd never dreamed of having a cushy lifestyle like this.

But the neighbors in Berchtesgaden avoided Diana and Max; the neighbors had avoided them from the start. They avoided them alright...it was more than mere avoidance, though. It was more like shunning. Or it was as if they'd been quarantined. It was as if they had some terrible communicable disease and the neighbors were afraid of contracting it. The old lady of the house next door did wave back once; and then the old woman looked down and away and quickly retreated from the patio into her house. The woman never returned another wave, another greeting. When the woman or her husband would come out from their house onto their terrace it seemed they refused to look in the direction of Max's and Diana's house. None of the neighbors would look at Diana or Max except for a quick glance maybe.

If it weren't for the little church congregation Diana, and eventually Max, had begun to attend Diana might have gone insane...or she would have gone back to her family in Austria or back to Berlin. How many times had she told Max she would be happy with a fourth of the money Pontius paid him, she would be happy with less than that, even.

We can make ends meet, she'd told Max a dozen times. Please, let's get away from him. Let's get away from all of them. We don't have to live in fear like this. We can go back to a small apartment like the one we had for years, she reminded him. It was tiny with only one bathroom but we were happy, she'd said. Maybe I can go back to teaching and we can go back to a two bedroom, two bath apartment like the one we had after our first apartment. We could go live in a cabin in the forest. Please, let's just get away from this!

But 2008 had turned into 2009 and now it was 2010 already and Max had not listened—-he had not listened to her pleadings and warnings for two interminable years as Diana wondered if Max would return home in the evenings, as she wondered if there would be a Gestapo-like pounding on their door in Berchtesgaden in the middle of the night.

And for the better part of the last two years they had attended the tiny little church congregation of thirty-three souls and had together read from the Bible each evening and her husband had begun to read it more and more and more by himself and, with his marker, highlight verses and, with his ball-point pen, underline words. He would spend two or three hours on the internet every night, taking notes and checking those notes with the words in the Bible and telling her what he'd found and asking her if she agreed or disagreed.

And Diana would answer that it didn't matter so much, right now, if she agreed or disagreed with this point of view or that point of view or this interpretation or that interpretation about a particular passage or prophecy. What mattered was getting free of the clutches of Pontius and those devils in that house high upon the Watzmann. Time after time she would tell her husband that he could research all those things, all those prophecies elsewhere...the internet was everywhere, computers and smart phones and those new iPads were everywhere, she had joked.

But it wasn't a joke. They had to escape Berchtesgaden and Pontius or they would die, she told him, finally one night, as they lay in bed.

"If you are so certain about this why don't you tell the pastor or tell one of the others? It might be good for you to tell someone besides me...it might be therapeutic."

It was quiet for two minutes as she considered the idea.

Then she said, "No. And I don't need therapy."

"Of course you don't...sorry."

"I won't tell them because I don't want to put them in danger..."

"Danger?" he asked.

"Yes, danger," she replied. Again it was quiet for two minutes. "And..."

He took another thirty seconds to reply to her "and..."

"And?"

"And even if I did tell them I'm not sure if they would believe me. I have no proof. I have only feelings. I have only my intuition. It's not enough."

"What does your intuition say?"

"That he, that they are weird and evil..."

Max took his wife's hand and held it gently. "Yes, they're evil...and weird...we know that don't we...but what else does your intuition tell you?"

Diana rolled toward him and said, "You have spent enough time studying the prophets, the apostles, and the Apocalypse, and hours on the internet, checking all those blogs and websites and their conspiracy theories and whether or not they match up with the words in the Bible. And you have been telling me everything. And I believe you! Why don't you tell me what my intuition might be saying?"

It was so quiet in the bedroom. It was so quiet in the grand house. It was such a quiet winter night in Berchtesgaden. It was almost quiet enough for their thoughts to be heard. The grandfather clock downstairs chimed. It was 23:00.

She waited for him to reply.

"You don't think...you aren't saying..." His voice trailed off and stopped as though he was afraid of the rest of his words.

"The passenger...they way you described him...and Pontius...and the others...none of it makes any sense... unless..."

Now she, too, was afraid of her words. So she didn't say them.

He turned out the light and said it was late and he was very tired and good night.

Five minutes later he turned on the light again and told her he planned to work for Pontius another year or so...by that time they would have a nice stash of euros. It was true because they'd been living on less than half the salary of 200,000 per year.

Then he added, "In one year or a bit longer we will have 300,000 euros or maybe even more. We can go live in Berlin. You like it there. You could teach again. I could find something to take up my time. Maybe some rich fellow in Berlin needs a chauffeur. It's going to be all right."

Diana echoed Max's last line, "It's going to be all right." And then she sighed out her next line, "And if it's not...all right?"

His answer came quickly, as if he'd rehearsed it. "We will withdraw our money and leave the country. We can go to Switzerland or Spain or Brazil or

Mexico...we can go the United States...to America or Canada. We could ask for political asylum."

"Political asylum?"

Now it was his turn to sigh. "I know. It would be difficult to prove."

"It would be impossible, "she said, knowing she was right.

"Well, we can't worry about that now, can we?"

"No, not now..." she said. "Turn out the light. We need our sleep," she said.

The next morning after breakfast, Max held Diana to his chest and kissed her forehead.

"I must go...I have to drive Pontius to Munich."

"Munich again?"

"He has another conference there...I will be back tomorrow afternoon...he has another conference at the villa tomorrow night...it's 120 kilometers to Munich." He didn't have to tell her how far it was to Munich. Of course she knew how far it was to Munich.

"It seems he has a conference nearly every day now." She said it as she studied his face.

"I will call on the other cell phone."

"The other cell..." She kept studying his face and asked, "Do you really think he doesn't know?"

"He's never seen or heard me use it."

"My husband the optimist..."

"No, not an optimist, a realist...he knows nothing about the other phone."

She looked down at his midsection. The razor-thin cell phone would be there inside a tiny Velcro-sealed pocket inside his boxer shorts. He'd sewn all those tiny pockets inside all his shorts a year ago as his fears, too, had begun to grow. But his fears weren't as great as hers, at least not yet.

She reached out and graced the spot with her fingertips. The cell was right there. It would be turned off. He only turned it on when he called her. And she would never call him unless it was a dreadful emergency akin to a nuclear attack or something maybe worse. If Pontius found out about the other cell phone he would be very displeased. She knew he would take revenge somehow.

Max sensed his wife's light, finger-tip touch and smiled a confirming smile. "Yes darling, the phone is there as always."

Then he asked her, "And what do you have planned for this fine, drizzly, dark day in winter?"

"Food shopping...plus I'm going to paint the windowsill above the kitchen sink...the paint has been peeling...it looks bad...I want to fix it...whoever painted it the last time did a poor job of it. I'm going to scrape it down good this time and lay on two thick coats that won't peel for ten years...maybe longer."

"I'm sure it will not," Max agreed with a sparkle in his eyes.

Diana declared, "The next occupants of this house won't have to deal with peeling paint at all." Her eyes, too, were twinkling a little...this small talk about house paint was almost amusing. It would be good if they could have small talk more often and tell jokes more often and laugh like they did before moving to Berchtesgaden.

"You are right. The paint you are about to lay down on the windowsill will last." He hugged her once more and said, "Ten years is a long time...but we will be long gone before ten years have expired."

The cute little exchange about paint and the reassurance from her husband was no help. If only they could leave tomorrow...once he'd returned from Munich. If only he didn't have to go to Munich today. She had a bad, bad feeling about it.

Diana watched Max and the black Mercedes pass through the automatic wrought iron gate, turn right and disappear into the narrow, tree-lined street in their posh section of Berchtesgaden. She stood watching at the window in a semi daze as the drizzle thickened into rain and made a tapping sound on the glass. Her mind was once more flooded with a thousand thoughts about Pontius and his weird servants, all of them living up there in that weird villa high upon the Watzmann.

She took a deep, determined breath, centered herself and mentally planned her day.

After food shopping she would change into a pair of baggy jeans and an old sweatshirt, the perfect uniform for house painting. She wanted to finish the job as soon as possible so there would be time left for her to go to the sports club. She needed to swim some laps and relieve her stress, a little of it anyway.

The rain had become a waterfall. The wipers on the windshield of the silver BMW 650i Coupe, another benefit from her husband's employment, could scarcely keep up with the deluge. Diana leaned forward over the top of the steering wheel to find her way down the blurry street that would take her to their street and to their house. Water gushed inside the wheel wells; the front fender was pushing water away from the car like it was the bow on a small boat.

It would be snowing in the mountains. The skiing would be fantastic tomorrow. Perhaps Max could take a few days off and they could go skiing. Perhaps if they were skiing he would be more relaxed and more able to listen to reason.

She pressed the button and the automatic gate opened and she pressed a second button and the automatic garage door slid upward. She slowed the car and came to a halt and pressed the buttons once more, one for the gate the other for the garage door. Being out of the rain storm and sealed in like this didn't make her feel safer.

She took another deep breath, turned off the engine, and popped the trunk lid and ferried the four bags of groceries to the kitchen. As she put things away she eyed the peeling paint. Yeah it would be good to fix that. It wouldn't take too long, maybe two hours? After she'd finished the job she would definitely go to the sports club and swim laps. She needed to undo this stress.

She changed into her work uniform—-the old baggy jeans and sweatshirt. She draped the small canvas tarp over the tap and the sink and the counter space beneath the windowsill. She fished out the scraper from the little box of tools. She was ready.

She was gripping the handle too tightly. Her knuckles were too white and underneath her fingernails the tissue was too red. Her wrists were too tense and so were her forearms. She was clenching her teeth, too. Her heart was beating so hard inside her chest it might jump out.

This must be what a panic attack feels like.

Slow down, okay? Breathe...breathe through your nose, she said to herself over and over. She sat down on one of the kitchen chairs. She calmed herself by talking to herself, telling herself that she would be all right, that her husband, too, would be all right.

She came to her feet. She felt better. She was okay. This had never happened before but she knew she was okay, at least for now.

The peeling paint was falling from the scraper in rubbery chunks onto the small tarp atop the sink and counter. Whoever had used this kind of cheap paint did not know what they were doing.

The last twenty centimeters were a little harder to remove. She would have to use a more delicate touch while still keeping the same pressure. She had to be careful. She didn't want to gouge the fine woodwork now revealed. She didn't want to score it up or she would have to patch it with wood putty and that would add time to this project. She still wanted to go for a long swim. It would help her relax and sleep better.

She lifted the last ten or so centimeters with one last scrape and the paint scrolled beautifully onto the blade. She shook it loose onto the tarp. She grabbed a rag and brushed away any bits of paint or debris. Now she would do a light sanding and then lay down the good stuff...the right kind of paint that wouldn't peel for at least ten years.

The letters and what must be words written, engraved into the wood caught her eye but didn't register in her brain, at first.

She blinked. She focused. She leaned over the windowsill. She studied the letters, the words. She was an archeologist reading the Rosetta Stone for the first time. She'd just discovered the Dead Sea Scrolls. She blinked once more and forced her mind to wrap itself around them.

Ja Farbe abziehend.

"Yes, peeling paint."

???

There were more words.

schauen Sie unter Eckfußbodenfliese im Vorlagenbad

"Look- under-corner-floor-tile-in-master-bath." She read the words one by one.

Look under corner floor tile in master bath. She repeated the words one by one in her mind.

All right, she would go there now and look. And she could guess which one it was; it was the loose one in the left corner, the one she'd planned to fix. It was another repair job she'd put off.

She knelt and slipped the fingers of both hands under the loosened tile. The tile gave her no difficulty.

Clearly, it had been loosened on purpose. Most of the cement had been scraped away. The tile had been resting free with so little adhesion. The only things holding it in place were a couple of strips of some kind of cheap glue. It appeared to have been a job done in haste.

She saw nothing.

There was nothing under the tile...nothing except the traces of cement and glue.

She set it in place once more and heard the crinkling sound, like paper crinkling...no, it was plastic crinkling.

She turned over the tile.

Someone had flattened a sandwich bag and taped it to the backside of the tile.

She removed the tape and took the little plastic bag into her hands and slid the zip-loc to the side, opening it.

She took out the contents: a folded page, a photograph...a man's wedding band and a woman's diamond ring and wedding band.

It was a middle-aged couple. Like Diana and Max this couple, too, looked like they had once been very attractive and still were somewhat attractive despite their age.

She set the rings on the floor next to her. She unfolded the page.

> If you are reading this you likely fixed the peeling paint on the windowsill in the kitchen. Yes, even peeling paint can serve some purpose.
>
> There is little time. My husband and I will be brief and to the point.
>
> The man is going to try to kill us. And you can be sure he will try to kill you. We are leaving Berchtesgaden and this house tonight.
>
> We leave our wedding rings as a sign and symbol that what we say is true. If he finds us at least he'll not get our rings.
>
> We regret ever coming here. We regret every euro he paid my husband.
>
> He is a devil. My husband has been shaken to the core of his being and so have I. We now know he has eliminated every previous employee once he suspects they know too much. It is nothing more than a game to him. He enjoys the chase between the hunter and the hunted. It is all some kind of twisted, perverted amusement.
>
> What goes on in that villa is beyond anything ever imagined. It must be so.
>
> Please leave this place too. Save yourselves.

Diana refolded the page and tucked it inside the sandwich bag along with the photo. She tucked the rings into her pocket. Later, she would put them in a safer place among her things. She would help make sure that Pontius did not get the rings. She whispered a prayer for the couple in the photograph, another chauffeur and his wife. She prayed they'd escaped and were living happily somewhere.

She was surprised how calm she was. All doubt was gone, now. This was confirmation. This was the Almighty telling them, shouting at them: Leave! Go away! Save yourselves!

Diana would go to the sports club and swim at least 2k. And then she would return to this house and wait for her husband's call. He always called around 23:00 hours.

She would tell him everything...

Her husband would know what to do next...

And...

And tomorrow they would be free...

THE PASSENGER

PART ONE

REVELATION 13

1 *And I stood upon the sand of the sea, and saw a beast rise up out of the sea,* having seven heads and ten horns, and upon his horns ten crowns, and upon his heads the name of blasphemy.

2 And the beast which I saw was like unto a leopard, and his feet were as the feet of a bear, and his mouth as the mouth of a lion: and the dragon gave him his power, and his seat, and great authority.

3 And I saw one of his heads as it were wounded to death; and his deadly wound was healed: and all the world wondered after the beast.

4 And they worshipped the dragon which gave power unto the beast: and they worshipped the beast, saying, Who is like unto the beast? who is able to make war with him?

5 And there was given unto him a mouth speaking great things and blasphemies; and power was given unto him to continue forty and two months.

6 And he opened his mouth in blasphemy against God, to blaspheme his name, and his tabernacle, and them that dwell in heaven.

7 And it was given unto him to make war with the saints, and to overcome them: and power was given him over all kindreds, and tongues, and nations.

8 And all that dwell upon the earth shall worship him, whose names are not written in the book of life of the Lamb slain from the foundation of the world.

9 If any man have an ear, let him hear.

10 He that leadeth into captivity shall go into captivity: he that killeth with the sword must be killed with the sword. Here is the patience and the faith of the saints.

[11]*And I beheld another beast coming up out of the earth*; and he had two
horns like a lamb, and he spake as a dragon.

[12]And he exerciseth all the power of the first beast before him, and
causeth the earth and them which dwell therein to worship the first
beast, whose deadly wound was healed.

[13]And he doeth great wonders, so that he maketh fire come down from
heaven on the earth in the sight of men,

[14]And deceiveth them that dwell on the earth by the means of those
miracles which he had power to do in the sight of the beast; saying to
them that dwell on the earth, that they should make an image to the
beast, which had the wound by a sword, and did live.

[15]And he had power to give life unto the image of the beast, that the
image of the beast should both speak, and cause that as many as would
not worship the image of the beast should be killed.

[16]And he causeth all, both small and great, rich and poor, free and
bond, to receive a mark in their right hand, or in their foreheads:

[17]And that no man might buy or sell, save he that had the mark, or the
name of the beast, or the number of his name.

[18]Here is wisdom. Let him that hath understanding count the number
of the beast: for it is the number of a man; and his number is *Six hun-
dred threescore and six.*

MURDER, MYSTICISM AND IMMORALITY

Sam Keen, author of "Fire in the Belly," gave the closing plenary message:

"...there was very strong agreement that religious institutions have to take primary responsibility for the population explosion...cut the population by 90 percent and there aren't enough people left to do a great deal of ecological damage."

The applause was deafening!

Kill millions of people? How? What happened to love, compassion, and concern for the poor? These leaders had called for poverty programs, gun control, and global financial redistribution as if they wanted to save lives. Were these schemes simply a stepping stone toward global control? Did no one care about the individual lives behind the faceless masses?

—Berit Kjos
Excerpt from her report on the *State of the World Conference*
sponsored by Mikhail Gorbechev, September 17, 1995.

"Finally there was Nietzsche's prophecy of the coming elite who would rule the world and from whom the superman would spring. In *The Will to Power* he exclaims: 'A daring and ruler race is building itself up...' The aim should be to prepare a transvaluation of values for a particularly strong kind of man, most highly gifted in intellect and will. This man and the elite around him will become the 'lords of the earth.'"

-William Shirer
The Rise and Fall of the Third Reich; page 100.

"The Hitlerian myth can be understood only if viewed in the context of the particular philosophical system that produced it, which is itself but one link in an historical tradition going back over centuries. Those who induced Germany to embrace the swastika are not dead. They are still among us, just as they have been in every era, and doubtless will continue to be until the Apocalypse. National Socialism was for them but a means, and Hitler was but an instrument. The *undertaking* failed. What they are now trying to do is revive the myth using other means."

—Jean-Michel Angebert
The Occult and the Third Reich

"And Caesar's spirit, ranging for revenge,
With Ate by his side come hot from hell,
Shall in these confines with a monarch's voice
Cry 'Havoc,' and let slip the dogs of war;
That this foul deed shall smell above the earth
With carrion men, groaning for burial."

—William Shakespeare

"Such subtle covenants shall be made
Till peace itself is war in masquerade."

—John Dryden

CHAPTER 1

6 June 2008
Wolfgang Amadeus Airport
Salzburg, Austria

Under the crystal-clear Bavarian night sky, under the full moon rising over the jagged mountains to the east, the black Mercedes-Benz S-Class 4-door sedan's headlights cut a wide v-shaped swath through the cool air, lighting up the tarmac as the car drew near to the Gulf Stream V and came to a halt. Two shadowy figures, suddenly illuminated by the Mercedes' lights, stirred at the top of the stairway that came down from the door of the jet.

The Mercedes' arrival was the cue for two perfectly-proportioned, Nordic-looking attendants with high cheekbones and military haircuts under black berets and dressed in immaculate uniforms of gray, single-breasted tunics atop perfectly-pressed black trousers tucked into black, knee-high jackboots to descend those stairs from the plane, and walk in sync, shoulder to shoulder, to the car. Maximilian, the chauffeur, once a military man himself, admired their precision. But Max hated the jackboots; he despised the jackboots. The jackboots made them look like Nazis. Max's hatred for Nazis trumped all his other hates.

"You will remain here," the passenger said, *matter-of-factly.*

One of the attendants stepped out of formation, opened the rear right-side door and held it, waiting for the passenger to exit. The passenger stepped out and stood stiff and erect. The attendant that had opened the door closed it behind the passenger and joined his equal. Both stood side by side at attention and waited.

The passenger gave them a slightly-abbreviated version of a Roman salute to which the attendants replied with a vigorous, full Roman salute of their own. The salute gave Max a momentary sick feeling in the middle of his gut.

The passenger moved toward the jet. In lockstep, the attendants followed him a few paces back. They waited at the base of the stairway until he had entered the airplane before pivoting in sync and returning to the car, once again in lockstep, to retrieve the passenger's luggage, black raincoat, and fedora.

One of the attendants pounded two times on the trunk with his black-gloved fist. It was the signal for the chauffeur to open it. Max pressed the button and the trunk popped up automatically. It was all right with him to stay seated in the car. Let them do the work.

A suitcase in one hand and the stairway railing in the other, the attendants trotted, one behind the other, up the steps. It was amazing that neither one showed the slightest amount of effort—-their jackboots did not miss one step, the attendants seemed to float upward hardly letting the soles of their jackboots touch the steps; they must have wings in those jackboots or rotating propeller blades like a hovercraft would have.

Max wrinkled his forehead a little and narrowed his eyes as he analyzed what he'd just seen...

...those bags weighed at least thirty kilograms apiece. Max blinked and focused and kept trying to understand what he was seeing.

Before entering the cabin, the second attendant paused a second and looked toward the Mercedes and the chauffeur. Max thought the attendant was, at that moment, more like an eagle or a hawk and possessed the vision of one of those birds of prey. Plus with a hooked nose like that, the man could very well pass for a hawk. Max could swear the attendant was staring like that to intimidate him; the attendant seemed to have a kind of snarl on his clean-shaved face. His right upper lip seemed to be curled back a little and the man was showing a fang like a wolf.

Now the second attendant, too, entered the jet. The stairway retracted and the door closed, sealing the cabin shut.

The whole thing was a well-rehearsed operation that had taken no more than ninety seconds from start to finish, intimidating look included...wolf's fang included.

Max ran his eyes along the length of the jet, studying it—-it was another bird of prey, a gigantic raptor waiting to leap from a branch and catch the wind and soar higher and higher and higher to spot a target and make the kill. The giant bird glittered all silver and white in the soft moonlight, its marker and navigational lights rotating and blinking, its twin jet engines revving up and whirring. The flaps were rolling out and down into takeoff position. The jet was unmarked except for the black serial number and letters on its flanks —-XB20041889.

Max was relieved to see him go...the grouchy passenger had sat silently there in his place in the back seat for the last fifteen minutes. He'd said he was tired of listening to Beethoven's Piano Sonata Op.27 No. 2—-Moonlight Sonata—-and didn't wish to hear it again. He'd told Max, the chauffeur, that he didn't want any more music, that it was quite enough. And he'd said it in perfect east coast American English, the presumptuous kind spoken by Ivy League academics. Max had noticed that kind of English before when he watched American television programs and news.

The passenger had turned moody—-sullen, cranky, morose, angry, glum, gloomy, dour, depressed and restless; the sullen, cranky, and restless passenger had sat there as Max watched him via the rear view mirror. A few times the passenger had taken a deep breath and let it out quickly as if to expel whatever it was inside his chest that was making him so tight. He had zippered his lips into a thin, straight line and looked out the window, with his steely, unblinking eyes, at the passing Bavarian countryside laid out under the moon. His hands were fidgety as if they were about to search for a pill that should be in the bottle in the medicine cabinet but wasn't.

Their eyes had met again a few kilometers back, collided as it were; but this time the passenger looked away as if he had no time for eye games. In an impatient tone he'd asked once or twice or thrice how far it was, yet, to the airport. He was a spoiled, petulant child asking his overindulgent mother how long it would be before they arrived at their destination. The passenger's bad temperament could be catching if a man wasn't careful.

By the time they pulled up to the Gulf Stream V, Max wanted to choke the ill-tempered passenger but thought better of it. He didn't want to risk the 200,000 euros per year salary that Pontius paid him and he most certainly didn't want to do jail time for a creep like this.

On the other hand, giving up his 200,000 euros per year might be a decent trade-off for choking the little jerk. It angered Max that the little jerk had so easily managed to bring out the worst in him in a period of less than an hour during the trip from Pontius' house to the airport in Salzburg...but just now, as Max had watched him exit the car and be escorted to the stairway by the two-man honor guard and ascend the steps to the waiting open door on the jet, the passenger had managed to bring out the best in Maximilian—-for a moment or two Maximilian had once again returned to his Germanic-Austrian-Aryan sense of nobility and greatness. He'd once again dreamed of things grand and glorious, and of flawlessly-tailored suits, fine cuisine, beautiful women and Mozart, Beethoven, and Bach.

But the image of Max's father would always appear in his head whenever he felt a wave of grandiosity. It was the image of father showing him the photos from the war and father weeping then, his neck bowed and his shoulders rounded, the few tears trickling out from behind his wire-rimmed glasses.

Another image would appear, right afterward; it was the scene from the pall bearers carrying father's simple wooden coffin under the wrought iron archway to the graveyard. It was winter, the ground was frozen, and the snow was thin and swirling about, leaving broad, bare patches among the tombstones.

The jet was turning now and heading for the end of the runway. Max would wait. He loved airplanes, especially jets. He loved to watch takeoffs and landings.

His father would take him to the Flughafen, the airport near Linz, when he was a young boy. Father had loved airplanes, too.

The Gulfstream V rotated and grabbed the air above runway 34 and went into a steep ascent. The exhaust from the screaming engines glowed orange-red.

Max let out a long exhale as if he'd been forced to hold his breath under water for far too long and was so glad, so relieved to resurface. The passenger was gone and Max hoped never to see him again. Max took a long inhale and savored the new air.

The landing gear was retracting into the jet's belly as it was turning to the right, turning east.

East...

That was a curious direction for a jet carrying an *Amerikan back to Amerika.* A jet returning to *Amerika* would turn left after leaving runway 34, not right, not east.

Max's father had hated the direction...east. It was the direction of Stalingrad. It was the direction of Russia, and all the places where father had begun to take the photographs. It was the direction of Operation Barbarossa and of starving, bleeding, and freezing to death. It was the direction of the Gulag, the direction into which millions had disappeared during the war and after the war, when the Soviets had seized control of Eastern Europe.

Max's father had been one of the lucky ones. *Ja glücklich.* Yes lucky. After being wounded in the upper right leg during the fighting in Stalingrad he was evacuated to Germany to recover. Yes lucky; he had returned from the Eastern Front only to be sent to the Western Front once he was able to walk or run without too much of a limp.

West. Father had hated that direction, too. Father had become somewhat of a xenophobe and had not gone out much at all during those twenty years after the war...but he had managed to take his young son to the airport near Linz and go to his job in the bakery. Mother had had to work to make ends meet and would often say she'd wanted to have another child or two perhaps but there was no money, you see.

The lights on the jet were fading—-smaller and smaller and vanishing into the blue-black sky. Max grasped the ignition key and almost started the car. But he set down the keys and placed his hands in his lap and waited.

Something was making him wait and keep looking toward the jet even though he could no longer see it. And something was stirring deep inside him as his mind became a black and white film montage of father and his photographs and mother weeping because she would have no more children. In the montage was an image of her weeping once again, the day her son, her precious Maximilian, reported for service in the army. It was the last time Max saw her alive. She died a month later; she'd had cancer and not told anyone.

Max picked up the keys again and inserted them into the ignition. The Mercedes whirred delicately. He pressed a button and switched on the CD player and listened another time to Moonlight Sonata.

As he pulled away from the tarmac and headed toward the fence and the gate he looked once again to the east, knowing the jet was long out of sight but he looked anyway...and recited the letters and serial numbers.

"X-B-2-0-0-4-1-8-8-9."

CHAPTER 2

Pontius' chiseled face with its perfect Roman nose was pressed firmly to the lens of the multi-million euro telescope. He adjusted the focus and kept the Gulfstream V in the center of the view. His mind was filled with a thousand times a thousand ideas, strategies the passenger and he and their minions would use to subvert the world when the time came.

He enjoyed tracking the jet, he relished watching it streaking east and gaining altitude in the cool, clean air of the Bavarian summer night. He enjoyed the rotating, blinking lights. He loved reading the serial numbers and letters; he adored those numbers and letters. Pontius loved and adored all things from this New Age, from this neo-Greco, neo-Roman world; he enjoyed all things Bavarian, Austrian, Aryan, all things Germanic, all things cultured and civilized; he loved his life of luxury in his fabulous villa high upon the Watzmann high above Berchtesgaden; he loved his never-ending stream of money. He loved and relished and ravished Aryan women but would never marry one; his destiny was tied to the man's destiny; the man and he were too great for the confines of matrimony. Their *bride* was the world, the world they would control and *re-mold even more into their own image*; and that completely re-molded, re-created world would later be their *wife and vicariously the wife of the Angel of Light.* Meanwhile, Aryan women and their charms was simply another thing to be enjoyed in the endless fabric of this wonderful life. More to the point, in the world they were about to re-create there would be only Aryan women and plenty of them for Pontius to enjoy forever.

Indeed he adored all things Aryan. It was obvious this Aryan people, this race, Pontius' people and his race were chosen. Like him, these people had been smiled upon by the gods and set apart to rule the world forever. This race, led by the passenger and Pontius and the Angel of Light, would one day subjugate all other races; this Aryan race would soon be the incarnation of the eternal pantheon; this race with its higher, inner sense of spirituality would pave the way to the collective Aryans' higher self. Pontius had been born of this most-blessed, highly-intuitive, spiritual, hearty, northern, Aryan race and he was part of it again. And now he would be part of the final Aryan conquest. The ritual of the labyrinth and the replication of the wounds had confirmed it; the man opening the iron case had proved everything prophesied was true.

"*Wissen Sie, welcher Tag dieses, Pontius?*" the man had asked.

Of course, Pontius knew the answer. And of course, the man had asked the question rhetorically that day back in April—-that 20 April 2008 when the man had walked *das labyrinth. Hail Caesar! Hail the Angel of Light!*

And today was 6 June 2008.

6 June. How appropriate. Today was D-Day, the Allied landings in Normandy had happened on this day—-6 June 1944.

6 June, appropriate without a doubt because D-Day would soon be avenged and the correct order of things would be ushered in once more. D-Day would be avenged, and there would be revenge for the humiliation suffered in 1918 at the end of the First World War and revenge for the 1945 debacle of the Second World War, as well. Everything would be made right when they would meet once again, in the not-too-distant future, at the appointed time, *Wenn das Königreich unsere ist*, the man had said.

When the kingdom is ours. When this New Roman world and this New Age led by the Master Race of the Aryan People covers the earth everything would be grand and glorious as it should have been all along. If not for certain contrary forces, in the past, it would have been. Soon those negative forces would be eliminated. Soon Babylon would return and be ruled by the King of Babylon, a king like no other.

Pontius kept admiring the beauty and grace of the streaking Gulfstream V as he kept watching it through the lens. He wondered if the man might be looking back now, over his right shoulder, enjoying the view of the Obersalzberg and the Watzmann.

In minutes the jet would make a sharp left turn north to fly over Leonding and Linz, the places the man had known so well. And a few minutes after passing Linz and Leonding the jet would turn right again, east again, and pass over Vienna, another place the man had known. For him Vienna had been a place of suffering, starvation, and rejection; that too would be avenged.

Pontius owed everything to the man. The man had secured Pontius' release from hell.

Pontius had been there, in burning torment for two thousand years, ever since he had committed suicide and the two grave diggers buried him in a wood near his villa along the Italian-Austrian frontier near Tridentum the place of his birth.

When he'd arrived in hell he knew it was wrong; he did not deserve it; he had only done his duty; and he'd done it well. He'd done it despite the depression and misery those Jews had brought upon him, despite that fateful dream and, during the years following that dream, all the unspeakable nightmares his wife had suffered ever since that day he'd washed his hands with the water and pitcher and bowl and had the Centurion make that sign and nail it to the cross above the Galilean's head. Yes, Pontius like his wife had suffered nightmares, thousands of them. There had been no escaping the nightmares for either of them. They'd been placed under some kind of curse by those evil Jewish sorcerers, devils all.

After Pontius had resigned his position as the 5th Procurator of Judaea, Claudia and he had returned to their small villa outside Tridentum to a life of self-imposed obscurity and exile. They'd needed to get away from everyone and everything. They'd only desired a bit of tranquility, a time of peace to be alone and forget Judaea. But forgetting Judaea and the Jews had been impossible. Claudia had died of sorrow mixed with madness six months before Pontius took his own life with his sword.

And he'd loved his wife, Claudia Procula, he'd loved her dearly. He should have listened to her and her dream. He should have released that *King of the Jews*. He should have sent him packing, back to Nazareth; he could have provided an escort of twenty Roman soldiers. He should not have let those other Jews; those other rabble-rousers have their way. Pontius should not have gotten involved in one of their ridiculous family arguments. He should have put the entire Sanhedrin in the dungeon for a week to make them calm down. He should have put them down in that dirty dungeon and chained them together, ankle to ankle, with that Barabbas in the middle. It would have been entertaining for the guards to watch them squabble and fight over the thin porridge and molding bread.

The man, *the Anointed One, the New Caesar* was right. Everything bad can be traced to the Jews and nothing would ever be right until they were eliminated, they and all those favorable to them plus all other inferiors.

The man, the Anointed One, the *New Caesar* had spent thirty years in that more hellish sector of hell—-he'd been in *the abyss* contemplating what went wrong and how he would do it differently if given the chance. Pontius had spent two thousand years thinking similar thoughts. And then they *met*—-their disembodied spirits colliding and mingling and nearly exploding from their combined pent-up rage.

Pontius had tried to free himself from the ghastly entanglement, thinking it was yet another demonic spirit there to taunt him and make his torment even worse. But the man had refused to let go and with a grip as strong as an iron vice had taken Pontius by the arm, wrist and hand and pulled him upward into a fleeting shaft of green-blue light. He'd told Pontius to hang onto him because the shaft of light would only come once. It would never come again, he shouted.

The shaft was a tunnel, and at first the suffocating tunnel was so narrow they'd hardly fit side by side. But it widened and widened until it opened into a vast, vaporous ocean of brilliant, white light crisscrossed with orange-red veins and arteries of lightning flashing and flashing and flashing.

Upward and upward and upward they floated through the vapor and lightning until they entered another airy zone, a place full of angelic beings singing the most beautiful Roman anthem Pontius had ever heard. The indescribable music penetrated the spirit, it revived the heart, it was sweet like honey, it was healing ointment for one that had burned in hell for so long and now was free. The angels smiled the most beautiful smiles as Pontius and the man passed through them. And the angels were cheering, applauding, and dancing a most beautiful dance, a dance full of energy and other-worldly sensuality.

Some of the angels had taken them by the arm and escorted them, helping them to ascend to another zone, a place of total quiet. Then the celestial escorts left them alone and faded back into the ether.

There was no more lightning and no more thunder and no more singing. Suddenly, the man had let go of Pontius and, crying out with a voice resonating like a hundred waterfalls, announced to Pontius that he, the man, would be born nine months later...

"On 20 April 1975...the same day you will rise from your grave, Pontius!" the man screamed as he spun away and vanished.

And it *was indeed* on 20 April 1975. What the man had said was true. Pontius had risen from the dead that day; he had risen from the unknown grave in the unknown wood near their villa outside Tridentum. Only now Tridentum was Trento and the country was Italy. Only now Pontius could speak Italian, and German, and Spanish and French and every other language on planet earth in addition to Latin and Ancient and Modern Greek and Hebrew and Aramaic and Arabic.

And Pontius' body had not aged. It seemed he would perpetually be thirty-three...the same age he was the day he arose from that grave in the wood.

He kept watching the jet and kept remembering and kept thinking...and it came to him then, another bit of knowledge from the all-knowing one, the Angel of Light. Perhaps now he would begin to age, he would begin to move forward in time now that they had met again, on earth, and were destined to meet once more. *Wenn das Königreich unsere ist,* the man had said.

Pontius scoffed at the idea of aging, of getting old and dying. Why would it matter if he or the man were to age a bit? Once they'd gained the kingdom they would be eternal. They would be like God. Pontius had been in hell for almost two thousand years and the man had been there, in the abyss, in a hotter area, for thirty. But they'd both been paroled and this proved they were destined to be eternal; being in hell and getting released showed who they really were. They were everlasting, immortal messengers, they were prophets specially selected from all the prophets who had ever been born and lived and died.

The man and Pontius, Pontius and the man had been sent back, *they had been chosen by the Angel of Light* to be the supreme leaders in the Kingdom of Light...in the kingdom where the moon was in the seventh house. It could only be them to lead that kingdom; it could be no one else. Their immortality proved everything...and soon the entire world of inferiors would believe it was immortal, too. Let the inferiors believe it...let them become deluded...let them forget who the Master Race really was...when their guard was down due to their delusion the Master Race would smash them and take all the spoils.

The jet's lights had disappeared despite the power of the multi-million euro telescope...

That resurrection day in Trento, 20 April 1975, a man had approached Pontius on the Via Roma and given him bank account numbers in Geneva and told him a car would be along shortly. He told Pontius they would take him to his house high on the slopes of a mountain called the Watzmann, in Germany.

Pontius had not asked for an explanation. Every detail about this new world, global affairs, every detail about planet earth was already in his head, in his mind. Clearly, the Angel of Light had infused him with this knowledge. Clearly, the Angel of Light, the creator of the tunnel of light, the escape route from hell, was the Almighty and the Almighty had intervened and rescued him from a wrongful sentence. Clearly, the Almighty Angel of Light had done the same for the man. Clearly, the Angel of Light had formed a Luciferian Trinity: 1-the Angel of Light, 2-the New Caesar, and 3-Pontius the Prophet. This trinity would go forward and conquer the world: The man and Pontius, Pontius and the man had been preordained by the Almighty Angel of Light to be his agents and bring unity and peace to the world and, more than that, to bring about union with him—-*the oneness of all things*....Immanency.

Clearly immanency was truth...immanency as understood by the Luciferian Trinity, that is. And clearly, Caesar and Pontius had been selected to cleanse the world of its undesirable elements: Those who would attempt to stop this Truth, this Immanency, and the Almighty's Sovereign Plan.

Ave Caesar!

CHAPTER 3

The passenger sat alone in his private section of the Gulfstream V's cabin, sipping a mineral water and staring down at the Obersalzberg and the Berghof. And over there, 1,000 meters above the Obersalzberg, bathed in silver moonlight, lay the Kehlsteinhaus, the house Bormann had built. The passenger was still afraid of the elevator that took him up to that rocky outcropping where the Kehlsteinhaus still rested. But despite installing the scary elevator Bormann was a good man and knew how to get things done.

Yes. Bormann knew...Bormann had remembered the vision...

The passenger touched the indentation, the scar on his right temple. Bormann was there that day with his vial in his pocket. Bormann had scooped up the blood. Bormann had seen to it that some of the blood went to Torino and the rest to Washington to Georgetown. *Das Klonen erfolgt in Washington. The cloning would be done in Washington...as for the scar and tissue damage to the brain that would be dealt with by Anatoly and his angels.*

Ah, Bormann, you were a good man, a good friend and it was good to recall, it was good to see the Kehlsteinhaus. It was a beautiful house, Bormann. It still is. Thank you.

The Americans had *changed* the name of the Kehlsteinhaus to the Eagle's Nest.

The Eagle's Nest—-it was a good name; it had a nice ring to it. One day he would see to it the Americans or what would remain of the United States of America were properly thanked for changing the name.

One day he would see to it that *everyone* who had changed anything he did not wish to be changed would be *properly thanked*.

He took another sip of mineral water and lifted his gaze to the Watzmann. Pontius would be there watching through that telescope of his. Pontius was a fellow traveler, a fellow passenger who would one day show his *gratitude* for the *changes* which had been foisted upon him, as well. And Pontius would be his new version of Bormann. If Bormann had been a brother Pontius would be a *twin* brother.

Pontius would be all the passenger's brothers and servants rolled into one: Goering, Goebbels, Himmler, Eichmann, Mengele, Heydrich, Hoess, Hess and all the rest; and Pontius would be the new religious leader, the new Reich Bishop Ludwig Mueller. Pontius had been chosen for this role, one among many; this role, too, was perfect for him. Of all humankind who could know as much as Pontius about religion and how to use religion as another weapon in the arsenal? After all, had he not allowed the other Christ to be put to death and then washed his hands using the pitcher and bowl?

Pontius was perfect for the office of Planetary Reich Bishop. Pontius, of all who had ever lived, could distinguish better than anyone, between the true Christ and the false Christ. Pontius, like the passenger, had clear vision. Clear vision!

The passenger lifted his eyes to the southern horizon where the long line of snow atop the main body of the Austrian Alps made a white, serrated knife blade end to end across the edge of the earth. He closed his eyes, imaging all the people of the world, right now, scurrying about, yes, scurrying about like well-trained, little religious worker ants...little spiritual, missionary insects with some imagined purpose in life, little bugs that had been waiting so long for someone to inspire them, deliver them, to preach to them, to confirm all their collective spirituality and goodness and to unite them in *truth*—-Pontius would indeed be welcomed as the great unifier, the great Prophet by all those scurrying, little ants, all those little spiritualists. When the kingdom was theirs Pontius would present the possibilities for greatness to all the little ants that wished to be at peace with their fellow ants and, hypocritically, also wished to be greater than their fellow spiritualist ants. Pontius would tap into their collective jealousies and give them everything for which the little, jealous hypocrites clamored. Pontius would testify of *the true evolutionary Christ,* the true Leader, the only one who could confirm, once and for all, that for humanity *the right way was every way* as long as one was sincere and did not bring harm to others. And the stupid, little bugs would believe it...

The passenger squirmed in his seat like a restless child. He clutched the armrests. His thoughts were just getting revved up like the engines on the

Gulfstream V. If they revved up too much he might take off like an airplane. He took a couple of short, deep breathes to reduce his tension and think more thoughts about Pontius.

Pontius was the only one who could bring all humanity into submission to the one, true Almighty God and his proxy, the Caesar...yes, Pontius would bring all the scurrying, little ants into submission to the one ruler of the universe and the one ruler of the earth, the one ruler of the one people, the one kingdom. The true Christ, the passenger, would be received gloriously as the world's savior and lord. He would be received as the only one able to save the giant ant colony from destruction.

The passenger was perspiring from his grand and glorious thoughts, the grand and glorious speech he'd just composed in his mind. Beads of sweat threatened to fall off his chin into the glass of water. He wiped the sweat away with his handkerchief; he clutched the handkerchief with both hands; he clutched it so hard his knuckles turned colorless. His eyes flashed and rolled back into his head.

The passenger could feel and yet not feel the blows upon his back. He could feel and yet not feel the beatings, the humiliation dished out daily upon him by his wrathful father. He recalled the day he'd decided never again to cry out against those blows. He'd decided, then, to be the true man of the household and protect his saintly mother and the others from that wretched, womanizing, government functionary, Alois, another scurrying, little ant, another no-account among millions and billions of low-life no-accounts. Father was an Aryan, it was true, but he had not lived up to that fact. He had betrayed his family and especially his son. Father should have died like a Jew or a Gypsy in one of the camps.

Camps. There would be no *camps* again because there would be no barracks. Housing and feeding all those no-account undesirables in barracks had been a waste of money. But the rumor that there might be camps and barracks out in a desolate desert somewhere would be carefully crafted. All those foolish, little, scurrying ants would think it was true. Such disinformation would plant great fear in their weak hearts and minds. The rumor would be another propaganda tool for controlling their emotions and behavior; the rumor would misdirect their collective angst.

A great leader knows how to play to that collective angst and mold it to his wishes. A great leader knows how to tap into those negative energies and make them, the ignorant masses, do things, and think things they would not otherwise do and think. A great leader knows how to use such dismal idiocy. A great leader knows how to use that stupidity, how to *sift through the material* and use a few of the stupid ones, *and make them believe they are leaders too,* in order to control their fellow members of their underclass, their inferior tribe or race...then a great leader knows how to turn them all against one another and thereby use the vermin themselves to carry out the necessary task of ridding the world of collective ignorance and non-viability.

But a great leader must always be aware that there are others who might see themselves as just as smart, just as great. These so-called wiser ones were another threat which in due time must be eliminated, as well. A great leader would know how to crush all threats, anything and everyone standing in the way. A bullet to the head and ask questions later or don't ask questions at all. The fittest was always the quickest with the trigger.

The swivel-mounted monitor above his seat showed the jet's exact position in comparison with the terrain below. The open laptop on the tray table in front of him showed the exact same data—-all the cities and towns and villages, the highways, rail lines, indeed all the infrastructure, above and below ground...the bridges over the rivers and the highways through mountain ranges...all of it scrolled by slowly on the map on the two screens.

The passenger noted a particular name on the laptop's screen and turned his head to look down at the tiny lights of the town of *Leonding*.

He could feel nothing for the town now. Perhaps he had felt something, some affection at one time but no longer. A minute later, the jet was over *Linz* and still the passenger could feel nothing for all the scurrying, little religious ants in those two towns and across the world.

No. There would be no camps for any of them; there would only be *detention centers.* The masses of insects would be told the detention centers were needed to control the misfits, all blood-sucking social parasites, all those miscreants that had made life so difficult if not impossible for all productive, decent persons. By the time the detention centers came into existence they would be welcomed by all...just as the *chip* would be welcomed.

The passenger would explain everything in his next book: *Mein Seig. My Victory.* It would be the sequel to the last book. He would write this book once he'd arrived in Mexico and taken up residence in the secluded villa specially built for him by Anatoly's angels posing as human construction workers. The villa had been designed by the Angel of Light centuries ago, millennia ago—-it, too, was part of the plan.

Mein Sieg would not be as lengthy as that first volume. After all, the passenger had learned much while in the abyss and would now say much more with far fewer words.

The passenger smiled a smile that wasn't a smile. His grasp of history had been forged in the fires and was surpassed only by the Angel of Light. And, as for this new book and its all-encompassing view of history, he would release it for publication once the world bowed their knee to him and him alone.

The book would not be for sale; it would be distributed free of charge and it would be required that all Aryans read it every day until they'd memorized it. There would only be Aryans in the future kingdom and *My Victory* would be the new Bible.

The passenger glanced at the map...

Vienna. The jet was over Vienna now. The passenger leaned forward and stared through the window at the thousands of lights dotting the old part of the city and the newer suburbs.

He closed his eyes and sat back in his seat. He pressed his spine against it. He opened his eyes once again and stared into space—-he could see his dear friend Kubicek. He could hear him playing Mozart on that old piano.

Had Kubicek been sent to the abyss? If so, the passenger wished him well...and not to worry...once the kingdom belonged to the passenger and Pontius, the passenger would send for his old friend Kubicek. He would send for him and soon they would walk together once more upon the streets of Vienna. They would attend the opera and later have long discussions about the music; they would talk long into the night.

Vienna, the city had been controlled by the Jews. It was their fault the passenger had suffered so despicably in Vienna. It was their fault he had not been accepted by the Vienna Academy of Art. It was that Jewish professor that had shut him out and sealed his doom. It was the Jews' fault the passenger nearly died of starvation like a mangy street dog or mangy alley cat. The passenger had been wronged; he'd been just another Aryan getting short-changed by the mercantilist Jews.

On the other hand, the passenger now realized that one of his greatest mistakes, once he'd taken control of the Reich, was mistreating the Jews.

He should have brought them in to help the cause of National Socialism just as the Marxists had brought in the Jews to bring about Communism. He would not make the same mistake this time around. He would expand upon this idea and concept once he began to write *Mein Sieg, My Victory. He would entice the Jews to be part of the plan—-before he sprung the trap.*

My Victory would be written in American English...it was the lingua franca now. So be it. After all, the Americans had won the war with a bit of help from Stalin and Churchill. *So be it.*

Anyway, it wouldn't matter which language would be used to wage war, any kind of war, a war with tanks or words, what mattered was who would be victorious. Writing *My Victory* would be just the beginning of the *New Form of Blitzkrieg* that was coming.

Blitzkrieg, the word was magic. And it would be the passenger who would conquer this time around. Odin and all the gods had smiled upon the passenger. All the gods were helping the Angel of Light to make sure the passenger would win...the Angel of Light would help the passenger and the selected Aryans to reinstate the passenger, the rightful Caesar, to his throne.

The Gulfstream V had settled into its cruising altitude of 12,000 meters and speeded along at 900 kilometers per hour. The plane was headed for Volgograd. The passenger had known it as Stalingrad. It would be good to go to Stalingrad, to Volgograd. The passenger had not gone there before. He had not visited his brave troops. He'd only depended upon reports from the Eastern Front from the wayward, indecisive generals that had commanded the brave troops of the Wehrmacht. It was those wayward, fumbling generals' fault Stalingrad was lost and the swine in the Kremlin, the malevolent rulers of the U.S.S.R. were not smashed. Moscow should have been razed and the Marxists strung up.

A *like-minded Aryan* waited there now, in Stalingrad, in Volgograd. He had been selected to help with the overthrow of Russia. The *like-minded Aryan* would do all the leg-work, guiding *three Aryan generals*. But once the right moment came the passenger would call all the shots. Yes, Russia would fall, then Ukraine and then all Europe, especially Germany...*Gomer and all her bands.* The time would come and all Europe and Russia plus the Balkans and Central Asia and later the rest of the world would redraw their borders and become part of the Ten Planetary Kingdoms.

And once the entire Planetary Kingdom was under the control of the passenger, of *Caesar* and Pontius all inferiors would be disposed of...and only the Aryans would be left...only the best and the brightest of the Aryans. There was a scarcity of the proper stock in the world but that would soon change once the gene pool had undergone correction.

Yes the jet was speeding toward Stalingrad and it was good to reminisce and to plan. It was very good indeed.

The attendant brought *Caesar* his dinner of steamed mixed vegetables and another bottle of mineral water and lowered the cabin lights as *Caesar* continued to plan and prepare as the Angel of Light continued to fill him with wisdom, understanding, and knowledge.

CHAPTER 4

The chauffeur's wife, Diana, had begun to read the Bible about a year ago, sometime in 2007. Max didn't mind it so much, as long as she didn't try to convince him of anything. He was quite able, on his own, to live a good, moral life; he was quite able to be respectful and decent just as his father had been a respectful, decent man and had taught his son well. Father, too, had read the Bible once in a while it seemed; or maybe he'd read it lot. Max couldn't be sure.

On a few occasions, as Max and Diana lay side by side in bed at the end of another day, Diana had tried to read some verses or even an entire chapter to Max. Most of the time he had politely declined to listen, saying that it was all right, that it was very good for her to read the Bible but...but if he wanted to read it he could do so on his own, in his spare time.

One night he had given in, though. He loved her so much and, truth be told, was pleased she had started to read that book. That book had some kind of power; she had changed into an even more patient person and she seemed to possess some kind of inner glow and an outer glow too. It was hard for Max to describe but he saw how real it was. And Diana didn't smoke anymore either...and Max hated cigarettes. His father had hated them, too. Father, despite his loathing of the Nazis, had admired their anti-tobacco fervor and had passed this fervor on to his son.

Because Max loved his newly tobacco-free wife so very much he had given in that night and let her read anything she wished from the Bible as long as it wasn't *too much*. It had been a long day and he was very tired, he told her. He knew she wouldn't listen, though.

Diana had chuckled and said she was going read *the entire book of Daniel*. She'd said it was part of the Old Testament. Max had humored her as she began, knowing he wouldn't be able to keep his eyes open, knowing he would fall asleep in ten minutes or less.

When she finished an hour and a half later he asked her to read it again, which she did, word for word, line by line, chapter after chapter until she'd again read the last word of chapter 12.

They lay together without speaking for half an hour until they fell asleep around 02:00, and Max had another dream about father and the war, and the photographs father had taken, and about mother and her grief from not having more children, and her untimely death from cancer.

Father was there in the dream, sitting at the table in the tiny spare bedroom. Like always, he had placed the photos atop the varnished oak wood table; he always placed them in a sort of chronological grid; from left to right, top to bottom the photos covered the table and told the story, at least father's part of it from 1939 to 1945. There were one hundred eighty photos in the grid, ten rows of eighteen...one hundred eighty photos, a fact no one knew except Max and, father of course.

Mother came into the tiny spare room, at that moment in the dream, and told father to put the photographs away; it was bad to look at them...*it does no good*, she said, *it is not helpful*, she said, before turning to the door and leaving the room. Mother's weeping could be heard from down the narrow, little hallway as she left; she had wept like that so many times before.

When Max shared his dream with Diana the next morning she stopped sipping her coffee and just stared at her husband, waiting for him to finish. And when he did, he waited for her to speak, to say something...it seemed she had wanted to say something as he spoke about his dream; but now she was holding back.

"I had the *same dream*," Diana said. "Your mother left the room, and was weeping." Max had not mentioned mother weeping. He'd said nothing about it.

His wife was speaking again. "And I know how many photos there are."

Max waited. Diana was going to say how many photographs in father's collection? No one knew that number, no one except father and him. And how did she know mother was weeping?

And...

Not even mother had known how many photos there were.

Diana was holding back once more, and taking another sip of coffee. She waited another three minutes, sizing up her husband.

"Okay, tell me. How many?"

"If I get it right, what will you give me?" A little smile creased her face and made her eyes dance a bit.

"You have to 'get it right' first."

"Of course... but what will you give me if I get it right?"

"What would you like?" He asked. However, he wasn't smiling.

"A promise..."

"A promise..."

"I want you to promise to let me read the Bible to you every night."

Now it was Max who was sizing up Diana and wondering how he'd let himself get into this...it must be his hatred for cigarettes.

"Every night?" He still wasn't smiling. And he was sorry he'd gotten into this mess. He was sorry he'd told her about the dream.

"Every night," she replied, repeating the requirement. She was looking deep into his eyes.

"How would I know you weren't simply guessing and simply got it right from pure luck? How would I know you hadn't...?"

Max caught himself. He would not say it.

"What? How would you know I had not counted them beforehand? Is that what you think?"

"No..." He was sorry for ever letting the thought come into his mind. He knew better.

She was right to call his bluff. She had never seen the photos. She didn't even know where the key to the metal box was hidden. Plus she'd never shown any interest in seeing them. She detested anything related to the war and the Nazis. Her father, too, had been drafted and had lost two-thirds of his left leg and left arm from the elbow downward and left eye and ear. The entire left side of his face had showed the horrible scars that followed him to his grave. Her mother had married her father despite the hideous injuries that made him into a freak. Her mother had been a saint.

"All right, tell me."

"One hundred eighty."

The cell phone was ringing, playing rather, the opening measure to Beethoven's 5th—-dot, dot, dot, dash... It was Pontius calling his chauffeur.

"Yes?"

"Take me to the airport. Be here in an hour."

Max stood to his feet and picked up his coffee mug one more time and finished the morning brew. Pontius had said one hour and one hour meant forty-five minutes.

"The master calls," Max declared as he straightened his striped powder blue and scarlet tie. The tie went perfectly with the white shirt and light gray suit. Pontius' clothing allowance for his chauffeur was excessive but what could Max say to that? It was Pontius' money, not his.

Max hugged Diana and kissed her forehead. She laid her head on his shoulder for a moment. Max loved her. Diana loved him and...

Max knew Diana hated Pontius. She'd told him she could be happy with a fourth of the money, with even less, she'd said. A couple of times she had suggested leaving Berchtesgaden and moving back to Austria or perhaps moving to Berlin. Once she'd said she was afraid...afraid of Pontius. But Max could not be distracted by her fear of the boss, not now anyway. Max had to concentrate on the mission of getting Pontius to the airport.

Another Gulfstream V would be waiting on the tarmac, another silver and white one; another raptor would be waiting for the chauffeur to pull up with the Mercedes. In addition to the pilot and co-pilot there would be a pair of attendants plus three or four women. There were always women flying in Pontius' jet...stunningly beautiful women, too.

Diana watched him back out of the garage and turn around the car inside the walled courtyard-driveway in front of the grand house. The wrought iron gate retracted automatically. They lived like royalty, her chauffeur husband and she...and they'd vacationed in the Caribbean, Dubai, Singapore, the Greek Islands; they'd gone to Brazil once...and she was still afraid of Pontius. All the vacations in the world would not help take away her fear of him.

Diana turned to go back to the kitchen and clear the table and wash the few dishes. She could afford a servant but was far too frugal for it, despite all the money and perks.

She stopped turning and faced the window once again. He was getting out of the car. He was walking back along the edge of the driveway.

She left the house and stood on the ornate flagstone landing in front of the twin, over-sized mahogany doors; the 3m x 3m landing lay under a beautiful vine-shaded pergola, the entrance to their temple of stucco and tile, their sumptuous Bavarian house.

She waited. He had something to tell her.

"Yes, one hundred eighty...you will have your *gift* but only for six months. Six months will be quite enough for a sinner like me."

"All right, Max. Six months."

He was still speaking. "And I want you to read the book of Daniel again...maybe two more times...and the last one..."

"The last one?"

"Yes...I forgot the name...my father would read that one."

It was true. He could recall it now. Father had read that one a lot.

"Ah, Offenbarung."

"Ja Offenbarung, that was it...and then, for the remaining months, you can read to me anything you want from your Bible...I don't like cigarettes."

CHAPTER 5

The passenger had rested very well in his private cabin. The comfortable, fold-out bed with crisp, smooth sheets had made for a good sleep for part of the three hour flight. And half an hour ago, after taking a fine, hot shower in the customized lavatory he had changed into a perfectly-tailored *uniform*—-a long-sleeved khaki shirt tucked into khaki trousers tucked into tan combat boots, the kind used in desert warfare. The olive drab belt was an army web belt sans holster and pistol. The belt required a sidearm; it would look incomplete without it. The passenger pulled out that sidearm from the cabinet now—-a Walther PPK 7.65mm. The pistol had a full load of ammunition: 7 rounds.

Now the pistol *rested* in his hand just as the passenger *had rested* during the flight from Salzburg to Volgograd. The pistol and the passenger were inseparable, they always would be.

He hefted the weapon a couple of times. It had a nice feel; it always had a nice feel in his hand. He had loved that pistol and he loved it now. A pistol, in the correct hands, was the miniature manifestation of world-wide power, conquest, and domination. That backward Chinese swine Mao and his ugly fat face had understood one thing correctly: *Power comes from the barrel of a gun.* But that useful idiot Mao could not have known that everything depended on *who* was holding the gun. Certainly the gun, the power could not be wielded by idiots like the Chinese and the rest of their non-Aryan brethren, the Korean dogs, the arrogant-kamikaze Japanese, and the inferior mixed races of Southeast Asia plus the half-breeds in the Philippines and the Pacific Islanders, mongrels all. History had proved this.

An announcement came over the intercom: "We will be landing in ten minutes, sir."

The passenger returned to his seat and peered through the window at the twinkling lights dotting the suburbs of Stalingrad. Cars and buses were still moving up and down the streets despite the lateness of the hour. There were more people than before... there were more of those unknowable Russians. *Enigmatic* Russians were all right with the passenger; they were more useful idiots, every one of them. They were not enigmatic to him. Churchill was a fool to call them enigmatic.

Now the Gulfstream V was making a sharp turn to the left to line up with Runway 29 at Gumrak Airport. The flaps made a light hum as they dropped down from the wings to slow the jet's airspeed. The landing gear made another whirring sound as it lowered from the belly of the craft. The pitch of the nose was slightly raised to slow it even more as it rode the glide slope to the threshold of the runway.

Gumrak Airport. The passenger knew exactly where the airport would be; he didn't need the scrolling map on the laptop's screen although he was watching it now. He was watching it because the map gave him pleasure—-it was a delight for the passenger to watch the scrolling map of the world because he knew that every square centimeter of it would be his: All Russia would be his and the rest of the planet including China, Japan, Korea, and Southeast Asia. He would dominate those oriental inferiors, and then he would systematically exterminate them. Plus he would eliminate all the Orientals' offspring—-the so-called native people in the Americas.

Gumrak, the *Flughafen*. The German 6th Army had used the airfield as a fuel and supply depot during the Battle of Stalingrad in 1942 and 1943.

Ah, the 6th Army and that fumbling General Paulus...he had given in to the Communists, he had surrendered to that cunning fox Stalin. It never would have happened if the passenger had been in the field with the great soldiers of the Wehrmacht. Things would have been different if the passenger had gone there and turned the tide against that swine Stalin and his vaunted Red Army of inferior men. But the passenger had not been able to leave his post in Germany or the Wolf's Lair in Poland. He'd had to depend upon fumbling generals like Paulus.

That General Paulus, even though he was an Aryan, was still a disgrace and a coward—-and to think the passenger had graciously promoted him to *Field Marshal* just before the surrender at Stalingrad in order to afford the cowardly traitor an opportunity to restore his honor, one final chance to redeem himself via comitting suicide. No Field Marshal in the Wehrmacht had ever let himself be taken prisoner but the coward Paulus had done just that. He'd let the Russians take him to Moscow. And in a few moments the jet would land near the place where that coward had betrayed his Fuehrer and his fatherland. But while Paulus' flesh and bones rotted in his grave and his spirit and soul roasted in hell the fatherland would go on; the Aryan Nation was still in the world as it would be forever... and a nation was, after all, the sum total of the individuals that make up the nation...but it was the nation that counts and not individuals like all those scurrying little ants, all those little individual cowards like Paulus...in a few short years the Aryan people would rise again, and destroy all others, and then the greater Aryans would rule the lesser Aryans. Aryans, too, had to undergo the normal, evolutionary process of natural selection. Rebellious Aryans had to be eliminated just like anyone else.

In a few minutes, the passenger would consult with Anatoly, the one that would manipulate everything in his designated sphere of influence and see to the overthrow of Russia. After all, Anatoly was perfect for this great work. He knew the Kremlin's lying, subtle ways. He knew the so-called enigmatic Russian mind. And Anatoly had picked two others to overthrow Ukraine and Germany and then go to work on neutralizing the rest of Europe including Britain. The other two were perfect for the work, as well. They, too, understood that the time had almost come—-in a little more than ten years the plum would be ripe for picking and the juice would be so good. The juice would be like new wine and the passenger would drink that new wine with his disciples when the kingdom belonged to him.

In a few minutes Anatoly and the passenger would take a long walk together on the Volga Promenade and finalize the plan for world domination and conquest. It had all been arranged, it had all been prewritten. It would all become reality in a few short years. The entire creation and all races and civilizations and societies had been longing for this glorious time and that great and final day when *eternal peace* would come. The passenger and *his helpers* would *give the races all the eternal peace they would ever need...as they moldered in their graves.*

The passenger gathered the seatbelt around him and inserted it into the buckle until it clicked; it was fastened now. He was *secure* now. The passenger almost laughed out loud about being *secure*. He would always be *secure*. Nothing could stop him. He was invincible.

He shifted his *super-computer mind* away from trivialities like seatbelts to other *aspects of the plan:*

Fiat currency would be destroyed and then abolished. The global monetary system was nothing except illusion anyway. And such illusion brought nothing except delusion to the masses; the deluded masses had been overdosing on those illusions, like overdosing on drugs. In a little while they would have to quit cold. But for now let them keep overdosing, let them be deluded.

Illusions and delusions—-more illusions and delusions were on the way in every *sphere of influence* in the world...

*Spheres and spheres of influence—-convergence—-emergence—-transformation—-synergy—-communitarians—-seismic shift—-new paradigm—-metaphysics—-orbs—-fractals—-*immanency*—-Pontius' specialty...spheres and all the sphere buzzwords... Environment, economy, equity, consensus, affordable housing, action, protect, preserve, quality of life, benefit of all, sanctuary, social justice, watershed, facilitator, traffic calming, best practices, outcome-based education, endangered species, invasive species, restoration, public-private partnerships, common good, regional, collaborative, inter-disciplinary, stakeholder, international baccalaureate, school-to-work, historic preservation, vision, sustainability, sustainable medicine...and everything is global this and global that...*

"If you tell a lie big enough and keep repeating it, people will eventually come to believe it. The lie can be maintained only for such time as the State can shield the people from the political, economic and/or military consequences of the lie. It thus becomes vitally important for the State to use all of its powers to repress dissent, for the truth is the mortal enemy of the lie, and thus by extension, the truth is the greatest enemy of the State."—-Joseph Goebbels.

Ah, Goebbels had been magnificent...and if only Goebbels could see the passenger now and if only Goebbels could be part of this campaign. Goebbels need not worry. The passenger would bring him back along with Kubicek and all the others; once the undesirables had been eliminated and the Angel of Light had been satisfied the power over life and death would be transferred to the *rightful power brokers—-the passenger and his public relations officer, Pontius.*

And the contemptible, scurrying little ants, the naïve little bugs had made all of this possible and did not even know it. On the other hand, despite the scurrying little ants' collective stupidity and naiveté, despite being know-nothings the scurrying little spiritualists *had missed* the passenger...yes they *had missed* him even though they might not immediately recognize that fact either. But it was true that they'd had a yearning in their easily-deceived heart for the passenger because they could not find self-actualization and total fulfillment until he arrived. And they'd possessed enough intuition to realize their deficiencies despite their ignorance and stupidity. They'd known they needed something to fill the void in them but until now the scurrying, little, contemptible bugs had not quite figured out *what it was all about.* This slowly-developing collective consciousness had been gradually, subtly shepherded into existence by the Angel of Light and now it would be further guided via the New Caesar as the *triumvirate* consolidated its power over the entire globe. One step at a time, one year at a time, one decade at a time, and one century at a time the Angel of Light had done it. He had done it one so-called *trend* and one so-called *phase* at a time, slowly, less slowly, a bit faster, and faster...and soon, via the New Caesar and Caesar's prophet, Pontius, the Angel of Light would spring the trap. Their triumvirate would win and all opposition be vanquished.

It was true that the little bugs had not quite figured out *what it was all about* even though *they'd so patiently waited for something; they'd waited for him* without knowing it and that, too, was according to plan. But soon the day would come for their blinders to fall off and *they would see that he was supernatural and therefore without equal in the world and was the answer to all their problems.* This time, after so many failures, so much wasted energy, they would get it right. And they would understand, truly understand that by receiving the passenger they would be fulfilling all their collective Scriptures, the Holy Books—-all their prophecies had predicted one and the same thing all these centuries and millennia and soon they would grasp that fact. Soon *they would open themselves to being channeled* by the passenger—-the New Caesar—-and *they would open themselves to being channeled* by Pontius and the Angel of Light and by all the other angelic beings of the sacred hierarchy. Soon humanity would *ascend* and take hold of its higher self and be transformed.

They would be channeled straight into oblivion.

The rear landing gear squealed as it touched down on the surface of the runway, making two clouds of smoke, followed by the nose gear making a third cloud. The spoilers popped up on the wings and the pilot put the engines into reverse thrust to slow the jet enough to exit the runway via the next taxiway.

The air this summer night in Stalingrad was balmy and humid and it was into this warm, lovely air of Stalingrad that the delighted passenger stepped for the first time. And for him this place, this city, this Stalingrad, would never go by another name; for him it would always be Stalingrad. Tonight it would be the place where he would begin his renewed campaign in earnest. Therefore, it was fitting that this city always be called Stalingrad and once the final kingdom belonged to him he would rename it Stalingrad. That would teach the sly fox a lesson. That would teach the sly fox that it was the passenger that ruled and could dole out names and titles any way he chose.Plus the sly fox wouldn't be getting out of hell like the others. The fox would never know the name of the city had been re-named yet again, in honor of him as he roasted forever and ever in flames.

The two attendants escorted the passenger to the waiting SUV, a silver armor-plated Tahoe. Anatoly was the driver; and, Anatoly was dressed in a similar *uniform* to the passenger except it was black. Anatoly was armed too, sporting a Glock 9mm in a shining black holster on his right hip. The weapon was superfluous; *nobody would bother this version of Anatoly* or any version of Anatoly for that matter.

Anatoly's face and physique weren't his real face and physique. Anatoly and his helpers had been infused by the Angel of Light with power to alter their faces and bodies. Tonight, *this* Anatoly was a young man of perhaps thirty-five with a wiry frame of perhaps 1.8 meters in height. Tomorrow he could be a fat man of sixty or a skinny man of forty-five with graying hair. He could become a woman if the situation required it. He'd done that a number of times and had had pillow talk with quite a number of adulterous heads of state.

Anatoly and his helpers could morph into anyone they wanted—-beautiful women, heads of state, military leaders, business leaders, CEOs of major corporations, anyone. Or, if necessary, they could simply return to their spirit-body form and occupy anyone they chose...except the true Christians. No one could occupy the true Christians. Anatoly and his helpers had attempted it a many, many times, too many times to count and had been without success.

The fake Christians were easy to occupy and rather amusing and fun but rather boring, as well. And there were so many of them now. Plus, truth be told, the fakes weren't of much use anymore. Even the so-called unbelievers knew most Christians were fakes. But those fundamentalists, they were a problem; at least for now they were. Later the fundamentalists would pay for their misguided fervor.

The passenger knew all about Anatoly and his angels and how they particularly enjoyed occupying heads of state, military leaders, and international financiers because that was where things got done. That was the arena through which the final kingdom would come into existence and remain eternally, once the Jews and those pesky fundamentalist Christians had been liquidated.

Anatoly, like his angels, like the passenger and Pontius, was another special messenger chosen for this great work. They were part of the chain of command of the true angels which proceed from the Angel of Light. The passenger had a special place in his heart for Anatoly. Anatoly and his angels had been there to implant the passenger in the womb as *the Aryans* gathered around her bed that night in Washington in Georgetown and held hands and prayed.

Anatoly drove through an open metal gate located on the north side of the airport far from the main terminal and other buildings. Two *guards* stood at attention on either side of the gate and gave a stiff Roman salute as the SUV passed by. The pair of guards was two more of the millions and billions of *helpers* under Anatoly's direct command. The passenger found it amusing to see them wearing Russian army uniforms with Russian assault rifles, standard issue Ak-74m, slung over their shoulders. The pair of guards closed the gate behind the SUV and disappeared into the gloom.

The passenger and Anatoly walked side by side on the promenade as the Volga flowed under a brilliant canopy of pre-dawn stars as the diminishing light of the yellowish moon faded in the west. To the east the horizon was bathed in grays and shades of rose. Their boots made a light crunching sound against the cement underneath. Their four military boots were the first of millions and millions and millions of boots to come.

They had walked and talked for an hour. They had finalized the plan: *Army Group A, a force of ten million,* comprising armies and air forces from Russia, Western, Central, and Eastern Europe, China, Japan, Australia, the *newly realigned* USA, India, the Baltic States, Scandinavia, the Western-sympathizing sectors of the Balkans and Western-sympathizing sectors of Turkey would deploy here. Five million men of *Army Group A* would go in the first wave to the south with another five million held in reserve.

Army Group B made up of troops from West Africa and Ethiopia plus Western-sympathizing Central and Southern Africa would deploy to the Sub-Sahara and be ready to aid *Army Group A* in case Libya or Egypt or Sudan and Somalia and other Muslim Africans became unruly. *Army Group B, a force of five million,* would be half the size of *Army Group A* with two and a half million soldiers moving forward to the Saharan salient in the initial stages of the campaign. The Mediterranean sectors, Red Sea sectors, and Persian Gulf-Arabian Sea sectors—-east, west, north, south quadrants of each body of water—- would be handled by a fleet of twelve hundred ships and submarines. The second wave of two and a half million men of *Army Group B* would be held in reserve in case the first two and a half million proved insufficient.

Everything would be timed for *Army Group A* to arrive in Israel first, in order to block the kings of the north, south, and east—- the kings of the north being Kazakhstan, Uzbekistan, Chechnya, Dagestan, Azerbaijan, Turkmenistan and others from that region...the kings of the south being Libya, Algeria, Morocco, Sudan, Somalia and others from that region...the kings of the east being Iraq, Iran, Afghanistan, Pakistan, Bangladesh, Indonesia...it remained to be seen with whom Saudi Arabia, Oman, Yemen, the Emirates and others from that global sector would side. But once the war began it wouldn't matter much anyway.

In addition, another massive navy would be deployed in the Eastern Atlantic, Indian Ocean, and the Pacific, effectively sealing off any threats from those regions of the globe.

And all of it would be created in order to provide the passenger with a *lethal scenario* from which *he would save the Jews by crushing the Muslims.* A horrified and grateful Israel would be in the palm of his beneficent hand. They would be overjoyed because they would be relieved of their collective fear, especially the fear that would come via the uprisings soon to occur in Egypt and Libya and Syria...in 2010, 2011, 2012, and 2013 and beyond.

Those uprisings of the ignorant, Muslim masses would be instigated by Anatoly and his helpers, as well. The uprisings were another part of *the preparations*...to frighten the Jews and make them ready to turn to anyone that offered them peace and safety.

And, once critical mass was achieved via the Angel of Light, via Caesar and Pontius and via Anatoly and via angels like him all minds on the planet would be channeled and controlled...and *the minds* that were not compliant, those few who might harbor rebellious thoughts would be rounded up and destroyed. And, naturally, all non-producers and other inferiors would be destroyed too.

Once the passenger conquered the Middle East and dealt with the Jewish problem, he would deal with the North Koreans...he would deal with everyone once he'd established order.

The passenger turned and faced Anatoly.

"I shall sign the accord with them 12 October 2024."

"Yom Kippur."

"Yes."

"Day of Atonement."

"The day I save them from their sins."

"Blasphemous."

A light wind came up along with the rising sun. The whole eastern horizon across the Volga across the steppes of Russia was bathed in blood red. The passenger's eyes reflected that red dawn and were the same color as Anatoly's...all four eyes were the color of blood. Anatoly smiled and his teeth glistened red, as well.

They returned to the airport and the refueled, waiting jet. The two attendants approached the SUV and one of them opened the door for the passenger while Anatoly exited his side, stood at attention, and watched the passenger and his two-man escort enter the aircraft and disappear.

As the jet left the runway Anatoly clicked his heels together and gave a Roman salute as the passenger caught a last glimpse of him through the window and turned once more to watch the scrolling map on the laptop and the monitor.

CHAPTER 6

The passenger sipped another mineral water and considered his position in geopolitical and demographic terms. If only he'd been granted this much power before, he could have brought about the kingdom then. But the Angel of Light has his ways, his special timing; the Angel of Light was sovereign and the passenger had to content himself with the fact that the Angel of Light had chosen him above all others to spearhead the Angel of Light's sovereign plan. Furthermore the passenger had to content himself with the fact that he had been chosen not once but twice to eliminate the Jews. The passenger took a celebratory sip of water and cast his vision toward Pontius.

He could see Pontius now, sitting in his tower and looking through his telescope. Or he would be working out, lifting weights and then going for a twenty kilometer run. In a few hours he would be peering through the cabin window of his own Gulfstream V, watching the Swiss Alps off to his left as the jet flew west and then southwest to the Canary Islands. Pontius, too, had a meeting to attend with some religious leaders and global bankers and global corporate leaders drooling over the prospect of financing and supplying billions of micro chips for the coming effort for total control of the great unwashed masses. And, just as the passenger had Anatoly and millions of lesser *angel-helpers* available to him, so Pontius had *Darius* and millions of lesser angels. And each of the millions of lesser angels had millions of angels of even lower rank available to them. The entire hierarchy operated in lockstep with the Angel of Light, the passenger and Pontius. The hierarchy was magnificent. It was perfect. It was genius.

Their great, coordinated work would be divided into the following major tasks: The passenger would be in charge of political affairs, global security plus military command and control and conquest and Pontius would be in charge of economic and religious affairs. Yes, yes, and yes...the passenger made himself feel giddy by going over it again and again inside his head; he loved to think about it; he loved to savor these thoughts; these thoughts were one and the same as the Angel's; the thoughts were in sync with the Angel of Light's bold plan:

Both the passenger and Pontius would answer directly to the Angel of Light and be aided by the Angel's minions. As *the great work* progressed during the next ten years more and more *angel-minions*, millions and billions of them, would be sent to help bring everything to its rightful and logical conclusion—-the handing over of the *keys to the kingdom* to the Angel of Light via his representatives on earth: the passenger and Pontius. It was a simple plan. The best plans always are the simplest.

And it was all so correct and logical, and now it would almost be effortless in a certain sense. The easily-seduced nations had been prepared to receive their *king*. And their king was the Aryan of Aryans. And once they realized who he was, it would strike mortal fear in them. They would have no alternative except to bow their knees and worship him. To the pathetic masses he would be like no one else. No one else had ever returned from the grave except that imposter...and, truth was, that imposter had not returned from the grave; no, that imposter had faked his resurrection and duped millions and millions of stupid, naïve little spiritualists...*believers all.* It was time to pay back the imposter and pay back his followers plus pay back the people that had foisted the imposter upon the world...the time had come to pay back those Jews and their ugly step-children, those fundamentalist Christians, those *true believers.*

The imposter had not returned from the dead as was claimed. Only the passenger had done that...and Pontius, of course. The passenger took another sip from his *sacramental* mineral water.

It would be good to depart now, to Magdeburg, to the place where they had buried him. It would be good to stand in that place, pay his respects and, after paying his respects, go to the river to the place where the reprehensible KGB devils had scattered the ashes. From that bridge he would pay his respects once more. It would be good to remember. If only his saintly mother could be with him; they would make this voyage through time together.

Ah mother, dear mother, dear Klara. He would bring her back, as well, once the kingdom was his. And he would bring back Eva. Ah, dear Eva possessed the same name as Adam's wife in *the book.*

The passenger drank once more from the glass and visualized more details of the soon-coming planetary kingdom...

Yes and *when the kingdom was his*, once everything had been established, as it should have been all along, there would be no room for anyone except the passenger, Pontius, the Angel of Light, and the hierarchy of angels ruling over the residue of obedient humans, the surviving Aryan classes. Yes eventually there would be no one left except well-trained, obedient Aryans. And from that time forward the passenger, in consultation with the Angel and Pontius, would decide everything. Their triumvirate would be supreme forever.

When the kingdom was his, when the kingdom belonged forever to their Trinitarian-triumvirate the millennium would begin. *Yes, the long-promised thousand-year kingdom would stretch from pole to pole and from sea to sea.* When the thousand year kingdom ended it would be swallowed up by a higher kingdom, even more beautiful, as the Trinitarian-triumvirate ruled without end and the best of the Aryans evolved into higher and higher selves. This was the ultimate goal. For this the passenger would give everything.

The passenger slapped his knee lightly; he was glowing with happiness, with glee. He could scarcely contain himself. He wished he had wings like this jet. He wished he could fly like an eagle. If he were an eagle he would soar high above the earth and look down with his sharp, eagle vision knowing everything below was his; once the kingdom belonged to him there could be no limitation on his power. He would be as God ruling over all his little, forever-evolving gods.

The passenger's eyes rolled back into his head. He shifted his torso from side to side. He was locked in a subtle dance with himself. His ego was a nuclear reactor held in check only because it would be *inconvenient* to show it...at least it would be inconvenient for now. The moment for showing his true self to the world would arrive once all the scurrying little ants' collective egos had been stroked long enough, once the fertile, self-centered self-images lying within the little ants had been *cultivated* and *prepared* for the final planting and the final harvest.

Once the low-grade humans of all races and creeds had used up all their petty *dialectic* conversations and debates—-*thesis, antithesis, and synthesis* ad nauseam—-they would fall into the hands of the passenger. Overthrowing nations meant overthrowing minds and those minds were very close to capitulation. Once all traces of the masses' collective remaining truth, their so-called moral values were eliminated and replaced with the lie, the bigger the better, anything was possible. But the lie that would soon replace *their remaining collective truth* was actually the truth and not a lie at all. The Angel of Light and the doctrine of Immanency was truth. God was in all things; all things were God. This fact, this truth was self-evident. And the passenger would be the God of all Gods—-and this the religionists did not understand. How could they with their petty minds? How could they know that their embracing of Immanency would be the trap that trapped them.

The passenger took another sip of his mineral water and continued to converse with himself and to commune with the Angel of Light. Again he sensed he was glowing.

Lies, the bigger the better; but the lies, which were actually the truth, had to come at the masses like a tidal wave building momentum and the momentum had to be sustained as long as possible...because as Goebbels had known so well, the masses can only be fooled for so long until the truth—-their collective delusions—-comes back in the form of a counter wave, another tidal wave that will decimate the first wave. Only if the timing was perfect could the first wave win the day and render any countering wave ineffective.

The inevitable result from this growing tidal wave of lies, lies which were actually the truth would be war.

Yes, war.

And the masses would have no escape once war came. Ironically, they would not want to escape war because they would view it as their destiny. They would, in fact, welcome war because war tapped into their collective angst and provided a release and relief from that angst, that nervousness, that anxiety. War would be to them as the release of rain was to a thunderstorm. Many, if not most, would see *war as greatly necessary*...they would see it as *a necessary evil... a necessary cure...a necessary liberating event to bring the world to the next higher level.* Naturally the masses understood that they were gods and capable of godhood. They only needed to see and then embrace their great lord and savior to confirm all they knew via their natural intuition.

The passenger wringed his hands as if wringing them and smearing that wrung-out sweat about his wrists and up his forearms would help consolidate his thoughts. He loved being the one that would confirm for the masses what they had known or at least suspected for so long.

He loved to think about war and conquest. He loved his grandiosity. He loved to consider how many *untermenschen,* how many *inferiors and non-compliants* he would get his hands on and destroy; yes, he would get his sweaty hands on their collective necks and choke the life out of them.

The passenger knew that the only reason the world was not as it should be was because of those *untermenschen, those inferior races, and those annoying non-compliant individualists who would dare to defy the Angel of Light and not understand their proper place in the food chain. Because of their ignorance and defiance they would be liquidated.*

Once the passenger had eradicated the inferiors everything would be as it should have been all along, thought the passenger once more.

The passenger drank again from his mineral water and swallowed slowly. The mineral water might as well be the blood of everyone he was about to kill.

How mistaken were the masses of petty spiritualists! Contrary to what they thought, there would be no *achievable* higher level of existence for ninety percent of them because they would all be dead. *Yes, they would all be dead via the selection process...the selection process, the dirty little secret the New Agers believed was their secret; the foolish New Agers thought they had developed the concept on their own.*

This *selection process* would come on several fronts—-war, detention centers, and *unfortunately* pestilence. Pontius would see to it the microbes were let out at the right time. Those little germs could do what three or four great armies could not...kill *a billion little bugs* before the pestilence would run its course.

The passenger wringed his hands and wrists once more and spread more perspiration up his forearms. Considering releasing pestilence upon the masses of undesirables gave him immense pleasure; it made him high; it fed his addiction to excitement; it was better than heroin, better than crack cocaine; better than meth—-he had not tried any of those drugs but he knew their power over the inferiors he was about to eliminate.

The first great test of releasing pestilence carried out by Pontius and his *angels* would be the discharge of black death—-*black death, Yersinia pestis, and small pox, Variola vera—-this first great experiment* would be carried out upon the mongrel South Americans as a sign, and as a warning of what the passenger and Pontius would do to anyone else once the Jewish problem had been solved and the Middle East stabilized.

The idea of killing so many South American mongrels made the passenger take a deep, satisfactory breath. He truly loved war and conquest and making everything right. He loved being the chosen one to accomplish this heretofore unrealized utopian dream. He loved being who he was. He loved himself. Loving himself was the same as loving the Angel of Light and that was exactly as it ought to be.

And, another thing would be exactly as it ought to be—-this time the passenger would not have to share the spoils of war with the likes of the Italians, Japanese and Russians. It was laughable how he'd ever tolerated such a foolish idea in the first place. But the times had been different. Now everything would be for him, Pontius and the Angel of Light, exclusively. There would be no sharing. The time for generosity and sharing had ended long ago.

Ah, Magdeburg, the place of his burial and cremation, the place to which the enigmatic Russians had taken Eva and him. It would be good to go there. It would be good to remember.

When the kingdom was his and he called to the river to give up Eva's ashes it would be at Magdeburg. He would be standing there on the bridge, waiting to take her hand and lift her resurrected body out of the water and greet her with a kiss and present Magdeburg to her as a gift. Thousands upon thousands of astonished Aryans would be there, watching, cheering, lining the streets as the motorcade wended its way through the city draped once more in the billowing red, white and black swastika flags of the Reich.

CHAPTER 7

Max eased the Mercedes into position at the end of the long, runway-like driveway—-the driveway that was really an extension of a two-kilometer spur off the long, winding mountain road that zigzagged, higher and higher and higher through the forest, up the Watzmann from Berchtesgaden until it finally arrived at the grand facade of Pontius' majestic and glorious three-tiered house of stone, stucco, tile, polished marble and bullet-proof glass.

The Greco-Roman pantheon, the statuary lining both sides of the driveway was always an assault upon Max's senses. The statuary was gaudy, garish and eerie. It was extravagant, tasteless and creepy. To sum it up: It was weird, it was bizarre and all of this not to mention the Egyptian obelisk on the left side of the villa. But Max would keep these opinions to himself. He was a chauffeur and a soldier at the same time and good chauffeurs, good employees like good soldiers do not express their opinions about things, especially not when it came to someone like Pontius.

The house servant or attendant or whatever he was, was marching toward the car with the two black leather suitcases. The servant seemed to be doing an odd, abbreviated form of a goose step. It struck Max as strange, as peculiar for the servant to walk like that with two suitcases. There had to be thirty or forty kilos worth of Pontius' belongings in each piece of luggage; but the man was indeed doing that weird goose stepping and not missing a beat either. The man, the servant, the attendant must be very strong in addition to crazy. Goose stepping?

Max pressed the button and popped open the trunk and exited the car to help the crazy, goose-stepping house servant place the luggage correctly. He might as well help the poor fellow and humor him. Perhaps he could even get the poor fellow to talk, to say something, anything.

For three years, ever since Max had taken this job with Pontius, he'd not spoken even once with the servant or with anyone else on the staff—-the grounds keeper always kept to himself, the one Max believed to be the chef always kept to himself, this one always kept to himself; there could be other servants in the house that kept to themselves but Max hadn't seen anyone else besides these three. At any rate, all of them were weird; they all must be mutes, *deaf non-talkers*, totally absorbed by their duties and totally devoted to Master Pontius. They were all mutes made of ice; yes, they were frigid blocks of ice wrapped up in a covering of flesh and bone and black uniforms. Truth be told, Max had grown to hate these *fellow employees*, these *icy mutes*. He might as well admit it because it was indeed the truth.

Max stood beside the open trunk and the servant set down the suitcases. Even if he hated this icy mute he would still try to get him to speak.

"Good morning," Max said and smiled, waiting for the servant to return the greeting. If he did it would be a first.

The servant only nodded and proceeded to lift one of the suitcases.

"Please, allow me."

The servant, a man of perhaps twenty-five, with dark, slicked-back, oily hair and dark eyes and olive skin *paused* and looked at Max the chauffeur. It wasn't just any look; it was a concentrated glare, it was as if his eyes were sending out fiery laser beams to burn a hole through Max. The look was one of disgust as if the servant was appalled this chauffeur would even dare to offer his help.

The servant was still in pause mode.

Before the servant could react to the chauffeur's offer of help, Max reached down and wrested the handle away from the servant. Then, he tightened his two-handed grip even more and tried to hoist the piece of luggage into the trunk. It didn't move; it didn't budge even though Max was a very strong man.

He tugged at it again. The suitcase might as well be bolted to the ground. It would not dislodge from the asphalt beneath. He grabbed and pulled once more. It still didn't move. It had to weigh more than two hundred kilos.

Max backed away and took hold of the other one. Its weight was *normal. It weighed the usual amount,* thirty kilos or so, enough clothing and whatnot for a two or three day spree to some conference site—-the typical duration of one of Pontius' typical trips with his usual entourage of two attendants and three or four gorgeous women. Yes, this bag was normal and must weigh about thirty kilos, maybe forty at the most. But that other one...

And that other one now lay inside the trunk.

The servant had just set it there using only one arm. He'd done it so quickly Max had scarcely seen the maneuver. One second it was on the ground, the next it was inside the trunk. *It was astonishing.*

Max tried to make eye contact with the servant but the man was already marching back to the house.

That *unmovable* suitcase must have been some kind of trick. It was some kind of *odd* joke.

Max's heart was racing from the sudden bombardment of thoughts about this odd place and all the odd things he'd observed, and not being able to move that suitcase. There were so many things about this house, this villa, this employer that were strange and different and odd. There were so many bizarre things Max had chosen to suppress and ignore because he loved the money and benefits. His love of the money and perks was as sure as his hate for the weird, icy, *deaf-mute* fellow employees.

Who else but Pontius would pay a chauffeur two hundred thousand euros per year and give him so much money for clothing and give him all the perks—-a liquor allowance, a travel allowance that let Max and Diana vacation lavishly, and an awesome car, an awesome BMW fully loaded; Pontius had even given Max fifty thousand euros in bonus, that first year when he had signed the employment contract. The bonus would be for anything Max might want, Pontius had said with a pleasant smile from across the table in the café in Berchtesgaden. And it was the only time Pontius had actually addressed him by his name: Max.

Max had gone out that same day and purchased the best multi-media equipment for his house: a to-die-for giant screen TV, a fantastic sound system, plus dozens of classical music CDs, new computers; the list went on.

The list went on...and what about the awesome, wonderfully- furnished house with walled courtyards and gardens in Berchtesgaden? Pontius had made that possible, as well. Max's and Diana's previous house had been a two bedroom, one and a half bath, little condo and now he was living like *the Kaiser* in a splendid six bedroom, four bath *palace*. It was beyond imagination for a humble man like him from a humble house in Austria.

Why should he give the servant's little trick a second thought? Why should he harbor ridiculous ideas that there had somehow even been a trick played on him? There had been no trick, there had been no deviousness. Max had been mistaken about the actual weight of the suitcase. Yes, he had truly been mistaken. Perhaps it was simply a matter of grabbing hold of it correctly and...

No. He knew he had not been mistaken. That suitcase did weigh two hundred kilos or perhaps more. And if that were the case what on earth was inside it? Rocks? If the contents were rocks they would have to be very dense rocks. They would have to be pure granite or marble. Or maybe it was full of gold bars. Or full of silver.

The servant had retreated to one of the side entryways to the house and disappeared. Max stepped to the rear door and waited for Pontius and tried to blank out the rush of sinister thoughts crowding his mind. He had to concentrate on getting his boss to the airport. He was a chauffeur and that was his job.

Max continued to wait and wait. It was unlike Pontius to delay this much.

Max moved his eyes guardedly toward the house but did not turn his head. He wouldn't reveal that he was curious.

Meter by meter, Max raised his eyes from the ground level to the third tier to Pontius' balcony and the floor-to-ceiling panoramic window behind it.

Pontius was there, in the window. Pontius was there, watching his chauffeur, Max.

Now Pontius was turning a bit to his left. The servant was there, saying something into Pontius' left ear.

The servant backed away into the shadows. Pontius resumed his watch upon the chauffeur as if he were analyzing him, as if he were sizing him up like a boxer does his opponent before the big fight.

Max lowered his eyes one or two meters down the front of the grand house, hoping Pontius had not seen him looking.

Five minutes later, Pontius emerged from behind the huge stainless steel doors that whirred and hummed as they opened. Like a great actor stepping onto the stage for the opening scene of the play, he stepped onto the flagstone courtyard in front of the house and paused for a moment between two ten-foot marble statues of Mercury on the right and Venus on the left; Pontius was waiting and watching his chauffeur once more.

The enormous stainless steel doors hummed again and closed behind Pontius as he approached the car. Max snapped-to like a *soldier* and opened the door for the *commander.*

Pontius was wearing a perfect gray suit, white shirt, and dark red tie. His leather belt was glossy black as were his polished Italian slip-ons. Pontius appeared to be in a no-nonsense mood. It was a departure for him. Usually he was jovial and talkative as he anticipated the flight in the Gulfstream V and being pampered by three or four perfectly-proportioned women.

Pontius was anything except good-humored. Today he was more like the passenger: somber, sullen, gloomy, and brooding. What was going on inside that unfathomable mind inside Pontius' head?

The next sixty minutes were the quietest of Max's life as, at Pontius' urging, he speeded down the Watzmann and speeded through Berchtesgaden, and down the highway to the airport. Pontius seemed to have no fear that Max the chauffeur would be stopped and cited for speeding. This had happened before and Max had repeatedly watched all around and in the mirrors for a police officer to pull him over; but it never happened. And Max knew the police had spotted him speeding and had registered his speed with their radar not to mention the traffic surveillance cameras that dotted the roads now. Max should have been picked up and ticketed long ago. This, too, was another inexplicable mystery.

Max pulled into the designated spot next to the waiting jet, the same spot to which he'd delivered the passenger only yesterday. It seemed a lifetime had passed since yesterday.

The serial numbers on the flanks of the silver-white jet read: *57914002.*

On the other side of the jet three women were exiting another car, a long, silver limousine with darkened windows. They were dressed to kill and that was an understatement. The women, in their mid-twenties, were walking like fashion models on the runway; they were moving in an easy lilt toward the base of the steps that were hanging down from the open door on the port side of the plane.

Two attendants with black berets atop their head and dressed in all black uniforms—-black tunics over black trousers and shiny black jackboots—-approached the Mercedes. Like the passenger's attendants they, too, formed an honor guard marching in sync, shoulder to shoulder, to the car. It had struck Max as odd before, just as it struck him as odd now, that the attendants wore such uniforms since they didn't seem to be part of any military...but it was just another oddity among many and who was he to question this too? It was just another thing he'd best not think about too much or he might go crazy.

Max grasped his door handle and started to open it. He needed to get out of the car and attend to the master.

"No, you will stay here."

"Yes sir." Max said it automatically as if he were a robot maybe. He hated feeling like a robot.

Now one of the attendants pounded twice on the lid of the trunk. Max pressed the button and opened it. Pontius remained seated for the moment...as the attendants returned to the airplane with the luggage. Max could only guess which of them had the heavier piece because it was impossible to tell from this position. Plus each attendant was equally sure of his payload and showed no unbalanced movement or body language. Both of them raced up the stairs to the jet and returned as quickly to escort Pontius.

The women were clustered together at the bottom of the steps waiting for their *benefactor*.

Before one of the attendants opened Pontius' door Pontius said, "Never touch another suitcase without permission."

The door opened, Pontius exited, and was escorted to the Gulfstream V.

Five minutes later, Max watched the jet racing down the runway and rotating upward. He watched it gain a thousand meters of altitude before turning left, west. He watched it until it disappeared.

He needed to go home and hug his wife and do a little gardening. The peonies were at their peak and so were the Siberian irises. He would bring some flowers to the kitchen for her to make a bouquet. It wouldn't be long and the daylilies would bloom and the poppies, as well.

CHAPTER 8

Pontius turned his head left and leaned toward the window, almost putting his Roman nose to the glass. He squinted and focused on the Mercedes and the chauffeur inside it. The chauffeur was still sitting there on the tarmac as the Gulfstream V rose from runway 34. The chauffeur and the Mercedes should have left the airport minutes ago. But there he was, still sitting there. There he was watching the jet taking off.

The *brave* chauffeur had done a *brave* thing in attempting to load that suitcase into the trunk. It wasn't that the chauffeur had never loaded a suitcase into the trunk for Pontius; it was that the chauffeur had butted in and grabbed the suitcase away from the attendant. That was very brave indeed and very foolish.

Insubordination, albeit committed in ignorance was still insubordination. The chauffeur had committed an act of insubordination against Pontius by interfering that way. Time would tell what measures would need to be taken to rectify things and make certain the chauffeur never did it again. Perhaps the stern warning Pontius had given him in the car would be enough.

Perhaps it would be easier if *all* Pontius' *employees* were *angels.* But, on the other hand, he enjoyed having a human chauffeur with a human wife and watching them self destruct. It was a game to Pontius; he loved being the cat and playing with the mouse and the mice.

In addition, perhaps it was a good idea having a human chauffeur. A human chauffeur was needed to provide *another layer of cover* for Pontius. Naturally, the Trinitarian-triumvirate had to keep their behind-the-scenes activities as low-key as possible before ratcheting up for the climax, the ultimate push to victory—-the destruction of the Jews and their step-children the fundamentalist Christians.

To prepare for this final push leading to the finale, the surrendering of the kingdom to its rightful heirs and ultimate victory, the *Luciferian-*

Trinitarian-Triumvirate needed some human beings...besides, noted Pontius for the thousandth time, humans were more fun than angels. Humans still possessed an element of unpredictability. Angels were completely set in their ways. Pontius would always enjoy the challenge presented by humans like the chauffeur and his attractive wife—-even though angels were so much smarter.

It gave Pontius immense pleasure to think about the challenges humans presented and...

And, the destruction of the Jews would prove no easy task. And neither would the destruction of their tenacious off-spring, the fundamentalist Christians. Both groups had some kind of innate power, some kind of inner drive, some kind of proud certainty about their beliefs. Both extremist groups were suicidal fanatics. Both extremist groups were fixated on some kind of overwhelming, overpowering worldview which gave them infinite strength to fight and an eternal unwillingness to surrender. They would die before surrendering their extremist, mistaken beliefs. So be it. Let the suicidal maniacs have their way. And it would be good to get revenge for the miserable life the Jews had foisted upon Pontius and his wife so long ago.

The Jews and Christians were *extremists* alright and they would be *tagged* with that label. That label would make the rest of the world hate them more and more as the Jews and the so-called *true* Christians would be seen as those who would dare to block the plan for world unity and solidarity. The New Agers' and everyone else's abhorrence for Jews and Christians would soon explode into violence against those two groups. Jews and Christians were doomed, without a doubt.

Indeed the *false worldview* of *the Jews and fundamentalist Christians* had to be tagged, and smeared, and isolated, and systematically destroyed in order for the *true* worldview to prevail. Pontius, the passenger, and the Angel of Light knew what the stakes were: The winners would be the Jews and their Torah and their progeny, the fundamentalist Christians and their false Christ, or the winners would be Lucifer, the passenger, and Pontius and Immanency. And the winners would, without a doubt, have *the power of life and death granted to them.*

Immanency...it was fun to *play* with that word, that word the religionists thought they understood but didn't understand at all. Playing with that word was as much fun as *playing* with the chauffeur. If the chauffeur showed any more disrespect Pontius would send an angel to take a closer look at the chauffeur's off-duty time and report back his findings. Pontius wanted to find out a little more about the chauffeur's wife, too. Pontius hoped the two of them were unprotected by the opposing angels.

The chauffeur's wife...

He'd met her once. It was shortly after hiring the chauffeur, one evening when Pontius had invited the couple to dine with him in Berchtesgaden. There'd been something...something in her eyes, her facial expressions, and her body language that had said much more than the cordial words she'd spoken that evening.

Certainly the woman was grateful for her husband's new job and all the benefits. He'd been unemployed for several months and things had been rather difficult. Now they would be back on their feet once more, she had said with a smile. The woman seemed pleasant enough, and naïve enough, not to mention she was quite attractive, as well, for a woman in her fifties. In addition, both she and her husband were Aryans which was another positive.

All the same, Pontius would arrange for a bit of spying once he returned from this trip. He would send a messenger to speak with *Darius* about it. Again Pontius hoped the chauffeur and his wife did not have a shield around them. Darius' would let Pontius know if such were the case. Until then Pontius would assume the chauffeur and his wife were typical human humanists and clueless as to what was really going on in the unseen dimensions.

Pontius pressed the button to make the seat vibrate and give him a massage. Once this massage had ended it would be time for drinks and then dinner. His entourage of beautiful ladies would sit around the table in the forward compartment and make small talk with their boss; they would flirt with him and when the moment was right they would all retire to Pontius' private rear section of the cabin with a fold-out, king-size bed. The Caesars had never had it so good.

Pontius returned to seriousness. At the conference in the Canary Islands he would release information on how to launch *counter-cyber missile attacks.* The Angel of Light had told him in a dream last night that the time for releasing the information was at hand. The Israelis had developed malware with the ability to decipher virtually every security code to virtually every security system in the world. The time had come to begin to teach those clever Jews an unforgettable lesson and turn the tables on them. Later, the three generals attending the conference would be instructed in *counter-cyber missile applications*. They would be told exactly what to do and when to do it.

CHAPTER 9

The passenger pressed his face to the window, narrowed his eyes to slits, and focused on the endless plains of Western Russia sprawling north to south and east to west beneath the rising, hot summer sun that was growing bigger and bigger by the minute, expanding into a gigantic, shimmering ball.

His *blitzkrieg* armored columns had rolled, rolled, and rolled across those dusty plains, churning them up while obliterating everything and everyone standing in their way. Whole towns and villages and thousands upon thousands of Slavic inferiors had been wiped out by the mighty forces of the Nazi warlord. The warlord's *Einsatzgruppen—-the mobile SS units*—-had followed the glorious and brave soldiers of the Wehrmacht and carried out most of the real dirty work, the necessary work of ridding the world of Jews and the Bolshevik Communists that were the brainchild of the Jew Karl Marx.

The passenger's four years in the trenches during the First World War had been validated by the work of the *Einsatzgruppen.* Never in recorded history had such a purging of the unfit taken place as that which began during the opening weeks of Operation Barbarossa. If only the passenger could have been down there to help...he would have taken pleasure in pulling the trigger on his Walther PPK 7.65mm and doing away with so many inferiors. Alas, being the Fuehrer had its drawbacks; he'd had to delegate those tasks to others...others *so willing* to carry out his orders. It was amazing how willing they were.

On the other hand, one should not be amazed. One only had to plant the seeds and water them and that ancient fertile ground of hatred and distrust and suspicion, that primordial desire for self-preservation would sprout and yield a beautiful plant and blossoms—-humans always, when pushed, resort to the most drastic measures to keep a roof over their head, clothes on their frame, and food on their table. One only had to understand the basic laws of the jungle and all else would be crystal clear. It was pathetic how many never grasped this simple truth. But useful idiots were, well, useful.

America...

The passenger pulled his thoughts away from the plains of Russia. He pushed them westward across the North Atlantic to the United States of America. Things were not going well for the United States of America these days...and they were about to get worse, a lot worse. And this was good, very good. The old America had to be undone and who better to accomplish this than the passenger and his minions? The upcoming *elections* would set the stage for the final conquest of America, the final reining in of America and her so-called cherished ideals. America had to be brought to heel and put in her proper place in the New World Order. There could be no doubt about this. America was too important to the passenger's overall goal to be left to her own devices. America was powerful and the passenger needed that power brought into proper alignment.

The time had arrived for a new kind of president to assume *control* in the USA. The time had come for a useful-idiot Marxist, a radical, an uncaring, brutal and clever leader to conceal the truth even more and deceive even the most observant, if possible. The time had come for the final dismantling of America's Constitution. This dismantling would lead to revolt, and revolt would lead to revolution, and revolt and revolution would lead to violence in the streets. The Americans would demand order and turn to anyone with the power to restore that order. A quasi *dictatorship* would be the result. *Then, once control was in the hands of the passenger, the useful-idiot-Marxist president would be arrested and tried for treason...and another election held and another useful stooge, perceived by the masses to be far better than his predecessor, would be installed. And the new stooge would be easily controlled and later overthrown.*

The quasi dictatorship would include Canada, Mexico and Central America, too. They would be forced into taking their places in one of the ten planetary-kingdoms. That was how it was going to be, like it or not.

But for now, fear alone of such a *dictatorship* taking over would be enough to make America weak in the knees and putty in the hands of the passenger. Via this new and upcoming Marxist president and a few brainwashed billionaire fellow conspirators, creations of Anatoly and his helpers, the passenger would take advantage of America's collective fear and soon set in motion everything necessary to provide that putty "in his hands"—-the next ten years, if all went according to plan, would prove to be a lost decade for the United States...so much strife, so much discontent, so much anxiety and sorrow would overcome the Americans as they lost hope, lost sight of what they'd once been—-a proud constitutional republic—-and saw what they had become—-a nation in rapid decline on all levels, in every area, in every sphere. The demoralized Americans, seeing their dreams slip away from them, would realize their final dissolution was right around the corner; their end would come about no later than the year 2018 perhaps sooner. The spectacle of the constitutional republic version of the United States of America's ceasing to exist would prove too much to bear. The vast majority would give up and yield to anything that offered some stability and the promise of food, shelter and clothing. And they would accept the new status quo like complacent, obedient Pavlovianized dogs.

Americans, all but a few die-hards that still possessed a long-term memory, had become fat and lazy and unappreciative of the sacrifices of their founders. The fat, lazy Americans had been living far too well for far too long. They were more than three hundred million spoiled brats that had had everything handed to them on a silver platter. And now the time had come to take away the silver platter and almost everything on it. The time had come to let them have a taste of suffering as they'd never before imagined...because in America's view suffering was for others, for the less fortunate, for the third world...suffering, deprivation, hunger and famine was simply impossible to fathom for Americans. And this would be the necessary shock to their communal consciousness...this coming time of famine would be the catalyst to bring her down and make her yield.

The passenger stroked his clean-shaved chin; thinking such beautiful thoughts pleased him. It relieved him from boredom. It was entertaining to visualize millions of once-fattened Americans wandering the streets in the cities and towns begging, all of them weighing less than a hundred pounds and dressed in rags. The waifs in those cities would be like the Warsaw Ghetto waifs. They would look like stray, mal-nourished animals.

But the real entertainment would begin when they realized there was no hope and turned on one another, especially when those dying of starvation realized not all their countrymen suffered like they did. No, some, maybe the majority would be kept rather fat to create more sense of injustice, more jealousy, and more angst and anger. This would be the point where Anatoly and his billions of angels would step in and stir things up more and more and more...millions of Americans would, in their desperation, be compelled to find a scapegoat. Someone always has to take the blame and that someone would be the Jews and those troublesome fundamentalist Christians. They would also turn upon anyone seen to be a social parasite draining the financial system via receiving welfare and staying fat while addicted to drugs and alcohol and cigarettes. The strong would readily turn upon the weak, the addicted, the social parasites and freely escort them to a detention center for liquidation. The strong would readily turn on those foolish government welfare workers and others naïve enough to help those who cannot be helped—-the strong understood that *all* the social parasites needed to go to a detention center and be *dispatched.*

The passenger gyrated in his seat. He loved hashing out these plans. He loved throwing out these ideas and playing with them like a cat plays with a captured bird. He knew the Angel of Light was watching him and enjoying this play right along with the Angel of Light's proxy on earth. In time the plan would crystallize more and more. Everything would gel. Everything would ripen. Everything would be ready for the harvest. *The grapes of wrath* would, without doubt, be picked, trampled and turned into wine.

2008 would certainly prove to be a critical year in the passenger's plan. Yes, indeed; and right now Pontius was on another *diplomatic mission...*it was amazing how well such diplomacy worked when a suitcase full of gold bars was opened, glimmering gold bars for all their sticky little fingers and hands to heft. The CEOs of the chip-making corporations were the greediest, greedier than the politicians and CEOs of other industries. The CEOs of the chip makers stood to gain the most, at least that's how it seemed to them.

The passenger almost let out an audible chuckle as he imagined those CEOs doing the quick math for the 1000th time—-there were 7-8 billion people on the planet right now, all of them needing to be chipped... 7-8 billion recipients of the RFID-nano tech chips not to mention all the scanners, parts and service; not to mention all the babies born every second, each one needing a chip implant. The greedy mercantilists' collective heads were spinning right now... those greedy heads were spinning this very moment while the passenger was sitting comfortably in his Gulfstream V watching the unfolding plains of Russia far below...those greedy, spinning heads were at this very moment sitting atop the shoulders of all those money-hungry, chip-making CEOs; they were all useful idiots, more putty in the passenger's hands as he sat here at this very moment knowing his time had almost come...*wenn das konigsreich unsere ist. Yes and when the kingdom belonged to the Angel, the passenger and Pontius they would send all those CEOs to the guillotine and lop off those greedy heads.*

The next America president had been pre-arranged. The man was perfect for the work. He would play upon their collective racial guilt and be elected with much fanfare. The election of that man would be lauded by nearly all as a great leap forward in bringing racism to an end in the USA. What nonsense!

According to plan that new president would implement his *Marxist* agenda and spread more and more fear and general discontent. He would overwhelm America by using his Leftist cohorts to *spend* her into oblivion. By the time the next president was finished it wouldn't matter much anymore what one's particular political persuasion was or had been. It wouldn't matter how powerful the USA had once been—-economically, militarily, and philosophically, even. Once the next president was finished draining the US Treasury, America would be a basket case and a bad joke.

The rest of the world would not mourn for America, though, because the rest of the world was already far more corrupt than America. The rest of the world would see America's demise as their opportunity to pick America's bones like vultures pick the bones of a lost and dying man in a desert. The last traces of *American exceptionalism* and the last traces of the much-vaunted Judeo-Christian ethic would be erased once the former version of the USA was discredited and discarded upon *the ash heap of history*. The new version of America would be perfect for the plan.

The ash heap of history—-at least Trotsky had done one thing right in coining that phrase.

The next American president would be nothing more than a Marionette puppet on the unseen gloved hand of the passenger, of Pontius, of Darius and Anatoly and their helpers. The other Leftist Marionettes that would make up his administration would strike the death blow and bring about the end of the once great USA through more regulations, higher and higher taxes, government bailouts of business, outright takeovers of many businesses; there would be more handouts, more welfare, a rapid down-sizing of the military; plus there would be a flooding of America with vice—-casinos everywhere, lotteries everywhere, drugs everywhere, sexual vice everywhere...this would give the moralists nightmares as they watched their beloved country sink into the sewer. It would make them so tired they would simply give up and let it happen. The moralists would become so demoralized they would believe they had nothing remaining inside them, no more power, no more moral energy with which to fight. They would believe they had been abandoned by the Almighty.

America would gradually break into two irreconcilable groups: the progressives and the conservative-fundamentalists. Elections held before the final collapse into quasi dictatorship would produce mostly stalemates. The courts stacked with Leftist, judicially-activist judges would exercise their power and prevent the conservatives, the constitutional republicans from ever regaining a foothold in the country. In ten years the USA would be completely conquered and never again possess its former greatness. Nations can indeed be overthrown...

It gave the passenger indescribable pleasure to think about the things that were about to befall America and how America was about to be absorbed into one of the soon-coming ten planetary political, economic and religious kingdoms. America would go down with little fight once the people saw the futility of resistance and *the grand and glorious benefits of taking their place in the New World Order.* Yes all this imagining and visualization gave the passenger a soothing inner peace and a certain inner assurance that what he had begun so long ago would indeed come to pass...National Socialism would rise again and this time it would never be defeated because this time the foes of National Socialism would be eradicated. This time the passenger knew precisely what he would do differently and that would make all the difference in the world and the universe for that matter. This time National Socialism would morph into Global Socialism and from Global Socialism into the elimination of all opposing forces except select Aryans serving their *Leader,* and all of them serving the Angel of Light.

This time around there would be no vacillation, there would be no delays; there would be no consideration given to any entity refusing to obey the passenger and his prophet and the Angel of Light. There would be no camps with barracks, there would be no expensive warehousing of resisters; there would be either adherents to the new dogmas or there would be dead dissenters and the elimination of those deemed, for any reason, unfit to live.

The attendant brought the passenger a mineral water and a plate of rice and steamed vegetables. The passenger only ate rice and vegetables. He could not countenance any sort of flesh. It made him ill to think of eating meat. It made him ill to think about drinking alcohol and smoking was forbidden anywhere near to the passenger. No decadent behavior like smoking or drinking was permitted around the passenger, period.

The western plains of Russia rolled on endlessly everywhere beneath the flight path of the Gulfstream V...north and south and east and west; but the cities, towns and villages were growing denser now, dotting more of that vast agricultural terrain, that bread basket of Europe. Bread basket indeed...until the famines strike, until the critical moment comes for the overthrow of Europe and Germany, of Europe and Ukraine and Europe and Russia herself...until the armies are called forth from humanity and mustered into service...until the time comes *to take a spoil* and once and for all end all the nonsense by bringing final victory.

My struggle is my victory. Mein Kampf ist Mein Sieg.

The passenger's eyes rolled about in his head as he smiled that strange little smile.

His face went blank. The smile disappeared. His genius mind went back to planning. But, in a certain sense, it wasn't really planning because all the planning had been done long ago. All that remained was to set the plan in motion when that one and only moment came...when that covenant would be signed.

He stared at his ring. He was Gog. And it was written that he would lose. But he would not lose. He would win and what was written would be proved false. He had not returned to earth only to lose once again. No. This time victory was certain. It had to be so. Otherwise he would not have returned. He was Gog.

CHAPTER 10

The jet approached the border of Poland, heading for Rastenburg and the Wolf's Lair. The passenger had already advised the pilots that he wished to do a special, nice-and-slow flyover of the Wolf's Lair. And after flying low over the Wolf's Lair they were to proceed to Magdeburg immediately.

Magdeburg, Magdeburg—-before continuing the passenger's journey of remembrance through Europe, before continuing on to North Africa the passenger had to pay his respects to Eva, and Goebbels, and to Goebbels' wife and children at Magdeburg....Magdeburg...the place where he would perform the first resurrections once the kingdom belonged to him.

After Magdeburg they would fly over some of the camps. It would do the passenger good, it would be a pleasure to review the handiwork of his former henchmen: In a moment the passenger would open the most excellent chart listing all the camps and all the *statistics.* Of course there would be no time to fly over all of the camps...however there would be time for Auschwitz-Birkenau, Treblinka, Majdanek, Sobibor, Dachau, Buchenwald, Ravensbruk and perhaps Theresienstadt .

The chart was in the black leather briefcase resting on the floor next to the passenger's seat. He reached for the briefcase now, relishing the action almost as much as he would have relished being there with his beloved SS on the plains of Russia. He placed the briefcase upon his lap and opened it and slipped the laminated chart from its soft white linen pouch printed with the Reichsadler and swastika in red and black. He set aside the briefcase and pouch and opened the chart and began to examine it just as he'd examined so many charts and maps of war in former times.

He let out a long exhale and spent the next ten minutes immersed with the names of the camps and the statistics. He could have done more. He could have done better.

He exhaled once more at the chart—-it had all been terribly inefficient. Such folly would not be tolerated in the future. The waste of manpower, the waste of energy and food had been astronomical. The folly of using so much slave labor had been a waste beyond all logic. Why had they wasted so much time using slaves to build things, to produce things? It had all been a colossal mistake...a gross error that would not be repeated.

In the future the detention centers would be the vehicle for dispatching the millions and billions...detention centers would be utilized plus the release of fatal viruses and bacteria. The next mass killings would have to be carried out in three years or less before any sort of resistance could be organized. The next genocide would make the former one look like children playing. The next time the *modus operandi* would be to bring them in, exterminate immediately, haul them away for burial in a pit or burn them in a blast furnace. That's it.

The yet unproved factor in all this rested with Pontius and his sector: The release of small pox and bubonic plague was the great unknown. The South Americans would be the first to undergo this test. And if it worked well on them Pontius would direct his efforts toward the East—-Japan, China, Korea, and Southeast Asia and India. If all went according to plan the entire *operation* could be finished in perhaps two years.

Only a few Aryans would be spared.

The Gulfstream V had slowed a bit and had been losing altitude for the last fifteen minutes. The land below seemed close enough to touch. The air above that land of Eastern Poland was crystal clear this fine summer morning. That *Lebensraum land* which had once rightfully belonged to the *Reich* would be absorbed, like all lands on the planet, into the coming global kingdom. The concept for *Lebensraum land available globally* for select Aryans would soon become reality.

It would be a hot June day down there. Perhaps it would be as hot as the July day Stauffenberg and his fellow villains used a bomb in a satchel to attempt to murder their chief. 20 July 1944—-*a day that will live in infamy*. The passenger had a notion to instruct the pilot to land. Surely there was still an airport nearby. The passenger had a notion it would be good to walk the grounds of the Wolf's Lair. However, he would not take the time. He needed to move the *remembrance tour* along...there were too many places on the itinerary before they would fly to Latin America, to Mexico and to the villa specially built for him.

20 July 1944. Those old wounds from that old bomb had disappeared when they doused Eva and him with gasoline in the courtyard of the Chancellery. The passenger stared at his hands and arms—-they were new hands and arms, the hands and arms of a young man of only thirty-three years. He looked down at his legs, also young and strong. His new eyes were perfect. He could see as an eagle sees. His mind was as clear as the air. He was as focused as a magnifying glass, as focused as a laser beam. His hearing was superior to any canine. And inside him burned an eternal flame spurring him onward to go out and conquer once again. He clenched his fists, relaxed them and clenched them again.

He brought his face nearer to the window and studied the topography as he would study a map. The scattered farmland west of the Wolf's Lair had vanished, being replaced by the forest, like the forest that surrounded the Wolf's Lair. The forest around the Wolf's Lair would still be intact and there would even be more of it now than before. The narrow, canopied roadway leading into the compound would still be there as well as the remnants of the bunkers and a few remaining buildings.

"We will be coming around the site on the north side, sir, and making a steep left turn at 300 meters altitude," one of the pilots announced over the intercom.

"Yes, good," the passenger replied into the intercom in his private cabin.

The pilot didn't have to inform the passenger of the aircraft's direction. The passenger knew precisely where the aircraft was in relation to the Wolf's Lair. He didn't even need the scrolling map on the laptop or the wall-mounted monitor to tell him where the plane was now.

And, as far as the Wolf's Lair itself was concerned, the passenger knew the fortress HQ in the forest as well as he'd known his wife. The passenger knew every tree, every clearing, every road and path inside and outside the compound; he knew every building and every bunker, especially his own bunker; indeed, he knew everything in the Wolf's Lair like a man would know every inch of his wife's body.

"Ah, Eva, when I am king you will be my queen." The passenger said it quietly and tenderly. She would always be his soul mate—and she would bring the passenger's soul back to life. She would revive him. She would make his cloning turn into a true resurrection.

Eva, the name of Adam's wife, Adam the first man. Eva, it was said, had been taken from Adam's side; and it was said this had been done while

Adam slept...a rib had been removed from the man and refashioned into a beautiful woman. It was fitting that Eva was the name of the passenger's wife. The passenger was, after all, the new Adam, the new man. He was the new man that would lead the world back to sanity...once the fast-approaching time of insanity and *purification* had run its course.

He was *the new man* that would bring about *the new birth of freedom* for the world. The man, Lincoln, had *coined* the phrase. If only Lincoln could be here and see who was *re-coining* it now. All the dialectical arguments had been preparing the world for the next phase of history...and Lincoln during his time had been just another contributor to the dialectic as the world was being made ready for this moment.

Yes, *this moment...*

*This moment...*was almost here. The hearts and minds of humanity had nearly reached critical mass. Once that critical mass was reached things would move along swiftly. Things would happen so fast almost no one would suspect what was actually happening. The few that might suspect something catastrophic, something cataclysmic was about to occur would be rounded up and dispatched.

"Indeed, may there be many who come to suspect, who come to realize exactly what is going on—-it will provide another excuse to eliminate them," the passenger whispered this conclusion to himself as he sat in his seat and watched the terrain below the jet and clenched his fists once more and imagined his SS purging the world of inferiors.

"Ah Eva...and I am doing this for you as well, my queen...my Queen of Heaven...my queen, my wife taken from my side as I slept." The passenger had turned poetic for a moment or two.

The passenger reached under the briefcase with the charts of the concentration camps. There was another brief case—-another, smaller leather briefcase containing his Bible.

The Bible was the same one given him by his auntie when he turned thirteen. He'd carried it everywhere. It was dear to him. *It held all the greater plans.*

At the military academy he'd drawn some annoying attention from other cadets because he'd so often sat alone under the maples reading the Bible. The cadets of West Point like the idiots at Harvard were fools. All of them were fools and useful idiots. All of them were easily used for the plan. None of them suspected anything. All of them believed *the law of uniformity*, the silly idea that everything would continue as it always had. All of them, too, had been blind and deluded. Good. They would go to their grave blind and deluded. They were not worthy of life.

He turned to Genesis 2: 21-24, the passage about Eva and the rib:

21 *And the LORD God caused a deep sleep to fall on Adam, and he slept; and He took one of his ribs, and closed up the flesh in its place.*

22 *Then the rib which the LORD God had taken from man He made into a woman, and He brought her to the man.*

23 *And Adam said:*
"This is now bone of my bones
And flesh of my flesh;
She shall be called Woman,
Because she was taken out of Man."

24 *Therefore a man shall leave his father and mother and be joined to his wife, and they shall become one flesh.*

Soon his Queen Eva would be joined to him once again and together with Pontius and the Angel they would rule the world...forever. All the gods had been waiting for what would soon take place.

He turned to the book of Daniel. The passenger was in that book, as well—-he was the main character of that book. That book was his theater. It was his feature film. The script had been written long ago...twenty-five centuries ago. And now he was here to play the role. He would make it come alive. The *Anointed One* had come at last. *The entire world is a stage* so it was said.

Daniel 7

1 *In the first year of Belshazzar king of Babylon, Daniel had a dream and visions of his head while on his bed. Then he wrote down the dream, telling the main facts.*

2 *Daniel spoke, saying, "I saw in my vision by night, and behold, the four winds of heaven were stirring up the Great Sea.*

3 *And four great beasts came up from the sea, each different from the other.*

4 *The first was like a lion, and had eagle's wings. I watched till its wings were plucked off; and it was lifted up from the earth and made to stand on two feet like a man, and a man's heart was given to it.*

5 *"And suddenly another beast, a second, like a bear. It was raised up on one side, and had three ribs in its mouth between its teeth. And they said thus to it: 'Arise, devour much flesh!'*

6 *"After this I looked, and there was another, like a leopard, which had on its back four wings of a bird. The beast also had four heads, and dominion was given to it.*

7 *"After this I saw in the night visions, and behold, a fourth beast, dreadful and terrible, exceedingly strong. It had huge iron teeth; it was devouring, breaking in pieces, and trampling the residue with its feet. It was different from all the beasts that were before it, and it had ten horns.*

8 *I was considering the horns, and there was another horn, a little one, coming up among them, before whom three of the first horns were plucked out by the roots. And there, in this horn, were eyes like the eyes of a man, and a mouth speaking pompous words.*

9 *"I watched till thrones were put in place,*
And the Ancient of Days was seated;
His garment was white as snow,
And the hair of His head was like pure wool.
His throne was a fiery flame,
Its wheels a burning fire;

10 *A fiery stream issued*
And came forth from before Him.
A thousand thousands ministered to Him;
Ten thousand times ten thousand stood before Him.
The court was seated,
And the books were opened.

11 *"I watched then because of the sound of the pompous words which the horn was speaking; I watched till the beast was slain, and its body destroyed and given to the burning flame.*

12 *As for the rest of the beasts, they had their dominion taken away, yet their lives were prolonged for a season and a time.*

13 *"I was watching in the night visions,*
And behold, One like the Son of Man,
Coming with the clouds of heaven!
He came to the Ancient of Days,
And they brought Him near before Him.

14 *Then to Him was given dominion and glory and a kingdom,*
That all peoples, nations, and languages should serve Him.
His dominion is an everlasting dominion,
Which shall not pass away,
And His kingdom the one
Which shall not be destroyed.

15 *"I, Daniel, was grieved in my spirit within my body, and the visions of my head troubled me.*

16 *I came near to one of those who stood by, and asked him the truth of all this. So he told me and made known to me the interpretation of these things:*

17 *'Those great beasts, which are four, are four kings which arise out of the earth.*

18 *But the saints of the Most High shall receive the kingdom, and possess the kingdom forever, even forever and ever.'*

19 *"Then I wished to know the truth about the fourth beast, which was different from all the others, exceedingly dreadful, with its teeth of iron and its nails of bronze, which devoured, broke in pieces, and trampled the residue with its feet;*

20 *and the ten horns that were on its head, and the other horn which came up, before which three fell, namely, that horn which had eyes and a mouth which spoke pompous words, whose appearance was greater than his fellows.*

21 *"I was watching; and the same horn was making war against the saints, and prevailing against them,*

22 *until the Ancient of Days came, and a judgment was made in favor of the saints of the Most High, and the time came for the saints to possess the kingdom.*

23 *"Thus he said:*
'The fourth beast shall be
A fourth kingdom on earth,

Which shall be different from all other kingdoms,
And shall devour the whole earth,
Trample it and break it in pieces.

24 *The ten horns are ten kings*
Who shall arise from this kingdom.
And another shall rise after them;
He shall be different from the first ones,
And shall subdue three kings.

25 *He shall speak pompous words against the Most High,*
Shall persecute the saints of the Most High,
And shall intend to change times and law.
Then the saints shall be given into his hand
For a time and times and half a time.

26 *' But the court shall be seated,*
And they shall take away his dominion,
To consume and destroy it forever.

27 *Then the kingdom and dominion,*
And the greatness of the kingdoms under the whole heaven,
Shall be given to the people, the saints of the Most High.
His kingdom is an everlasting kingdom,
And all dominions shall serve and obey Him.'

28 *"This is the end of the account. As for me, Daniel, my thoughts greatly troubled me, and my countenance changed; but I kept the matter in my heart."*

The passenger was ecstatic. He especially loved verses 5, 8, and 20...he loved the idea of the *three horns* being pulled out by the roots, and the three horns being cast down. This described exactly what he would do to America, Europe and Russia—-these nations were the three horns, the first three planetary-kingdoms of the ten...and he was the little horn coming up from among them...he was from these people...as Gog he was destined to lead them...he would first become *their* Fuehrer before he would become Fuehrer of the world...and once he was Fuehrer of the world he would send Anatoly and his angels to empty all jails on the planet to provide personnel for the coming SSF-CAC, the Special Security Forces and

Citizens Auxiliary Corps that would also help put into operation *the plan.* In addition, Anatoly and his angels would rally the Muslims and use their Sharia law to threaten all non-Muslims. The non-Muslims' deathly fear of Sharia law's implementation would further solidify the passenger's control as he showed the non-Muslims the way to neutralize the Sharia-Muslims; and he would use the Sharia-Muslims' and the so-called moderate and liberal Muslims' undying hatred of the Jews combined with the rest of the world's undying hatred of those hapless people to re-create a worldwide *Roman Empire* the Caesars never could have imagined. Fear and suspicion would rule the day; *fear and suspicion,* these two things would combine with the universal need of humans for law and order, the law and order that the passenger would give them. The masses would cry out for him, they would beg him, the passenger, to come and give them that law and order, and give them stability, and liberate them from certain destruction. *Ave Caesar!*

The passenger re-read verses 23-25:

23 *"Thus he said:*

'The fourth beast shall be
A fourth kingdom on earth,
Which shall be <u>different</u> from all other kingdoms,
And shall devour the whole earth,
Trample it and break it in pieces.

24 *The ten horns are ten kings*
Who shall arise from this kingdom.
And another shall rise after them;
He shall be different from the first ones,
And shall subdue three kings.

25 *He shall speak pompous words against the Most High,*
Shall persecute the saints of the Most High,
And shall intend to change times and law.
Then the saints shall be given into his hand
For a time and times and half a time.

The fourth beast—-the fourth beast would be as Rome x 1,000 or x a 1,000,000. And within ten years the *new* Rome would be ruled by him, the passenger; he would be Caesar. And the new Caesar, Gog, would defeat the other three beasts on earth, the lion, the bear, the leopard and force the new planetary *Roman Empire* into the already-established ten planetary-kingdoms—-the ten political-economic-religious planetary-kingdoms. And he, Gog, would be *different* just as the text said. And the ten lesser kings of the world would give all allegiance to him their savior and the savior of humanity.

And his words might be considered *pompous* by a few or perhaps by many; it did not matter. What mattered was bringing in the kingdom of the Angel of Light and if he, Gog, had to change some *laws and times* he would do it. If he had to eliminate all who opposed him he wouldn't hesitate to do that either. The passenger savored his repeating thoughts of destruction...the destruction necessary to bring in the final resolution, the final peace.

"For a time and times and half a time...yes, three and a half years..."

It was remarkable how accurate this book of Daniel was...this Daniel, this Jew had written the truth; he had foretold what was about to happen. This Daniel, this Jew had written intelligently and accurately. But now it was the passenger's responsibility to fulfill the prophecies the way the Angel of Light wanted them fulfilled...the passenger was the *True Messiah that would bring in the True Kingdom.*

The passenger lifted his eyes from the Bible and watched the earth below. His graceful, bony hands were trembling a little but his gaze was steady—-and his hands only trembled because of the excitement welling up once again inside the passenger as once again he thought about his fantasy becoming reality. And he would see to it that every *human* believed that their fantasy too, whatever it was, would become a reality. Each one of those little mystics would achieve deity; everyone would so identify with the Caesar that they would be one with him—-oneness combined with unity-in-diversity combined with Immanency. Gimel, Vav, Gimel—-Vav, Vav, Vav. *Immanency* was a grand notion, and useful.

It would be pure pleasure to write the sequel to *Mein Kampf.* If he weren't so distracted by this journey of remembrance he would begin to write *Mein Sieg* immediately. However, he would wait. He would let all the concepts and ideas age like fine wine. At the right time the wine would be poured out into a chalice and served to the world—-the passenger was waxing poetic once again.

He would allow the storm clouds to gather even more before he unleashed the wind and lightning and thunder and rain...before he would *'let slip the dogs of war'*...then, after he'd conquered the whole world, they would know exactly who he was... and *that day* they would bow down and worship him.

Then the saints shall be given into his hand

For a time and times and half a time.

Nothing can stop the unstoppable. Nothing can alter history. Nothing can undo the words of Daniel the prophet and the other prophets that wrote about the passenger so long ago...so long ago.

He turned to Daniel chapter 9. This chapter contained another of his favorite passages; it contained another prophecy about him. It was another prophecy the passenger would be pleased to fulfill. For what was prophecy if it cannot be fulfilled, if it cannot be made to come true? It would be a lie. The passenger would see to it that this passage and many others came true *in the future.*

He ran his eyes down the page. He placed his long, skinny index finger on the verses. He ran the finger to the bottom of the verses, enjoying the experience. He lifted the finger slightly and let it drift to the top once more. He narrowed his steely-blue eyes. A bead of sweat trickled down his forehead.

This beautiful, exhilarating passage penned so long ago by the Prophet Daniel was some of the prophet's best writing.

The passenger closed his eyes and visualized his army groups poised for the attack, ready for the assault on the Middle East and Israel and Jerusalem. He visualized his massive armada covering the southern flank of Europe and the vanguard moving into place off Israel when the right moment came. The passenger would turn Jerusalem into *a cup of trembling* for the world. Jerusalem's conquest was the key to everything. He opened his eyes once more and read:

24 " *Seventy weeks are determined*
For your people and for your holy city,
To finish the transgression,
To make an end of sins,
To make reconciliation for iniquity,
To bring in everlasting righteousness,

To seal up vision and prophecy,
And to anoint the Most Holy.

25 *" Know therefore and understand,*
That from the going forth of the command
To restore and build Jerusalem
Until Messiah the Prince,
There shall be seven weeks and sixty-two weeks;
The street shall be built again, and the wall,
Even in troublesome times.

26 *" And after the sixty-two weeks*
Messiah shall be cut off, but not for Himself;
And the people of the prince who is to come
Shall destroy the city and the sanctuary.
The end of it shall be with a flood,
And till the end of the war desolations are determined.

27 *Then he shall confirm a covenant with many for one week;*
But in the middle of the week
He shall bring an end to sacrifice and offering.
And on the wing of abominations shall be one who makes desolate,
Even until the consummation, which is determined,
Is poured out on the desolate

The passenger closed his eyes once more and remembered his days in the Wolf's Lair—-if he could have seen himself then as he saw himself now he would have done twice as much, three times as much to win the war. If he had won the war the kingdom would already be his—-these great and beautiful prophecies would have already been fulfilled. Eva would be with him now; his mother would be with him now. All his adoring followers would be with him now.

He opened his eyes and looked through the window. He turned to the monitor.

According to the data scrolling on the monitor and the screen on the laptop it was still 200 kilometers to the Wolf's Lair. The jet's altitude was now 7,000 meters. Its speed was 350 kilometers per hour. There was still time to study more of these prophecies. There was still time to savor the words.

He scanned the page as more beads of sweat rolled down his forehead. He wiped them away with the back of his hand. He was back in Nuremburg giving a speech. He had hundreds of thousands gathered before him, line after line after line of believers worshiping him.

The passenger had conjured up the spirits and sent them out from the dais at Nuremburg to take control of each of his hundreds of thousands of devoted followers. The powers emanating from the Angel of Light had been one with the powers emanating from the passenger. In Nuremburg the Angel of Light had overshadowed him and melded into the passenger's being; in Nuremburg they were one. Soon the whole world would become a Nuremburg Rally. Soon the Angel of Light would overshadow the passenger and Pontius. Soon Pontius would call down fire from heaven and baptize the masses with the fire.

The airplane bounced about in the turbulence. It yawed right and left and right. Orange and white lightning flashed in the air outside the jet. Satiny black thunderclouds had come up suddenly out of nowhere, shrouding the Gulfstream V with inky darkness.

The cabin interior lights came on automatically. The passenger reached for the chart again and ran his eyes over it, right and left and right and up and down, massaging it with his steely eyes. He could barely contain his delight, his euphoria from looking at the numbers. And this was nothing more than an appetizer for the main course to be served upon the world in a few short years. This chart only represented a beginning of the birth pangs, a beginning of the sorrows...

He set his eyes upon Daniel chapter 9 once more. He read verse 27:

27 *Then he shall confirm a covenant with many for one week;*
But in the middle of the week
He shall bring an end to sacrifice and offering.
And on the wing of abominations shall be one who makes desolate,
Even until the consummation, which is determined,
Is poured out on the desolate

He, Antiochus Epiphanes, he, Gog, would indeed make a covenant with the Israelites. And it would be a delight to see them fall into the trap. The Jews believe they are clever, smart, intelligent, talented, and self-reliant. The passenger would use all their collective, so-called talents, their collective advantages, their collective beliefs about being superior to the rest of humanity; the passenger would be using it all to his advantage, not theirs.

The peace accord the world had been waiting for, the peace accord the planet had been longing for; the peace accord the entire globe had been craving would come at last. Peace would be established...peace, peace...there would be jubilant billions on the planet dancing and dancing and dancing. It would be a global party, a global feast without end. The passenger would extend the seven year agreement; he would make it *ad infinitum...*

And there would be a chicken in every pot, a car in every garage; every planetary citizen would have complete medical care provided by their ten planetary-kingdom governments...and these ten kingdoms would be answerable to the passenger, Pontius and the Angel. Peace indeed. There would be peace...until the detention centers were ready...until the staff for the Special Security Force and Citizens Auxiliary Corps had been released from all the jails of the world. The SSF and CAC would do exactly what the passenger wanted. The SSF-CAC would be completely devoted to carrying out their master's plan; they would all be told about the great rewards awaiting all of them once the world had been subdued and the keys to the kingdom delivered up to the passenger. And once that happened and the SSF-CAC were no longer needed they, too, would be eliminated.

The passenger read the next two lines of the verse:

But in the middle of the week
He shall bring an end to sacrifice and offering.

The passenger would bring an end to the Jews' rituals and then he would redirect their worship to him and the one true god—-the Angel of Light. The passenger would have to do this as punishment for the collective mistake the Jews and their ugly step children the Christians had made; they had let themselves become deluded into thinking they worship the true god. No, no, and no! The Angel was the true god, and the passenger was his son and Pontius the mouthpiece for the son. The passenger was the only true Son of God. Pontius was the Holy Prophet and the Angel of Light was the Almighty.

As part of redirecting the worship to the one, true Almighty God, the passenger would stop the sacrificing of animals. It was wrong to kill animals; it was wrong to shed their blood cruelly; it was a nasty business and would not be tolerated, among any religion on earth, once the passenger had taken his place in the Temple. The only lawful food and drink would be planetary-kingdom approved food and drink—-vegetarianism would replace eating meat. This would provide a two-fold benefit for humanity:

1. All humans would be healthier.
2. Limiting diets to fruits and vegetables would allow grazing lands to return to their natural state.

The passenger loved visualizing all those gullible New Age vegetarians believing Pontius and him. The passenger could hardly wait until that day arrived. He could hardly wait to see what the idiots would do when they saw Pontius calling down fire from heaven and when the little deified narcissists saw that fire spreading to every place on earth...when they saw the tongues of fire resting upon every deluded, mark-taking man and woman and their children.

The Gulfstream V bounced a couple of times in the turbulent air and the passenger turned to the book of the Apocalypse. It was another book he admired...it was as good as the book of Daniel. The passenger loved how those writers and prophets had coordinated their respective histories.

The passenger located chapter 13:11-13.

11 Then I saw another beast coming up out of the earth, and he had two horns like a lamb and spoke like a dragon.

12 And he exercises all the authority of the first beast in his presence, and causes the earth and those who dwell in it to worship the first beast, whose deadly wound was healed.

13 He performs great signs, so that he even makes fire come down from heaven on the earth in the sight of men.

The passenger had underlined that beautiful part of the prophecy, the prophecy of Pontius calling down fire. What a spectacle that would be...the final battle for the planet, the world, the globe, the final battle for *the kingdom* would be engaged; and, that final battle would be an extension of the Battle of Berlin just as World War 2 was an extension of World War 1. And to think the Great War had begun on *Tisha b'Av*. What irony! *Tisha b'Av*, the very day the Jews remember the destruction of their first two temples was the day the Great War had begun.

It was good to remember these things. It was good to return to the battle fields, and it was good to go to the camps. It was good to be alive, to be eternal. These were *the days of awe* and it wouldn't be long before he would provide the most awesome *Tisha b'Av* imaginable.

CHAPTER 11

And on the wing of abominations shall be one who makes desolate,
Even until the consummation, which is determined,
Is poured out on the desolate.

The passenger read the last few lines from Daniel 9:27 and contemplated the text.

He, and the angels serving him, would cause desolation. He, and the angels, would cause a thousand arguments, a thousand philosophical fights in a thousand places on planet earth to evolve into a thousand struggles of class warfare, a thousand versions of racial division, a thousand versions of *Mein Kampf*. He would cause inconceivable suffering for all who dared to defy his iron rule. There could be no other way to bring about the Kingdom of Light. There would have to be a time of desolation, of great tribulation, of great pain; there would have to be a time of birth pangs in order for there to be a birth. And some may believe him to be an abomination. However, they would be mistaken. He was no abomination. He was *the Christ*. And the only desolate ones upon whom the *consummation* would be poured out were all the disobedient people in the world, anyone that would not comply, and especially the Jews and the foolish Christians allied with the Jews.

It was horrible to think that there had always been that foolish cadre of Christian fanatics unintelligent enough to fall for the Jews' treachery. Both groups, Jewish and Christian, had to be annihilated once and for all.

The jet was flying smoothly once again. The sudden storm clouds had disappeared. The plains and forested areas of Eastern Poland created a lovely green and straw-yellow patchwork. Soft, puffy clouds drifted a thousand meters above the earth; their shadow-shapes could be taken for giant, dark tattoos on the land. The Gulfstream V's altitude was now 5,000 meters and the IAS—-indicated airspeed—-was 275 kilometers per hour.

The passenger read the last few lines of Daniel 9 once more, savoring each word. It was good to know the exact meaning of each word, line, verse and chapter and book. Clear vision was essential. Anatoly and his angels would see to it that this clear vision which the passenger possessed and Pontius possessed, and most certainly the Angel of Light possessed would not be permitted for the Christians and Jews or for anyone else, for that matter. Anatoly had special envoys to make sure the Jews and Christians stayed in the dark. They had to stay confused. They had to be blinded. It was unfortunate, though, that certain Christians, and certain Jews, still were protected, by Michael, from blindness and confusion—-but one day that would change, at least it would change for most of them. Most of them would lose their protective shield.

In the meantime, Anatoly's *special invisible forces* would keep close watch on the protected ones and on anyone else among the Jews and Christians that might begin to show signs that he or she had figured out what was happening. Anatoly's angel-helpers would know just what to do. They were excellent strategists and well-trained counter-intelligence specialists. They would plant doubt if doubt needed to be planted in the mind of any budding prophecy experts in the world. They would spread dissention and discord among the Christians and Jews and make them fight each other instead of cooperate with each other. Anatoly's helpers would prevent a large portion of those misguided fanatical, true believers from gaining any kind of *countering critical mass* and thus persuade the masses of humanity concerning what was happening. Anatoly's helpers would try to kill any *awakening* trouble makers if it became necessary. But it would be best to neutralize them in a less severe manner to avoid arousing suspicion. The time for making martyrs of them would come soon enough but it was important not to jump ahead prematurely.

The passenger's eyes rolled about in his sockets. He smiled his smile that wasn't a smile. He took a sip of fizzy mineral water flavored with bitter, sour lime. It was good to be here, it was good to be back. The passenger loved himself. He was enthralled with himself, and with his great plan. The passenger adored himself. The passenger was ecstatic over himself. He was thrilled, overjoyed, elated. He was euphoric. What he and Pontius and the Angel and Anatoly and Darius and all the angels were about to accomplish would be an event without equal. Truly the end of this age had almost arrived. Truly a New Age was coming. And he was the New Age King of the New World Order.

The passenger could hardly wait for the day he would raise from the dead all who had devoted themselves to him in the former kingdom, the former Reich. If Pontius and the passenger could be brought back all of them could be brought back, too. The passenger could hardly wait to see the surprised expression on Himmler's face the moment that little chicken farmer understood what had happened. He would be a most grateful little chicken farmer. And, imagine Himmler, once he realized he would be given one last opportunity to annihilate *a few more*. Imagine the look on Heydrich's face, as well. And the look on Goering's fat face, and Hess' face, that ape...and the look on the faces of Streicher and Rosenberg and Hans Frank and Mengele. It would be unforgettable.

But the passenger would not raise all of them from the dead. No, no, and no. He would leave quite a lot of those wayward generals rotting in the grave; he would leave their souls in hell. They deserved their fate. They had not done their duty. They had betrayed their Fuehrer.

And the assassins? The passenger had a notion to raise them from the dead so he could torture them once more before sending them back to the unquenchable fire....Count Von Stauffenburg and the rest of the despicable cowards. They did not deserve to wear the uniform of the Wehrmacht.

The passenger set aside his Bible for the moment and opened up the *My Documents* program in the laptop.

He clicked on the icon that read: *Biographies.*

The file opened to a page titled: *Nazi leaders.*

There was the list...the beautiful list containing so many names, so many *talented men.*

The passenger would only read one biography. There would be time to read more once the remembrance tour was over once the airplane was headed west across the Atlantic...the passenger could see himself now, sitting poolside in his chair in the villa in the Yucatan. To be sure there would be plenty of time then, to study the rest of the biographies and decide *the order* for the next hierarchy. As for who would be *the leader* of the resurrected Nazis? The passenger had almost chosen Bormann. And then he had reconsidered. In spite of Bormann's devotion to his Fuehrer there could only be one choice for the coming leader of the revitalized party. There could be only one choice for the man that would carry out the last purges of humanity just prior to bringing in the final resolution when the Kingdom of Light would cover the earth and only the select, chosen Aryans remained.

He clicked on the name: *Reinhard Heydrich.*

The file opened:

Reinhard Tristan Eugen Heydrich (7 March 1904– 4 June 1942) was a high-ranking German Nazi official. He was *SS-Obergruppenführer* (General) and *General der Polizei,* chief of the Reich Main Security Office (including the SD, Gestapo and Kripo) and *Stellvertretender Reichsprotektor* (Deputy Reich-Protector) of Bohemia and Moravia. In August 1940, he was appointed and served as President of Interpol (the international law enforcement agency). Heydrich chaired the 1942 Wannsee Conference, which discussed plans for the deportation and extermination of all Jews in German-occupied territory. He was attacked by British-trained Czech agents on 27 May 1942 sent to assassinate him in Prague (see Operation Anthropoid). He died approximately one week later due to his injuries.

Contents

11.1 Film

11.2 Fiction

12 See also

13 References

13.1 Notes

13.2 Bibliography

14 External links The passenger scanned the rest of the file, absorbing all the data in three minutes.

His eyes rested on one of the last pieces of info:

As of 2008[update], Heider, Marte and Silke are reported to still be alive.

So. The children were still alive. If the passenger had more time he would pay them a visit. However, there wasn't extra time.

The passenger read the last two paragraphs:

Summary of career

Service record of Reinhard Heydrich

Heydrich's time in the SS, often stated by historians to be a "murderous career," is a mixture of rapid promotions, reserve commissions in the regular armed forces, as well as front line combat service. During his 11 years with the SS, Heydrich truly "rose from the ranks," being appointed to every rank from private to full general. He was also a Major in the Luftwaffe, flying nearly one hundred missions until he was shot down behind enemy lines by Soviet anti-aircraft fire while flying a combat sortie. After this he was ordered personally by Hitler to return to Berlin and resume his SS duties. Furthermore, his service record gives him credit as a Reserve Lieutenant in the Navy, although during World War II Heydrich had no contact at all with this military branch and the entry was likely made due to his prior service.

Heydrich was also the recipient of several high ranking Nazi and military awards, including the German Order, Blood Order, Golden Party Badge, bronze and silver combat mission bars and the Iron Cross First and Second Classes.

Some parts of the biography were absurd. Some parts were ridiculous. It was preposterous to read some of the things these so-called historians had written about dear Heydrich. His was not a *murderous career.* Eliminating inferiors wasn't murder. Eliminating inferiors and trouble makers was a high calling. The real murderers were the Jews and their lackeys, the Christians. If not for them there would have been far less trouble in the world.

As for the so-called historians that had maligned Heydrich—-they would pay for their crimes.

Heydrich, like all the talented men soon to be resurrected, would know exactly what he must do to them all once he was brought back from the grave. In addition, Anatoly and his helpers would make sure that Heydrich, too, had all the necessary tools at his disposal.

The passenger looked at his left hand. There was the *Totskopfring* Himmler had awarded to Heydrich...there on the ring finger was the remolded, *resurrected ring with three letters*—-Gimel, Vav, Gimel...Vav, Vav, Vav...Vav, the 6th letter of the ancient alphabet. Three Vavs—-666. Gimel, Vav, Gimel—-Gog.

The passenger turned to Revelation chapter 13 verses 17 and 18:

> 17 *and that no one may buy or sell except one who has the mark or the name of the beast, or* <u>*the number of his name.*</u>
>
> 18 *Here is wisdom. Let him who has understanding calculate the number of the beast, for it is the number of a man: His number is 666.*

Gimel, Vav, Gimel=Vav, Vav, Vav—-666.

Could it be any clearer?

Unfortunately for the Jews and Christians and indeed for most of the spiritualist ants the message was *too clear.* For that reason alone most would not believe it. Their petty minds would not grasp it. They were all so deluded already. And their collective delusion would grow exponentially.

Gog...the number of his name...666 and the name would be imbedded in the chips...this would be the universal code all would receive in addition to the rest of their political, economic, and religious data plus their DNA data, their medical records and all other aspects of a person's existence. All would be tracked, all would be listened to, all would be monitored. Nothing would go unnoticed. And all dissenters, all those refusing the take the chip, and other non-essentials would be rounded up and sent to the guillotines and furnaces or exterminated using small pox and bubonic plague. Small-scale killing centers would still do it the old fashioned way using machine guns, rifles and pistols.

The passenger looked at the file again and re-read the part about Himmler giving the ring to Heydrich.

Totskopfring--Death's Head Ring. The SS insignia. Another sign of things to come...another sign that the sound of millions of combat boots would, in a little while, be heard across the globe. *Totskopfring. Gimel, Vav, Gimel. 666. Gog.*

The passenger moved his eyes back a couple of paragraphs in the dossier and read about the children once more:

As of 2008[update], Heider, Marte and Silke are reported to still be alive.

Heydrich's children, if they were still alive when their father was brought back, would be delighted to see their dear father once again. Imagine! And if they were dead, the passenger would remedy that. It would be a grand family reunion for them.

CHAPTER 12

The Gulfstream V was cruising at 200 kilometers per hour now. The altitude was 3,000 meters. The wings were slicing into the tops of the puffy clouds and cutting them into small, wispy pieces. The distance to the Wolf's Lair was less than 50 kilometers. There would be time to *savor* one more passage from *the book* before the plane did the flyover.

The passenger closed Heydrich's file in the laptop and opened *the book* once more. He could easily read the passage on the computer but he preferred the feel and smell of the black leather-bound volume. He loved to run his fingers over that black, shiny leather and rub the entire book with his palms. He loved to warm up the leather. Warming that black leather might warm his *black, cold* and *unfeeling* heart.

His black heart...

Once the kingdom belonged to the Trinitarian-triumvirate all the former sensibilities would come back. He would no longer be the cold man cloned from the cooling blood Bormann had scooped from the floor. He would be a real man and not a clone. He would be capable again of feeling the world as Wagner must have felt it and as his friend Kubicek had felt it. The world he would soon conquer and remake would be perfectly designed for the right sensibilities—-the correct sensibilities only selected Aryans possessed.

He opened the Bible to Revelation 13 and read verses 1, 2, and 3.

> 1 *Then I stood on the sand of the sea. And I saw a beast rising up out of the sea, having seven heads and ten horns, and on his horns ten crowns, and on his heads a blasphemous name.*
>
> 2 *Now the beast which I saw was like a leopard, his feet were like the feet of a bear, and his mouth like the mouth of a lion. The dragon gave him his power, his throne, and great authority.*

[3] *And I saw one of his heads as if it had been mortally wounded, and his deadly wound was healed. And all the world marveled and followed the beast.*

The passenger pressed down on the indentation at his right temple with his right index and middle finger. The cloners had decided to manipulate the genes and chromosomes in such a way as to make the scar reappear. The *technology* for achieving that had been dictated to them by Anatoly.

The Shroud of Turin...

Some blood from the head wound had been smeared into the shroud at precisely the location of the right temple. One of Anatoly's angels was *stationed* to watch over the shroud to make sure none of the scientists analyzing the shroud from time to time nor any of the faithful that came to view the shroud in the Cathedral of Torino would *see* the additional blood—-the time would come later when the angel would be ordered to retreat and that blood would become visible. Wait until the masses see that blood stain. It would be another great *sign and wonder*. The masses love to be deluded. They love to have their fantasies become real. At heart the masses were Gnostics anyway. And some were better Gnostics than others. And all were little, New Age mystics.

The passenger read the verses again, and again, and again. The prophecy would come true—-but not exactly in the manner described. The passenger was not a terrible beast. In truth, he was a benevolent man. He would be doing everyone a favor. He would be sending most of them to their sacred afterlife sooner. They all must die anyway so why wait? Let them go to their reward. Perhaps the Angel of Light would allow the passenger to bring them all back after they had suffered *a proper sentence in the fires*. Perhaps they could then be dispatched to other parts of the universe while the passenger ruled the kingdom here with his selected Aryans, his new race: *Homo Noeticus*.

The passenger was clenching his fists and shaking his head. He pounded the tray table like he'd pounded many a conference table while scolding his generals. He gnashed his teeth and his mouth dropped at the corners.

No, no, and no. There would be no returning to life for anyone who had opposed the passenger. They deserved what they were soon to receive. They were miscreants and misfits all. They had to go. Nothing would ever be accomplished until they were sent into oblivion.

The passenger calmed himself, wiped away some sweat from his brow with the handkerchief, and massaged Revelation 13:1-3 with his fingertips.

The words were dancing; the very letters were vibrating; they were leaving the page now and floating in the air around the passenger's head.

The words, the letters lined up and stiffened into a short Roman sword, *stabbing* the indented scar at the right temple, and exiting the left temple. The words and letters swirled about like a miniature tornado in front of the passenger. They migrated upward toward the top of his head and swirled horizontally and settled there, forming a crown.

The crown of letters and words floated upward and swirled in the air in front of the passenger and became a perfect 3-D likeness, an exquisite hologram of a Walther PPK 7.65mm.

The weapon came undone as the letters and words spun around once more and circled his head and lined up in the correct order, going single file and returning to the page and sticking there.

He put the tip of his right index finger to the first word and dragged the finger to the right, reading the words out loud in his east coast American English:

> *"1 Then I stood on the sand of the sea. And I saw a beast rising up out of the sea, having seven heads and ten horns, and on his horns ten crowns, and on his heads a blasphemous name.*
>
> *2 Now the beast which I saw was like a leopard, his feet were like the feet of a bear, and his mouth like the mouth of a lion. The dragon gave him his power, his throne, and great authority.*
>
> *3 And I saw one of his heads as if it had been mortally wounded, and his deadly wound was healed. And all the world marveled and followed the beast."*

Wait until the masses *hear* his voice, wait until they *figure out* who he is. In the near term the passenger would alter his voice a little to conceal his identity. He wasn't concerned about anyone recognizing his face. He was, after all, only thirty-three and who among humanity would believe it was him? The answer: No one would believe it was him until the day he would enthrone himself in the Temple and demand worship.

And all the world marveled and followed the beast...

He read once more about the dragon giving him his power. How dare they refer to the Angel of Light as a *dragon*? And how dare they refer to a blasphemous name written across the seven heads? And yet, this is exactly what the prophet said would happen.

But they would not get away with blaspheming the Angel of Light and the Angel's servants. Those who did that would pay for their crime.

The seven leaders of the seven empires...each of them in turn had done what they thought was right. The passenger, the seventh leader, had done what he thought was right during the time of the Reich. Every man does what he thinks is right given the circumstances of his particular time in world history. This is logical.

The updating information on the map showed it was 20 kilometers to the Wolf's Lair. He turned to Revelation 17:9-11.

9 *"Here is the mind which has wisdom: The seven heads are seven mountains on which the woman sits.*

10 *There are also seven kings. Five have fallen, one is, and the other has not yet come. And when he comes, he must continue a short time.*

11 *The beast that was, and is not, is himself also the eighth, and is of the seven, and is going to perdition.*

*And is going to perdition...*and this is where the struggle would be most difficult... but this is where the passenger would win...he would prove he is god and can change times and laws...he would prove he can change prophecy.

The passenger read verse 10 once more...

The seven kings were seven kingdoms—-Egypt, Assyria, Babylon, Medo-Persia, Greece, Rome and the Third Reich...the first five had vanished into history before the writer recorded the prophecy...and Rome was in existence when the prophecy was given...and the Third Reich had not yet come...and when it came it lasted a short time

The passenger read verse 11.

The beast that was, and is not, is himself also the eighth, and is of the seven...

The beast that was...20 April 1889-30 April 1945...*and is not*...he had been absent from earth 30 April 1945 until 20 April 1975...*is himself also the eighth*...the passenger was indeed the eighth world ruler...*and is of the seven*...he was without a doubt one of the seven...he was *the seventh*...he was *Hitler*...and now he was *Gog*...and soon he would be *Caesar*...and then he would be *King of Babylon* incarnate.

The Gulfstream V was 4 kilometers northeast of the Wolf's Lair. The pilots had brought the plane to less than 400 meters in altitude and were making the right turn to the northwest. They would fly the jet just to the northeast of the Wolf's Lair making several left turns—-west and southwest and south and east and north and west once more, completing the circle.

The air at this low altitude was hot. The outside air temperature read 30 degrees Celsius. If it was this hot at this altitude it would be 20 percent hotter in the Wolf's Lair. It would be at least a 100 Fahrenheit. How many sweltering days had the passenger spent down there as the Wehrmacht rolled into the U.S.S.R. in 1941 in Barbarossa? How many sweltering, anxious nights and days and nights and days, sending and receiving messages? Those were sweltering days and nights of glory. And they would have been more glorious if the passenger's armies had wiped the Marxists from the map in 1941.

The passenger would have seen to the execution of Stalin personally...after the scoundrel had been given a *fair trial.* And the passenger would have selected the piano wire for stringing him up. He would have had the execution filmed and would have enjoyed watching that sly dog squirming at the end of the metal rope. The idiots in Britain, beginning with Churchill, and the idiots in America, beginning with Roosevelt, had committed a grave error by allying themselves with that dog. That dog was their true enemy, not the passenger. But Churchill and Roosevelt were too dim-witted to know it.

The jet turned hard to the left. The passenger put his eyes to the window. There was his main bunker. There he had commanded his armies. From there he had sent millions to their death.

Soon he would send billions more to their death—-this would be the price exacted from the world for having rejected the Fuehrer. The billions about to die would avenge the millions of brave soldiers of the Wehrmacht. Billions for millions was a fair trade when comparing the inferior mongrels with the Aryan men of the Wehrmacht.

But there could be no real comparison between Aryans and others. It would like comparing apples to oranges or rather like comparing swine to thoroughbred horses.

In the coming kingdom there would be no more *swine.* When the passenger sat on his throne in the Temple it would be *the sign* that no more *swine, nor more inferiors* of any sort would be tolerated or allowed to exist. The great purification was at hand—-take the mark and worship the passenger or die like a sacrificed pig.

The jet turned left again, sliding through the air at 200 kilometers per hour, skirting along the west side of the compound. Sections of the canopied roadway leading into the Wolf's Lair from the west showed when there was a break in the trees. How many times had the passenger traveled that road?

The jet made another turn, heading east. The wind whistled under the wings of the silvery raptor, making the raptor let out a shriek. The raptor was hungry and needed to find some prey, some unwary *rabbit in the weeds or a fish in a lake.*

The passenger stared at his long, bony fingers and formed them into an eagle's talons and closed his eyes.

He had seen enough of this place. It was time to go to Magdeburg.

CHAPTER 13

The Gulfstream V had accelerated to 600 kilometers per hour. The *pilots* would bring the shining, sleek bird to an altitude of 6,000 meters for the rest of the flight to Magdeburg. This segment would take a little more than an hour. In a little while the passenger would shower and change into an appropriate gray suit, a crisp white shirt, and a blood red and black striped tie—-the passenger adored red and black and white...as he adored the seven colors of the rainbow...the colors of the archway, the gateway back to the Antediluvian Kingdom of Atlantis, *seven* colors when spun turn into an *eighth* color—-dazzling white, a clean slate, an immaculate foundation upon which to rebuild and remake the world.

One of the attendants knocked and entered the cabin and asked if the passenger was hungry or if he could bring him anything else.

The passenger replied that he wasn't hungry at this time. The attendant bowed and then stood erect again and spun around on his heels and exited the cabin and closed the door once more. The passenger appreciated the attendants Anatoly had trained—-and once the invasion of the Middle East began each human soldier would have an invisible angel *attendant* assigned to him, to empower that soldier, to make that soldier do exactly what that soldier must do.

The passenger typed in a request for the current weather in Magdeburg.

Clouds, 40 kilometer winds gusting to 50;10 degrees Celsius with moderate to heavy rain, the data read. A cold front had just swept through the area. Before disembarking, the passenger would don the black raincoat and the fedora. He would pull up the collar to keep out the rain and chilly wind.

At the same time he would take pleasure in that rain and cold—-it would remind him of the rain and cold of those miserable and heroic trenches during the Great War. The rain and cold would remind him of running and slogging through the water and mud of those gigantic labyrinths, delivering messages and dodging the shells.

The shells and their white-hot, sizzling fragments would whine and whistle and screech. The fragments would go *thud, thump, thump, and thud* as they embedded themselves into sandbags and boards and logs and dead, bloated bodies that had already turned blue-black in the putrefying grip of death.

The Angel of Light had guided and protected him even as the shells fell upon thousands and thousands and thousands of less fortunate men. Every shell that had missed him had proved he was chosen...every one of those shells had thundered out the endorsement of the gods. Every voice he'd heard, telling him *go here, don't go there* was the voice of providence. Although it was true; he had been hit in the leg one day and was gassed just before the end of the war. But that was necessary to toughen him further and make his medals for bravery shine brighter.

The passenger longed for those exhilarating days of shellfire and machine gun fire and rifle fire...days of proving providence was smiling on him...days of danger...days of death and dying...days of hunger and of purging...days of separating the wheat from the tares...the true soldiers from the look-alikes...he wished to deliver one more message...soon he would get his wish—-soon he would conquer the world—-soon he would walk the *greatest labyrinth* for the last time...*the greatest labyrinth of his rise to power that would be the pathway to the Temple*...and the final dispatch...the final message that would be: *Bow the knee and worship me.*

The jet's rear landing gear touched down on the 2 and the 7, the numbers of runway 27 in Magdeburg. A five-meter plume of water shot upward behind the plane and swirled in the blast from the twin engines. The water fanned out right and left as the nose settled into the concrete, making another plume fly up and slap against the belly of the aircraft. The pilot reversed the engines. More water spun up on either side of the Gulfstream until it slowed enough to turn right onto the taxiway at the west end of the flying field.

Through the water-streaked window the passenger observed the car—-a silver 2008 Volvo S60 waiting in the general aviation parking area. The driver was standing outside the car, wearing a tan raincoat and a brown tweed, waterproof Irish walking hat; the driver was oblivious to the rain and wind.

And the driver would know exactly where to take the passenger first—-to *Klausener Strasse 23*, to the Smersh Unit's Headquarters, to the place where once there had been a cement courtyard but now there was grass and walkways and a couple of trees. Now the courtyard was empty. No longer did ten skeletons lie there.

The driver opened the passenger side rear door and snapped to attention. The passenger sat down but did not remove his fedora or raincoat. Why would he? It was but a short drive to *Klausener Strasse 23* and it looked like it would rain the rest of the day and night and probably tomorrow as well. The fedora and raincoat would remain in place.

The passenger observed the driver in the rear view mirror. The driver was one of Anatoly's alright. Of that there could be no doubt. The driver wasn't like the chauffeur in Berchtesgaden—-the Austrian chauffeur, living in Berchtesgaden, the one that worked for Pontius.

The passenger wondered for a moment how well things were going for Pontius' chauffeur. The passenger might just give Pontius a call one of these days and ask about the fine clothes-loving and classical music-loving Austrian chauffeur and his Austrian wife. The passenger knew why Pontius kept hiring humans to be his chauffeurs...Pontius' chauffeurs lived in the town and not in the villa and sooner or later would suspect something was very, very odd about Pontius and his servants in that villa. Sooner or later a chauffeur or his wife would develop a loose tongue or would do something that gave them away. Pontius enjoyed watching his clever chauffeurs and their clever wives begin to suspect something was amiss. Pontius enjoyed setting them up. Pontius enjoyed letting them attempt an escape before he would track them down and kill them. Pontius enjoyed reeling out just enough rope for the chauffeurs and their wives to hang themselves.

The wipers on the windshield kept time with the pelting rain. The passenger ordered the driver to put in a CD and play Wagner.

The driver placed *The Ride of the Valkyries* into the player and pressed the button.

The Ride of the Valkyries...

*The Ride of the Valkyries...*the passenger was lost...lost in time and space as he raised his arms and elbows and moved his fingers and hands in sync with the tune. The magnificence of the piece carried the passenger away; it transported him to another world the world of the gods dwelling in the far north—-the world of the Valkyries...the female goddesses that would choose which warrior should live and which warrior should die when the time of battle came. But the passenger was beyond the reach of the Valkyries now—-he now transcended them just as he transcended Odin, as well. The passenger was untouchable and unstoppable—-only Pontius came close to the power of the passenger—-and only the Angel of Light was more powerful than the passenger—-and soon all the Angel's power would be vested in the passenger.

The music ended as the driver turned the Volvo to the left onto *Klausener Strasse*. The rain had not let up; rather it had become a deluge. And there was lightning and thunder and more and more wind. The trees lining the street swayed right and left and bowed to the passing auto. The trees could be the bowing masses of expectant humanity welcoming their conquering king.

The passenger crossed his arms in front of him in a gesture of defiance—-he would be the conquering King of the World. There had never been anyone like him in the past. And in the future there never would be anyone like him again. Oh, there had been a few that had eliminated more of the human ants than the passenger—-Stalin and Mao had eliminated at least a hundred million. But they had eliminated those ants for the wrong reason. They had eliminated them because they would not accept the Marxist dogmas and lies. The passenger would eliminate the ants because the ants had the wrong blood, the wrong DNA. The passenger would eliminate ninety percent of so-called humanity because they were unfit to exist. They possessed no essential merit.

He condensed his thoughts into words and declared:

"I will be King of the World."

The driver nodded his head up and down and said, "All will be fulfilled." The driver knew who the passenger was. The driver knew...

The passenger was standing at the podium in Nuremberg, waiting for the multitude to grow quiet before he would fill their ears and minds with *the truth*.

And another day would come for making speeches. The day would come when the entire world would be as it was in Nuremberg. The day would come when the whole world would become Nuremberg, the entire world would bend the knee to the Fuehrer.

"Spielen Sie es wieder."

The driver played *The Ride of the Valkyries* once again as the car came closer and closer to *Klausener Strasse nummer* 23.

The car slowed to a crawl; there was the place the Soviets had buried the passenger's remains. There was the place they had buried Eva. There Goebbels and his family had lain. There was the concrete courtyard or what once had been a courtyard of concrete—-there was *the cemetery*, now empty. No longer did any bones lie there.

The Ride of the Valkyries played on and on and on as the passenger sat in his place in the back seat of the car, gripping the door handle with his right hand and gripping his left knee with his left hand. The knuckles of both hands had turned white from the tension and the fury rising from deep inside the passenger—-it was fury for all the years he'd spent in the abyss, burning for crimes he did not commit.

He was frozen in his place, his eyes half closed. He was rotating his head right and left and right over the grassy area and walkways; he was visualizing the Russians in 1946 digging the holes, the graves and laying down the remains. After the burial they sealed everything in concrete before retreating to the Smersh HQ building and drinking vodka and eating smoked caviar spread out on the finest thin crackers the West could make; the vodka went down well that cold, nasty day in February; the caviar went down as well as the vodka.

Russia and Russians would pay—-once the kingdom was the passenger's he would make all of them pay. Russia and Russians would never be part of the coming kingdom; never.

The driver opened the door and the passenger's black leather shoes sunk into the soft, wet pathway of crushed limestone. He pulled up the collar on the raincoat and lowered the brim on the fedora. He drew his shoulders upward toward his head. He thrust his hands behind him, clasping them together. He stepped forward, his shoes making a squishing-scraping sound.

For a moment he was no longer King of the World. For a moment he was a pathetic little Charlie Chaplin, a depressed little clown in a 1920s Vaudeville play. He was a hunched-over black and white image from a grainy Nickelodeon flick; he had just dropped a nickel into the slot, a nickel he could have used many times as he starved in the flophouses of Vienna.

He lifted his gaze. There. That was the place she had rested beside him for twenty-five years. And there, that was the place the passenger had lain. And over there—-there was the place of the children, the beautiful children. And there Goebbels and his wife...

Enough! Enough of this!

The passenger turned on his heels like a soldier. He marched to the car, his arms and hands swaying at his sides, in sync with his steps.

The driver opened the door and closed it behind the passenger and proceeded to his place at the wheel.

"Nehmen Sie mich zur Brücke durch Biederitz."

"Ja mein Fuehrer."

The driver would take the passenger to the bridge near Biederitz. The driver could drive there blindfolded.

The driver was there that night of 4 April 1970, when the KGB scattered the ashes from the bridge into the river by Biederitz. The KGB did not see the driver because he was in his disembodied state. The driver was one of many of Anatoly's *angels* assigned to the passenger from the moment of his birth—-Easter Sunday, 20 April 1889. And the driver and many *angels* were there, in Georgetown, 20 April 1975. The invisible *helpers, the invisible angels* had surrounded the woman and the cloners as the cloners held hands and stood in a circle around her bed. *The helpers had mimicked the humans and held hands, as well. The Angel of Light had descended into the room and hovered above the woman as she screamed and the child was born.*

The passenger recalled everything once again—-from the moment he was placed in her womb...the gestation period, the birth; everything. He recalled his parents' death in the airplane crash. He recalled his Aunt Paula, his years in school, his years in the academy, and in the army; the army was glad to be rid of him; everyone had been glad to be rid of him; and that, too, was according to plan—-however, one day they would all welcome him once critical mass was reached.

The highway curved a bit to the right. There lay the bridge. To the left and below the bridge lay the sandy parking area. The driver eased the car into the lot and stopped and opened his door and stepped out and went to open the door for the passenger.

The passenger stood on the left side of the bridge and placed his hands upon the low wall and watched the dark water. The river was rising fast from all the rain. The swift current had become a mosaic of swirling pools and foam. The river was talking to the passenger, reminding him of that day the river had carried him into the ether.

The ashes were tossed into the river, thrown to the wind here; they were scattered from here, from this bridge, the bridge they called the Pig Bridge.

The ashes landed down there on the dark water. But the passenger had returned. Never again would any river carry away his ashes.

The Pig Bridge—-Like Antiochus he, too, would desecrate their Temple. The passenger, too, would bring *the abomination which causes desolation spoken of by Daniel the prophet.* The passenger would do even worse than merely sacrificing a swine in their Temple—-the passenger would set up his image and make them bow to it, to him, and to the Angel of Light.

The Pig Bridge—-it was a good name.

The passenger gazed into the black water. The rain came harder. The wind came harder. It was time to leave Magdeburg. He had paid his respects.

It was time to go on with this journey of remembrance and visit the death camps and the battlefields; and, in a few hours, the jet would leave the North African coast and fly to the Yucatan and the villa. And once there, there would be one more meeting, one more rendezvous with history past. There would be one more touch point between what could have been and what would be. There would be one more friend to greet and then to bid him farewell until the kingdom would be theirs.

Then the passenger would write *Mein Sieg.*

My Victory...

CHAPTER 14

The Atlantic coast of Morocco, bathed in pinks and umbers and purples by the elongated rays of the setting sun, lay twenty kilometers behind the Gulfstream V. The jetty and inlet which defined the harbor of Mohammedia was still visible to the passenger as he turned his head hard to the left to look back.

Farther south on the coast sprawled the city of Casablanca where Churchill and Roosevelt had met after the end of the Africa campaign. Beyond that Moroccan shoreline, beyond Casablanca, far to the east, far inland, far across the sands, far inside Algeria and Tunisia and Libya and Egypt the passenger's Afrika Corps had nearly done it—-they had almost managed to encircle the Middle East by meeting up with the Wehrmacht operating in the Balkans and Greece. The mighty German army had almost managed to join forces with Nazi sympathizers among the Arabs in the Middle East—-they had almost managed to capture all that oil—-the passenger's army had almost taken Palestine; the army had almost sealed off the Jews' last place of retreat and refuge, their last line of defense.

The next time it would go differently. The next time there would be no victorious meetings in Casablanca or anywhere else for enemies of the coming kingdom—-the next time the passenger would prevail—-the next time clowns like Churchill and Roosevelt would be dispatched immediately once they had been captured. The next time the passenger's armies—-Group A and Group B—-would smash their way into Israel and the surrounding terrain. The next time would bring the ultimate revenge. The Valkyries would be smiling upon the passenger and his armies. The Valkyries, the twelve handmaidens of Odin, would ride over the battlefields and escort the souls of the passenger's fallen enemies *to their Valhalla*.

The in-flight telephone was beeping. The number on the monitor showed it was Pontius.

The passenger pressed the button for taking a hands-free call and answered with a dead pan voice:

"Yes."

"You have finished your tour...I wanted to congratulate you..."

"Yes..." The dead pan voice remained dead pan.

The passenger lifted his cold blue eyes and gazed into the southern horizon of the North Atlantic. The Canary Islands were out there on the other side of the horizon. Pontius must be in the Canaries, still. Pontius had left the villa on the Watzmann one day after the passenger and had planned a several-day conference in the Canaries. "You are still in Puerto del Carmen?" Pontius had gone to Puerto del Carmen on the Island of Lanzarote to meet with the bankers and chip-makers and the rest.

"I departed Arrecife an hour ago...and now I am on the left side of your aircraft."

Pontius' Gulfstream V swung up to a position barely fifty meters off the port side of the passenger's Gulfstream V. The wings tips were lined up to perfection as the jets streaked through the thin, sub-zero air at 600 kilometers per hour.

Pontius was saluting and saying: "Hail Caesar!"

The passenger nodded his head; Pontius saw the nod; Pontius, too, had five senses as good as any wolf or dog. His vision was as the eagle.

"And the conference, Pontius?"

"The *Round Table* discussion was short...only three hours. The attendees had all been *well briefed* and were most cooperative. They were eager to hear *their part* of the plan—-especially the bishops and the other religious leaders."

"Bishops?"

"Two bishops—-*one Catholic, one Protestant.*" Pontius said the words *Catholic* and *Protestant* with contempt. Pontius knew how corrupt the two bishops were, he knew what hypocrites they were. He knew what power-hungry little thieves they were. "I gave *them* some of the gold. The rest went to the bankers, the generals, and the chip-makers...and a few of the *other* religious leaders."

"Two bishops...and other religious leaders..."

The passenger repeated the words *two bishops and other religious leaders and* let his voice trail off...

"Yes, two bishops, and a few others," Pontius said. "They had a *wonderful* time after the conference," Pontius added. "It seems the bishops and the others love women as much as I. And it was most amusing to observe the bishops and the other religionists, sitting there at the conference table, sharing their vast knowledge of philosophy and theology and science. They are I tell you, enamored with *Immanency—- their own version* of it, not ours."

"It is good to let them have *their own version* of *everything*...it is good to give them all they want...all they desire."

"Yes—-and they love their dialectical arguments, they love to discuss and argue and discover how much they share in common, and they love to find *solutions*. They love to show their tolerance and mutual respect. *They love their fractals and orbs, and quantum spirituality linked to quantum physics*—-one of the religionists was the chief rabbi of one of the largest synagogues in America. *He loves getting along* with everyone, especially with the two bishops. The esteemed rabbi has even written a book—-*Quantum Everything; the Call to Knowledge.* Plus they all *meditate*. They go to *the thin place*. They feel *the presence*. They feel *the light*. They are all *on the same page*, the Protestant Bishop told me. He even said they are all *change agents*...and that they have been waiting for *this moment in history...that only comes once*. And they want to make me the head of all religions...they want me to be their spokesman, their prophet, their teacher, their Minister, their Priest, their Rabbi, their Imam, their Guru, their Shaman...they want to bestow this power upon me...they think it is their duty to give me such titles. They believe they actually have a choice. "

Pontius could not hold back. He finished his speech by thundering out a long string of laughter and then repeated the title of the rabbi's book: *"Quantum Everything; the Call to Knowledge."*

Then Pontius declared, "They are all in the villa at this moment, having a grand time with the women I brought in. They are all meditating." Pontius laughed once more and then said: "And they believe in the Illuminati too."

"And *the generals*?" The passenger was asking about the *three* Aryan generals.

"The generals did not stay...they left immediately after the conference. They cannot wait to hear more about *counter-cyber missile applications and how to defend against electro-magnetic pulse warfare."*

Pontius was laughing again and repeating, "The executives and bishops and the rabbi believe in the Illuminati...and the Bildergbergs."

The passenger did not laugh. And if Pontius wanted to laugh it was his own business.

The three generals would prove very useful in a few short years. Each clever general held great influence in his homeland. Each general would be the key to the coming power grab, the key to taking control of the other *wild beasts of the earth*. The generals would be another *catalyst for the transformation*. These New Age generals had just the right amount of altruism, too. If they did everything according to instructions the passenger might keep them around so they could get their share of the spoils, maybe.

The passenger changed the subject.

"And the chauffeur and his wife?"

Pontius did not respond right away. Pontius was considering the question.

"I must give them more time..."

The passenger waited for Pontius to finish but he did not.

"And?"

"Darius informed me that the wife and now her husband have been *studying...*"

"Studying..."

"The prophets...the apostles...studying *them*...and Darius told me that the wife attends a congregation..."

"A congregation..."

"A fortress congregation."

It was silent for a long fifteen seconds. The passenger narrowed his eyes. Pontius waited for the passenger's reaction.

"Michael." The passenger showed no emotion as he said the name.

"The congregation is one of *Michael's*, yes." The irritation in Pontius' voice was plain as he confirmed what the passenger had just said. And because the chauffeur and his wife were under the protection of *Michael* they could not be destroyed by the *Angel of Light* or by any of the other *angels or by any other humans.* But they could be destroyed if they ever stopped trusting in their God to save them or if they were to act in a way not in accordance with the will of their God. Pontius might have to find a way, at some future time, to make them act foolishly. And there were many ways he could think of to accomplish just that. There were *many, many* ways...

The passenger whispered the name *Michael.* He seemed unaware that Pontius could hear him saying the name into the phone.

Pontius declared, "This is why I must wait...this is why I must give them more time to...*to act*...after they have become desperate...then...then we shall see what fate awaits the chauffeur and his wife." Various scenarios were already taking on form inside Pontius' genius, calculating mind.

There was more silence in the phone. The passenger was waiting, Pontius was waiting.

The passenger spoke.

"It is good to speak plainly about these matters, Pontius. When you take the necessary measures, do not fail. The chauffeur and his wife could present a problem. They are credible, Pontius. I saw it in the chauffeur's eyes...and a man with such eyes would only marry a woman of equal valor to him."

For a moment the passenger saw his mother, he saw Klara; he saw her credible eyes. For a moment the passenger saw the face of Doctor Bloch. The passenger had not harmed Doctor Bloch, the Jew. Doctor Bloch had done all he could for Klara. Doctor Eduard Bloch had earned the right to live. The passenger had given the doctor special protection after the occupation and annexation of Austria by the Wehrmacht, the SS, and the Gestapo. The passenger had made Doctor Bloch untouchable.

Pontius was talking.

"This is the first chauffeur, and wife, like this. I should have been more careful. It won't happen again. I should have told you about them before. On the other hand..."

"They will be more of a challenge." Once more the passenger finished Pontius' sentence for him.

Pontius pondered the passenger's words, and said, "*Iron sharpens iron.*" Then he said, "The wife is the *stronger* of the two. But one of Anatoly's angels informed me that the husband has asked that she *read* to him every night...from *the book*. Now he grows *stronger*, as well. The protection given the fortress congregation now extends to him...although he doesn't realize it yet...but I will get them..."

"*Iron sharpens iron*, Pontius, your words."

"Caesar..." It was the first time Pontius had called the passenger *Caesar* during a conversation. "Caesar, there is something else about the chauffeur—

his father served in the Wehrmacht...was wounded at Stalingrad...the father was an exemplary soldier...except for one thing. He took photographs—-of the SS and their *work*. It seems he took a lot of photographs. The father died twenty years after the war."

The passenger's knuckles were turning white as he made two fists. How dare a soldier of the Wehrmacht betray the Fatherland and how dare he betray the Fuehrer?!!

Pontius was still speaking.

"The wife's father also was in the Wehrmacht. He also was wounded, terribly." The passenger relaxed his hands and fingers. Pontius went on, "It may take a year, perhaps two. Then I will strike—-it will be my best game yet."

"Until I enter the Temple, they and all like them will remain protected by Michael...unless they do something foolish before that day comes." The passenger took a deep breath and said, "The chauffeur's father died young. That could mean the son has been lonely. He could be depressed. He might have a void in him. You must explore this aspect of his character. You must sift him, like potter's clay, Pontius."

"I will sift him. I will find the weakest point—-that is where I will strike. Perhaps he grows bored with his wife. Perhaps he is like the bishops and the rabbi?"

"Perhaps, Pontius, perhaps."

"I will get him...and her." Pontius said it as if making a pact. However, Pontius knew as well as the passenger that if the chauffeur and the wife did not act unwisely they would remain untouchable until Michael was withdrawn and the moment *critical mass* was reached.

"There are few left like the chauffeur and his wife, Pontius. Give them two years, maximum. Then you must strike. We cannot allow them to upset the plan. In two years they will have come to understand too much. They must be eliminated lest they become *a catalyst for preventing critical mass and transformation*, Pontius. And I repeat, there are few left like the chauffeur and his wife...very few...but numbers mean nothing if they become *a catalyst for preventing...*"

"Critical mass..." Pontius relished the term as much as the bishops and the rabbi and the rest of those deluded New Age fools relished talking about quantum this and quantum that. When *critical mass* was achieved Anatoly and Darius would unleash all the power of the Angel of Light.

When *critical mass* was achieved the passenger and Pontius would stand on the threshold—-of the ultimate kingdom, the final rendition of what should have been theirs all along.

"Pontius—-*seven heads and ten horns*...billions are about to morph. They will be intoxicated with euphoria from their greatness, from their grandiosity. They will be drunk with their ascendancy to deity. And they will be soft clay in our hands as we press them, kneading them, fashioning them more and more and more into our image—-they will be soft and pliable until we have them where we want them. Then we bake them. And *we will* bake them in *the oven*, Pontius. They won't suspect until it is too late, until they feel the boot kicking them into the oven...or until they are strapped onto the guillotine."

The passenger was clenching his fists again.

"The day I bake the chauffeur and his wife in an oven cannot come soon enough." Pontius was showing his irritation again. "I will kill them by baking them. I will have the oven built on the mountainside above the villa. And I will throw their ashes to the wind and watch them floating downward to Berchtesgaden...I may lop off their heads before I bake them. And I will not hire another human chauffeur. No more games. He is the last." Pontius doubted he'd really bake them...because another *plan* was taking a more defined shape inside his head. But he would wait and see if it would indeed be the correct *plan.*

"You will keep me informed."

"Yes, Caesar."

The two jets turned away from one another—-Pontius' jet circled to the left and back to Europe and Bavaria. The passenger's jet turned a bit to the right, accelerating to 900 kilometers per hour, and heading out over the open ocean to Mexico and the Yucatan.

Their vapor trails mingled, twisting themselves into a long piece of braided hangman's rope before the wind blew the rope apart and the jets vanished into the approaching night.

CHAPTER 15

The Gulfstream V made a final course adjustment and lined up with the three-thousand meter asphalt runway in the jungle. It was pouring cats and dogs, *gatos y perros*, or more fittingly it could be pouring invisible evil spirits that looked like some Mayan version of a gargoyle...evil spirits were falling down to earth, here, this tempestuous day in the Yucatan as lightning, thunder, and more lightning turned the rainy, blurry, pancake-flat landscape into a dazzling combo of green and gold. Every few seconds the lightning flashes made the millions of green and gold trees turn silver and then back to green and gold in the steaming, soaking forest. Evil spirits once again occupied the Mayan temples and the altars of human sacrifice as the Gulfstream V touched down.

The trees swayed in the wind in a kind of lilting dance—-the trees were happy, they were bowing down. They made for a triumphal entry, welcoming the passenger to his new residence, to his new home where, for a time, he would dwell among these Mexican inferiors, these Mayan cats and dogs.

The grand villa with its lap pool and gymnasium, and courtyards and fountains, lay in the sultry forest south of the runway. The forest, the jungle would operate as a protective *moat* around the *feudal castle;* the forest, the jungle was a protecting *sea* full of poisonous snakes—-coral snakes, rattlesnakes and other vipers plus boa constrictors. The jungle was crawling with millions of spiders and swarming with billions of ants. And there were scorpions, waiting with their tails curled up in strike position.

At the outer edges of the 10-hectar villa-estate a 3-meter high electrified fence guaranteed any intruder foolish enough to attempt entry that way would be zapped and toasted into a smoking ball of charred flesh and bone. In addition, the electric fence was topped with razor wire to create yet another deadly hazard. Emergency generators would provide emergency electricity in case anything ever shorted out or was struck by lightning.

Movable, revolving cameras had been positioned at 20-meter intervals on metal poles standing six feet higher than the fence itself. More cameras were mounted atop the thick 5-meter high masonry wall which lay inside the perimeter defined by the fence; the wall, along with everything else, totally encapsulated the villa, insulating it from all intruders...but the fence also contained hidden outlets, hidden panels that could be raised automatically to let out *the dogs* to deal with any invader.

The carved stone and stucco and tile-roofed villa itself, the house, the citadel was, except for the observation deck on the middle section of the roof, mostly a one-story affair. One-story structures resisted hurricanes better and one-story villas would be even harder to spot in the flat terrain of the Yucatan jungle unless some hapless Mexican-Mayan happened upon it. Or unless some wayward aircraft did a flyover—-but instructions to prevent that had already been sent to the governing authorities: There will be no flyovers permitted...unless the passenger gave an order to allow it. Plus the proper authorities had been bribed with a good amount of gold.

The villa's *security personnel* had been put in place by Anatoly. The *security personnel* would use human technology as much as possible for keeping the passenger protected. It would be best this way; it would arouse less suspicion if they relied on human technology. However, if human technology ever failed them they could always resort to *other methods...they could release the dogs:*

During the flight from North Africa the passenger had been informed via an encrypted text message from Anatoly that just three days prior there had already been a bit of trouble with some members of the drug cartels—-it seemed the Beltran-Leyvas and the Zetas had gotten into a shootout a few kilometers away. A chase followed with several SUVs stumbling onto the spur road leading through the jungle to the villa. But the warring cartels were met by a pack of a hundred dogs that had just been unleashed from the villa. The monstrous dogs, a cross between a Wolfhound and a Doberman, had killed all the cartel members, ripping them apart and eating them. When the passenger had been informed of the dogs' work the passenger had smiled that weird, perverse smile.

The passenger would deal with the cartels later, once the kingdom belonged to him and Pontius and the Angel of Light. But for now, it would be best to tolerate them and only kill them if they were foolish enough to come that close again. Besides, the cartels kept the drugs flowing and the drug addicts happy.

The brief trip from the landing strip in the silver Chevy Tahoe with the darkened windows was making the passenger fidgety. He'd had enough of jets and cars and now this SUV. He fidgeted with the door handle now. He could hardly wait to get out. He could hardly wait to shower and change into proper attire for a sauna like this miserable Yucatan jungle—-he would change into some black leather sandals, a pair of baggy, khaki slacks held in place with a black snake skin belt. He would put on a loose khaki shirt—-both slacks and shirt made of thin Egyptian cotton. This would be his *new uniform* during the coming years as he lived in the villa and composed *Mein Sieg* and continued to plan the final destruction of the Jews and Christians and everyone else except a few chosen Aryans. The passenger loved to repeat the basic thrust of the plan over and over and over inside his creative mind. He loved to envision the final plan, the final of final solutions. He loved to cast the vision upward to the gods and to the Angel of Light where the vision would be recognized as a kind of sacrifice.

After showering and changing into his new uniform, the passenger would walk the villa, the house, the courtyards, and the pool and gymnasium areas...he would inspect everything...then he would go to the roof and watch the long segment of the driveway from where it emerged from the jungle to where it arrived at the wall and electronic iron gate in front of the villa. He would listen for the sound of an engine approaching on the canopied road in the jungle. And the moment he would hear that sound...

He would come down from the roof. He would go to the library-study and seat himself in the great leather upholstered golden swivel chair which was more a throne than a chair. He would place his back to the 4-meter double mahogany door entryway to the room. He would wait for the knock; he had waited a very long time...

The knocking upon the door came softly and rhythmically—-*tap-tap...tap-tap...tap-tap. One-two...one-two...one- two.*

"Enter." The passenger said it, staring into time and space, and remembering.

The *security guard,* dressed in gray-green camouflage jungle utilities and black combat boots, swung open the great double doors and an old man stepped forward and stood at attention as best he could. The old man was dressed in tailored clothing to fit his thin frame—-a long-sleeved, white cotton Guayabera shirt, and dark, pleated linen trousers straight out of the 1940s. The black leather shoes were from the 1940s, as well.

The old man remained in place in the doorway; his left hand gripped a varnished walking cane made from acacia with a carved Death's Head symbol just below the handle; his right hand held a glass vial.

His chin was properly aligned with the front of his neck. His eyes blinked a couple of times behind the thick lenses of his wire-rimmed glasses. He had gone bald decades before and had shaved his head ever since. His skin was still smooth. Only a few tiny wrinkles showed at the corners of his mouth and eyes. Some of the skin on the head was semi-transparent, showing the veins and arteries and bone structure of the skull beneath it. The once youthful pudginess of the man's face had vanished with his hair; the long years of exile had done their work, sculpting the once youthful man into the image of the old man standing here now.

The old man took three more deliberate steps forward and stood at attention again and waited. The security guard used the opportunity to close the mahogany doors once more, sealing off the library-study from the anteroom.

The chair swiveled to the left and stopped; now it was turning to the right; now it was facing the old man in the white cotton Guayabera shirt and 1940s pleated trousers and 1940s black leather Winthrop shoes. The old man was trying his best to stay standing with his cane.

The passenger sat there, motionless, his arms and hands resting on the arms of the gigantic chair. His spine was pressed against the back of the throne and his feet were positioned parallel on the cool, terracotta-colored Saltillo tile floor. The passenger's eyes did not blink.

"Mein Fuehrer."

As the old man gently and reverently uttered the words, the fingers of his right hand loosened and the glass vial fell in slow motion to the floor, shattering into a *thousand* infinitesimal pieces. The shattering echoed across the room. Perhaps each of those thousand pieces of glass stood for a *year* of the *Reich* that didn't last as long as it should have...thought the old man as his left hand trembled as he tried to keep holding the cane and tried to remain in place.

The passenger lowered his eyes to the shattered glass sparkling on the floor. The passenger raised his eyes and looked at the old man once again.

"How old are you now, Martin?"

"I am nearly one hundred and eight, *Mein Fuehrer*." The old man trembled out the words.

"Well done, Martin."

"*Mein Fuehrer*...the vial...it was to be a gift, *Mein Fuehrer*."

The old man's voice still trembled but came on a little stronger now. The old man's thin frame was trembling but he stayed at attention.

The passenger ignored the confession about the broken glass and said, "Come, Martin...come closer."

The old man's shoes began their 5-meter trek to stand in front of the Fuehrer.

The passenger came to his feet and stood at attention, too. He stretched out his arms, his shirt sleeves riding back, his wrists showing, and revealing his scars.

"Touch the scars, Martin, and doubt no longer."

The old man graced each scar with the fingertips of his bony right hand. He looked downward at the passenger's ankles. The khaki trousers made it impossible to see...

"There are scars there, as well...and upon my back, my brow, and my side."

The old man raised his eyes and gazed at the passenger's brow, studying the hairline. These scars were less visible but they were scars nonetheless.

The passenger had told the old man what he intended once he had returned—-the passenger had told him of the vision—-of the labyrinth, the iron case, the whip, the spear point, the hammer and spike, and the crown of thorns; the passenger had told the old man of the vision one day as they stood side by side at the edge of the stone patio atop the Obersalzberg, the patio in front of the Eagle's Nest with the view of the Watzmann and the view of Berchtesgaden far below. The passenger had told Martin about the blood, and how to preserve it. The passenger had told Martin everything and then had told him to wait for him. The passenger had said that Martin would be all right, that he would escape, and that they would look for him but never find him.

"Martin. Do you still read the prophet? Are you still *un aficionado de Daniel?"*

"My eyes, *Mein Fuehrer*...they are weak...I cannot read anymore. But I am still *un aficionado..."*

The old man's body wobbled as he said the words.

The passenger reached out to steady him. Martin reached out to touch the scars with his right hand once again and pronounced, "My redemption draws nearer."

"Martin."

"*Mein Fuehrer*?"

"Is there anything else? Is there anything I can do for you?"

Martin blinked several times and took a deep breath and tried to recite everything just as he'd practiced it so many times for so many, many years.

"*Mein Fuehrer*. I had a wife here, in Mexico...a Jew. I had a son with her." Martin blinked several more times and waited a moment. "And the son of a Jewish mother..."

Bormann's left shoe found a piece of glass from the vial, one of the thousands of pieces, and ground down on it, making an unpleasant, scraping sound that echoed through the library.

"...is a Jew." The Fuehrer finished Bormann's words for him.

"My son is a physician...and a *geneticist.* He possesses *expert knowledge.* He lectures about the *subject* around the world, at conferences, in academia, and wherever he can find an audience. He is against *it."*

The Fuehrer cocked his head. His steely eyes didn't blink as he sized up Bormann, Martin Bormann who had married a Jewish woman. "Against *it*, against *what*...he is against what, Martin?

"Cloning." Martin took another deep inhale. "And he knows who I am."

The Fuehrer's eyes kept studying Martin.

"And you wish that he be protected."

"He is my son...a Jew...but he is still my son."

The Fuehrer remembered Doctor Bloch, another physician he'd protected.

"Martin...go...go in peace."

The passenger returned to the observation deck on the roof. The old man returned to the car. Before he entered it he turned and gave a Nazi salute. And it wasn't a feeble salute; no, it was quite strong and vibrant and full of meaning. The security guard had to grab him, though. Saluting had made the old man lose his balance yet again; he'd almost fallen into the crushed limestone and shells of the driveway. *But he did not fall.*

The passenger had seen the salute and Martin Bormann nearly falling and then not falling. Martin Bormann, almost one hundred and eight years of age, *had not fallen*; he had not lost faith in his beloved Fuehrer.

And the passenger had returned the salute with a smile that wasn't a smile...as crisscrossing grids of lightning seared and scarred the churning clouds and thunder pealed and it began to rain and rain and rain as the passenger christened the villa: *Wolf's Lair 2.*

PART TWO

All the world's a stage, and all the men and women merely players; they have their exits and their entrances; and one man in his time plays many parts, his acts being seven ages.

-William Shakespeare

CHAPTER 16

Berchtesgaden, Germany.
6 December, 2010

Diana stood there and looked into the dark glass of the window. Her reflection mingled with the night and the semi darkened scene outside the house.

The rain in Berchtesgaden had changed to snow. It was a heavy, wet snow, it was a heavy, wet blanket that stuck to everything.

The snow was piling up on the ledge outside window above the kitchen sink. But before it could pile too high, slushy chunks of it would melt off and plop down to the ground because of the warmth of the window glass. Despite her dislike of this house, Diana was grateful for the warmness this cold, wet night in Berchtesgaden.

The slushy chunks would fall away every few minutes as Diana would glance at the clock on the other kitchen wall, constantly checking the time—-ach, looking at the clock every minute was like watching paint dry. And Diana was doing that, too. She was actually watching paint drying. She chided herself. She ought to know better. Paint dries no matter what the painter does in the meantime.

For the last ten minutes she had been staring at the two thick coats she had laid down on the windowsill earlier that day, as she waited now for her husband to call. She could laugh about this—-this ridiculous scene of watching paint dry and waiting for her husband to call. But none of it was laughable. None of it was funny.

And, in a few minutes, when Max called Diana, she would tell him what she'd seen: the carved message in the windowsill, the loose tile in the master bath, and the letter and photo inside the little plastic sandwich bag taped to the back of that tile. And when he arrived safely home, she would hand him the two wedding rings and give him *the letter written to the future* by that other chauffeur and his wife—-the letter of warning embellished by the gold of those two wedding rings, the letter telling them to leave, to escape, to flee from that evil man and his minions in the villa on the Watzmann.

Diana would tell her husband that they had to withdraw their euros immediately and get away from Pontius—-perhaps they should go to Switzerland first and find a hotel in a town somewhere, a place to hide out and think things through...yes, they had to think things through. They had to make a plan, a good plan, and the best plan. Their chance to escape would only come once. Of that she was certain.

No. She wouldn't tell Max what they must do. She would wait for him to come up with the plan. She would defer to him. He would know what they must do. If he didn't know what to do *then* she would tell him her plan.

It was 22:50 hours. Max would call in ten minutes. He always called on the secret cell phone at 23:00 hours unless he had told her otherwise. At 23:00 hours her own cell would play the opening measures to *Bach's Aria in G*. It had always been her favorite Bach composition. It had always comforted her when she most needed to be comforted. The music was from heaven. Diana was certain of that as much as she was certain that their chance of escape would only come this one time and never come again.

They had to get to Switzerland to Martigny and Chamonix. Perhaps they ought to go to the Mont Blanc Tunnel and go to Torino in Italia or to the south of France, to Marseille or Arles or Avignon. Perhaps they ought to go to Spain, to Barcelona. From Spain they could go to Mexico or Brazil or maybe to America. Yes. Her husband would know where they ought to go. He was a good man—-the best. He would know what to do. But first he had to call. First her cell phone had to play *Aria in G by Bach*. First she had to hear her husband's voice.

It was 22:55 hours in the hotel bar in Munich and Pontius was insisting on buying his chauffeur another Jack Daniel's over ice. The chauffeur had already drunk two—-and his limit had always been two, never three...and he'd just told his boss he didn't want another...and here was the boss ignoring the chauffeur and the bartender was sliding the third drink in front of the chauffeur and now two gorgeous women slithered out of the murky ether of the hotel bar—-one had medium-length, straight blond hair and one had wavy jet-black hair that came to her shoulders. And one of the women, the one with the dark hair was placing her hand upon Max's right hand and whispering something into his right ear as the other woman watched and smiled. And Pontius was smiling, too, and the chauffeur's watch said it was 22:57.

Diana would be waiting and maybe pacing back and forth or doing some late-night chores; or she would be looking out the window, peering into the black winter night and looking every few moments at her cell phone waiting to hear *Bach Aria in G.*

Max had to stay sober. He had to drink slower. He had to find an excuse to go to his room. He had to make the call.

Pontius had a third woman, a redhead, sitting next to him on the bar stool on his left. He was holding her about the waist with his left arm now as he was saying something to Max...

Pontius was hoisting his own glass in a toast:

"To my chauffeur! He is the best!"

Max's watch said 22:58.

Max returned the gesture and said, "To the boss." He put his lips to the glass and took a shallow sip and locked eyes with the boss over the far edge of the glass.

The boss wasn't smiling anymore. The boss was sending out burning laser beams with those two wicked eyes of his. The boss' eyes were scanners trying to read the chauffeur's many thoughts.

Now Pontius' eyes were fixated on the chauffeur's glass of whiskey. Pontius was noticing that it had not gone down.

Pontius was toasting again and smiling again.

"*Zum Frieden in der Welt*...to peace in the world! And to beautiful women...you do like beautiful women? " Pontius was tempting Max with these women now.

Pontius gave the toast in perfect Berlin-accented German and equally perfect American English. It was astonishing how *talented* Pontius was with languages—-it was far beyond mere talent, though. And the passenger had spoken in flawless German and American English, too.

Max's glass of whiskey seemed to get heavier by the second, by the minute. He tried not to look at his watch because Pontius was once more studying him with the laser-beam eyes. Max took another shallow sip.

The ice made a small tinkling sound. The whiskey didn't taste good any more.

He set the glass on the bar but kept it wrapped in his right hand. Pontius' eyes were going down yet again and looking at the drink. Now he locked eyes with his chauffeur. Pontius was onto the game, the game being played by the *best chauffeur in the world*. Pontius was still smiling but his lip was curling a little.

Max placed his left hand on the left side of the glass, further concealing it, cordoning it off from those devilish lasers. The cuff of his left shirt sleeve peeled back. The watch's face was exposed—-it was 23:00.

Diana would be praying for him. She would be asking the Lord for her husband to call. She would be in the bedroom, kneeling at the foot of the bed. She would be looking up at the dresser where the clock read 23:00 hours in glowing red numbers. His wife would watch the numbers change from 23:00 to 23: 01...which is exactly what they did, right now on Max's watch.

Pontius had leaned turned toward the gorgeous red head that had draped her body over his left shoulder; her arms were around his head and neck; she was kissing his neck; Pontius was returning the favor and cuddling up to her. The watch said 23:02.

Max would go to the men's room. That's what he would do. He would go into one of the stalls. He would call his wife from there. He would mutter an excuse for leaving. After all, everyone must go to...

"Excuse me but..." Max did not finish his words.

"What? Where are you going?" Pontius had stopped carrying on with the red head and was asking the question. Pontius did not look pleased about his chauffeur going anywhere.

"I have to..." Max patted his lower abdomen.

"Ah..." Pontius raised his eyebrows and tilted back his head and examined his chauffeur. He was smiling a weird smile.

Pontius laid his eyes on the chauffeur's glass of whiskey sitting there in plain view. Pontius weird smile vanished. The level of the liquor had hardly gone down at all. In fact, the color was less rich because the melting ice chips were diluting it.

Max slipped off the bar stool and turned toward the sign—-*Herren*. The sign was above the arched entrance to a hallway about 10 meters away—-10 meters that felt like 10 kilometers to Max as he tried not to walk too fast to the arched entryway as he felt Pontius' laser eyes warming his backside and scrutinizing each step.

The men's room walls and floor were made of off-white, glossy tile. The lavatory countertops were black granite. The sinks were porcelain. The faucets were gold plated. The ceiling was arched. The whole place was a *stony echo chamber*—-a stony, rocky canyon or cavern. Max's steps echoed. He would have to speak very softly or his voice would echo too. Everything would echo in here. The cavernous men's room appeared to be empty.

Max opened the creaking door to the stall, closed it, and slid the bolt into the slot. The movement made an echo, a little echo but an echo nonetheless.

The door to the stall was floor-to-ceiling. That was good. But the door had openings for ventilation, of course. That was not good. That would make it easier for Max to be heard.

He loosened his belt a notch. He reached into his boxer shorts with his right hand. He tugged on the Velcro tab. It made a little scratching noise. He placed his thumb and index finger on the razor-thin cell phone. He tugged at it. He must not drop it.

He heard the grating sound of leather shoes. He stopped to listen closer. Someone had entered the men's room. Max had to know who it was.

He put his face to the ventilation slats. He tried to get a look. The slats were running in the wrong direction, though. Only if the shoes came nearer would he know. He knew which shoes would be Pontius' shoes. Pontius, like Max, had impeccable taste for shoes, for clothes, for whiskey...although Pontius only dressed up when he traveled; at the villa Pontius wore only his workout clothes and jogging suit, it seemed to Max.

The black leather shoes were parked right outside the stall door. They were Pontius' slip-ons. They were plain, supple leather...black and without tassels. They were Italian, naturally. They were Bruno Magli Ashtons, the same ones Max had seen Pontius wearing before, when relaxing after a conference.

The black trousers were cuffed. All Pontius' suit trousers were cuffed.

It was Pontius, had to be, and he still had not moved. He was still standing right there, facing the door to the stall where Max had just stopped pulling his cell phone from its secret place in the waist band of his boxers.

A faucet was dripping.

Max's watch said it was 23:06.

The shoes and trouser cuffs were moving.

Max let the thin cell phone drop back into its pocket. He heard it fall and rest there. He breathed through his nose. His heart thumped in his chest. He felt the flow of hot blood in both his carotid arteries.

The door to the next stall was creaking. The slip-ons were making a grating, unpleasant sound. Pontius cleared his throat.

It was 23:07.

CHAPTER 17

Diana was kneeling at the foot of their king-size bed with the maroon duvet atop it. Inside the duvet was their down-filled comforter. She loved the duvet and comforter. She loved being comforted. She needed to hear from her husband. She needed to hear his calming voice.

Beneath her knees was the giant throw rug from Iran that covered half the beautiful oak wood floor. The bedroom had a stone hearth. The hearth was behind her at the far side of the grand bedroom. The stone hearth and chimney rose up between two large bay windows. Diana could see those windows and the mantel above the hearth in the 2.5-meter tall mirror spanning the wall behind their bed. It was a lovely, luxurious bedroom fit for a duke and duchess.

Diana put her forehead to her folded hands. She was no duchess and she really cared nothing for this opulence. She only cared for her husband. For a moment or two she lifted her head again to look at her watch.

The Rolex said it was 23:07. Something was going on, in Munich. Something had happened. Max should have called by now. It had to be that devil, Pontius, keeping him from calling.

Pontius had sidetracked her husband. It was Pontius keeping her husband busy or entertained or whatever.

She chided herself. She didn't know if it was true. How could she? She was here, in Berchtesgaden, in their house, in their bedroom, in the middle of a winter storm 120 kilometers from Munich. She didn't know anything. She couldn't be sure about anything.

"Lord, please, let my husband find a way to call me. I need to know if he's all right, Lord. And I need to tell him about the letter and the other couple."

The room and the floor beneath her felt like it was spinning. The place where she was kneeling was a drain or maybe a black hole in space. She felt the presence of evil spirits in the grand bedroom. She knew they were there watching her. She felt as if the ceiling could come crashing in on her. The evil spirits could make it fall on her if they wanted. At least that's how it seemed.

Lord, protect me and...

"Lord, what must I do?"

She had no answers. She could only pray. It would have to be enough, of course it was enough. Prayer was always enough. And the Lord would answer when he was ready. Or the Lord wouldn't answer at all. It was up to the Lord to figure things out tonight and every night and every day. It was up to him to find a way for her husband to call.

The oppressive feel of the lavish bedroom was growing more oppressive. The oppression of this extravagant house was growing more oppressive. The oppression of Berchtesgaden and Bavaria and the Obersalzberg and the Watzmann and all the dark mountains surrounding the city, and walling it in, had become unbearably oppressive.

And this overwhelming oppression brought the answer to her prayer. The Lord was telling her, speaking to her via the oppression. He was telling her, and he was telling them, Max and Diana, to get away.

And the Almighty was telling her to wait for her husband's call. At this moment, the Almighty was telling her to allow the Almighty to act when the Almighty wished. The Almighty was perfectly able to find a way for her husband to call her on that thin, little cell phone he kept hidden in the Velcro-sealed pocket in his boxer shorts.

It was 23:12 hours.

It was 23:15.

23:17.

Max had been inside the stall for twelve minutes, give or take a minute. His watch said it was 23:17.

Pontius had been clearing his throat and making that annoying sound with the soles of his fine Italian slip-ons. And Pontius was still in the next stall.

It had to strike Pontius as odd by now, that his chauffeur was lingering so long in the men's room.

On the other hand, Pontius couldn't stay in the next stall for much longer either lest he arouse the chauffeur's suspicions or lest the chauffeur sneak away quickly and go back through the hallway, and through the hotel bar and to the elevator and to his room.

23:18.

Should Max make a break for it? Should he slide the bolt and unlock the door and slip away?

If he did he would make noise. There could be no avoiding it. His shoes would scrape against the floor and make a lot of noise like Pontius' shoes. Max's quick steps would echo and echo and echo.

Max could do nothing about making noise, making an echo. So be it. And...

Once he'd left the men's room he would scamper down the hall and keep a brisk but slower pace as he crossed the bar. The women, if they were still there, maybe wouldn't notice him. The effect of the low lights in the bar would hide him. In less than ten seconds he would have crossed the barroom and entered the hall on the other side, the hall leading to the elevator. And once he'd reached his room, and closed the door, and locked and bolted it shut, he would be free to speak with his wife.

It was 23:19.

Pontius cleared his throat once more. Pontius was playing cat and mouse. Pontius was enjoying this game. Max was so weary of Pontius and his games and his arrogance, his conceit, his haughtiness.

Max inhaled, and exhaled, and placed his hand to the bolt and whispered a prayer—-it wasn't so much a prayer as it was a sigh but it was a prayer, too.

Max turned the bolt and slipped it out of the hole. He had not made any sound. That faucet was still dripping.

Max turned the door handle and pulled the door to him and slithered past it, pretending he was invisible, pretending he was a ghost.

Max stepped across the large grid work of tiles. The grid work seemed endless at this point in time at this moment in his life at this moment in the history of the world. It seemed to Max that he was carrying the whole world at this moment. It seemed he could be crushed like a bug on this tile floor if he didn't get across it soon.

Max had made it to the other door, the door to the hallway that led to the bar. He pushed the swivel door open and as he did he heard Pontius' shoes grating again.

Max was in the hall, and running. He had to run. How could he walk?! Pontius was coming, he was coming and Max had to get to the bar before Pontius left the men's room.

The arched entryway to the bar was one meter away. Max converted his running into walking. He forced himself not to look back.

Do not look back and do not look toward the bar either, he repeated to himself. Keep your eyes on the other side of the barroom...keep them on the other hallway on the other side of the barroom. Don't look back, he repeated once more. Do not...

Max looked back...

Pontius was there.

Pontius was marching toward him like a Nazi Storm Trooper. If Pontius caught Max he would grab him by the neck and...

And Max would have to fight back, he would have to engage even if he didn't want to engage. He would have to kill his employer...but Pontius seemed to be made of steel. His body was a weapon. Max had been taught in the army to know his enemy. And now he knew, for certain, that Pontius was his enemy. Pontius was the cat and Max was the mouse.

Max's mind was flooded with a vision of being arraigned in court. He would be accused of felonious assault even if it had all been caused by Pontius. In court, the lowly chauffeur would be forced to stand mute before the judge and admit to his *crime.* There was only justice for the rich. Ownership was 9/10 of the law.

Max did not, not, not wish to engage in a fight with his employer. What good would it do? What good thing could possibly come from it? Max only wanted to return to his wife and figure out what they should do next.

Max was now in the other hall. He dare not run. There could be other hotel guests. The lobby wasn't far off.

He kept stepping, he kept walking, he did not run.

Max had arrived at the elevator. He pressed the button. The hotel had four floors and the light above the elevator door said the elevator was on the fourth...so he waited.

4—-3—-

3—-2—-1...the stainless steel door opened, making a slight whirring sound, and Max stepped into the elevator and pressed the number 4.

He waited and waited for the door to seal him in the elevator, for it to close him off from Pontius.

He heard Pontius' angry, imperialistic footsteps coming from the far end of the hall where it left the barroom. The footsteps were marching faster and faster, they were running! Pontius the mad marathoner was running!

The door was closing.

It was only open a few centimeters, now.

Pontius was right there. Max's eyes locked with Pontius' eyes.

Pontius was smiling, grinning. His teeth were perfect, his chiseled face was perfect. He looked like the sculpted, polished bust of some ancient Greek or Roman general.

But the smile, the grinning mouth, the chiseled face, the glistening teeth did not hide from Max what Pontius was thinking. Max could read Pontius' mind; he had learned to read it; he'd had nearly three years of practice—-studying Pontius and reading that diabolical, wicked mind of his. Max didn't know everything about Pontius but he *knew enough.*

And Max knew that Pontius knew that Max *knew enough.* Pontius knew that Max knew this cat and mouse game had only begun. And Pontius was the cat and Max and Diana were mice.

CHAPTER 18

Max shifted from side to side on his feet and noted how sweaty his hands were. The air inside the elevator was a mixture of chilly and hot. Cold sweat was trickling down his burning forehead. Cold sweat was running in his warm armpits. It was gushing there. His whole body was icy and hot and warm and cold at the same time. His face felt flushed.

The elevator was nearly to the fourth floor and in a moment or two the door would slide open and he would step down the corridor to the hotel room.

And it came to him. Pontius may have bugged the room. If the evil man, the devil-man, the little satan was stoking up the heat now, ratcheting up the tension now, beginning the final quarter of the deadly cat and mouse game now, he might indeed have placed a listening device somewhere in the room; or he'd had someone else place it, hide it. Maybe one of those weird attendants had come here, to Munich beforehand, before the conference, and hid a tiny little *ear* inside the room.

It was 23:24. The small chime sounded. The elevator door opened. Max stepped into the corridor and picked up the pace. He rotated his head and glanced behind him fearing Pontius may have taken the stairs.

There was no one back there, for the moment. But Pontius could easily have taken the stairs and got to the fourth floor in no time flat. The man was an athlete par excellence. That devil was able to fly up and down the spiral staircase to the top of that ugly Egyptian tower where he would spend hours watching the valley below the Watzmann, watching the streets of Berchtesgaden, watching the chauffeur's house perhaps, and watching the mountain roads, the highways. Who knew what else Pontius watched through the lens of that exclusive toy that wasn't a toy? Certainly he watched the Obersalzberg where the Eagle's Nest laid perched high above the world. The man probably watched the tourists milling about the Eagle's Nest in summer and whenever the weather was clear and good.

But, truth be told, Max didn't really know what Pontius did in that tower. Truth be told, all he could do was guess.

Max fished out the *key* from his inside lapel pocket and slid the magnetic strip down through the slot. The tiny indicator light was green. Max turned the doorknob, opened the door and shut it, and locked all three locks as rapidly as possible. He remained in place for a couple of seconds, trying to concentrate, trying to grab hold of his thoughts that were racing by like the fast-moving scroll at the bottom of a TV screen showing the latest headlines or the current stock market status or the price of gold and silver.

He shook his head. Maybe it would help stop his racing thoughts.

He had to go to the bathroom—-he'd not done that during the entire time he was in the men's room. He'd held it in, as he'd listened for the slightest sound Pontius might make.

He finished his business and let out a long, relaxing exhale and turned to the sink to wash his hands. He splashed cold water onto his face, onto his hair. The cold water was bad so he opened the hot water tap and waited. Now he splashed the warmer water to his face and hair. It was good, oh so good. His close-cropped hair didn't need combing. Keeping his hair this short helped Max feel like he would be more ready for bad things, for any crisis. He looked once more at his face in the mirror...he almost laughed about his short hair and thinking that would somehow help him.

He toweled off and began the search for the listening device. He had to find it, if it existed, before he called her.

Max looked everywhere: under the bed, behind the headboard of the bed, along the sideboards of the bed, inside the wardrobe, inside all the drawers in the wardrobe, the back panel of the wardrobe, behind the wardrobe on the wall, under the wardrobe, inside the drawers in the desk, under the desk, along the legs of the desk; he searched the drawers on the nightstand, he searched the bathroom, behind the toilet, inside the tank, under the lavatory, in all the bathroom drawers, inside the shower stall; he looked inside the three lamps in the room and inside the light fixture near the door; he lifted the two framed prints above the bed. He searched all around the window.

He stopped in front of the window glass and caught his semi-transparent, ghost-like reflection and observed the twinkling lights of the street and the lights of the city of Munich. He wished he wasn't here. He wished he was with his wife. He closed the drapes and turned toward the room once more.

It seemed clear that nothing had been planted in the Max's hotel room...ah...the heating vent. He would look there now.

He fished out his pocket knife and managed to remove the two screws. He finagled a bit more and took off the vent cover by using the knife as a wedge. He set aside the vent cover. He poked his nose inside the duct and peered right and left and up and down. There was nothing there either. To make double sure he reached as far as possible inside the dark shaft and felt around with his hand and fingers. There was only some dust.

Pontius had not bugged the room. It had to be true. The evil man had not bugged his chauffeur's hotel room. All the same, Max would speak softly to Diana.

Diana looked at the clock in the bedroom. It said 23:30. Max had not called. Max was thirty minutes overdue. Something was wrong...something had...

Her cell was playing *Aria in G* by Bach. And it was her husband's number. Of course it was. Who else would be calling at this hour? She was sorry to have worried so much. She should have had more faith, in her husband, and especially in God.

"What's wrong?! What happened?"

"I couldn't call...Pontius...he was..."

"Was what?" she asked. "Speak up, I can't hear you."

"I'll tell you later...and I have to speak softly...there might be a bug." He wouldn't burden her with all the theatrics that had just gone down in the hotel bar and the scary scene in the men's room. "Are you all right?" he asked.

"No."

Diana had to tell him about the peeling paint and the carved message in the windowsill and the loose tile in their bath and the letter and the photograph and the rings. She had to tell him in as few words as possible. There was no time for a long rendition of the day's events. She had enough of a basic plot for a thriller but she had to condense the entire manuscript into a hundred words or less. She had to make him know it was true, she had to make her husband understand. She prayed he wouldn't think it was some delusion or some fantasy she'd had about seeing those words and the letter and the rings.

"Why are you not all right? What's going on?"

Diana told Max everything in less than sixty seconds and asked what they must do now, tonight.

Max's head was spinning from what he'd just heard. He blinked his eyes and tried to focus. He'd always thought they would have more time to plan. He'd been a fool to think it would go that way. He'd been a fool for trusting Pontius. Pontius was a deadly weapon and *possessed* many deadly weapons waiting to carry out the assassination of the chauffeur and his wife. Pontius was a fiend; he was a demon. Max shook his head again and squinted his eyes, tightening every muscle in his forehead. He relaxed his muscles and opened his eyes and took a deep inhale.

"We're going to Switzerland."

Diana's mind went blank. She didn't know what to say, how to respond. Her husband was there, a 120 kilometers away from her, in a hotel in Munich. She needed him with her right now this moment.

She looked at the clock on the night stand. It was 23:34.

Her mind wasn't blank anymore. It was whirling. And she was pleased. He had come up with the same plan as she.

"What do you want me to do, Max?"

"Pack the car with clothing for all seasons. Save room for a suit or two for me and some dress-up clothes for you but that's all...the rest must be casual wear and some camping wear, winter coats, jackets, gloves, hats, hiking boots, the rucksacks, the go-bags, canteens and sleeping bags and the pup tent...in case we..."

Diana finished Max's sentence. "In case we have to go live in the forest or the mountains...or in some desert." Diana could see herself trying to sleep, cook, bathe and whatnot deep inside some dripping-wet, cold forest or bone-dry, hot desert full of poisonous snakes and scorpions.

Max was speaking again:

"And pack a case full of snacks and drinks...and don't forget your passport or the laptop...we may have to leave Europe."

"Leave Europe, Max?"

"We'll talk about that later, Diana, okay?"

"Okay, Max..."

"Diana, go to the bank as soon as it opens and withdraw everything in *cash*...no..." Max closed his eyes. Closing them would help him think. "Leave 25,000 euros in the account. It will raise less suspicion."

"Okay...okay..." Diana said it twice as if it would help. And then she asked: "Cash? Won't that make the bank suspicious?"

"We must have the money in cash. Pontius may have the account frozen. We would be left without money."

"All right. Cash."

"Have the teller put most of it in 100-euro bills and the rest in 50s. Put the money in a satchel and keep it with you at all times."

"Of course." Of course she'd never let so much cash leave her sight. Never!

Her heart was racing. And she didn't even have the cash on her yet. She hadn't even been to the bank yet or done anything yet. Her husband Max was speaking again...he was asking a question.

"The car...does it have a full tank?"

"I filled up this afternoon. Yes. It's full."

He let out his breath and said, "Good."

Max was relieved. It was one less thing she would have to do. Later he would tell her what they must do with the car. He didn't want to load her up with too many details. Later, he would tell her they must get rid of the car, somehow, and purchase another. They had to purchase a less conspicuous car. The BMW was too nice. Besides, Pontius may have had it bugged. He prayed that was not the case. He prayed Pontius wouldn't be able to track her as she drove to Zurich. Max should have checked for bugs on the car. He should tell her now to check the car for any sort of tracking devices...

He heard her weeping...

"Diana...listen to me...we can do this...." He said it firmly and as gently as possible. He wished he could be there and hold her. But he was in Munich and she was in Berchtesgaden, 120 kilometers away. *"We must do this."*

"All right..." Her voice was still trembling but carried some resolve in it now.

"We'll meet in Zurich. I'm leaving the hotel tonight and purchasing a train ticket: Munich Zurich...one way." He said *one-way* and didn't know why. It wasn't necessary. "It's five hours to Zurich by rail...I will arrive first and find a hotel and call you from there."

Diana went over to one of the big bay windows in the sumptuous, grand, palatial bedroom and stared into the winter night and the swirling snow. The snow wasn't wet anymore. It was dry and wind-driven. There was a blizzard in Berchtesgaden and Bavaria. After the phone call she would turn on the TV and get a complete weather report.

He was speaking.

"Are you still there?"

"It's snowing."

These were words he didn't want to hear.

"How bad is it?"

"Bad."

"All right." It wasn't *all right* but what else could he say? He didn't want to worry her even more. "We can't change the weather. We will still do everything I just said. And tomorrow morning you will still go to the bank and then head for Zurich. If there is a problem, call me."

She looked down on the patio below. The security light showed snowdrifts building along the hedgerow and the Belgian fence and the stone wall. The drifts were at least a meter high already.

"I will call..." Her voice trailed off...

"We can do this." He tried to sound as affirming as possible. "We *can* and *we will* do this." He was repeating himself but he had to; he had to sound as positive as he could...despite winter storms and the dark night, despite the blowing, drifting snow, and the howling wind.

"And the church?" she asked as she kept staring through the big window at the snowdrifts and the hedge and the Belgian fence and stone wall.

"What about the church?"

"Should I let them know...so they can pray for us?"

"No."

"No?"

"No."

Diana understood. No one must know. Besides, the dear souls in the congregation would notice, sooner or later, that Max and Diana had vanished. And they would pray for them anyway. They would always be remembered by the congregation no matter where they might have gone and no matter how long they might be away. Plus they would not endanger the lives of the kind people of the congregation. If Pontius even suspected the people there knew a fraction of what his chauffeur and the chauffeur's wife knew or suspected he would try to harm them too.

Besides if Diana or Max did tell the pastor or the others would they even get it? Probably not. They would probably think Max and Diana were lunatics.

She wondered, for a second or two, if she and her husband indeed were lunatics.

"Okay, I won't tell them."

"Call me in the morning after you make the withdrawal...I love you," he whispered his last three words. He loved her, he adored her so much. She was the bravest woman he'd ever known.

"I love you too." She choked up as she said it and almost closed the cell phone but her husband was saying something.

"The Glock. You know where it is."

Of course she knew where it was...the 9mm was in the closet in their bedroom inside a gun case. Inside the case lay the pistol inside a holster plus four boxes of 9mm rounds.

"I know where it is."

"And the rifle—-it's under the floor in the storage room, in the corner. The boards are loose there. The box with my father's photos is there...and the key."

"The rifle?" She didn't have to ask that question. She knew about the sniper's rifle with the bipod and scope. She just didn't know where it had been hidden, until now. She didn't know where the photographs were, until now. But she did know how many there were. One hundred eighty. She would pack them with the rest of their belongings.

Diana knew Max had been trained as a sniper in the army. He'd been hesitant to tell her that, given the history of their families, given what had happened to his father and her father in the war.

The rifle would be inside it's metal case and broken down into several pieces. Once, years ago, he'd shown her how quickly he could assemble the weapon. His dexterity had astounded her. He and that rifle were one. She could still see him screwing in the barrel with its fire suppressor. She had never seen him shoot but she knew he was good, very, very good. Her husband would always be a soldier. It was in his blood.

"I will see you in Zurich. I love you."

She said *I love you too. Ich liebe dich auch.*

CHAPTER 19

It was 23:40 hours. She had nine hours and twenty minutes until the bank opened. Nine hours and twenty minutes should be enough time.

If only she wasn't so tired.

She was exhausted. She had to admit it. She might as well face the truth. She was so tired she could hardly think.

She had not been sleeping well these days and here she was, even more tired from the lap swimming and tired from the terrible stress of waiting for her husband to call from Munich. She considered lying down on the bed and trying to sleep a couple of hours but no, that wouldn't work. She had to do as her husband had said. Besides how could she sleep now with all this adrenalin rushing into her arteries?

First she would make a list. Yes. She had to make a list; and, she had to get away from the big bay window and from watching the snow swirling about. It only depressed her.

But being depressed wouldn't change anything. It would not change the next question popping into her mind and mixing with the rest of her racing thoughts: What if the driveway was waist-deep in snow by morning?

She answered the question with another question, the *question* was really the only *answer* there could be—-So what if it was waist-deep in snow by morning? She would have to clear it. There was a snow blower in the garage. She had watched her husband use the blower once before, during their first winter in Berchtesgaden. It had not snowed so much since that winter...but it was snowing an awful lot now.

Lord, why are you letting it snow so much tonight? Please make the snow stop, Lord.

She scolded herself for telling the Lord what he should do. She had no right to do that. And she had to stop this questioning. It would do no good.

She went downstairs to the study-library and found a notebook in the huge mahogany desk. She grabbed up a pen from the drawer and headed for the kitchen. She didn't like being in that big, dark library-study with its walls and shelves of dark-stained wood. She didn't like the heavy, velvety drapes at the massive window. The drapes were all dark greens and purples. She preferred the airy, light kitchen. Its walls were creamy off-white. The cupboards were creamy, off-white, too. The kitchen was the best room in the over-size house—-the house that had always been too large for just the two of them; the house that had become more like a mortuary now.

She would sit on a stool at the breakfast bar and make the list there. And she would make coffee. She needed coffee.

The coffee was ready; the mouth-watering aroma filling the kitchen said so. She poured a full mug. The mug was a gift from her husband—-it was glazed in streaking patterns of blue and gold; it resembled candle wax melting. Coffee always tasted the best when drunk from that mug. She took a sip.

It was strong and good but not as good as it would be in happier times. She sipped again and set down the mug. She closed her eyes, trying to visualize the list.

She opened her eyes and wrote the number *1*. Then, she wrote *clothing items for my husband* and began to list her husband's clothes, all the clothes she knew he would need for their journey, their great escape from tyranny and death. She listed socks and shoes and boots. She listed the jackets, both light weight and heavy. She listed gloves and hats. She listed underwear for her husband, boxer shorts and t-shirts. Trousers. Jeans. A couple of belts. Two suits. Two sweaters, two sweat shirts. Regular shirts, two for dress, five long-sleeved and five short-sleeved for casual wear. Bermuda shorts, two pair. Ah, his long-sleeved cotton t-shirts, those over-size things. He loved those baggy, sack-like shirts, the black one and the gray and the dark blue one. She hated them. They made him look like a Rugby player. But she loved her husband more than she hated those ugly, sack-like shirts.

She took another sip of coffee and laughed out loud about the shirts. She went to the great room which lay just off the kitchen. She stood in front of the giant screen TV and the rest of the media center. She might as well fill this big lonely mansion with music. She would play *Bach's Toccata and Fugue in D minor for organ.* She would let it play over and over and over again as the snow piled higher and higher in Berchtesgaden and Bavaria and in the mountains of Austria and Switzerland. The skiing would be fabulous come tomorrow. Would she ever ski with her husband again? Probably not.

She put away the thought and instead savored the opening measures of another of Bach's celestial compositions. She returned to the breakfast bar and her coffee and took another sip. It was said that Bach had loved coffee, as well.

She put the pen to the paper and kept listing item after item after item, keeping in sync with the music, until she had filled three pages.

It was 01:00 in the morning. Making the list had taken more than an hour. She had drunk all of the coffee, too. She didn't want any more, not now, maybe later, but not now. She poured a glass of water. The coffee had left her thirsty. Coffee always had that effect on her. She drank deeply from the glass, nearly finishing it. Now she had to relieve herself. She would get to packing in a minute or so. She needed to go to the water closet immediately. She had been so excited and hopped up on caffeine and dedicated to finishing the list that she'd scarcely noticed how much she had to go.

She finished and looked at herself in the floor-to-ceiling mirror in the dressing alcove in the bathroom. She was still wearing the baggy jeans and baggy sweatshirt. She had worn them to the sports club. She had been so upset by the writing on the windowsill and the letter and the photograph and the wedding rings from that poor couple that she had not changed into other, better clothes. Just before leaving this big house in Berchtesgaden she would throw them in the hamper in the laundry. She wouldn't need them anymore. There were many things she wouldn't need anymore.

She thought about Pontius...Pontius could accuse her husband and her of committing a crime, of stealing, of embezzlement, maybe. Pontius could inform the police that his employee had left suddenly without notice. The man could get the police to inform Interpol, maybe. She could not imagine having to hide from Interpol or from any law enforcement. On the other hand, Pontius would more than likely keep secret this little game of cat and mouse. The man was perverse enough to enjoy tracking down his employee and his employee's wife. And if Pontius didn't do the actual tracking one of his bizarre attendants would. Yes, that's how he would do it...Pontius would have the chauffeur and his wife caught and brought back to that villa where he would kill them. She was certain she was right about all this.

Or maybe she was wrong about this? Maybe the Almighty would keep those bizarre attendants, or whatever they were, away from her husband and her. Dear God may it be so. She whispered another prayer for the previous chauffeur and his wife.

She stared at her face in the mirror. There were few lines on it. She was still beautiful. Her green eyes were like emeralds, her husband had told her so many, many times. And it was true, that she was still beautiful. She had shoulder-length, auburn hair with no gray at all. Her figure was still hourglass. Her breasts were still in place. Her legs were strong and her arms toned and strong. She was indeed beautiful for a woman in her fifties, that last decade before the candle wax begins to melt. Men always seem to age better than women. It was true. However, it was also true that having no children makes it easier for a woman to keep her figure. She put away the wave of thoughts flooding her mind once again. She'd known for a long time she could not bear children and she didn't need to be burdened by these thoughts, not here, not now. She needed to be positive mentally, spiritually...and it was a positive that she'd kept her figure and most of her energy despite being in her fifties. She would need all that strength to get to Zurich, to find her husband, and to hide from Pontius. If this were 1943, and she were Jewish, Pontius would be Himmler and would hunt her down like a rabbit and gas her.

That Pontius seemed never to age. That devil had discovered the fountain of youth up there on the Watzmann. That's what her husband had started to notice about a year ago—-Pontius seemed *locked in some kind of different dimension of time* her husband had said and shrugged.

She stopped looking into the mirror...it was silly to do this at 01:00 in the morning. She had to concentrate on getting packed and getting out of this house and getting to the bank and getting on the road to Zurich.

She headed down the long hallway to the stairway, her running shoes making a squeaky noise on the tiles. She had a notion to start running right now. The caffeine was still affecting her and the adrenaline was coming on again. She would not run, though. She had to stay calm and centered and do this right. This great escape chance would only come once, she reminded herself again.

They had to give that evil Pontius the slip; they had to *get out of Dodge* as the Americans say.

CHAPTER 20

Max was wearing a black woolen top coat over his charcoal gray suit and black gloves on his hands and rotating his head to the right and to the left, scanning like an automatic, remote-controlled camera, looking about the hotel room one last time.

He grabbed the black leather overnight duffle bag from atop the disheveled white duvet draping the end of the bed. The crumpled mass of whiteness reminded him of all the snow outside, of all the snow covering all Bavaria and the Alps and all of Central and Southern Europe, probably. The storm was a big one; maybe it was *the storm of the century*, of this new 21st century. Maybe it was the first of many *storms of the century to come.*

Max slung the duffle over his shoulder, turned about face, and flipped the switch to turn off the wall-mounted lamp. He turned to the door, opened it as quietly as possible, trying to avoid making a clicking sound, and headed down the corridor to the elevator.

He imagined his shoes were moccasins, silently padding through the woods. He pretended he was one of those American Indians he'd seen in the movies as a kid. Max's favorite Indian had always been Geronimo the Apache.

One thing that gave him some relief and comfort was the fact that Pontius' room wasn't on this fourth floor. Pontius' grand suite was on the first floor on the opposite side of the hotel where there was a beautiful patio-garden in summer. Max had driven Pontius to quite a number of conferences in Munich and they'd always stayed at this hotel. It was good that that hotel suite lay on the opposite side. It was good that it was only 04:00 hours. There was little chance that anyone would be up at this hour. There wouldn't be anyone except the night receptionist at the front desk. And with a bit of luck Max would be able to slip past the front desk and slip out the door without being seen.

Of course, Max could be seen later, on the security camera video. It wouldn't matter much because by the time anyone viewed that video he would be on the early train to Zurich which departed the Hauptbahnhof at 05:37. Max hoped he was right about not being spotted and arousing too much curiosity this morning. Anyway, he would try to keep his face turned down and away from the camera. It might help unless there was more than the single camera covering the hotel desk, the only camera he'd ever noted in that section of the hotel...there were more cameras covering the street, though, cameras operated by the City of Munich. Once Max was in the street he would walk *indifferently* like a normal business man headed to catch the early train or headed out early to work in his office.

The chime sounded and the elevator door opened. The door didn't make too much sound—-that was good, very good. Max poked his head out ahead of the rest of his nearly two-meter frame. He looked right and left.

There was no one. Of course there was no one. It was 04:01 in the morning on a cold winter's night in Munich. Nobody would be out and about unless they were crazy...like *the crazy chauffeur.* Max almost laughed at how crazy this was to be down here attempting to escape the hotel at this ungodly hour. All the same, he would play, as best he could, the part of that business man headed early to the train or to the office. He would win an Oscar for playing the role perfectly. He would pretend he wasn't crazy. Of course he wasn't. Anyone in his shoes would do the same if they knew about Pontius and those devils in the villa high on the Watzmann. If only he'd come to his senses sooner. If only...if only he had listened to his lovely, dear wife. Diana had been so patient with him.

Max kept walking and reminding himself not to rush. If the desk clerk saw him it would be bad enough; but it would be even worse if the desk clerk saw him hurrying through the lobby. And it would look even more odd once the desk person had noticed that the chauffeur was carrying his overnight duffle. And certainly the desk clerk would think the chauffeur was headed to his car and the desk clerk knew that the small, fenced-in parking lot next to the hotel was locked at this hour and the chauffeur would have no access to the car unless he had made arrangements beforehand. And certainly the desk clerk would wish to know why the chauffeur was headed out at such an unusual hour. Max prayed the desk clerk wouldn't see him.

If only he could just get through the door and onto the street. Getting through the door and onto the street were all the challenge he needed for the moment—*get through the door, get to the street, turn to the right and go...go...go...*

Max was wearing a suit. A suit was Max's work uniform. It was good he didn't bring casual clothing along with him. He might have been tempted to wear it. It was good he was at least wearing his work clothing. He was, after all, a professional chauffeur. If the desk clerk saw him he would think the chauffeur had some sort of official reason for being up at this hour. Maybe...

Maybe the desk clerk would think the chauffeur had trouble sleeping and was only going out for fresh air? But that, too, would seem weird. It was bitter cold at 04:00, in winter. It was frigid in Munich. Anyone with sense would be zonked out under a fine, warm comforter with his or her head buried in a fine, soft pillow or would have his arms around a beautiful, warm woman.

Max stepped into the lobby and scanned the room. He scanned the desk area. Good. It looked like it was going to be easy. There didn't seem to be...

"Can I help you, sir?"

The question had come from the left side of the lobby. It was the desk clerk. It had to be.

Max had been startled by the man's voice but tried not to show it. He simply stopped and held his position for a moment.

The fiftyish, bald clerk had some magazines in his hand. The clerk must have been tidying up the lobby, getting it ready for the morning.

The clerk was still there, his eyes fixated upon the chauffeur. It appeared that he had noticed the duffle. The clerk appeared to be cocking his head a little.

"No, everything's all right, quite all right...I have to..." Max the chauffeur was scrambling to find the right words of explanation. "I...I should have made arrangements for the car."

"The car, sir?"

"My employer needs...he told me...he told me last night he needed some files for the morning...he left them in the car...they are in the trunk...I forgot to fetch them before retiring to my room."

The desk clerk cocked his head once more. He could tell the chauffeur's explanation was vague and lame. Or maybe he couldn't tell at all.

"I can call security, sir."

Max's brain was crowded with a dozen thoughts, all at once. He focused on one thought and replied, "Yes, thank you...I will go to the parking lot now."

Hopefully the desk clerk would think the duffle the chauffeur had brought with him was for carrying files. Hopefully the curious clerk wouldn't notice how the duffle sagged a bit from the weight of the chauffeur's belongings inside. Hopefully nothing more would come of this little encounter at 04:00 in the morning in Munich. Hopefully Max could now fake out the security guard as easily as faking out this simple desk clerk. For a second Max considered turning to the right once he was on the street...he would not go to the parking lot...it would be easier to avoid the security guard altogether.

The clerk was talking on the telephone, telling the security guard about the chauffeur heading out the door to parking lot. Max didn't wait for the clerk to say if it was okay or not. He didn't wait for the clerk to hang up.

He almost turned right. He stopped himself. No. The security guard had been alerted. He would be expecting the chauffeur in a few moments. There was no time to turn right and escape down the street and head for the train station.

He turned left from the hotel entrance. A blast of wind hit him head on. It was a bitter wind. It made him think of his father, fighting against his will with the Wehrmacht at Stalingrad and later in the Ardennes sector of Belgium. Thinking of his brave father gave Max courage. He had to fight against Pontius and the passenger with all his might; somehow he had to find a way to undo their plans. However, he and his wife had to escape Pontius first. They had to get far away from that monster to a calm, safe place where they would have time to consider all options.

The security gate opened. The guard had seen him coming.

The guard was a young man, maybe thirty years old. Max wished he could be thirty again. He had wished the same thing when first he'd seen the passenger that drizzly dark night that seemed an eternity ago.

The guard was following Max to the car now, staying back by three or four paces. It irritated Max to have this young man following him. He had a notion to ask him to return to his post. But he refrained from saying anything. He would have to play this game right. It was 04:06. The train to Zurich departed in an hour and thirty-one minutes and Max would have to be aboard at least ten minutes before that. He couldn't be seen running, dashing to catch the train. That, too, could arouse suspicion and stick out in the mind of some railroad terminal employee. And later that employee would tell the police what he'd seen.

Max fished the car keys from his trouser pocket. He pressed the button on the remote and the trunk lid popped open a half meter or so. Max lifted it another half meter or so but avoided opening it all the way. He might be able to use it to shield himself and what he was doing. He could use the lid to block the guard's view...if he could get the guard to back off or move to the side.

Max opened the trunk lid a bit more and halted. He turned around, half smiled at the guard, and raised his eyebrows. It was a semi-pleading look, a pleading gesture to get the guard to back off a little...

The guard got it, and did a half turn away from the chauffeur.

Max didn't waste a second—-he faked rummaging around through *papers* in the trunk. It sounded like rummaging through files or file folders and whatnot...it must sound like that because the guard appeared uninterested; the young man was stretching his arms above his head and letting out an audible yawn. Max had to conclude this little game now. The guard might be getting impatient. Thirty year olds are still young enough to become impatient very quickly. The guard was probably wishing he was back in the cozy little guard shack with the heater turned way up to fight against the bitter cold at this ridiculous hour. The guard was probably thinking he should be napping right now but here he was, waiting for this forgetful chauffeur, this chauffeur retrieving files at 04:07 in the morning.

Max opened the zipper on the duffle, making that irritating, *zipping* noise. He zipped the bag shut, making more of that noise. He closed the trunk and spun around.

The guard had been watching that last maneuver. He had seen the fake unzipping and zipping, Max was certain of it. The guard seemed fascinated by Max's antics.

Max made a declaration: "All right, I'm finished. Thank you."

The security guard didn't move. He just kept staring at Max and the duffle bag.

Max pretended not to mind the staring, by focusing on the far end of the parking lot where he'd entered from the street. The automatic gate over there was closed, of course. Max began to walk.

And Max kept walking, pacing himself, heading toward the gate. The nosy guard once again followed him, staying back two meters. Max could feel the guard staring at his back and at the duffle bag.

Now Max stood before the closed gate, looking through the fence at the snowy street and lamp posts. The guard had veered to the left to enter the warm guard shack. Max prayed the guard would stay there where it was wonderfully warm. Max prayed the wonderful warmth would distract him enough so he could go on...and all this fuss would be over and...

The gate began to slide open. Max raised up on the balls of his feet in anticipation. He was a race horse, the bells were sounding, and his gate was about to swing open. He was about to win the famous Triple Crown. He took a breath and again reminded himself to stay calm and not hurry away...

The gate stopped. It reversed direction. It clanged and clicked. It was closed again.

"Sir?"

"Yes?"

The guard had stepped outside of the shack.

"Sir, I must inspect the bag."

"What?"

"The bag, I must have a look."

It was true then. The overly-zealous, curious security guard had noted something incorrect. He had seen the fake zipping and unzipping. He had *not* been completely turned around. And that yawning had been feigned at *that* moment. And now the overly-dedicated, curious little guard wanted to know if there were files in the overnight duffle bag or not. It seemed the guard was as good as Max at faking things.

The watch read 04:13. Max had to be at the Bahnhof in no less than forty-five or fifty minutes to purchase the ticket. And the Bahnhof lay at least eight blocks away, perhaps ten. A ten-block hike would be no easy thing in cold this bad and in wind this bad.

"All right. You may look." Max shrugged it off and made it look like he was not at all worried. However, Max was as worried as a man could be. And he could *not allow* this security guard, this lowlife parking lot attendant to look inside the duffle bag.

The guard motioned him to the guard house.

Max did not want to kill this young man...

CHAPTER 21

Max clutched the hand straps on the duffle bag and didn't realize how tightly he was clutching them. It was an unconscious effort to keep that bag where it belonged, in his grip, and out of the grip of the youthful, overly-curious security guard. Max's shiny black driving gloves would hide the whitened knuckles on both his hands. It was good the gloves hid at least some of his tenseness. Max hoped the tenseness wasn't showing too much in his face or in his body language.

Max got a quick look at his watch, visible now because his left sleeve was pulled back. The watch said 04:15. This unfortunate encounter at 04:15 in Munich with this fool of a security guard had to end. The guard had to be *neutralized* and Max had to get to the railroad station and the train to Zurich.

Max didn't want to kill this man. But he would kill him if the man made an attempt to open the duffle. Max was not about to let this guy keep him from getting on the train to Zurich. This guy wasn't going to keep him from meeting Diana in Zurich. This guy wasn't going to keep Max and Diana from escaping Pontius.

The security guard was sizing up the chauffeur—-he must be comparing the chauffeur's physique to his, and the chauffeur's age to his, and wondering if this clever chauffeur knew anything about self-defense or maybe the chauffeur was too old and fat, too slow to do much of anything.

Max noticed that to the right of the security guard in the far corner of the guard shack was a 1 meter by 1.5 meter table, give or take a few centimeters. The table was bare and the Formica top was the color of putty. It was an ugly table and not worth more than 5 euros. The luxury hotel wasn't about to spend any more money than necessary to make this guard shack any nicer for this uneducated security guard.

Or maybe the guard was smart? Maybe he was brilliant? Maybe he was a frustrated university student, a frustrated graduate with a degree in law and could not find a job as a lawyer? Maybe this security guard was angry because he had to work the night shift, fighting off drowsiness by watching boring movies—-there was a small TV and DVD player in the other corner of the shack, sitting on another , smaller table...the power cords were showing behind the TV and player. What else was in this dirty, little guard shack? Ah...

A photo of a pretty, blond Bavarian girl was tacked into the cork bulletin board. There were other photos of the same girl. One was her in a skimpy bikini, standing there on a beach somewhere, smiling into the camera. The girl was pretty indeed.

"Your girlfriend?"

The security guard blinked at Max's question.

"Yes...she is."

And that's all the guard said and now Max was sorry he'd asked such an stupid question. What could a question like that do for him? Answer: nothing. It didn't distract the security guard. It didn't make him more conversational. It didn't get rid of the guard's curiosity. And the question seemed to have irritated him.

The guard was talking.

"The duffle bag? I need to have a look inside it. Please set it on the table."

Max didn't move. He was still clutching the bag.

"Sir. The bag."

"Why?!"

The question startled the guard.

Max repeated his question: "Why?"

The guard was squinting his eyes. He looked like he was either going to cool off or heat up. It was hard to tell which one it would be. The guard was weighing the pros and cons: Did he wish to have a confrontation with this chauffeur at this frigid hour, in this dirty, little guard shack? Was it worth it? Did the hotel pay him so much that he should feel obligated to be this insistent? Why would it matter to him if the duffle didn't contain any files? Why would it matter to him if the chauffeur was disingenuous?

No. It did matter. The security guard was a good security guard. Plus he had always been a good boy and a good teenager and a good, decent, hard-working, conscientious young man and a good student, too, in the university, and later in the school of law. And one day he would find a good job with a good law firm in Munich. And he wasn't about to change his work ethic now, no not for this chauffeur, not for anyone. He was going to have the chauffeur place that duffle bag on that table and unzip it.

"Place the bag on the table and open it."

Max had been trained well in the army and he'd never forgot that training. He knew how to deflect and divert an attacker and then kill the attacker with one hit. Max's hands could convert into vice grips. He'd never lost a fight while in the army. His fellow soldiers had put him up against the best of the best from the other regiments. Nobody could beat Max. Max knew how to kill using just his thumb, right or left. If Max got a grip on an opponent's neck he could crush it by crushing the wind pipe. Max had had to hold back from doing that during many of those matches because he'd not wanted to kill anyone. Those matches, those fights were for sport or training purposes only and not for killing.

"No. I am not going to place the bag on the table. And you are going to open the gate and I am going to walk out of here and you are going back to guarding or watching movies or napping or whatever you wish to do."

The guard frowned, making his thin, brown eyebrows into upside down Vs. His eyes bulged out a little. His mouth was a thin black line turned down at the ends.

The guard's face relaxed and with it his mouth and his eyebrows. He was taking a deep breath. He was looking at the cell phone perched in the windowsill. He was thinking about making a call, maybe. Maybe he wasn't thinking much at all. Maybe he was scared and was trying not to show it.

Max had called the guard's bluff...or maybe it was not a bluff.

"Sir, you're not going anywhere. Set the bag on the table and unzip it."

The guard had not been bluffed.

"No."

The guard stepped forward and...

Max dropped the bag to the floor and, with his lightning-fast right arm and right fist, struck the young man in the throat.

The young man was shocked and was tottering and gurgling blood, trying to spit it up and out of his mouth as he held his hands to his throat. He fell with a crash against the back wall of the guard shack and slid down onto his backside. He was still gurgling and rasping and blood was bubbling from his mouth and spilling onto his uniform and chest. His face was white. His eyes were glazed and staring at Max. His arms were limp at his sides. His legs lay limply in front of him atop the cold concrete. Max had made the man a quadriplegic in a half second.

But his eyes weren't paralyzed. And he seemed to be telegraphing with them: Asking why, why did you do this? Why did you take away my life? Why did you ask if she was my girlfriend? Yes, yes she was...and she was my fiancée. We were to be married this spring.

The gurgling stopped. Max checked the pulse. The guard was dead.

Now Max had another problem in addition to getting to the Hauptbahnhof at least ten minutes before the train to Zurich departed; now Max had to dispose of the body of this sad and stupid and very dead security guard.

Max pulled back the left sleeve of his top coat and suit jacket. It was 04:21. This business had taken six minutes. Now Max had exactly one hour and six minutes to be on that 05:37 train to Zurich where he would meet his wife. And if the police found this body and then interviewed the hotel desk clerk Max's face, and the face of his wife, Diana, would be all over the news all over the internet all around the planet no later than noon today. Every border guard and customs official in Europe would be on the lookout for the murderer and his wife.

Max took a deep breath and kept staring at the dead face of the dead young man...there was a dumpster at the rear of the hotel...it was cold in that dumpster...it was cold in Munich...it was way below freezing...a body would not rot and give off a foul smell under these conditions...and the garbage truck must be coming soon...if Max could get the body into the dumpster and then get back to this guard shack and clean up any blood he could buy some time...and as the saying goes: *no body, no crime...or is it: no body no murder?* It didn't matter how the phrase went, what mattered was getting the body into the dumpster...right now!

There, hanging from one of the four pegs on the wall was another winter coat. It was an army parka...gray-green...yeah, Max would wrap the guard in it to keep blood from getting onto his own clothing...it might work...it had to work.

And to get to the dumpster Max would have to go around the parking lot. He would have to walk on the sidewalk outside the 2.5 meter chain link fence. And the cameras of Munich would see him...Max was frozen from the thought...he was as frozen as the air, as frozen as the snow, as frozen as the city of Munich with its all-seeing cameras. Maybe it would be best to leave the body and return to the hotel and kill the desk clerk and destroy the security camera in the lobby?

Sweat poured from Max's arm pits. It streaked his forehead and flowed into his eyes, the saltiness burned them. He blinked away the sweat. He tried to dig the sweat out of eyes with his gloved hand and fingers...he was blind...blinded by the salty sweat, blinded by the cold that was making the sweat freeze upon his skin; he was blinded by the hopelessness of everything...but he had to get to Zurich...blind or not, freezing or not he had to get to Zurich.

CHAPTER 22

The alarm was beeping...and beeping...and beeping...

Max opened his eyes.

He wasn't blind.

He wasn't freezing.

He was sweating. He was soaked.

It was only a dream...only a nightmare. *Only a horrific nightmare...*

It was 03:30. It was time to get up, shower, finish packing the duffle bag and leave the hotel and walk to the train station.

He wasn't a murderer. He was just a simple chauffeur with a pretty wife that adored him. He was a man that only wanted to live free and in peace. He wanted to die in peace when the time came.

The sheets were soaked. The pillow was soaked. He was soaked; he was sopping wet. He needed that shower. He needed to wash away the nightmare with soap and shampoo. He needed to wipe away the nightmare with the bath towel. He needed to get to Zurich and, from there, his wife and he needed to find a place to hide, somewhere, somehow. And they might have to get out of Europe.

A clearer sketch of an escape plan was forming along the edge of Max's mind. In the sketch they were on a jet to America, to Mexico, to Costa Rica, to Colombia, to Chile...in didn't matter right now what the destination might be as long as they were headed west across the Atlantic. Or they might have to find some place in the EU before they found a way to cross the Atlantic. They would not go east, to Russia or Central Asia or China. What could places like that offer? Answer: They could offer nothing except more danger and the world was dangerous enough without places like Russia, Central Asia, and China. Max mentally set down the sketching pencil inside his mind. He had to concentrate on getting ready and leaving the hotel and getting on the 05:37 train.

The shower was good, oh so good. It was the best shower Max had ever taken except for the first time he'd showered with his wife on their honeymoon. Soon he would see her. Soon they would find a hotel in Switzerland. Soon he would sleep with her again. Soon everything would be *normal.*

Normal? No. Nothing would ever be normal again for Max and Diana. Too much had happened. And Pontius knew that they knew too much or at least *suspected* too much. Normal? How could they ever live a normal life with Pontius searching for them? And how could they just disappear?

A weird thought grabbed Max. It was a weird thought he'd had before: Perhaps he ought to kill Pontius. Perhaps Max ought to be the hunter and Pontius ought to be his game, his little mouse to play with before squashing him. Weird thought, indeed. Max put away that foolish, weird thought. He would be no match for a devil like Pontius who was surrounded by lesser devils eager to do whatever their master wished. All the same, it would be a pleasure to kill Pontius and spare the world...it would be a pleasure to kill the passenger, too, and spare the world...

And spare the world...spare the world from what? Max couldn't even put words to his thoughts...his thoughts were too horrifying. And the passenger, who was he? Who was he?

He shook his head once more to rid himself of these thoughts...these terrible, dark visions creeping about inside his head.

Max was a good man, good and decent like his father. And Max had *not* killed the security guard. Max had never killed anyone. Max had not gone to war. It was good not to have killed anyone. His father had been unable to say the same about himself. Poor father.

Max scanned the room like a security camera and sensed a wave of *deja vu* washing over him. He had been here before. The crumpled white duvet on top of the bed looked like one of the towering Austrian Alps in winter, with steep, razor-like ridges running off in all directions, serpentine ridges with deep valleys lying between them, deep valleys that saw little sun in summer or winter or fall or spring. Max felt like he was deep inside one of those valleys, trying to find his way out, trying to find the sunshine. This hotel room had become a deep, dark place. But he was leaving it. Thank God.

Max stepped to the window and looked down at the street. The street lights were blurred disks in the swirling snow. They seemed to be the only lights in Munich. For a second he seemed like the only man, the only person in Munich. He seemed like the only person on earth.

He glanced at his watch. It was 04:00. He turned about face and walked to the door, pausing to turn out the wall light. He opened the door to the corridor and looked both directions. The corridor was silent and empty. The way to the elevator was clear. The path to freedom was opening, it was widening, it was making way for Max. He prayed his wife could get the car out of the driveway in Berchtesgaden. He wished he was with her now but he wasn't. He was here in this hotel and now he was in the elevator and the door was closing and the numbers were reversing: 4-3-2-1...

The small chime rang and the door opened. Once again Max looked right and left. Once again the corridor was silent and empty.

The lobby was empty...the security camera above the desk was not pointing in the direction of Max as he'd feared—-no, it was pointing too far to the left for his digital image to appear later. All the same, he would keep his face pointed downward and to the right.

Max pushed open the double glass door to the street. He turned right, away from the door and away from that dreaded parking lot and that young guard he did not kill. Max's heaviness was gone. His feet had wings. The duffle bag was half its weight. He was on his way to Zurich...no, not quite, but he was on his way to the Hauptbahnhof and the 05:37 train to Zurich. He was on his way to the train indeed, as the adrenalin coursed his arteries and giddiness filled his mind, as he thought about that miserable Pontius lying in his grand hotel suite probably with two naked women draped over him that scandalous, monstrous man. It pained Max to find himself thinking about Pontius again. If only he had not met the man. If only he'd not taken the job.

Max would definitely kill Pontius if given the chance. But could Pontius be killed? Could Pontius die? Was he mortal? What was he? Who was he? And again, who was the passenger? And could the passenger be killed? Perhaps Max would never know. Perhaps it didn't matter. Getting away from such monsters was all that mattered. Getting away from Pontius and staying away from him was all that mattered for now.

Maybe Max would tell someone, someone with legal authority, about Pontius. Maybe the police would listen? Maybe someone in the Austrian or German government would give Max the chauffeur a fair hearing?

No. No one would listen. No one would believe the crazy, unemployed chauffeur named Max. If anyone did hear the story they would tell Max the chauffeur to see a doctor to get some medications. It seemed there were few people in the world with any understanding. It seemed Max and Diana were the only ones. How could this be? How did this happen? And what would happen next if Pontius and the passenger and those evil creatures in the villa high on the Watzmann were not stopped? And how many more of those evil creatures were in the world? What were they planning? *And who was the passenger? Who was he???*

CHAPTER 23

Max quickened his pace as the bitter wind beat against his head, his ears, his neck. His hands were numb. His feet were numb. Everything was numb...even his mind might go numb if he didn't keep concentrating on getting to the train station and getting out of this nasty storm.

A blast of wind and snow mixed with some ice pellets struck Max. He turned his back to it and put his chin to his chest. The wind and snow and now a wall of sleet mixed in with the snow almost knocked him to the sidewalk. He turned into the gale once more and staggered side to side like a drunk.

Max had forgot to put on his gloves plus the black stocking cap that lay in his coat pocket. He fished out the cap and pulled it over his head. He fished out the black leather gloves lined with rabbit fur and slipped into them. Again he turned his backside to the wind, barely escaping another pelting of snow and sleet. The wild wind staggered him again and almost pushed him backward.

Max held his ground and resumed his march to the train station. He had already covered one block and was now crossing the street to the next one and his head was warmer now and his hands and fingers, too, as he thought of his father lying in a shell hole in Stalingrad at -30 C.

Father had crawled into the shell hole believing the myth that lightning never strikes twice in the same place...father's misguided belief had saved his life because a few minutes later a shell had landed there and wounded him...he got it in the leg...he was evacuated to Germany on one of the last planes out of that frozen hell...Stalingrad.

The 05:37 would be for Max his last train out of this hell. And he would do this for his beloved father and for his mother may they both rest in peace. Max's father would be proud of his brave son. And his father would do the same as his son. His father had showed him the photos from the war. The photos were father's act of defiance against...

Against the Nazis and against Hitler. Father had only pretended to fight for them in order to survive the war. Father did not want to kill Russians and later Americans in the Ardennes. But he'd had to do that. And it was the guilt that had shortened father's life. It was the nightmares full of shocking images plus guilt; yes, that was it. It was all too much for father to bear.

As Max thought about Hitler and the Nazis and the war and his father he walked and ran and walked and ran and ran and ran for nearly five blocks. Thinking about the Nazis made him run. If only his father had seen what was coming perhaps he could have run like this too, perhaps he could have got out of Austria and gone to America.

Max paused for three seconds to catch his breath and peered ahead into the swirling snow. He wished he could see the train station. Seeing it would confirm that he had taken the correct route. Max knew the station lay in this direction but he could be off course, right or left, by a block or two or three. He hoped this wasn't the case. Being off course would only waste more time and there was none to waste.

The watch said it was 04:20. If Max wasn't off course and the station was only three or four or at most five blocks ahead he would arrive there in approximately twenty minutes. He would arrive at approximately 04:40. There would be plenty of time to spare to purchase the ticket and be ready to board the train. There would be time to get a cup of coffee and a pastry except Max wasn't hungry.

Perhaps his appetite would return once he was on the train and the train was barreling down the tracks to Zurich. Perhaps Max would feel a little safer then.

He saw his mother lying there in the coffin made of varnished pine. The coffin was lined with some kind of velour with pleats. The velour was the color of blood. Mother had been dressed in her only nice dress and nicest sweater. Both were black. Mother's face was smooth, it was stretched and showed the form of the skull beneath. Her hair had gone gray and had been combed back. It seemed her hair had been all brown the day young Max left for the army. And it had turned to gray in one month.

Max would dedicate his escape from terror to his parents—-just as death had delivered them from suffering in this world of pain this escape would deliver Max and his wife from Pontius and the passenger and the devils. Max and his wife had to live to tell the story. They had to live and maybe tell someone about Pontius and the passenger and the house high on the Watzmann.

Max walked and ran and walked another block as he imagined telling someone about Pontius and the passenger. It was hard to keep hold of the image of him actually telling a willing listener about these last two or three years and about his wife's angst and about the grand house in Berchtesgaden and the cars and the two hundred thousand euro salary plus the benefits. Again he thought about telling the authorities—-the German or Austrian or Swiss police, Interpol. Maybe he would tell the American FBI or the CIA? The NSA? Ha!

Max was feeling even more crazed and crazy. He had to stop thinking about telling the police or anyone else. If he told the police or the FBI or CIA about Pontius and the passenger they might *recommend* Max be taken some place for *evaluation*. Then they would throw away the key and Diana would be questioned next and she, too, would be taken somewhere for evaluation and that would be the end of the little chauffeur and his little wife. Their life would be over and the authorities would chalk it up to another day's work protecting the world from insane people like Max and Diana.

Max crossed another street and was grateful it was so early and there wasn't any traffic. Anyway, how could there be traffic with snow this bad?

No. Max and Diana would tell no one. They would simply fade away, they would disappear, they would find that magical place to hide and be sustained with enough food and drink to be happy. As the years passed they would get grayer and grayer and a little fatter and then the day would come for one or the other to die...he would bury her in a forest and...

He put away his silly thoughts about getting grayer and grayer and fatter and fatter. He focused ahead to the railway station, to the train that would take him to Zurich, to the moment when he would be calling her, and later meeting her at a hotel. Once *safe* in the hotel they would plan the next chapter in their *novel* about escaping Pontius except this wasn't a novel, this wasn't fiction, and Pontius did indeed want to kill them, and Pontius wouldn't stop trying until he'd succeeded.

Max's watch said 04:35. The station lay just five minutes away out there in the blinding, swirling snow. It had to be there...he leaned into the wind and watched his feet and legs marching...forward, forward, forward...he had not slept well nor had he slept enough and he was so tired and it was still so early as he marched, marched, marched and marched. And there it was, the train station and the watch said 04:40. Max had been right all along.

Max turned to look behind him...

There was nobody there...there was nothing except the street lamps blurred by the blowing snow. The lamps could be the stars in Van Gogh's painting. The lamps could be ghosts watching Max except Max didn't believe in ghosts. Max believed in getting on the train to Zurich and calling his wife.

He prayed for an extra measure of strength to fill his mind, his soul, his spirit, and his body. He had to trust the Almighty like never before...only the Almighty could deliver Diana and Max out of Munich and out of Berchtesgaden and later out of Zurich and the EU.

Max's watch said it was 04:42 as he entered the main entrance to the Munich Train Station. The 05:37 to Zurich lay off to the right, resting quietly on the tracks as the train's personnel went about their work, preparing the train for departure.

Max brushed some snow from both his shoulders and tried to appear unhurried. He tried to appear like a typical business man on his way to another conference. Max looked back to the main entrance and was glad the station was empty...well, it appeared to be empty except for the train's crew and a few dark figures standing a few feet back from the train and a few dark figures farther down the line where the train ended.

Max would go to the ticket machine instead of the ticket counter. It would be one less point of contact with humans. As soon as the announcement came to board the train he would find the right car and the right seat and keep his composure and pray that Pontius would not realize his chauffeur was gone, and wasn't coming back, until it was too late to do anything about it. Max and Diana needed as much time as they could get.

It gave Max pleasure to imagine Pontius' displeasure with his once-trusted chauffeur.

Max's pleasure faded as he thought of Diana digging her way out of the driveway and trying to get to Zurich in the middle of the worst snowstorm in Europe in perhaps a hundred years.

He looked at his watch. It was 04:50.

CHAPTER 24

Max slipped the train ticket into his lapel pocket and walked to the pastry shop and stopped. No. No pastry shop. No letting his face be seen by more people than necessary. He turned to his right and spotted a bench along the wall. He would sit there for a few minutes and wait.

There were more passengers entering the station and dotting the platform now. They, too, were taking the 05:37 to Zurich. They, too, were leaving Munich and Bavaria...but they would return this evening or maybe tomorrow or the day after tomorrow. Max and Diana would never return...and that thought hit him head on now. It struck him like the icy wind had struck him. The decision to jump ship on Pontius had no way of ever being changed. What was done was done...and the game, the deadly game had begun. And the game that was no game could not be stopped. Either Max and Diana would win or Pontius would win. There would not be a truce or an armistice. There would only be a winner and a loser.

A security guard walked past Max and stopped three meters away. The guard turned around. The action made Max recall the nightmare from barely two hours ago. The guard was looking at him now, observing him. It was the same guard from the dream, the nightmare. It was the guard the chauffeur did not have to kill.

A smile seemed to emerge on the guard's youngish face. But the smile froze and turned into a slight frown as if the guard was remembering the chauffeur, the chauffeur that had murdered him in the nightmare and kept the guard from marrying his fiancée, the chauffeur that had kept the guard from having a happy life with a beautiful wife and the three children they'd planned.

Max made direct eye contact with the guard but remained straight-faced. What could this silly security guard do to him now?

And how silly to think it was the same person from the nightmare!

But he was the same person from the nightmare. And he was approaching the bench now like a lawyer approaches the bench in a courtroom except in this courtroom the judge had not summoned this lawyer, this security guard with the youthful looks.

The guard sat down on the opposite end of the bench and folded his hands on his lap and stared into space in front of the bench and said, "I wish I could leave on the 05:37 train...I wish I could leave Munich and go to Switzerland and ski...I love to ski..." The guard was making small talk. "It is supposed to snow more than five meters in the mountains...they say it's the storm of the century...and they are closing most of the highways in Bavaria...it was on the news just a few minutes ago." The guard's small talk was no longer small. All Max could do now was think about his wife preparing to leave Berchtesgaden and here was this guard informing him the highways were being closed. Was it true?

It had to be true about closing the highways in Bavaria. And only a miracle would allow Diana to escape Berchtesgaden. Only a miracle would get her and the loaded car with the full tank of gas out of the garage, the driveway, and down the street and out of the town and on the way to the highway to the Swiss border and later Zurich.

The security guard was making small talk again but it didn't matter to Max. Max could not hear him as he thought of his wife—-as he imagined her now in the house, packing, finalizing everything before she would leave for the bank where she would withdraw most of their euros. And...would the bank be open or would the bank keep its doors closed because of the storm? Would the bank stay closed until this *storm of the century* spun itself out and moved away? Max and Diana would need many miracles to see one another again.

The security guard was speaking once more...he seemed to be reciting words.

Max squeezed his eyes closed and opened them—-the guard was gone.

Max moved his head right, left, and right again—-the guard had vanished. He had gone *poof* into thin air. Max shook his head and closed his eyes again and opened them again. He stared at the spot on the bench where the guard had been sitting. A small square of paper lay there...it was a gum wrapper or a candy wrapper. The security guard had been sitting on it.

Max looked both ways again, leaned over, and grabbed the paper wrapping. He focused. On the small piece of paper was a word and three numbers: *Psalm 121.*

Someone had left a bible reference on a public bench. The security guard had been sitting on it. And now Max had the reference in his hands. He had no idea what Psalm 121 said. Maybe he would look it up later, in the Bible, in the hotel room in Zurich or he would look it up on the internet.

He looked at his watch. It was 05:20 and a female voice on the public address system could be heard across the platforms. Her voice reverberated under the massive roof, it bounced against the walls. It was the call to board the 05:37 to Zurich. The confident, reassuring voice was making the announcement in German, and now French and now English. Max folded the piece of paper, put it in a pocket, picked up his duffle and moved toward the waiting train. He stopped and peered into the multitude pressing in on the 05:37 to Zurich.

The security guard was nowhere to be found among the people. It must have been a ghost.

CHAPTER 25

The muted silver light of daybreak appeared beyond the bedroom window and beyond the rooftops of Berchtesgaden. In spite of the low, dark, wooly clouds, in spite of the thick snow, falling straight down now, the first light could be seen out there in the frozen world. And despite Diana's decision not to sleep, she had slept for nearly two hours. She could sleep for twenty more but instead she would take a five-minute shower, put on her make-up, and get dressed in her travelling clothes, and go to the bank, and withdraw the money.

Diana slid down off the huge bed and turned toward the window. She grabbed the edge of the mattress and steadied herself. The grogginess from only two hours of sleep hadn't left her yet.

Diana stretched her arms above her and yawned. She took a deep breath and let it out slowly and began to organize her thoughts as she fought back the tiredness.

Before heading to the bathroom and her shower she had to look down onto the driveway. She had to check it out. She had to know.

It was a little hard to tell but the driveway didn't look so bad. Drifts seem to lay on either side but the center section of it couldn't have more than twelve centimeters of snow. It must have been the wind...the wind had blown in such a manner as to carve out a pathway in the center of the driveway. At least now she knew she would be able to get to the street on the other side of the wrought iron gate.

Diana squinted her eyes and focused on the street. The grayish, pinkish, yellowish, silvery light was now strong enough for her to see the street and from what she could see, it too, wasn't all that bad. However, this could change in ten minutes if the wind came up and blew from a different, less helpful direction.

It was 07:30 hours. It was fifteen minutes drive to the bank under normal circumstances. It could take twice that long in weather like this. She had to leave no later than 08:20...and she needed that shower...and she needed to eat something...and she needed to go outside and look closer at the driveway and then walk out to the gate and see if it was true about the street not being so bad.

As Diana was about to turn toward the master bath a ray of bright light caught her tired eyes. No. There were two rays of bright light. It was a delivery truck passing by just outside the gate. Delivery truck indeed. The street was drivable then. And this meant the city plows had been working, perhaps working all night long; this meant the storm wasn't bad enough for the city to call off the plows. If it was this good in Berchtesgaden the other highways leading out from town must be all right and the highway to Switzerland, the E 52, must be all right and later today, this afternoon or this evening, she would meet her husband at the hotel he'd chosen and everything would be all right.

CHAPTER 26

Max lifted the duffle above his head and shoved it into the luggage compartment above his seat—-the duffle seemed to weigh a ton. But it was only his worry and anxiety weighing a ton, worry and anxiety he'd transferred onto his duffle bag. But he was relieved to be rid of the bag for now.

He sat down and took a deep breath and looked out the window. More passengers were pressing in on the train. Most of the passengers were business people, he figured. There were few tourists this time of year in Germany and Europe. Europe in winter was too windy and cold, too snowy or rainy, too dark and gray. The business people pressing in on the train were dressed mostly in dark grays and browns—-dark gray or brown trench coats with dark gray or brown scarves, and black leather gloves...their clothing matched Europe's winter weather.

Max spotted a young couple. They weren't dressed for business; they were dressed in blue jeans and khaki cargo pants, and black down-filled jackets, and stocking hats in bright colors, colorful gloves, hiking shoes, bright red and powder blue woolen scarves and carrying backpacks. The couple, too, was going to board the 05:37 to Zurich. The couple must be American or Canadian. Max, like most Europeans, could spot Americans or Canadians from a half kilometer off—-although it was slightly easier to tell if they were Americans...*Americans always had that look about them.*

The couple disappeared from view. They'd likely got on the train much farther down the line, down the platform. Max would not see them again or at least not until they'd arrived in Zurich. He didn't want to talk to anyone on this trip let alone a couple of Americans.

Max was wrong about not seeing them until Zurich. He would not be alone on this trip to Switzerland. That couple had found their compartment and their seat—-the compartment was Max's compartment and the two seats about to be occupied were facing his. Ach. He'd so hoped to be alone and have it totally quiet so he could get some good sleep. He needed more sleep. He needed to be sharp. Pontius would try to kill them, murder them. Pontius would be furious when he discovered his chauffeur had mutinied and the chauffeur's wife had stolen the BMW.

The couple managed to slide their unwieldy backpacks into the luggage compartment. They sat down in their seats. They both looked up now and...

And...

And, if they spoke to him, he would speak to them in German only. He wanted to see if they spoke German. And if they did, so be it. If not, it would give him a chance to eavesdrop. His English wasn't the best but it wasn't the worst either.

The man, around thirty years old, spoke first.

"Hi." He said it and grinned.

Hi. Hi was a universal greeting. If Max replied with a *hi* of his own it wouldn't reveal if he spoke English.

"Hi." Max didn't smile as he returned the greeting. He was in no mood for smiling.

The woman, however, smiled too and said, "Hi." Then she said, "Good morning..." and smiled once again.

Max would reply in German and not smile.

"Guten Morgen."

Now the man grinned, again, and began to speak slowly.

"Mein... unser... unser Deutsch ist nicht sehr gut..uh...my ...our...our German isn't very good. Do you speak English?"

"Mein Englisch ist nicht gut...my English...not...not...good."

Okay, so it was a lie. The truth was Max could understand at least 90% of a conversation in English. Truth was, he could sometimes understand 100%. Truth was, he understood 100% of English most of the time. Truth was, for years he'd watched a lot of American and British TV.

"Well," said the man, "maybe I can teach you English and you can teach me German."

"Yes," said the woman, "it would be a nice way to pass the time until we get to Zurich."

Max almost spoke in English but checked himself. He did not want to engage in conversation with this American couple. Yes. That was an American accent, they were Americans. And now Max had to figure out a way to tell them, politely, that he did not wish to converse, he only wanted to sleep or at least close his reddened, burning eyes.

"Where are you from?" The woman was asking the question.

Max kept his eyelids sealed shut. Perhaps if he kept them this way for a minute or so the woman would give up.

Ach...what's the use? He opened his eyes. She was smiling and waiting for a reply. The man was smiling, too. It would be funny if Max wasn't so tired. It would be funny if Max wasn't so worried about Diana and about Pontius and his devilish servants wanting to kill them.

Here was this naive American couple, not much older than thirty or so, trying to have a conversation with him, on the train to Zurich. How could this naive couple have any idea what was going on with Max and Diana? How could anyone have any idea? They couldn't. No one could know. No one would know. What was happening to Max and his wife would remain a secret. It would remain a secret between Max, his wife, and Pontius. The deadly game of the hunter and the hunted would remain a deadly secret. And for Max and Diana, simply to get away from Pontius and the devils and surviving would be winning the deadly game. All Max and Diana could hope for was to escape and live out the rest of their time on earth in some yet unknown place. To escape and live would be winning. Max put away these troubling thoughts that would come over him every hour or so and smother him.

The woman repeated the question. "Where are you from?"

"Oostreich..."

"Austria." The woman smiled at her success translating the name of Max's native land, and continued speaking. "Austria was so beautiful. We were there a week ago. Went to Innsbruck...Vienna...Vienna was beautiful...Innsbruck was beautiful...the Alps were beautiful...we went all the way to the Brenner Pass!"

"Yes," chimed in her husband or boyfriend, "we did go all the way to the Brenner Pass...that's where some of those Nazis and SS guys escaped. They would hike some back trails over the pass on their way to..."

"To Bari!" She was proud of her knowledge, proud she'd remembered that detail.

The woman was far too enthusiastic for 05:37. This trip was going to be longer than Max could have imagined. How could he endure this enthusiastic woman and her enthusiastic companion while Max was so worried about his wife? What could he say to get them to be quiet, to leave him alone and let him get some sleep?

"Honey, let's go to Bari after Switzerland."

Honey mulled over her suggestion.

"Yeah? You wanna?"

"Yeah, let's go to Bari. It would be nice to go somewhere a bit warmer... and yeah...Bari was where a lot of Nazis escaped from Europe after the war...remember? We saw that documentary about that British intelligence officer who said he and his men had spotted Martin Bormann in one of the cars up there in the mountains...so they trailed them into Italy...they followed Bormann and the others all the way down the Italian coast, all the way to Bari...they watched them loading their cars, trailers and all, onto one of the ships...the intelligence officer insisted until the day he died that he'd spotted Bormann. He knew it was him. He had seen so many photos of Bormann, newspaper clippings with photos too, and even some films. The Brit said they gave him orders to follow Bormann but not apprehend...they were to let him escape...I love all that Nazi stuff...it's so scary..."

She was panting. She'd said so many words in such a short time. It had made her short of breath. And it struck Max as odd for this woman to have such an interest in Nazis. She'd recited all those details without skipping a beat.

It was her husband's turn to speak once again. It was his turn to offer his *well-thought-out* opinion about Nazis.

"Nah, I don't believe it was Bormann. I believe he was killed in the Battle of Berlin. I believe it was Bormann's bones those construction workers found back in the 1970s or 80s or whenever...I believe the German government wanted to clear up the matter...so they did some research and came to the conclusion that that skeleton was Bormann..."

The man paused and smiled at Max and asked him what he thought about it. But Max didn't offer any opinions.

"Nazi stuff...it doesn't interest you?" The man wasn't smiling now.

Max turned toward the window. The visibility was poor. The wind was blowing harder out here in the country away from the city. It appeared to be snowing harder, as well. The storm had not let up at all. It had grown worse. The weather outside the train made Max think of his father again and the Wehrmacht and Stalingrad and later, when father had to fight the Americans in the Ardennes.

Max turned to the man and said, "*Mein Englisch...*"

"Oh yeah, that's right...I'll talk a little slower for ya...Nazis...are... you... in-ter-est-ed in Na-zis?"

Max didn't answer right away so the woman said to her husband, "Honey, maybe his family...maybe they were Na..."

She was staring at him now. Her eyes didn't blink. She was serious. She was being offensive and taking it seriously.

Max didn't blink either.

Now the man was talking again. "My grandpa was in the 3rd Infantry Division. Yep. He was in Italy during the war. And before Italy he was in North Africa. He won the Silver Star. He musta' killed a lot of Nazis to win the Silver Star!"

Max wanted to grab the stupid man by the neck and...no, he wouldn't do it...Max would just let the stupid, ignorant, foolish man keep talking.

"My grandpa was a pilot." The woman said it, as her unblinking eyes remained focused on Max. "He flew a big bomber."

"A B-17," said the man. Then he formed his two hands into a makeshift airplane that looked more like an eagle or hawk. "Woosh...woosh..." the man was making noises like an airplane or bird swooping down on its prey. This man was still in middle school or maybe high school in his head. That's how his foolish gesturing looked to Max as he visualized giving him a good paddling and sending him home with a note of reprimand.

The woman was speaking.

"Yeah, a B-17. He flew thirty-five missions over Germany. That's what my dad told me, anyway." The woman continued. "He bombed about every German city there was...he bombed Dresden, too...I saw a documentary about that...it was bad...the whole city burning...all those people burning...but that's what happens when you vote for Nazis."

Max recalled the dreadful wounds his father-in-law suffered while serving in the Wehrmacht. The war had left him a freak. Max thought of all those people in Dresden, the people of the city this woman was now blaming for their own demise. Max thought about Pontius and his Berlin accent. He thought about the passenger and his flawless Austrian-German accent. Max would hold his tongue. He would let these stupid Americans talk all they wanted. He would try to be amused by them. Max thought about his wife again, and the snow storm and her escaping from Berchtesgaden. It would be hard to be amused by this stupid couple with everything that was happening to Max and his wife.

"Yeah, why would anybody ever vote for a guy like Hitler?" The man was speaking again. "It never ceases to amaze me how foolish people can be."

It was getting harder and harder for Max to hold his tongue here on this train to Zurich in the middle of this savage storm. It was hard to listen to this high school student pontificate about the war, about things he could not understand.

The woman was talking again. She was holding up some kind of brochure. She was asking a question: "Have you ever been to Chartres Cathedral?"

Now why would this woman suddenly start talking about the cathedral in Chartres? First she talks about Bari, and Nazis, and bombing Dresden, and...and now...now she was pointing at the cover of that brochure, that booklet. The cover contained a photograph of the labyrinth in the floor of the Chartres Cathedral.

"We walked the labyrinth," the man declared, as if that was quite a feat. "It's very soothing to walk the labyrinth, any labyrinth...it transcends...it's transformational...it is as if all life's journeys, all our lives' journeys are compressed in time and space when ya walk the labyrinth."

Max had not walked the labyrinth, *any labyrinth* anywhere. He sized up the man and said: *"Oh ja, das labyrinth..."*

"Ja, das labyrinth..." the man repeated Max's comment in German.

The man was smiling. He was enjoying talking to Max. That's how it looked anyway.

"Das labyrinth—-trans-for-ma-tion-al...do you understand what I mean?" Now the man was giving Max a tutorial of some sort.

"Ja...transformations."

"I don't think he gets it, honey," she said.

Suddenly she popped out her smart phone and began to type on the screen with the tip of her index finger. She turned the phone around so Max could see the small screen. The screen was peppered with little blue dots.

"I just did a search for labyrinths in this area...look at how many there are!" She was typing again. She showed the screen once again to Max. "This is Southwest Michigan where we're from...look how many labyrinths!"

It would appear the woman was as taken by labyrinths as her husband and was quite proud there were so many in Michigan. And it would appear this chatty couple was just plain weird. Maybe they were crazy, too.

"Ja." Max said.

"Ja." She replied and smiled.

Max felt a wave of nausea. He felt depressed. He turned again to the window. It would be dawn soon. Already the eastern horizon was showing pink-gray despite the heavy, low clouds full of snow. He wished he was with his wife on this train instead of with this chatty crazy couple. He wished they would stop talking about Nazis and the war and labyrinths and whatnot. He wished he could sleep if only for a while if only for thirty minutes. He wished he could step out of this dream...this dream which had become a nightmare. He wished he could be free. He wished he could laugh. It had been so long since he'd laughed, since he'd felt free to laugh and free to relax.

He wished his father could take him one more time to the Flughafen where they would watch airplanes landing and taking off and disappearing behind the puffy clouds or behind the mountains with their patchwork of summertime snowfields stretching out in long, narrow lines among blue fields of granite. He wished his father would take him by the hand and walk with him down the cobble stones in the village and buy him a waffle dusted in powdered sugar and cinnamon. It was all father could afford so he didn't do it very often. Father would always purchase an extra for mother.

CHAPTER 27

It was 08:40 and Diana was ten minutes from the bank. The bank opened at 09:00. If everything went all right she would leave the bank around 09:15 or 09:20, with the money, and there was no reason everything would not go all right. On the other hand, it wasn't every day a person makes a withdrawal of more than 200,000 euros. For a moment she debated whether or not just to withdraw all of it. Diana wondered if she or her husband would ever have the opportunity to get the rest of the money, the last 25,000. If she withdrew it all it would total about 235,000.

Ah, go for it all. Don't leave anything. There was no way she and Max would ever return to Berchtesgaden. No way!

Diana liked being this decisive. If her husband were here he might do it differently. He might leave money in the account. But he wasn't here. He was on the train to Zurich and he was probably taking a long snooze. She wished she was on that train, curled up under a blanket, her head on his shoulder, and napping alongside her husband. She wished, again, she had not been so cooperative when her husband had announced the job offer from Pontius. She should have been more decisive then like she was now.

That day, when Max told her about the job, seemed so long ago now; it seemed it was ten or twenty years ago instead of only two or two and a half. Where did the years go? 2011 would arrive in a few short weeks.

Diana had not been able to bear children. That news had come hard for her husband. It had depressed him for a long time as he'd struggled to find work and struggled to get out of bed in the morning and struggled to keep his waistline trim. Her inability to have children had brought back the bad times from his childhood and his mother not having more children and later dying of cancer after he had gone off to the army. But Diana's infertility made escaping Berchtesgaden easier. Her infertility was a blessing for her and for her husband now. It was too bad she had such thoughts but the truth is the truth. If they'd had children they would have had grandchildren and that alone would have made leaving Europe impossible.

There was the bank. It was 08:55. Diana would use the time to find a parking slot which wouldn't be difficult. She had only seen five other autos and a couple of delivery vans on her way to the bank. Most of the parking slots in the city center would be empty.

Diana pulled into a spot scarcely a minute's walk from the bank. She turned off the ignition and whispered a prayer. She thanked the Almighty for her tiny church congregation. She'd not really gotten to know anyone there but she knew they cared about her and about her husband. In the end that's about all that counts. In the end...

The end for Diana and Max could come very soon...

She took a deep breath, and put her hand to the door handle on the front door to the bank. In spite of her warm gloves she felt the cold steel of the door on her fingertips.

Diana entered the lobby and slowly and deliberately walked across the polished tile floor as her knee-high, black winter boots made a soft padding sound. She had tucked her khaki-toned, flannel-lined trousers into the boots. Even though the pants plumed out a bit they still showed how stylishly tailored they were. Diana would always look her best no matter what she might be doing unless it was fixing a bad paint job.

Her winter coat was a version of a U.S. Navy Pea coat cut long so it reached mid thigh. She loved this coat and she loved the soft cotton sweater, the navy blue one she was wearing now. She loved wearing soft cotton underneath the warm Melton wool and nylon blend of the Navy coat. She loved her Russian fur hat...she loved being comfortable, and safe...she didn't like the idea that she and her husband may have to go live in the mountains, forest, or desert or in some dingy neighborhood somewhere in some third world hellhole.

The bank teller, standing 3 meters behind the counter, was a woman in her late thirties or early forties. She was wearing a gray skirt, knee-length, topped with a black, single-breasted blazer with pewter-toned buttons. Her blouse was white. The gold chain about her neck sparkled. Her hair was shoulder length and dishwater blond. Her makeup was flawless and so were her nails. She wore a pair of black pumps. The lenses in her eye glasses were a bit thick. She looked a little like a schoolmarm. The lenses made her eyes look larger than they really were. Maybe the poor girl had spent too much time reading or studying and not having enough fun?

It was ridiculous to have such thoughts...thought Diana.

"May I help you?" The teller said it as she walked up to the edge of the counter and faced Diana head-on.

"I wish to make a withdrawal."

"Your account number?"

Diana gave her the bankcard with the account number. The teller studied the number for a second and turned toward her super thin monitor and keyboard. She tapped out the account numbers on the keyboard and waited for the account information to appear. She paused and blinked her eyes several times as if she had some debris in them or her eyes were dry. She continued to bat her long eyelashes. Diana could hear them brushing softly against the woman's high cheek bones. Diana tried to read the other woman's mind.

"And how much do you wish to withdraw?"

"All of it."

Their eyes met. The teller wasn't blinking now. The teller was studying Diana. Now it was she who was reading thoughts.

"That would be 234, 553 euros..." The woman took short breath and held it for a moment. It was obvious she was more than a bit impressed by the amount.

"That's correct..."

"And how do you wish to...?"

"Cash."

The young woman, this young female teller looked up abruptly and stared at Diana. The teller would make a decent poker player.

"Cash?" The teller asked and kept staring with her poker face.

"Yes. Cash, please." Diana wished she had not added the word *please* to their little exchange. "And I want it in 100-euro bills...I want 210,000 of it in 100-euro bills. And the rest in 50s."

Diana took a deep, slow breath and let it flow out through her nose without making a sound. She was too nervous and it showed; she had sounded *too rehearsed*. She could win an Oscar for being nervous. She was playing the part of a nervous person perfectly. She could hear the applause as she accepted the award. She could hear the applause as she thanked everyone that had helped her win an Oscar for playing the part of the nervous person in the film, in the bank, in this bank in Berchtesgaden.

"There may be a penalty." The teller was still staring.

"No, there will be no penalty. The money isn't in an interest-bearing account."

The young woman teller looked at her computer screen once again and said, "You are right."

Diana noted how much the teller's eyebrows were raised and how much her forehead was wrinkled. The teller had to be wondering why anyone would have so much money just lying there in the bank and earning no interest. The teller was trying to piece together the parts of this unfolding story, this scene in this small bank in Berchtesgaden...she was probably trying to do her own personal profile of Diana. And maybe this teller, this bank employee had a loose tongue and would tell her boss about this *incident* in the bank. Maybe she would call her boss as soon as Diana departed the bank. But what could the teller do or say? Diana wasn't doing anything illegal. The money was in a joint account and belonged to her and her husband.

Now Diana wished she'd come to the bank before, if only once or twice or thrice during the past one, two or three years during their stay, during their sojourn in Berchtesgaden. If that were the case maybe this teller would recognize her and they would be somewhat familiar with one another. But her husband had been the only one to make the deposits. And this meant Diana was an unknown person to this bank and to this bank teller, this overly-curious bank clerk.

Diana wished they'd simply kept the money in their big house in Berchtesgaden. But Max had insisted on using the bank. We cannot keep so much money lying around here, he'd said.

But Max had said that back in the days when his fears weren't as great as Diana's. If only they'd moved the money earlier she would be on the highway to Zurich now. If only they'd hidden the money in their house from the beginning. If only this all hadn't happened so suddenly, they could have been prepared.

Diana centered herself and thought about her mother and her father. Her father had been terribly wounded in the war. Her father and all like him had been subjected to the worst tyranny...tyranny brought on by monsters like Pontius.

Diana would consider these few, nervous, tortuous minutes in the bank as combating tyranny. This time spent in the bank, standing in front of this curious woman bank cashier, to withdraw their money was another step on the road to freedom. It was another step on the road to victory. And where would this road take them?

The only way to know the answer to the question was to keep on taking steps, keep on walking, keep on driving ahead into the storm.

After placing the packages of bills in the satchel, Diana thanked the teller but the teller did not respond, as Diana turned and headed for the door, as she felt the eyes of that woman following her through the door and out to the street.

Diana placed the satchel with the money on the passenger side floor. She put the key in the ignition and started the engine. She looked at her watch. It was 09:15.

The snow had not let up at all but the wind was still calm.

CHAPTER 28

Pontius punched in the numbers on his cell phone and waited. His chauffeur, his clever, little chauffeur, Max, would answer in a moment.

Pontius would invite his chauffeur to sit with him at his table in the hotel's breakfast room. Pontius wanted to watch the chauffeur squirming as the events of last evening would replay inside the chauffeur's head. Pontius would say nothing as he stared at the chauffeur. Pontius would let him simmer there, he would watch him slowly cooking in his own mental juices. Pontius would act as if nothing had happened or that it had all been nothing more than good fun. But it had not been just fun—-Max had not taken the bait. Max had not fallen for one of the women.

The American woman was trying to rouse Max.

"Sir?" She kept tapping his knee and saying, "Sir? Sir?"

"Hmmm...hmm? Huh?" He had been in a deep sleep for at least an hour and did not wish to wake up for at least another hour.

His cell! His regular cell phone! It was playing that short riff from *Eine Kleine Nacht Muziek*. Max loved Chopin. Ah! Pontius! That devil was calling!

Why hadn't he turned off the phone?

Max had to answer, now. He had to answer his *boss*. His boss! Ha! Pontius may have been Max's boss for a time but he would never hold that title again. Never. Never again.

Max fished out the phone from his pants pocket, opened it, and placed it to his ear as the American woman and now her husband watched. This couple had no manners.

Max got up quickly and slipped open the Plexiglas door to the compartment. In a second he was in the narrow corridor of the train car. He took a few steps to the right. Now he could speak without having to endure the watching eyes of that stupid American couple.

"Yes?"

"It is 08:00. You will join me for breakfast at 08:30."

This was the first time Pontius had invited him to have a formal meal together. Max would act as if surprised.

"Breakfast? You want me to..."

"Yes. 08:30." Pontius was agitated. The agitation could be heard in his voice despite his perfect Berlin accent and despite his cultured, sophisticated ways.

Max would play him a bit.

"But...we have never..."

"Be there. 08:30. All right?"

All right. Pontius had said *all right*? Pontius never sounded so conciliatory.

Max would say it once more: "But, sir, we've never eaten an entire meal together." Max closed his eyes and waited for Pontius to respond. And it was true that they'd never eaten an entire meal together and it was also true that until last evening they'd never had a drink together.

Pontius continued to sound conciliatory: "Yes, I know. I think it's time for that to change. You have been a good employee. I want to get to know you better. You have earned my trust."

Max opened his eyes and looked out the window. The snowstorm was still raging as the train pushed through it, onward down the tracks to Zurich. The snow flew up and away from the window and dusted the frigid air outside the train.

Pontius inviting his employee to join him for breakfast? It was as if last night's charade or whatever it was had not happened. It was as if Pontius had forgotten the whole thing. However, Pontius never forgets anything. And right now, Pontius was mocking him by saying that Max had earned his trust. The bizarre incident with the suitcase came to mind. And Max heard, once again, Pontius' warning. Max took a deep breath. He had to keep his cool and...

And Max would play his boss one more time...

"08:30? Okay, I will *try* to be there at 08:30."

"*Nein*. You *will be* there at 08:30."

Max could see Pontius clenching his teeth as he said the words. He could hear the wrath. He could hear it in the way the words came through the phone, words that had been compressed, squeezed like a sour lemon gets squeezed. Max wouldn't play his ex-boss anymore. He'd riled him a sufficient amount. And this would be the last time he spoke with him. Enough was enough.

"Yes, of course. I will join you at 08:30. It would be a *pleasure."*

Pleasure indeed, thought Max the ex-chauffeur as he closed the cell phone. He re-opened it and turned it off. Good. There would be no more phone calls from the boss. At least there would be no more phone calls from Pontius on this phone. And once Max got to the hotel in Zurich he would disassemble this phone and dispose of it well. He didn't want to risk throwing it from the train because it might be found by some railroad maintenance crew or perhaps some farmer with land near the railway line.

Max stuffed the phone into his pocket. It felt good to play his boss, his *ex-boss* now. Max hadn't felt this good for a long time. Yes, despite his depression, it felt good. He couldn't wait to tell Diana what he'd said to Pontius.

Max looked at his watch. It was 08:04. Diana would be heading to the bank soon. He whispered a short prayer for God to help her. He wondered how it would go once the bank teller saw that Diana was withdrawing so much money in cash. He was sorry now that he'd told her to leave 25,000 in the account. It made no sense to leave any of it. They would never go back to Berchtesgaden or Germany or Austria. Never.

They had to get out of Europe undetected, somehow. But how? How would they do it if Pontius contacted Interpol? And what if he reported the *BMW 650i Coupe as* stolen? Max would have to find someone to take the car off their hands. He would find someone looking for a bargain, someone discreet, someone living on the margins, someone *living in the shadows* as they say. And there were plenty that fit that description if one knew where to look.

But getting rid of a BMW 650i for next to nothing might not be quite so easy. That car was worth at least 60,000 euros. Max would have to find someone with connections, someone with wealthy clients outside the EU in the Middle East perhaps or Morocco perhaps. Trying to sell it for say one-fourth its value could provoke too many questions. However, Max would get rid of it one way or another. The car had to go. That was a certainty.

Once they'd settled into their hotel room Max would visit a few bars in the area. There would be someone in one of those bars with the connections, with the information Max needed. Someone in Zurich would *appreciate* the BMW. Someone with connections to car thieves or smugglers would get rid of the BMW for Max. And later, Max would purchase another car, a less conspicuous car like a used Toyota or a Honda or maybe a Volvo...even an American jeep. And he would pay cash...they would use cash for everything from now on...they had to cover their tracks...and somehow he would find someone to make new passports...Max could grow a beard, too, and Diana could change the color of her hair...

The American woman watched Max slide open the compartment door. She watched him take his seat once more. Max looked at her and showed no emotion. He placed the train blanket over his front from feet to chin, wrapping himself inside as best he could. He leaned toward the wall by the window and closed his eyes.

She was speaking and she was placing her hand on his shoulder.

"Are you all right?"

Max opened his eyes again. "Ja...all right...I...am good...I am all right."

"You don't look all right."

"No?"

"No."

The American woman was right, Max supposed. He should have gone to the WC and looked at his face in the mirror. He should have thrown some cold water on it. Perhaps then he would look better. Perhaps then he wouldn't draw so much attention from this woman.

Pontius looked at the clock on the wall. It was 08:35 and his chauffeur had not arrived yet. He pounded out the numbers on his cell phone once again. He waited as the phone rang, and rang, and rang. The computerized voice came on, asking him to please leave a message after the tone. Pontius was almost spewing fire now as he exhaled like a surfacing whale and waited for the tone.

"It is 08:36. Get down here now. I have a schedule to keep."

He slammed down the phone next to his coffee. He took a sip from the cup. His coffee didn't taste good anymore. The fresh-baked roll with butter and jam didn't taste good anymore. Nothing tasted good, not even the omelet the breakfast room attendant had just delivered to the table.

Something was amiss. And Pontius would figure out what it was. He pushed back from his linen-draped table, threw down his linen napkin, and stormed off to the see the desk clerk. He needed to know if the clerk had seen his chauffeur.

The poor desk clerk was fidgeting and avoiding eye contact with Pontius while Pontius interrogated him. The clerk's shiny bald head was showing tiny beads of perspiration. A few of the beads were coming together to form a small river that was flowing down the side of his head into his crisp white shirt collar.

"No sir. I've not seen him," the clerk said the words and looked up, finally. He looked down again. Pontius' eye were daggers, they were laser beams burning a hole through the clerk's forehead and melting his brain.

"Come with me to his room! And bring the key!"

"Yes sir."

The sixty seconds it took to go up to the chauffeur's room had seemed like sixty minutes to the desk clerk as he swiped the card through the slot next to the door handle. He could not wait to get away from this madman. The clerk was having an unlucky day working as a temp at this unlucky job. The clerk had once been a pilot and had flown commuter jets throughout the EU but the economy had tanked and now here he was stuck in a job he hated; here he was with this angry hotel guest that was looking for his chauffeur...this rich guy that could still afford a rich lifestyle, including a chauffeur and a large expense account.

The clerk opened the door for the irate guest and the irate guest stormed into the middle of the chauffeur's room and let out a string of expletives.

Max had vanished.

The desk clerk didn't know what was going on but somehow he sensed the chauffeur was long gone and far away from the hotel. It made the clerk happy. Even though he did not know the chauffeur or what was going on he was glad the chauffeur had made Pontius so angry.

Pontius stormed out of the room and into the corridor once more, leaving the desk clerk *behind in the dust.* He got on the elevator and pushed the button to close the door. Let the desk clerk take the next elevator ride down or let him take the stairs. Pontius could care less about the stupid, inept, incompetent clerk. All he wanted now was to return to his room and grab his luggage, the luggage which he'd ordered the two whores to pack for him last night.

And once Pontius had his bags he would head out to the parking lot and get the Mercedes and drive back to the villa...he was absolutely furious with himself and the world for allowing his chauffeur to slip away like this. He was livid. He would explode.

If the passenger knew what had happened, the passenger would be far more furious than Pontius. After all it was the passenger that had sprung Pontius out of hell with the help of the Angel of Light. The passenger had helped the Angel of Light during the selection process and had helped choose Pontius. Of all history, Pontius was the only one with the right qualifications.

Pontius pushed open the door to his hotel suite. The women were still in his bed.

"Get out! Now!"

The two women hardly moved under the huge, rumpled comforter so Pontius ripped it away and flung it across the room. The two hookers started to complain as they slid off the bed and headed for the bathroom.

"Shut up and get dressed...no bath, no shower!"

Pontius stood to one side with his arms crossed, glaring at the women, the women he now loathed. He had used them and now he was abusing them. They were unworthy of anything else.

He pushed and prodded them through the door as one of them was still buttoning her blouse.

"Wait." Pontius reached into his lapel pocket and pulled out a roll of bills. He gave a bill to each. "Here...!"

"That's it?! Fifty euros???!!!" It was the hooker with the half-buttoned blouse asking the question. The hooker was not happy, not happy at all.

"You are not worth fifty. You are not worth five. Go!"

The other hooker stuffed the 50-euro bill into her bra and said to her companion, "Come on."

In an instant the other woman jerked a revolver from her handbag, stepped back, and leveled it at Pontius' face.

"Give us one thousand a piece!"

The color in Pontius' face faded to gray. His eyes became the eyes of a Timber Wolf. He cracked a smile and flared the nostrils of his Romanesque nose. The smile was the smile a wolf would make if a wolf could smile. Two or three of Pontius' front teeth sparkled.

In a split second Pontius had the hooker's revolver in his own hand. It was he that now leveled the weapon at the defiant whore.

The women's jaw fell open. Her eyes were bigger than saucers. This man wasn't human. No normal man can move that fast.

"You have one second to leave or you die."

The terrified prostitutes turned around and headed down the corridor and began to run. They had to get away from this devil, this monster, this killer.

Pontius grabbed the two pieces of luggage and headed for the parking lot next to the hotel. He hated having to drive the car himself. He hated the chauffeur and the chauffeur's wife.

CHAPTER 29

The dashboard clock said it was 09:15. Pontius would be in Berchtesgaden by 12:00 perhaps sooner, if the snowstorm didn't get any worse.

The first thing Pontius would do upon arrival in Berchtesgaden was call on the chauffeur's wife, living in the splendid residence he had paid for and had used to house all his chauffeurs and their wives.

And where was his latest chauffeur now? He must have taken the train to Berchtesgaden to fetch his wife. Surely the chauffeur wouldn't go anywhere without fetching her first, especially with weather this bad. Yes, that was it—-the chauffeur had gone to Berchtesgaden because that was where his wife was and that was where their BMW was, the BMW into which they would pack as many of their things as possible as they attempted to escape their master.

On the other hand, maybe the chauffeur had not gone to Berchtesgaden. The passenger had alluded to the valor of the chauffeur and his wife. The chauffeur might indeed go somewhere other than Berchtesgaden. The chauffeur might have told his wife to meet him elsewhere. And where would that be? It wouldn't be Munich. No, not Munich. The chauffeur wouldn't stay in Munich. Perhaps he would go north to Frankfurt or Hamburg or Berlin.

The chauffeur and his wife would need money and Pontius knew where their money was. He knew the chauffeur had been making regular deposits in a savings account in that bank in Berchtesgaden. Pontius needed to call the bank and have them freeze that account. Pontius had the power to do it. The bank's general manager had been bribed, and *mildly* threatened too.

Pontius held the phone in his right hand and punched in the number for the bank with his right thumb as he drove the Mercedes with his left hand. He could use the auto dial for calling the number, he supposed, but punching in the numbers was just as easy since he carried thousands of phone numbers in his super memory. Truth be told, Pontius' brain contained the phone numbers of millions. And yet, the passenger was right; despite their powers, despite their super brains, despite all that the Angel of Light had given them they could not harm *any believer* under the protection of Michael unless that believer deliberately brought himself or herself out from under that protection by deliberately giving up, by deliberately losing faith or by taking matters into their own hands perhaps.

Ruminating like this made Pontius' anger grow and grow and grow. He could not wait to catch the chauffeur and his wife, take them to the villa, and roast them. And he hated the concept—-he hated admitting what was true, that if the chauffeur and his wife or any like them could not be harmed as long as they did not lose their faith, as long as they remained under the control and guidance of their god. This belief defied evolution and the survival of the fittest, the victory of the strongest over the weak. The notion that all one needed was faith in that false Judeo-Christian god...and that that god might win was intolerable for Pontius and even more intolerable for the passenger. For this reason they had to crush these Judeo-Christian dreamers and anyone that dared to defy the Angel of Light and his followers.

A female bank employee was answering the call:

"Hello?"

"I want to speak with your manager." Pontius said it in a monotone voice designed to mask his anger.

The young woman looked toward the rear of the bank to the manager's office behind the floor-to-ceiling, bullet-proof glass panels. The office was empty. The snowstorm must have made the manager late. She turned around in time to catch a glimpse of a silver BMW passing by in front of the bank. A sudden ray of sunshine showed through what must be a break in the low, winter clouds. The ray bounced off the driver side door of the car and sent a penetrating beam into the teller's eyes. For a second or two she was blinded by the light. But she had not been too blinded to see the other woman driving the BMW, the same woman that had just withdrawn more than two hundred thousand euros from the account.

"I'm sorry, sir. He has not arrived yet."

Pontius was about to let loose a long streak of swearwords about the bank manager being late for work. But he held back. He would get this stupid girl to freeze the account.

"I want you to freeze my employee's account...that would be my chauffeur's account." Pontius' tone had morphed from monotone to nasty.

The teller had chatted with the chauffeur on quite a few occasions when the nice man had come in to the bank to make deposits. She liked the chauffeur—-in a father-daughter sort of way. The chauffeur had made her feel sorry for him, too. There was always something sad or tragic about him. The man seemed to be much more than just a chauffeur. He seemed like a tragic, reluctant hero or like one of Shakespeare's characters, perhaps.

The teller didn't like the way Pontius was speaking. She didn't like his nasty tone. It made her feel protective of the chauffeur like a daughter would protect her father if her father were threatened or attacked.

"I'm sorry, sir. The account has been closed."

It gave the teller pleasure to say these words. She took a couple of deep breathes, hoping the nasty man at the other end had not noticed her slightly emotional reply. Yes indeed. It made her feel good to say these words about *the account being closed.*

Pontius' eyes bulged like a frog's eyes would bulge just before the frog croaked. His pulse went to one hundred fifty. His armpits were sopping.

Like a snake, Pontius hissed into the cell phone: "Closed?! Who closed it?!!!"

"His wife was here a few minutes ago. She withdrew the money and closed the account." Again the teller felt enjoyment in saying these words. The words were delightful and amusing because she knew how angry they made the nasty man talking to her now.

Pontius' eyes glowed red. His face turned the same color. He nearly crushed the phone in his hand. And he almost cursed at the teller.

He looked at the clock on the dashboard. It was 09:20. The bank had opened at 09:00. The chauffeur's wife must have just left. And where was she headed? And which route would she chose for leaving Berchtesgaden? Surely she wouldn't head into the mountains in a storm like this. No she wouldn't do that. She would go north, farther into Germany. Yes, she would go to Germany to meet her clever, conniving, disrespectful husband.

They'd had it all planned for a long time, probably—-the chauffeur would catch a flight or a train out of Munich and the wife would drive the BMW. They would meet up somewhere, somewhere in Germany or...

Or Italy or Switzerland or France or Holland or Belgium or...Germany, yes, Germany. It made sense to head away from the Alps. It would be easier to cope with a snowstorm away from the mountains.

He had bugged the BMW. Once he'd returned to the villa he would go to the computer—-he would check the screen. The icon for the car would tell him precisely where she was.

CHAPTER 30

Diana looked at the dashboard clock. It was 09:25. In her haste she had not studied the map, she had not decided which route, which road she would take to get away from Berchtesgaden.

Berchtesgaden. The name was toxic for her now. It was the name of the city below the *Berghof*. It was the city, however beautiful, and it was beautiful, that would always be ugly for her. Adolf Hitler had spent much time up there on the *Berghof* above Berchtesgaden. Adolf Hitler had stood there on that mountain-top veranda and stared into the valley, into the abyss below, and studied the town of Berchtesgaden while he devised his evil plans for taking over the entire world. Adolf Hitler had destroyed her father and the fathers of millions of German and Austrian girls. Diana had loved her father and felt badly for him having to endure his short life so disfigured from the wounds he'd suffered in the war.

A half kilometer out of Berchtesgaden, Diana eased the BMW onto the right shoulder of the road and came to a halt. She would study the GPS and the road atlas she kept between the console and her seat. She had to do this right. By now, Pontius was on his way back from Munich. He had to be. And Pontius had to be mad, he had to be furious, he had to be foaming at the mouth like a wild-eyed stallion or a rabid dog. Pontius would be spitting nails, he would be seeing red, he would be seeing the red blood of his disobedient, insubordinate chauffeur and the red, warm blood of the chauffeur's insolent, disobedient wife. He would be imagining how he was going to kill them, as he drove that black Mercedes down the autobahn, east to Berchtesgaden.

Outside Diana's car it was snowing hard. The flakes were the size of crepes and filling the air. They were dry, fluffy snowflake-crepes, the perfect snowflakes for making a perfect week for skiing in the mountains. Maybe when all this was over she and her husband could go skiing. Maybe they would go to Kitzbuhel or maybe to the Dolomites in Northern Italy. She had always wanted to go there, to the Dolomites, and watch the sunset turning the rocky cliffs and peaks into the softest, most exquisite pinks on planet earth. It was another unfulfilled dream Diana had had for a very long time. No, they would never see the Dolomites, they would never take another vacation.

Diana pressed the button on the GPS to widen the map. She had to get to the E 52 which would take her to Irschenberg where she would catch 472 which would take her to Miesbach and Bad Tolz. Diana wouldn't go via Salzburg even if it was easier. No. She would go the other way, the other route to Inzell via Schneizlreuth. Highway 20 would take her there.

Diana turned on the windshield wipers to remove the snow. The wipers whisked it away in two swipes. The snow was so dry, so wonderfully dry and feathery. If the wind held off for just two or three hours she would have a good chance of making it to the autobahn without trouble. If the wind picked up, this feathery snow would make high drifts that would cover the roads, and ruin her plans. This dry snow whipped up by the wind could make the authorities close the roads she was about to take. But she had to chance it. She hoped that by going the back way she would not cross paths with Pontius on the autobahn. That man had the eyesight of an eagle and might spot her and give chase.

Diana traced her route from Berchtesgaden on Highway 20 to Bad Reichenhall. In Bad Reichenhall she would go south, on Highway 21, to Schneizlreuth. It looked easy on the map. Maybe it would be as easy as it looked.

A wave of exhaustion came over her. She had a five-second fantasy of finding a hotel along the way and sleeping. She could feel the warm comforter around her neck and shoulders and her body going into a semi-fetal position, and then she would let go of this miserable world for just a few hours of precious sleep.

But she would not do that. She would not sleep until she saw her husband again. Her husband was good to her. She loved him so much. They'd had a good life and she wanted to have more of that good life with him. And any life without Pontius in it would automatically be good...even if they had to live in a cabin in the forest or a tent on the beach or live in some nowhere town or city or country it would be good never to have anything to do with that madman again.

Diana took a deep breath and refocused on the map. From Scheizlreuth she would go to Inzell on Highway 305 and 306. And from Inzell she would go to Siegsdorf and the E 52.

She finished programming the GPS and said a short prayer. The wipers were still running although it was unnecessary. The snow had stopped, for now. She turned them off and put the car in drive and accelerated slowly. To get to Highway 20 she would have to backtrack a little. She would have to cross most of Berchtesgaden. She would have to go near the old neighborhood. She didn't want any of her crazy neighbors to see her. They might suspect something was amiss and might call the police. Her crazy neighbors might be crazy enough to do it.

Diana ought not to think like this. Being paranoid would do no good. She had to concentrate on getting to her husband and then, together, they had to concentrate on getting away from that weird monster in that weird villa with all its weird servants and that weird obelisk where Pontius spent so much time, according to what her husband had observed.

And what sort of person builds an obelisk and places it next to his house? Ah, Diana put away these thoughts, too. She was being paranoid again.

The clouds closed in all around and draped the sheer sides of the blue-green-gray mountains. It grew dark even though it was still morning. Up ahead, beyond the town one of the clouds separated itself from the rest and became a long, twisted white-gray sheet. The lone, separated cloud reminded her of a shroud. It reminded her of mortality. It began to snow once more, the whiter snowflakes stood out in relief against the darker, grayer tones in the cloud that looked like a shroud. Diana turned her head away from it for a second. She looked at it again. The shroud had vanished.

Diana was waiting for the traffic signal to change at the intersection where the street to the right would take her back to the house and the old neighborhood. It would take her to that big house that had been more of a prison for her than a house.

On the other side of the intersection, on the street corner on the right, stood a woman. She was bundled up in black winter clothing. She wore a black woolen scarf about her head. She was slightly bent. She was the neighbor lady from the old neighborhood, the one that had only stolen glances at the chauffeur's wife. But she wasn't stealing glances now. She was staring at the silver BMW and at the driver of the BMW, at Diana.

The light went to green. Diana pushed down on the accelerator, careful not to drive too fast, careful not to make the car fishtail in the soft, slippery snow.

The old, bent lady from the neighborhood was lifting her black cane and pointing it at the car and the driver. She was moving her mouth, her lips. Now her ugly mouth formed a black *O* like she was saying "woe to you" or pronouncing some sort of curse. The old woman could be a witch for all Diana knew.

Everything was in slow motion as Diana passed the old *frau*. She could almost hear her evil words, her evil incantations. She could see the old frau's narrow eyes and the bags and wrinkles on her half-sunken face. The old *frau*, that old witch knew something wasn't right. And she would report what she'd seen to Pontius. Diana was being paranoid again.

It was 09:45. Pontius would be half way back to Berchtesgaden now. But the chances of their passing one another on the autobahn would be nil. Diana was sure of it as she watched the old woman, still pointing her cane and moving her mouth, fading away in the rearview mirror, the image losing itself in the falling snow.

Diana pressed the button on the CD player. She selected Beethoven's Moonlight Sonata. It was one of her husband's favorites, a rendition of the piece played on a classical guitar. Even though it was still morning it seemed appropriate to play a song written for night.

The clouds came lower. The snow came harder. Diana started to weep gently. It was good to shed a tear or two or three.

Diana patted her cheeks with her soft handkerchief. Her mother would do this when Diana was a little girl. She wished she could call her mother now...

CHAPTER 31

She came to Bischofswiesen. The road until now had been good. There had been no wind. The road had been plowed not more than thirty minutes ago and had remained clear. If things continued like this, getting to the E 52 would not be a problem. It might even be easy.

Diana turned on the radio. She needed to find a weather report. Maybe the worst part of the worst storm in a hundred years had passed? Maybe there would be no more wind? Maybe it would stay calm? She hoped she could stay as calm as the wind was right now.

She picked up a Salzburg station. The broadcaster was saying something about Afghanistan and the Taliban. That war would never end. It was 2010 already and they were still fighting there. It seemed they'd always been fighting there. Diana wondered if Pontius had anything to do with it. She wondered if the passenger was involved, somehow. These days, these years there seemed to be some invisible, some almost imperceptible force moving everything along toward some predetermined something or other. It was hard to sort out. It was hard to put into words. But something was in the works. Something was in the offing. Something lay on the horizon. She knew it in her gut. Her intuition told her so. It told her the world as she and her husband had known it was coming to some kind of catastrophe, some kind of horrific end. Everything was headed for some kind of collision...

Diana didn't believe in conspiracies, at least when it came to things on a global scale she didn't. But this time was different. Max had told her many things since that night they had twice read the Book of Daniel. Now those things were making more sense. Some kind of critical mass was going to be reached—-this year, next year, in five years or ten—-and compared to the span of human history five or ten years was nothing. It only took Hitler and the Nazis about that long to seize control of Germany. And almost no one had taken him seriously at first. And then, suddenly, overnight, he was the Chancellor of Germany. That obnoxious, little corporal and a few hundred devotees had done it. And eighty million Germans had enabled him to do it. Resisters, the few there had been, were arrested and jailed or murdered.

And it could happen again. The economic winds could change, and then the political winds could change. The world was not immune to another beast like Hitler. And given technology, and the weapons available now, another beast like Hitler would possess ten times the power of the first Hitler; he would have twenty times, a hundred, or a thousand times more power. Her husband had told her this and she had agreed. Anyone with common sense would have to agree. Anyone that knew anything about the prophecies would have to agree.

Oh yes, things could change overnight or in a moment, just blink your eyes.

The wind picked up. The snow was swirling about. The snow came harder and thicker. She turned off the radio. She had to concentrate on her driving. She gripped the steering wheel. She was glad there was no other traffic. She lightened her grip on the wheel. It was not good to grip the steering wheel so tightly.

Suddenly Diana felt very, very, very alone on this road in this storm. She felt the pressing weight of the evil, nasty, heartless world; it was crushing her, pushing her down into her car seat; it was pressing down on her shoulders and arms. It was so heavy it made her feel like letting go of the steering wheel and letting the car float off to the right or left and go down an embankment and get buried in a snowdrift. It would be the end of this nightmare for her.

If only she were a bird, if only her weighed-down arms were wings, she would leave this car and fly away to some nest or somewhere high in the dark mountains that jutted straight up on her right and left.

Now the wind came directly at her. Diana released the accelerator and let the car slow to 20 kilometers per hour. She could hardly see more than 20 meters in front of her.

Diana hit the brakes and by a hair's breadth managed to stop in time. She'd almost rammed into the two cars blocking both lanes of the highway. There was a third car on the other side of the two cars. It was a police car and its lights were flashing. One of the cars directly in front of her was stuck in the snow in the shallow ditch on the left. It looked like the second car was trying to pull the stuck car out as the stuck car was spinning its tires atop the ice and snow. They were spinning so fast there was smoke and a few sparks spewing out from them. It was weird to see smoke and sparks and ice and snow all mingled together like that.

The police were getting out now. The other two drivers were unaware of her presence. They hadn't noticed how close she'd come to smashing into them. She put the car in reverse and backed away ten meters.

Diana looked at the clock. It was 10:20. And she was halted on this narrow, two-lane highway, and there was nothing she could do about it. 10:20. She should have been much farther along by now.

One of the police spotted her and started to walk toward her.

She pushed the button and lowered her window to hear him.

"Are you all right, madam?" The patrolman asked and did a quick scan of the interior of her car. Cops were like that. Cops always do that. Cops are always curious.

Diana was glad she had laid her coat atop the satchel with all that money in cash.

"Yes...yes...I'm all right. Thank you."

"You must know it's very dangerous to be on the roads right now."

"I know, but I...have to get to Munich...my mother called. She's not well and she's all alone."

Okay, so it was a lie.

The patrolman, not noticing her lie, declared: "We can close these roads anytime. If that happens, what will you do?"

"I...I will find a hotel...of course."

The patrolman didn't seem to be buying it but there was nothing he could do or say except: "Madam, if you proceed you are doing so at your own risk. If I were you I would turn around and try to get to Berchtesgaden. Are you from Berchtesgaden, madam?"

"I am...but I must go to my mother's house in Munich. I have no choice. She is old and she needs me."

The wind was blowing even harder now. Diana had to raise her voice, almost to a shout, to make herself heard above the roar.

The police officer shook his head and threw up his arms. The gesture ended their conversation. He turned and loped back to join the other officer. The car that had been stuck had been freed. The police car disappeared into the whiteness, it's flashing lights vanished too. The other two cars also headed north and disappeared into the storm.

Now Diana was really alone. She turned on the radio once again and tried to find a Salzburg station. An announcer was reading the news. She waited for the weather report that always followed the news. She toyed with calling her husband. He had asked her to call him after withdrawing the money. But she'd forgot.

Diana put away that idea. If she told him about her predicament he would worry too much. Why upset him? There was nothing he could do.

The storm, the voice on the radio said, would last at least two days, yet. The roads could be closed at any time. Everyone should avoid driving. And please make sure there is enough food and water in your house. Make sure you have batteries or candles handy. This is a serious situation, the announcer said.

Diana turned off the radio. She already knew how serious the situation was. Ja, serious. She put the car in drive and went forward at a crawl. At this rate it would take twice as long to get to the autobahn.

She got through Bischofswiesen without problem. There was no one out and about. They'd all decided to heed the meteorologist's warnings. They'd all decided to do the smart thing, the right thing, the only thing that made sense in a tempest like this. They were all huddled around their kitchen tables or their TVs or snuggled up on the sofa or in bed.

Ahead and slightly left a pin prick of light pierced the veil of heavy, falling snow. It grew into a bright white sphere. It was the inter-city train.

She ought to be on that train only going the other way. But if she'd taken the train it would have been impossible to pack so much gear. It would have been chancy to pack the 9mm and the other firearm. But it would have been safer to go by train. She could have gone to Munich then caught another train to Zurich.

Perhaps they would have to get rid of half their belongings anyway.

Suddenly Diana was more worried than she'd been ever since her husband had called late last night. The money, the cash, all those euros—-what would she do with that money when she arrived at the Swiss border? It wasn't illegal to have cash but it certainly was crazy to carry that much. It would certainly make the Swiss customs agents and border guards curious. It might make them suspect something very bad. And then, if they found the firearms things would look a hundred times more suspicious.

Now she *really* wanted to call her husband. She needed to hear his advice. She *needed* to hear his comforting voice.

No.

Diana would not call Max about the money and the guns. She would not upset him.

She would figure out what she would do before she got to the Germany-Switzerland border. She had time to figure something out.

She could hide the satchel in the trunk where the guns were now. She could put it under the seat. She could leave it right where it was...right there beside her and let the agents see it and go through it, count it even, if they wanted.

Or she could put the bills inside her pants, inside her underwear, or in the pockets on her coat. She could put a few packs of bills inside her fur hat.

Diana almost laughed out loud. It would look silly if they found the money scattered all over her body in all those pockets and whatnot. And then it wouldn't be silly at all as they asked her to come into some office for a *chat about so much cash and two firearms...a pistol and rifle.*

Diana gripped the steering wheel and made the decision—-she would leave the money in the satchel. And she would leave the satchel exactly where it was right now...in front of the passenger seat. She would try to be as relaxed as possible as she passed through the border. She hoped the Swiss border agents wouldn't think she was trying to avoid paying taxes in Germany by depositing money in a Swiss bank account. She and her husband had scrupulously paid all the taxes. At times they had paid too much just to be *safer.*

Safer? Safe? What did that mean? Nothing was safe in this world.

Diana wished she'd read more of the Bible—-but her parents were agnostics. It was sad, it was tragic, it was...she had no word at this moment in this storm to express her feelings about her parents' unbelief. They weren't alone, though. They were like most of Europe. Her parents, her family of origin had lost its way after World War Two. They'd given up on any Christian beliefs they might have had before the war. It was to be expected, she supposed. Her parents, like the rest of European parents from that generation, had had their fill of war and misery and despair and the complete loss it had brought down upon them. They'd only wanted to reconstruct what they could, and live in relative comfort, and treat others with respect. They'd made the Golden Rule their official religion and hoped others would do the same. They'd placed their trust in the new kind of government coming after that war; they had embraced democratic socialism and the *live and let live* attitude that made Europe such a great place to live once everything had been rebuilt and everything had gotten back *to normal.* But those Bible prophecies were still there. And Diana knew they were true. Her husband, Max, knew it as well.

And that was why she was in this car, trying to get away from Pontius. And that was why her husband was on that train, trying to get to Zurich. Their escape would confirm what they knew to be true.

Her bladder was full and there was no place to find relief. There was no town, no service station. There was nothing except the wind and snow and this narrow road. She would try to hold it as long as she could. And if she didn't come to a town with a service station she would have to pull over and do the deed in the snow.

Twenty minutes later, after pulling to a stop, she struggled to push the iced-up door open, got out and did the deed amid the swirling snow, sleet, and spitting rain. She was so, so cold. She put herself back together as best she could. She pulled down the woolen coat. She turned toward the car.

The snow here had turned to sleet mixed with freezing rain. The freezing rain had already laid down a coating of ice on the BMW's roof. The driver's side door was even more coated now. In two minutes, the time it had taken her to relieve herself, the ice had become at least two centimeters thicker. The door handle was coated. It had all gotten coated with ice so quickly. What a horrible, nasty storm!

Diana tried to pull on the door handle. It slipped from her hand. She put both hands on it and pulled again. Both hands slid off and recoiled upward and smacked her in the chin. The motion nearly upended her like a bowling pin getting hit by a bowling ball. She was overjoyed now that she'd been smart enough to turn off the car, take out the car keys, and put them in her pocket. She could not imagine being here now, unable to open the door, and the keys still in the ignition and the car running.

Diana touched the pocket now to reassure herself that those precious keys were there...she stuck her gloved hand into the pocket and fished around with her fingers.

The keys were not in her pocket. They were not, not, not in her pocket. She checked the other one, knowing they weren't there. She took off her gloves for a moment...maybe if they were removed she could feel the keys better with bare fingers. But the keys were not there.

The freezing rain and sleet was pelting and stinging Diana's face. The wind was making it impossible to stay standing. She hunched over and put her back to the terrible wind. She backtracked to the spot where she'd relieved herself. The keys must have fallen out when she'd lowered the trousers.

How stupid she was! How dumb! Why had she let the keys fall out?

Diana scanned the snow, the ground, the area where she'd relieved herself. She tried to spot the yellow spot but it had been covered by drifting snow. She tried to spot the paper napkin. It had vanished. It had blown away. She wondered if she was at the right place or was it to the left or to the right?

A blast of wind and snow and freezing rain and sleet slammed into her. Her footing gave way and she hit the ground hard, banging her knees and elbows into the ice now coating the snow. For a moment or two or three she just laid there. She thought of dying, again. It wouldn't be so bad, to die. Dying had to be better than this, better than lying here in the bitter wind and ice and cold without the keys to start the car.

Diana rolled over. She closed her eyes. It would be easy to let her eyes freeze shut.

She opened them once again, maybe for the last time...and there were the car keys, embedded in four or five centimeters of ice.

She crawled to them on all fours and began to dig out the keys with her bare hands and fingers. She needed some kind of tool for chiseling or digging but there was no tool. There were only her hands and fingers.

She kept clawing at the keys until she saw blood oozing out from her nails. She got to her feet and kicked at them staccato-like, trying to free them with the tip of her boot. A chunk of snow and ice broke off. The keys lay there, ready to be grabbed if she didn't wait too long. In freezing rain and wind like this they could become frozen in place again in seconds.

She snatched up the keys and dashed back to the BMW. At least now she could use the keys to chip away the ice on the door handle. She could put her mouth to the handle and exhale as much hot air as her lungs could hold. She wished she had a cup of hot water. That trick had worked before.

There was even more ice on the handle now. She started to chip at it. She chipped and chipped and blew on it and chipped and chiseled some more.

She pulled on the door handle one last time and cracked open the door along the top of the window. She wedged in her hand and pulled it open completely.

She got inside, put the keys in the ignition, and started the car. She whispered another prayer of thanks and wondered if God heard her, knowing he did.

She stared at her reddened, bleeding fingers and chipped nails. She fished out the gloves from her pocket and slipped into them. Her hands were so cold she had no sensation in them.

Diana would call her husband. She had to let Max know she was all right. She pressed the numbers and waited.

Nothing happened; there was no signal; the mountains were too steep, too high; she was walled in. There would be no phone call to her husband until later or she would have to wait for his call to her and hope he got through.

The freezing rain and sleet had changed to all snow. Diana accelerated gradually, not wanting to spin the tires. The BMW found traction...and forward she went into the wind and drifting snow and into the steep, dark mountains.

CHAPTER 32

Max stepped from the train and paused and shifted the duffle bag on his shoulder. He was a little disoriented. And he was so tired. He was exhausted.

He didn't notice that the couple, *his travelling companions* from the 05:37 from Zurich, were standing motionless behind him.

Max turned about and noticed them now. The woman was speaking but Max wasn't listening. All Max could do was think about getting to a hotel and calling Diana. It was almost 12:00. It was 11:42 to be precise and he had to know if his wife was all right. He had to know if she had made it to the E 52. If Diana had not, it could only mean one thing—-she had got stuck somewhere in the storm, somewhere in the mountains south of the E 52. And if that were the case it could be a very bad thing because practically all the highways in that sector were narrow two-lane affairs. And they were many times more dangerous in foul weather, in a bad winter storm like this one. And if the authorities closed the roads in that area there would be no one left to find her until the storm had passed.

Max had to locate a decent hotel nearby, get a room, and call her.

Now the young couple were coming toward him. Why couldn't they just disappear? Why couldn't they just leave him alone. Max had had enough of them. And now he regretted hiding the fact that he could speak fluent English. He should not have done that. And he should have told them how ridiculous their comments about Nazis were. Such comments, any comments about Nazis always flooded Max's mind with a zillion competing, sometimes debilitating thoughts. Or sometimes such comments, or anything he might see on TV or read in a book or magazine or on a website about Nazis would put his mind into overdrive and he would have to fight back some elusive desire for revenge, whatever that meant.

For a moment he considered going to the men's restroom. He could slip away from this couple just as he slipped away from Pontius in the hotel bar last night. It seemed a lifetime ago since he'd been there with Pontius and Pontius' women. Pontius had been trying to get Max, his chauffeur, to do something illicit with one of the women, Max was sure of it. Pontius had wanted *to dirty* Max by getting him to play around on the wife. Criminals always try to do that. Pontius had wanted to have a reason to blackmail Max.

"Sir. You never told us your name." The young woman was asking the question.

There was no way Max would give away his name. He had to end this conversation now. He had to get away from this couple now.

"You..never...told me yours." It was true. They had not told him their names.

"Oh, you are right! We didn't!" She exclaimed as if suddenly making a great discovery.

The man was talking. "My name is Ryan and my wife's name is Meredith."

They were smiling at him and waiting. It was the signal for Max to tell them his name.

He would give them a made-up name. He would give them his father's name.

Max said, "My name is Erich Remark." Well, it was a lie. At least the last name, Remark, was a lie. But the first name, Erich, was the truth. It was not a full lie. It was only half a lie. Max's father's first name was indeed Erich.

"Nice to meet you, nice to know your name, Erich Remark." The man was shaking Max's hand. The woman was agreeing with her husband and saying, "Yes. And I am Meredith Smith and my husband is Ryan Smith. Easy enough to remember, don't you think? Smith? Pretty common last name."

"*Ja, Schmidt*...Smith."

All this small talk about names was tiresome. It was foolish and tiresome and taking way too much time here on the platform of the Main Railway Station in Zurich, Switzerland in this snowstorm.

"Are you going to be staying in Zurich for long?" Meredith was speaking.

Max ignored her and scanned the train station, looking for the sign that read *Herren*. He would try to find the men's room and, from there, see if he could ditch these people.

Max spotted the sign and turned around and said, "So, it was nice to...meet you...have a nice day...*auf wiedersehen...ciao...*"

Max pivoted and headed toward the men's room, hoping no one would follow him, hoping he would be left alone, hoping he could disengage from this couple and leave it at that.

He reached the entrance to the men's room and looked over his shoulder. He wasn't alone. Ryan had decided he, too, would go and use the men's room. Ach, so be it. It was fate, Max supposed, except he didn't believe in fate. He used to believe in fate but not anymore.

Max entered one of the stalls. He would stay in it for a half hour if he had to. He would stay in it for an hour.

He'd told them his name was Erich Remark. Max almost laughed. Max's mother's name was Maria. And another Erich Remark had written a book, a famous one: *All Quiet on the Western Front by* Erich Maria Remark...Remarque, using the French spelling. The man had wanted to honor the French he'd fought against. And he'd wanted to honor his dear mother by adding her name to his. And the Nazis had wanted to turn Remark into a Jew. They'd said his real last name was Kramer, or Remark spelled backward, and sounded Jewish so he must be a Jew. The Nazis had banned *All Quiet on the Western Front*. It was subversive to the Nazi cause and to the Fatherland, they'd said.

Perhaps Max should not have told the couple *his name*, even if it was a lie. Perhaps they would figure it out, that he'd been playing them a bit, that he'd lied to them. Max wouldn't do such a thing again. He would stay focused on reuniting with his beautiful wife, Diana, getting rid of the BMW, finding another vehicle, and finding a place to hide until they decided either to remain in Europe or leave. But somehow he knew they would have to leave the Europe, eventually.

Max heard the door to another stall creaking. It had to be Ryan. For a moment Max considered leaving immediately. Once outside he would vanish into the crowd inside the Zurich Railway Station. He would get away from Meredith just like he would get away from Ryan now.

It was 11:58. Diana would be worried. She would have to realize the 05:37 train from Munich to Zurich had arrived. Max had to get to a hotel, and turn on the television to get a weather report. He had to know how bad it was in the area of the E 52. And then he had to call her, reassure her, and tell her he loved her. And Max could not forget to tell her to check the BMW for tracking devices, any strange electronics, any sort of bugging. He should have told her to do that last night before she'd left Berchtesgaden.

Maybe he should call her right away? It was tempting. But he wanted to get away from the American couple and find a hotel first. It would be more reassuring for her if he had a room. Then he could give her solid directions. Yes, firm directions; she needed to know exactly where to go in Zurich. If the weather wasn't too bad she could still make it to Zurich by this evening or by midnight, perhaps?

A massive blast of frigid wind, straight out of the north, almost knocked him over like a like a linebacker would the quarterback in American football. Max should have put on his stocking cap. His ears were numb already. At least he'd remembered the gloves.

Max slipped on the cap and let his eyes adjust to the brightness of the snow—-the blowing, drifting, and falling snow. The storm was a blizzard. There was little traffic. Nobody would want to drive their car in such a storm. A snowplow passed by on the street in front of him, its blade and tires making a soft, muffled noise. To his left and across the street was a bridge. He would head to the bridge and cross it and get to the taller buildings which lay across some sort of frozen river lined on both sides by barren wintertime trees.

Above the streets and the bridge the lights on top of the utility poles seemed to vibrate. It was an optical illusion caused by the thickly falling snow and his weary mind. Max moved his eyes away from the weird lighting and located the street corner. He picked up his pace. He had to cross to the bridge and get across that river. The American couple could pop out of the Train Station at any moment and he did not want to be around when they did.

Ten minutes later, after weaving a path through a labyrinth of streets, first south along the river, then north on another street, then east, and left and right and right again he came to the top of the *Leonhardstrasse*. Directly across from him was a hotel...the Hotel Leon, a five-story structure of stucco and brick walls and a tile roof. It looked like a very good hotel and a probably a little expensive, too. He didn't care...he figured they might as well have a nice place like this for a few days before they might have to go live in the forest like wild animals. Anyway, they had more than 200,000 euros.

It suddenly occurred to Max that he might not find work, ever again. It suddenly occurred to him that his future might be bleak, very bleak indeed. It could be he had no future at all. It could be he was finished. It could be Max and Diana would become like forest animals. It could be they would have to live like squat, little gnomes in the woods, in a hole made into a house under or inside a big pine tree. Max would have floppy stocking hat, a silly white beard down to his belly, and wear scratchy leggings, and ugly leather shoes with big metal buckles. Diana would sprout a wart or two on her cheeks or on her nose.

These last ridiculous and depressing thoughts were the thoughts he dragged with him into the Hotel Leon as he passed through the doors. These thoughts plagued him as he asked for a double occupancy room, as he signed the registration form, paid for the room in cash, collected the key card, and headed to the elevator. These thoughts could become a cancer in his mind if he allowed it. These thoughts could make him insane.

Max slid the card's magnetic strip down through the slot and a blinking green indicator light said the door was now unlocked. He put his shoulder to the rather heavy door and entered the room. It was a very nice, adequate room with a nice size window and view to the *Leonhardstrasse* four floors below. Max placed the duffle on the low luggage rack and took a long, deep breath. The terrible thoughts had not left him. He had to call her. Hearing her voice would make his hopelessness go away. At least it would go away for a while.

Max slipped out the secret cell phone from his boxer shorts. It struck him as odd that he still kept it there. His fear of Pontius had made him do it. That fear would always be there, always in his mind, in his head. But he wouldn't put the phone there again.

With his finger tip Max poked in the numbers. He placed the phone to his ear and waited.

It was ringing...and ringing...and ringing. The recording came on, telling him "sorry I missed your call" and to "please leave a message" and "I'll get back to you as soon as possible." It was her voice.

Max ended the call and looked at the phone's screen. The time was 12:40.

CHAPTER 33

The silver and gold railroad clock, with its giant Roman numerals, on the wall of Pontius' enormous office-den-library said it was 12:40.

Pontius turned to the computer and typed in the data for up linking with the satellite. He waited a moment or two.

There she was, in Siegsdorf—-almost to the E 52.

She must be headed west or north or both. She must be going to Munich.

Pontius was ecstatic. She had been too stupid to consider a tracking device. Or, if it had occurred to her, she had been too stupid to look for the tracking device under the spare tire in the trunk. Placing the bug in the trunk under the spare was too obvious—-it was *so* obvious she had not thought to look there. Pontius smiled. The chauffeur's wife, as gutsy as she might be, was stupid.

This was going to be too easy. All Pontius had to do was wait until the BMW arrived at its destination and he would go there. If the weather remained bad he would go there in the Mercedes, tracking her by using an iPad. If the weather cleared he would go there in the jet. Pontius would go there and round up the two prisoners and fly them, in style, back to the villa—- after all, it would be their last ride on an airplane.

Pontius would have his servants serve the chauffeur and his wife the best dinner they'd ever eaten as he, Pontius, would assure them it had all been a misunderstanding...that things need not be so difficult between his employee, and his employee's wife and their forgiving employer. Pontius would even offer to pay the chauffeur more, perhaps another thirty percent more and more vacation time, too. Yes, more vacation time for them and perhaps the wife would like to see the house in Berchtesgaden receive a facelift? A remodeling? Perhaps they would like a Jacuzzi installed in the garden?

By the time the Gulfstream V arrived in Salzburg the chauffeur and his wife would be well fed, well drunk, and well on the way to reconciling with Pontius that wonderful man. Pontius would play the part of a father and take them into his confidence and promise them anything they asked.

And it would be most amazing to observe their reactions the moment they realized they were not going to their house in Berchtesgaden but rather were headed to the villa. At that moment the chauffeur and his lovely wife would understand that something was in the works. But they would be too clever to show it. They would suppress their fear. They might even offer silent prayers to their god.

Once the chauffeur and his wife had entered the villa they would not leave it again...until their ashes fell into the valley far below.

CHAPTER 34

Max let his bone-tired body sink into the crispy-clean white comforter atop the double bed. He closed his eyes and waited a couple minutes.

He opened his eyes and redialed her number. The phone rang until he heard her recorded voice again. He didn't wait for the recording to finish because of the static.

It must be the weather or it must be she's still in the mountains south of the E 52 or it's both; she's still in the mountains plus the weather...it's a combination of the two: bad weather and high mountains equal static. He could see her driving those curvy, icy, snow-covered roads. He could sense her angst. It was the same angst he was feeling now.

Not knowing why, Max reached into the pocket that held the piece of paper he'd found on that bench in the Munich station. He unfolded it and read the word and numbers again: Psalm 121. He located the hotel bible and looked up the psalm.

Ich hebe meine Augen auf zu den Bergen von welchen mir Hilfe kommt.

He read the entire Psalm. He tried to imagine the man who'd written it. He must have been in big trouble. He must have been in trouble like Max and Diana. He must have been fighting someone like Pontius, maybe.

Max read that last line again:

der HERR behüte deinen Ausgang und Eingang von nun an bis in Ewigkeit.

Whoever had written this had indeed been in a lot of trouble but was sure things would be all right. Once Max had Diana back he would make a point of finding out who the author was. He felt like he knew him already, though.

He refolded the paper and put it back in his pocket and redialed the number and waited.

It rang three times and: "Hello? Max? Max?"

Diana's voice had a tremble in it. She was frightened, he could tell. He could hear her distress, her fear, her unease.

"Where are you?" Max tried to ask the question as calmly as possible. He needed to be calm for her.

Diana could barely hear him from all the static.

"What? I can't hear you. Say it again." She really couldn't hear him.

Max repeated the question: "Where are you?"

The reception was clearer now, all of a sudden.

"Siegsdorf."

Diana was in Siegsdorf. That meant she'd been travelling very, very slowly. It meant she couldn't make it to Zurich until very, very late, until the wee hours of the morning, perhaps.

"And the weather?"

"The worst since this morning. I cannot believe the roads are still open and I've made it to Siegsdorf."

At least he could hear her better now. At least she could hear him now, as he gave her the instructions.

"Darling...you must find a safe place to pull over and check the car for bugs...for tracking devices."

Diana's head was spinning. It didn't help that she'd not eaten since leaving Berchtesgaden. She was feeling faint and having difficulty making sense of her husband's orders. She should have eaten a snack, a cracker or cookie, or a piece of fruit.

She tried to concentrate on what her husband had just said.

"Tracking? Oh no..." That devil Pontius could be watching her right now. He could be listening to her speaking to her husband. He might know exactly where she was and what she was saying. It gave her a weird, scary, sickening feeling. It made her even more dizzy, and angry at the same time.

"You must find a place to park the car and check everything from front to back, under the hood, under the dash, seats. Check the trunk. Check...ah, check where the spare tire is located, under the trunk matt in the well in the floor. Look inside the headlight covers. Tail lights. Look everywhere."

"I'll find a service station here in Siegsdorf before I get on the E 52."

She said it to reassure herself as much as him.

"Yes. Get to one and check for bugs. He may be tracking you right now. And speak softer. He could be listening." Max glanced at his watch. It was

12:47. "As soon as you check, and are sure there are no devices, call me...and try not to draw attention to what you're doing. And purchase some fuel—-it's best to keep the tank as full as possible in this weather...and use cash. No debit or credit cards. And check for a device while filling the tank. Look inside the trunk. Pretend to rummage around through the luggage. Then lift the hood and pretend to check the oil or the reservoir of window wash fluid...then check the other parts of the car, interior, exterior...don't forget the wheel wells and bumpers."

"All right." Diana had no idea how to de-bug a car but she would try. She didn't like to waste time filling the gas tank. She had enough to make it to Zurich, except her husband was right. If she became snowbound she would need fuel to run the heater. She put away the horrible thought. Running the engine while stuck in a snowdrift could cause carbon monoxide poisoning.

"Call me when you finish looking..." Max almost hung up but caught himself. "If you find a device do not destroy it. Simply unplug it. Or it may have a switch...simply turn off the switch. But do not throw it way."

"No? All right...but..." She spoke as softly as possible, fearing a hidden microphone somewhere inside the car.

"I'll explain later."

"Do you have a room?" Diana had to know she if had a place to go in Zurich. She needed to know there was a safe place to sleep once she'd made it through the storm.

"Hotel Leon on the *Leonhardstrasse.* I just checked in. The number is 1 8001, *Leonhardstrasse*. Program the GPS, okay?"

"Okay." She spotted a service station fifty meters ahead on the right side of the street. "I'm coming to a service station."

Max got up from the bed and went to the window. The snow was so heavy the dull gray buildings on the other side of the street were hard to see. But the wind had lessened.

"All right...call me in a few minutes," he said once more.

Max set the phone on the wooden table to the left of the window and kept gazing into the whiteness as a small voice inside his mind told him Pontius had indeed bugged the BMW.

Diana had to find the bug. She had to cut off Pontius' ability to eavesdrop on her and follow her to Zurich to this hotel. If that sly devil tracked her much longer he would figure out where she was going.

It was 12:51.

CHAPTER 35

Diana hardly managed to set the nozzle and begin pumping the fuel before a giant, frigid blast of snow and ice pellets broadsided her, nearly knocking her onto the ice-covered concrete surface. Just in time, she grabbed the driver's side door handle and clung to it with her numb fingers, staying as vertical as possible in the driving wind. Checking for tracking devices or listening devices today was going to be miserable.

The nozzle made a sudden clicking noise, steel against steel. It had not stayed in the set position. Diana would have to dispense the fuel herself and it would cost more time. It was 12:57 already. But it seemed a lifetime had passed since leaving Berchtesgaden and that big house. It seemed like ancient history since the old *frau* with the walking cane had pronounced her curses upon Diana.

Diana's right hand was totally numb so she switched the nozzle to her left. It, too, became totally numb in five seconds. The temperature must have fallen to -5 or lower. She couldn't feel her face, her cheeks, her nose. She couldn't feel her toes despite the warm boots. It would be easy to die in this weather—-from freezing to death after losing control of the BMW and sliding into a ditch or swale or down an embankment and becoming buried alive in a massive drift along the E 52. She'd heard of that happening to others. And it could happen to her.

The pumping was finished, the tank was full. Diana decided to go and pay the attendant before looking for the device. It would be best to have already paid for the fuel before trying to de-bug the BMW. It would make the attendant less curious, maybe. Or maybe not. It didn't matter. What could an ordinary gas station attendant do to her?

There were no other drivers getting fuel. There was no traffic on the street. It was snowing harder than ever. Diana must look crazy to the attendant as he took the 100-euro bill and gave her the change. He was a man of about forty with pinkish skin and a bulbous little button-like nose that would be tempting to squeeze and make him honk or beep or squeal. His beady eyes looked like they belonged to a plump little field mouse or a rat. The attendant looked dull-witted. Diana was tempted to offer him a bribe, a little extra cash, to let her pull the car into one of the service bays in the garage connecting to the right side of the service station. Or maybe he would do it for free? It wouldn't hurt to ask.

She might as well ask it. She might as well say it. What could this peasant from Siegsdorf do to her?

Diana cancelled the idea and went to the car—-she would look for the tracking device while outside the station, here, by this fuel island. She would not call attention to herself any more than necessary. This gas station attendant could be smarter than he looked. It would be miserable to look for the device outside in this weather but even more miserable if this ugly, little rat called the police.

She considered pulling away from the fuel island and the roofed-in area. Maybe she should drive half a block down the street, park, and search there. But that would make the search ten times more difficult. It was snowing so hard now. Diana needed the protection of the roof even if it wasn't much.

She brushed off the snow sticking to the two headlights and peered into the each one, examining, trying to focus, trying to spot something, anything that looked odd. There was nothing there, as far as she could tell.

Diana got in the car and popped open the hood latch and closed her eyes for a moment or two. She wanted to give up, she was so cold—-her hands, fingers, fingertips were numbed out. Her face was frozen in place. She looked into the rear view mirror. Diana could see how tired she was. Her eyes were reddened from sleep deprivation. Her forehead had deep grooves in it. Her face seemed to have moved two centimeters downward. She'd aged twenty years since yesterday.

Diana shook her head and gave herself another pep talk. She had to open up the hood and check everywhere Max had told her to check. She had to do it now. Diana had to get to Zurich, to the hotel, and to her husband, Maximilian.

Diana had to find rest. She could not go on for too many days like this. But what if another storm was headed for Europe on the heels of this one? It could happen. It had happened before and it could happen again. And the next storm wouldn't have to be as bad as this one to keep Diana from getting to Zurich.

She pushed her way up from the driver's seat and lost her grip and fell back into the seat. She was made of lead, of granite; she must weigh a thousand kilos. It was so hard to get out of the car and do this search. She tried again but it was no good. She let go of the door.

Diana felt a wave of nausea. She felt like vomiting. She should eat one of the snacks she'd packed. Her head was spinning. Her blood sugar was low. Too low. She could not faint here. No, no, no...

She fell back into the seat.

She lost consciousness.

When she woke up she was clammy all over. The clamminess felt icy too. She was sweaty and almost frozen. Was she even alive anymore? Maybe she was dead?

Her head was still spinning, and now her hands were sweating, now her armpits were sticky-wet.

Diana ran her right index and middle finger up and down her left wrist, trying to find her pulse. She should be searching for the tracking device but here she was feeling for her pulse and wondering if she had the flu, and wondering how she would get treatment if she did. How could she check herself into a hospital while carrying so much cash?

Diana took a long, deep breath and let it out slowly. She had to find the box of snacks she'd packed and placed in the front section of the trunk. She had to get her blood sugar back to normal. And she had to grab a bottle of water, too, and rehydrate. She hoped the case of water bottles had not frozen up. She couldn't wait for a bottle of water to thaw. She needed that water.

The dashboard clock said it was 13:15 hours. She'd been unconscious for more than 15 minutes. And the stupid gas station attendant hadn't even been curious? She could still see him sitting there reading a newspaper or some tabloid, probably. What was wrong with him? Diana knew the answer: He was from the next generation of airhead zombies that populated the EU. They were clueless about everything. They cared only about themselves. They would make excellent cannon fodder for the coming Reich.

Just thinking the word *Reich* was enough. Diana got out of the car. She knew exactly where the water and snacks were. She had to drink water and eat something before doing the search for bugs on the BMW.

She could do it...and she would do it for her father. She would dedicate this fight, this new war to him. Her father had been unable to escape the Nazi tyrants, the Fuehrer and his henchmen, the Nazi commissars and *Gauleiters*, but Diana and Max would.

For a second or two she wondered where Max planned to go after leaving Switzerland. He'd suggested France or Spain or maybe Andorra. He'd said they might have to leave Europe. Diana couldn't imagine going to live in Andorra. What kind of life would that be? And if they left Europe where would they go?

She stuffed three crackers into her mouth and took a drink of water. The water had not frozen. She grabbed a carrot and chomped down on it like that cartoon rabbit Bugs Bunny. She ate the whole carrot in three large bites. She took another drink of water, put the bottle in the cup holder on the console, and began to look under the hood.

There was nothing there so she looked inside the front bumper. There was nothing there either so she looked inside both front wheel wells. She ran her numbed hands and fingers all around the inside edge of the wheel wells and found nothing. She remembered Max telling her to look inside the spare tire well under the matt in the trunk. She would skip the interior of the car for now and go directly to the trunk. It could be the device was there. It could be Pontius had put it in there, where it would be obvious and easy to find. Perhaps it was another part of one of his psychological games. Maybe he thought Diana and Max wouldn't think to look there because it would seem too easy.

She dug through the luggage, setting things to the right and left to create some space. There was the matt. There was the well. She peeled back the matt.

The tracking device was a small, square black box about 20 centimeters x 20 centimeters x 4 centimeters thick. It was a little larger than a deck of cards. Two black wires came out of one side of the box and ran down into the bottom of the wheel well. Diana pulled, gently, on the wires. They detached easily from the little black box.

She slipped the device into her coat pocket, rearranged the trunk, grabbed another carrot, and closed the trunk lid.

She'd done it. She'd been triumphant. She could see Pontius' face—-his eyes, his nose, his mouth, and his perfect pearly white teeth as he curled back his lip. She could see him pacing about, stomping the floor like a mad bull, maybe. She could see him foaming at the mouth and snorting. Pontius could be beaten. Pontius wasn't quite the god he thought himself to be.

Diana started the car and departed the service station. She glanced to the right. The attendant was watching her now.

"Good bye you fat little rat." She said it out loud and laughed. It was an act of defiance, and a bit silly at the same time, but it helped Diana center herself and focus on getting through the storm.

She remembered the address Max had given her for the Hotel Leon and entered the data into the GPS. It felt good to do that.

CHAPTER 36

Pontius uttered a swearword through his clenched teeth and pursed lips. A bit of saliva spewed out of his evil mouth along with the curse. The spit rested on his chiseled, square chin. He wiped it away with the back of his hand and swore again.

He kept glaring at the giant flat screen looming in front of him on the desk as large as a soccer field. He wanted to grab the monitor, the giant screen and fling it against the gray stucco walls of his office. He wanted to cast it to the floor and stomp on it.

He pushed the button under his desk and spoke, ordering the servant to come into the office:

The servant, in his perfect black tunic and slacks, stood at attention in front of Pontius, waiting for more orders.

"She has found the device. I want you to go to where she is and bring her here! Immediately!"

"That is impossible, sir."

"Don't tell me that...go get her...and bring her here!"

"That is impossible, sir."

Pontius got up and circled the desk and proceeded to grill the servant like an army sergeant would grill a new recruit.

"Don't tell me that. Don't tell me you cannot get her!"

The servant did not move. He simply repeated, for the third time, what he'd just said twice.

Pontius knew the servant was right, of course. Max and Diana, Pontius' clever chauffeur and his wife, could not be touched...as long as they did not defy the prophecies and *take matters into their own hands*...as long as Max and Diana remained humble there was nothing Pontius or the passenger could do.

The previous chauffeur and wife did not have such protection. Pontius had caught them himself just a few kilometers north of Salzburg. He took them back to the villa and had them dismembered and burned. It had struck Pontius as odd that the couple weren't wearing their wedding rings. They had seemed so much in love and so devoted one to another. They were good, little European agnostics, though. They were touchable, they were vulnerable, and they had paid for it.

Pontius turned to the huge floor-to-ceiling window. He raised his eyes to the Obersalzberg. The passenger had lived there. And he would live there again in the coming kingdom. And Pontius would rule with him.

Perhaps it was true the chauffeur and his wife were untouchable, for now. But that could change. Humanity could be so vain. The quest for fame, and the fortune that often comes with it, had conquered far greater men than this chauffeur and his pretty wife.

Pontius would wait...he'd waited two thousand years...waiting a few more would be nothing...

Killing chauffeurs and wives had been entertaining, a good way to pass the time until the kingdom came. But Pontius would not hire another human.

Ave Caesar.

CHAPTER 37

The dashboard clock in the BMW said it was 14:00 hours. Diana could have called Max a few minutes ago, in Siegsdorf, but she'd wanted to get on the E 52 first. She needed to feel the triumph of getting to the E 52. She wanted to be able to tell Max she was on the E 52—-it would ease his worry.

She was following a big truck with a huge snowplow. She wished the plow would go all the way to Zurich so she could simply follow it, letting it clear the road just for her.

All of a sudden the truck hit a deeper stretch of snow and almost came to a stop. A huge batch of dry, fluffy snow came directly over the top of the truck and landed on top of the BMW's hood.

Diana was driving blind!

She hit the brakes and slid sideways and nearly smashed broadside into the back of the truck. She came to a halt not more than a meter away from it.

She craned her neck and looked up and could only see the steel bumper and big black tires on either side of the big steel box on the back of the truck.

And just like that, the truck spun those huge tires, dumping still more snow onto the BMW as the truck pulled away and kept on plowing down the E 52. The driver hadn't even seen her.

Diana was shaking inside and out. She could have been killed. What if the snowplow had backed up? It would have crushed her. It would have flattened the car. It would have flattened her. It would have turned her into a crepe. She wouldn't follow the plow so closely. She should have been smarter than that.

Diana took a deep breath and pressed the button on her cell phone and called Max. It only rang once. She tried to keep breathing calmly so Max wouldn't pick up on how scared she was, how she was still shaking, how she had almost perished a minute ago.

"Did you find anything?!"

"Yes."

"Where was it?"

"Under the matt in the trunk, in the well."

"Where is it now?"

"My pocket."

Max closed his eyes and thanked God.

"Did you program the GPS?"

"Yes."

"Where are you now?" Max paced the hotel room floor and stopped to look out the window. The snow had not let up at all.

"I'm on the E 52, about twenty kilometers west of Siegsdorf."

Max looked at his watch. It was 14:02. Diana was moving very slowly. It meant the snowstorm was as bad as ever.

"Are you okay?"

Diana waited a few seconds and said, "I'll never be okay, Max. Not anymore."

Max waited a few more seconds and said, "I love you."

There was silence on the phone for thirty more seconds. What else could he say? What else could she say? Their world was falling apart and now what would they do? Where would they go? How would they get there? What would happen when their money ran out?

"I'm only traveling at 40 kilometers per hour. I can't go faster, Max."

"It's okay, 40 is okay. At least you're moving."

"Max."

"Yeah?"

"It will be dark soon."

"Diana, if it's too difficult...I mean, if it's too much to drive in the dark, find a hotel. Try to get to Munich or...or the E 54...try to get to Landsberg, maybe, and get a hotel room there."

"I'm not going to stop, Max. I am coming to Zurich tonight...if I make it..."

"Where are you going to cross the border?"

"Konstanz."

"Good."

Max was glad. Diana had programmed the route correctly. Crossing the border at Konstanz would cost her extra kilometers but she wouldn't have to cross into Austria again. It was one less border, one less chance of getting caught with so much money in cash and two firearms. He prayed once again that his wife could make it to Zurich. He prayed the snow would stop. He prayed the storm would go away. Max had not prayed so much in all his life.

He rotated his head right and left and right again, watching the street below the Hotel Leon. The light was changing already. Twilight comes early in December. Night comes early in winter. The buildings across the street were glazed in soft pink. The wintry air was shimmering in a kind of powder blue. Flakes the size of saucers fell from the low clouds blanketing Zurich. There was no wind.

Max and Diana had met as children. She was his sweetheart. She would always be his sweetheart. And Max would always be her first love, her last love, her forever love. Both their fathers had suffered in the war. Both their fathers had died way too young. Max's mother had died way too young. Diana's mother was older when she died but it was still way ahead of her time. Max was an only child. Diana had a sister and brother. But Diana was different than her brother and sister, she had always been different. She had always questioned things. Diana had always been suspicious of the status quo. She had always been suspicious of politicians, the government, and especially of citizens that seemed more like sheep, more like lemmings than rational persons.

"Max?"

"Yeah?"

"Pontius...who is he?"

The question made Max stiffen up and clutch the cell phone too tightly. The question made him think about taking the passenger to the airport. Max could see the passenger's unblinking eyes in the mirror. Max could hear the classical guitarist playing *Moonlight Sonata*.

"I don't know, Diana. Like I don't know who the passenger is. Nothing makes sense. The world makes no sense, Diana."

Max's voice sounded dry and a bit hoarse. And it had a tremor in it. Max's desperation could be heard in the dryness, the hoarseness, and the slight trembling of his voice. It all indicated how desperate he felt at this moment, at this time in the history of the world. It took a lot to put her Max in such a state of mind.

Diana wanted to say something but what could she say? She and Max were alone and always would be. There would be no turning back. They could only move ahead but what would that mean? Diana was glad this world was not the end. And she knew Max was glad, as well.

234,553 euros would not, could not last forever.

CHAPTER 38

Max looked at his watch and then looked through the window again. His semi transparent reflection turned him into a ghost. The reflection made him look like a wandering, transparent, disembodied spirit traveling without purpose through this tiresome world.

He turned away from the window, and his ghost, and faced the hotel room. He had to stay centered, he had to concentrate.

"Diana, it's 14:06. If you can keep moving you should make it in eight or ten hours. Even if you can only go 40 kilometers per hour. You can do it."

Max's words had not registered in Diana's mind.

"Max."

"What?"

"I think I know...I know who they are."

Max sat down on the foot of the bed and stared at his feet.

"I think I know what you are going to say, Diana...but don't...don't say it...it won't help us...we need to focus on you getting to Zurich and then we'll talk...we can talk about anything, then, okay?"

"Pontius...he's..."

"No, darling...stop...don't say it."

"Okay...okay, Max."

"Diana, do you have food and water with you, inside the car?"

"Some crackers, fruit...a bottle of water. There's some cheese, but it's still in the trunk...I could get to it but would have to exit the highway."

"Alright...and you just fueled up...that's good. If you can, try to get some coffee...only if you can, only if it's convenient...and get some of that cheese and more crackers. You need to keep up your energy."

Diana checked her speed. It was back to 40 kph. The Snowplow was going faster than her and pulling away. That's okay. She would keep her distance from that monster truck and plow. And she would never tell Max about nearly colliding with it or about the possibility of getting flattened by it. She would put the incident behind her; she would put it out of her mind; she would hold the steering wheel firmly but lightly; she would keep monitoring her speed; she would try to find coffee. For a second or two she fantasized about a cigarette. Smoking would help her focus and stay awake. Maybe she should buy a pack? Maybe the situation called for such a drastic action? Diana still had her lighter.

No. No cigarettes. No smoking. No, no, and no.

She pressed the button on the CD player. She needed to hear some Bach or Beethoven or Albinoni or Mozart or some Chopin. She kept the volume low. Max was still on the phone.

"Diana, did you remember your passport?"

"It's in my handbag."

"Okay."

"Max, are we really going to leave Europe?"

"Maybe. But not right away. We have to think this through. Once we decide, we cannot go back."

"Max, why is this happening? Why us?"

If Max could answer this question he could answer any question, he supposed. But he didn't have an answer.

"I don't know...it's..."

"It's what, Max?"

"It's just another thing I don't know...another thing among many things."

Max wished there was something he could do, some action he could take, something, anything. It wasn't in his nature to let things slide by...to let things just happen to him or to his wife. Perhaps the hardest part of the fight ahead would be letting go...letting go of the world...letting go of their previous life...perhaps it was the only thing Max or Diana could do. Perhaps not...

Max put away the thought that had been gnawing at him from time to time. It would do no good to have a thought like that. But the thought would not go away. And he knew it.

"Max?"

"Yeah?"

"Have you eaten?"

"No, not really, not since yesterday."

"Eat something, Max. Call room service or go to a cafe' or restaurant...okay?"

"Okay."

"I'm going to hang up now, Max. Call me if you need to talk."

"And you call me, too, if you need to talk...and be sure to call once you cross the Swiss border."

"I will..."

Diana hung up and set the phone on the console. She kept it plugged into the charger. She needed that phone charged and ready. The phone was her only link to her husband Max. She had no one else in the world except Max, and the Almighty.

CHAPTER 39

It was 23:55, or five minutes to midnight as the doomsday people say, and the Swiss-German border lay 200 meters ahead. On this side lay the ancient German city of Konstanz and on the other side lay the equally ancient Swiss city of Kreuzlingen. A few blocks to the east was Lake Konstanz. Diana had vague memories of going to Lake Konstanz with her parents and siblings once, when she was about nine.

The snow had stopped a few kilometers back as she approached the northern fringes of Konstanz. Now the winter sky was syrupy black and the stars that weren't hidden by clouds were yellow points of light doing their best to sparkle in the frigid darkness. Diana had always wondered what might exist beyond the stars, beyond the sky, beyond the galaxy and beyond the universe.

She narrowed her red, tired eyes and concentrated on guiding the car into the correct lane to the booth in the center of the border crossing where a guard or two would be waiting for her to stop, show her passport, declare what she might be bringing into Switzerland, and go on...on to Zurich. Getting to Zurich would only take an hour or maybe a little more...

Diana could hardly believe she had made it through the terrible storm...she...

She took one last look at the satchel with all that money. She would not look at it again until she'd crossed the border. Looking at it, even once more, could bring bad luck except she didn't believe in luck. She'd stopped believing in luck a few years ago. Everything happens for a reason.

Diana inhaled deeply and exhaled slowly. The border was only 50 meters ahead now. A border guard was coming out of the booth now. He was turning toward her now. He was only 25 meters away from her now. It was 23:56 now.

She pressed the button and lowered her window. The border guard was a young man of maybe twenty-five maybe less. His face was smooth; his high cheek bones were too pronounced, too chiseled. He looked underfed. It might indicate his wife or maybe his mother had neglected him or maybe he had an eating disorder.

The young man was looking at his watch as Diana drove the last 3-4 meters and stopped.

The guard probably hated working nights and could not wait until his shift ended.

Diana had to stop trying to do psychoanalysis on this guard and just get through the border...just get through the border....just get through...

"Good evening. Passport please."

Diana reached over and pulled it from her handbag which was resting on the passenger seat next to her. She had made sure the passport would be at the top of her handbag so she wouldn't have to fumble around looking for it and make the guard wait.

She was careful not to look at her Navy blue woolen coat covering the satchel with the money. She had laid out the coat in such a way to make it look like she'd simply placed it there, neatly, to have it handy, ready to grab whenever she had to get out of the car and face the snow and cold.

"Thank you," said the young man, the young border guard with the gaunt face.

The guard went into the booth for a minute or so. He was studying some data on a computer screen. Diana tapped the steering wheel nervously and caught herself. Stop doing that!

The guard was stamping one of the inside pages of her passport. He was returning to the car with the passport. Everything would be okay.

The guard shined his flashlight all around the interior of the BMW. He'd pulled the flashlight from its holster on his belt or maybe he'd retrieved it from his desk in the booth. Diana could not be sure, everything was happening so fast.

"And what is your destination this evening, *fraulein*?" The young man was smiling slightly. Using the word *fraulein* instead of the age appropriate *meine frau* struck Diana as both cute and curious.

She would play to it...

"*Fraulein*?" she laughed softly. "It has been a very long time since anyone called me *fraulein*. Thank you, very much. I like that." She smiled at the guard and waited for him to say something. He could be her son if she'd had a son. She would have fed him well, dressed him well, made sure he'd done his homework, and watched him graduate from medical school or law school or...

The guard wasn't smiling anymore. He simply repeated his question: "Where are you going in Switzerland?"

"Zurich. I am meeting my husband. He is on business in Zurich...and once he's finished we are taking a vacation."

That extra information would explain the trunk so full of luggage and clothes and whatnot in case the guard decided to have a look.

"Ah, a winter vacation."

"Ja...a winter vacation."

The guard appeared to accept Diana's story as he put the flashlight in his jacket pocket and handed her the passport.

He was saying something.

"Your left rear tire needs some air...it is a tad low."

"Ah!" Diana didn't know what else to say except "ah" as she prayed a short, wordless prayer for this young border guard to wave her on to Switzerland.

He was saying something again.

"It should be all right. There's enough air in it for you to get to Zurich...it's rather late for putting air in a tire, *fraulein*. It's midnight...and it's very cold."

The guard was sympathetic plus he'd called her *fraulein* once again. The guard liked her once again. Everything would be okay. All her worries about crossing the border had been for naught. And how many more borders would she and Max have to cross in the future?

Diana waited for the guard to wave her on but he didn't.

"Is there anything else?" she asked

"Well, *fraulein*, you tell me...if there is anything else." His eyebrows were raised about 10 centimeters.

"Oh, yes, of course...I have nothing to declare."

"And what else, *fraulein*?" Now his eyebrows were raised even higher. "The toll, *fraulein*—-you must purchase a sticker for the car. It's forty Swiss francs or thirty-five euros."

"Of course..." She reached for her handbag to fish out her wallet. She paid the toll. The guard brought her the sticker and explained where to place it inside the windshield.

The guard waved her on and yawned. For him it was just another cold winter night on the border of Germany and Switzerland. Now he would probably go back to the booth to get warm or he would cross the street to chat with his German counterparts. Diana could not imagine having a job like that. But she could imagine what would have happened if the guard had opened the trunk and gone through the luggage and found Max's weapons...and she could imagine what would happen if the guard had done a thorough search of the interior of the BMW. She would certainly not be crossing into Switzerland this moment.

She pressed the call button on her cell. Max would be asleep but he wouldn't mind if she called to tell him she was in Switzerland.

She spotted the highway sign and the arrow that pointed the way to the A 7 and Zurich.

She cancelled the call. She was shaking so hard she could barely hold onto the phone and the steering wheel. She would pull over up ahead and wait until she'd calmed down. She began to weep and then started to laugh...and had to tell herself to stop it. If someone saw her like this they'd cart her away to a mental hospital.

She pressed the button on the CD player—-and found Beethoven's *Moonlight Sonata*. It would be the perfect piece for this moment as the storm moved away, and the clouds, as the stars shined as bright as she'd ever seen them. She accelerated gradually to the rhythm of the music and drove to the A 7. Diana would call Max in a few minutes.

CHAPTER 40

Max rolled over in the bed and faced the night stand and the digital clock's shining numbers. Those numbers were too bright. They hurt his eyes.

It was 01:45. Diana had not called. Or...!

Or he had not heard his cell phone ringing because he'd fallen asleep after taking that long, hot shower more than five hours ago. Max almost swore for falling asleep like this.

His cell lay there atop the nightstand and he reached for it now. He had to call her and say how sorry he was for not being awake to take her call.

01:45! Almost twelve hours had passed since she'd called him just after getting on the E 52. She should have made it to Zurich at least four hours ago.

Twelve hours! She must have gotten a hotel room somewhere in Germany. Whatever the case she would have called him but he had not heard his phone ringing because he had been asleep.

Or...

Max didn't want to think about her stuck in a snowdrift somewhere...somewhere out there in the storm...out there in the black night.

He checked the phone for incoming calls...and yes...she had called...

He pressed the call button and waited...

And waited...

And waited...

Her recorded voice came on. Max canceled the call and laid his body down on the bed once more.

His head was spinning. His mouth was dry. His heart was beating too fast.

Tap-tap...

Tap-tap-tap...tap-tap...

Diana!!!

Max spun himself 90 degrees and slipped from the bed to the floor in a half second, got to his feet and nearly tripped over himself, trying to get to the door and open it. He fumbled with the locks. He opened the door.

Diana collapsed into his arms. Max held her to his chest. She could barely stand up. He could feel all her 55 kilos weighing against him.

Somehow she managed to lift her head and look at his face and say, "Max, I called you after crossing..."

Max took the handbag and the satchel from her shoulder and the small duffle bag from her hand. With his other arm he guided her to the bed. He set aside the bags and sat down next to her and put one arm and hand around her and covered her two cold hands with his other hand. Diana pressed her head into his shoulder. They didn't speak for two minutes.

"I'll draw a hot bath for you."

"Okay, Max, okay..."

Half way to the bathroom he stopped and turned around.

"The car, Diana?"

"It's in the secure parking behind the hotel."

"You did well."

Diana managed a weak smile.

He returned to the bed after opening the faucet and testing the water, making sure it was perfect.

Diana was fast asleep. She'd simply laid back, her feet still on the floor, and fallen asleep in her clothes—-jacket, winter boots and all.

Max did his best to remove the jacket and boots, her trousers, her sweater. Diana was as floppy as a ragdoll. She didn't wake up as Max shifted her into a proper sleeping position, and pulled up the sheet and comforter, tucking both under her chin. He clicked off the light on the nightstand but left on the one on the table.

He kissed her cheek and said good night and sweet dreams. He went to the bath, turned off the faucet, and let the water drain out of the tub. It made an annoying suction sound.

Max knew he couldn't sleep for a while so he went to the window. The snow had stopped falling. From the semi darkened room he could clearly see the stars above. Max wished he could see the future as well as he could see the stars. He wished he knew what they should do next. Where should they go? And what should they do once they got there?

He returned to the bed and stared at the ceiling for at least thirty minutes as he conjured up one scenario after another, one possibility after another.

He fell asleep at last and dreamed—-he was in the house of his youth again, and there was his father again, and the photographs, and mother weeping.

The images on the photographs came to life and left their place where they'd forever been frozen in time by father pressing the camera's button so many times during the war. The dead soldiers and civilians, no longer dead, were in the room with Max and father and mother. Young and old men, old women and young mothers holding young children, some of them infants. The mothers were crying and screaming as the soldiers pushed them down the hill to the edge of a pit and ordered them to take off their shoes and clothes. The soldiers shot the mothers and their children and the old men and the young men and the old women.

Max woke up. The room wasn't dark. Morning had come. A warm sunray streamed in and cut through the air and bounced off the wall. The clock said it was 10:00. Diana was still asleep. In a few minutes he would order room service. It was time for breakfast.

His terrible dream, the nightmare, broke into a thousand pieces and disappeared along the edges of his mind, the places where he kept his hates. Max didn't like that part of him. It was something he'd always had to fight. He knew how dangerous he could be.

CHAPTER 41

Diana opened her eyes, looked at the clock, and looked at her husband, Maximilian, standing there a few feet away. She closed her eyes again, she wasn't ready for the day. She wasn't ready for anything in this world.

She could hardly remember last night—-it seemed she'd been dreaming or had been lost in some kind of surreal haze as she drove the final ten or fifteen kilometers through the northern outskirts of Zurich. She vaguely recalled passing the international airport; it was on her right, she'd thought. A few minutes later, as she put all her faith in the GPS, she'd driven through a labyrinth of streets lit with a thousand lights, and finally she was in the city center—-she vaguely remembered parking the car in the secure lot behind the hotel, after first parking on the street in front of the hotel, and going to the reception desk, and identifying herself, and asking about her husband...and asking for the room number and for permission to park in the secure lot...but after that, it was all a blur...parking the BMW...retrieving the satchel full of money...and her purse and her wool coat...and another bag from the trunk and...it was all a blur...everything was a blur...

Max poured the warm cream into the coffee cup, giving it a half stir. The cream formed a side by side swirling pattern; the patterns could pass for a couple of miniatures of Van Gogh's spinning stars from that famous painting.

The two swirls vanished into the coffee and Max took the cup to Diana and softly said her name.

"Diana..."

She rolled onto her back and propped herself up on her elbows, her eyes only half open. Max fixed the pillows to make a backrest.

Diana took the first sip of coffee and closed her eyes once more. She still wondered how she'd made it from Berchtesgaden to Zurich.

Max fetched the remote control from the nightstand and clicked on the television. He clicked a couple more times and found a news channel.

"Let's see if we can get a weather forecast."

"I withdrew all of it, Max."

Diana's statement made Max stop clicking the remote for a second or two.

"All 234,553, Max."

Max let his eyes fall on the satchel and imagined all that cash and what would have happened if the guards at the Swiss border had wanted to take a closer look. But, obviously, they had not. Obviously, Diana was here and so was all the money. 234,553 euros. How long could they make it last?

"You did the right thing, Diana."

She took another sip of coffee and said: "I knew we'd never return to Berchtesgaden. There was no point in leaving anything in the bank." She felt a small wave of euphoria, a slight feeling of satisfaction, and said: "Max, we're never going back to that house...that terrible, dark house with..."

"No...never..."

"I have their wedding rings, Max. And the photo and letter. Maybe we could find them, Max. Maybe we could speak with them." Diana knew that would not happen but she said it anyway.

"No...we have to disappear...we can't go looking for people we don't know...what good would it do? Plus we don't even know if they are still alive. We have to disappear, Diana, and we have to think this through...we cannot make a mistake."

Max focused on the TV. At the bottom of the screen information about the storm was scrolling by so fast it was hard to catch it all:

Snowfall to resume by late afternoon, winds increasing to 40 kilometers per hour, expect flight delays or cancellations at Zurich International, avoid driving except for emergency, advise all remain home, storm forecast to last three days yet...

Diana was reading the information too.

"I don't think we'll be leaving this hotel for a while, Max."

"I don't think so either. Would you like something to eat? There are poached eggs, bread and jam...you must be starving."

Diana didn't reply because she was busy opening the drawer on the nightstand and now she was holding the hotel room Bible.

"We need to read this...the entire book start to finish...we need to figure out everything we can, Max. And then we can *think things through*, as you say."

Max got up and went to the window. It was already snowing again, snowing hard.

"All right, we will...it looks like we'll have time for it."

Diana set down the Bible and came to stand next to her husband. She took his right hand in her left and watched the snow falling, falling, and falling.

Max tensed up and leaned forward. Something in the street below had grabbed his attention. He narrowed his eyes and let out a long exhale through just his nostrils. Something was irritating him.

Diana, too, leaned forward to study the street.

A man and woman, dressed in blue jeans and black down-filled jackets were plodding through the powdery snow on the sidewalk and walking in a silly fashion on purpose. They were playing around like teenagers, happy, silly, carefree...now the woman was scooping up some snow and trying to make a snowball...he was shielding his face with his two hands...they were laughing...now the man pulled the woman to him and together they started to waltz.

"I wish we could be like that again, Max...young and cheerful...we were, once, you know."

"They were on the train...we shared a compartment...they talked too much..."

"You met them?"

"Yes, unfortunately...they were the reason I hardly slept on the train...well, they weren't the whole reason..."

The couple was turning around and heading toward the hotel entrance where they disappeared beneath the overhanging roof. Max waited for them to return to the street. But they didn't.

"What did they talk about, Max?"

"About Nazis and the war and bombing...and something about labyrinths in Michigan and in Europe and whatnot...and about the Brenner Pass and Italy..."

"Italy?"

"They said they might go to Italy because it's warmer there...or something like that..."

"They have a point, Max. Italy sounds good to me, too."

"Diana, where is the bug?"

"Bug?"

"The device..."

"It's still in my coat pocket...it has to be there...why?"

Max retrieved the woolen coat from the small closet and fished around in the pockets. He found the little black box and returned to the window and leaned forward, looking right and left down the sidewalk. He looked at the opposite side of the street. The Americans had not returned to the outside. They were still inside the hotel. They must have gotten a room. It had to be so.

CHAPTER 42

1 week later.

Diana was sitting at the table and reading the final chapter of the Book of Revelation:

1*And he showed me a pure river of water of life, clear as crystal, proceeding from the throne of God and of the Lamb.*

2*In the middle of its street, and on either side of the river, was the tree of life, which bore twelve fruits, each tree yielding its fruit every month. The leaves of the tree were for the healing of the nations.*

3*And there shall be no more curse, but the throne of God and of the Lamb shall be in it, and His servants shall serve Him.*

4*They shall see His face, and His name shall be on their foreheads.*

5*There shall be no night there: They need no lamp nor light of the sun, for the Lord God gives them light. And they shall reign forever and ever.*

6*Then he said to me, "These words are faithful and true." And the Lord God of the holy prophets sent His angel to show His servants the things which must shortly take place.*

7*"Behold, I am coming quickly! Blessed is he who keeps the words of the prophecy of this book."*

8*Now I, John, saw and heard these things. And when I heard and saw, I fell down to worship before the feet of the angel who showed me these things.*

9*Then he said to me, "See that you do not do that. For I am your fellow servant, and of your brethren the prophets, and of those who keep the words of this book. Worship God."*

10*And he said to me, "Do not seal the words of the prophecy of this book, for the time is at hand.*

11*He who is unjust, let him be unjust still; he who is filthy, let him be filthy still; he who is righteous, let him be righteous still; he who is holy, let him be holy still."*

12*"And behold, I am coming quickly, and My reward is with Me, to give to everyone according to his work.*

13*I am the Alpha and the Omega, the Beginning and the End, the First and the Last."*

14*Blessed are those who do His commandments, that they may have the right to the tree of life, and may enter through the gates into the city.*

15*But outside are dogs and sorcerers and sexually immoral and murderers and idolaters, and whoever loves and practices a lie.*

16*"I, Jesus, have sent My angel to testify to you these things in the churches. I am the Root and the Offspring of David, the Bright and Morning Star."*

17*And the Spirit and the bride say, "Come!" And let him who hears say, "Come!" And let him who thirsts come. Whoever desires, let him take the water of life freely.*

18*For I testify to everyone who hears the words of the prophecy of this book: If anyone adds to these things, God will add to him the plagues that are written in this book;*

19*and if anyone takes away from the words of the book of this prophecy, God shall take away his part from the Book of Life, from the holy city, and from the things which are written in this book.*

20*He who testifies to these things says, "Surely I am coming quickly."*

Diana paused to look at her husband standing at the window. The window was glazed in gold. Max's face was glazed in gold as the sun disappeared behind some foothills west of the city.

"Do you want to read the last words, Max?"

"Do you want me to read them?"

"Yes."

She went to the window and placed the open Bible in Max's waiting hands. Now they would both be glazed in gold by the glorious sunset.

Max read the words in a soft voice...

Amen. Even so, come, Lord Jesus! [21]*The grace of our Lord Jesus Christ be with you all. Amen.*

The sky was gold, the few puffy clouds were gold, the air in Zurich was saturated in gold, the tops of the buildings were square plates of gold, the other thousands of windows facing the sun were gold. It was the most beautiful sight Diana had ever seen.

For one whole week they had remained cloistered. For exercise they'd done stretches and some aerobics. For food they'd called room service. And they had read the entire book, verse by verse, chapter by chapter, book by book—-every letter, every word, every paragraph, every thought, every truth...and they would pause from time to time to discuss a verse, a chapter, a book; they would pause to pray, too.

Their situation had not changed. They were still alone with no one, on earth anyway, to help. But the Almighty was there, as He'd always been, as He blessed them now with this unbelievable sunset, as He spoke to them in the still small voice Elijah had heard.

And they would go on now...

They would survive as long as possible and do what they had to do.

"Now what should we do, Diana?"

If Diana knew she would tell Max, she would tell him this very moment.

"Sorry. I don't mean to burden you, again."

"You don't have to be sorry, Max. We've been over this...too many times...I...I think the next thing is to go out for a long walk, get some fresh air, go to a restaurant and celebrate. How many people can say they read the entire Bible this week, Max?"

"Not many..."

Max tensed and leaned forward. The American couple...there they were, walking down the gray concrete sidewalk. Max had been right, they had rented a room at the hotel and they were still here, still in Zurich. They too, had decided to stay put and wait out the storm which had finally ended yesterday.

Diana had spotted them, as well.

"Diana, we have to get rid of the car and buy something less showy—-like a used Land Rover or maybe a Jeep."

"How would we get rid of the BMW, Max? We can't just take it to a car dealer and trade it in...there would be too many questions raised...as you have said, Max."

"My American 'friends' might help."

Diana tried to read Max's thoughts and had a faint idea what he meant. And she didn't like it.

"Is this why you asked about the tracking device when I first arrived here? Max, where are you going with this?"

"They might help us..."

"You said that, Max. But it wouldn't be right to put them in danger."

"We could ask them...we could explain it to them...I wouldn't try to trick them..."

"And how would you do that, Max?"

"We will invite them to have dinner with us and I will offer the car...they said they wanted to go to Italy, to Bari...I will offer them the BMW so they can *take the tour in style*...and we'll tell them a bit about Pontius...we'll make them think they are saving us...we'll make them think they are like James Bond...or something like that...besides, if they don't stop until they get to Bari, Pontius won't be able to get to them...all they have to do is keep moving. Once they are in Bari, they park the car on some street and walk away...simple...and we can even offer to pay for the fuel...we could give them a thousand euros to make it really worth their time."

Diana didn't say a word. Max knew she wasn't convinced.

"Max, why don't we just give them the car without the device? And, as you said, give them the thousand euros. Tell them to go wherever they want with the car..."

"No, Diana...the longer they have the car the more they risk being stopped by the police...or they could have an accident. We must simply ask them to take the car to Bari and leave it there...and..."

"And what, Max?"

Max's brain was in a whirl, Diana could see it.

"And we will ask them to plug in the device only after they arrive in Bari. Pontius..."

"Max, Pontius won't fall for that."

"Diana, the car has already disappeared from Pontius' radar ...it has been more than a week...what difference would a few more days make?"

Max had a point.

"Our goal is to throw him off our trail for as long as possible...I believe he will go to Bari after picking up the signal again...I believe his curiosity will get the best of him...he's so evil, Diana...he loves to play these games..."

"But it's wrong to put the Americans at risk. Pontius might kill them."

"Look, I don't like it either, Diana, but what other choices do we have? "

Max answered his own question:

"We could ask around Zurich...we could find someone to take the car for next to nothing...someone who knows a way to get it out of Europe...we could leave it here...but..."

Diana finished Max's thought for him: "But the hotel already knows about the car, they know it's ours...they would report it...and then the police would come looking for us...Interpol would get involved...and..."

Diana was shaking a little. Max gave her a quick hug.

"And what else, Diana?"

"I don't want to go looking for car thieves to help us...car thieves could be more dangerous than everything we're talking about here..."

Diana was right. And Max agreed. He didn't want anything to do with car thieves either.

And there was no easy answer. There was no easy way to get rid of the car. This whole thing was getting more complicated and depressing.

"I could drive it to the mountains and run it over a cliff...but if someone spotted me we could be in even more trouble."

Diana didn't comment. She simply nodded her head.

Max took a deep breath, thrust back his shoulders like a soldier coming to attention, let out the breath and declared:

"Then we will have dinner with the Americans and ask them to help us with *Plan A*...we'll be upfront with them, tell them as much as we can about Pontius, and offer them *ten thousand euros*...the four of us will go to the Italian border, we'll pretend we're traveling together, that we know one another, that the Americans are our relatives and we are taking them around Europe...once we cross the border, they keep the car and we return to Zurich by train, buy another vehicle and move on. If I were that young and someone gave me ten thousand euros to get rid of his car, I'd do it. Ten thousand euros would be enough to pay for their entire trip, airfare included."

"What are their names, Max?"

"Ryan and Meredith Smith...from Michigan."

Max was right. Plan A it would be....the revised Plan A with the device unplugged and nine thousand euros more for the Americans.

"*If* we can convince Ryan and Meredith, Max. They might say no."

CHAPTER 43

Torino, Italy...2 days later.

Max handed the keys to Ryan, gave him a bear hug, and said: "God bless you...and thanks."

"Your English, Max, has greatly improved since we met on the train."

"Ach, I vas nervous, you know. I don't speak English so much. I vas out of practice."

Max could see Ryan didn't believe him but it didn't matter. Besides, Max had come clean and told them his real name. That alone had exonerated him. That and telling them as much as they knew about Pontius. Well, they didn't tell them everything but they had told them a lot. Max and Diana had decided not to burden the Americans with too much information when even Max and Diana could not be completely certain about Pontius.

Meredith didn't seem to be bothered by any of it. She'd been the first to accept Max's offer of ten thousand euros. And once they'd returned to the hotel room after having dinner, after sharing a couple bottles of Italian wine, after eating like kings and queens, and especially after Max had counted out ten thousand euros, in fifties and hundreds, and handed the money to Ryan, Meredith had laughed a giddy, little laugh. She could not contain her joy.

Diana and Meredith were on the other side of the BMW and giving one another a hug. Diana was thanking Meredith. The plan was going to work.

The women came over to Max and Ryan and all four gathered in a small circle and grew silent, letting the winter sun warm their faces. It was an unplanned moment of reflection for each. The time had come to carry out the mission.

Max hoped, prayed they wouldn't back out, as they stood here, reflecting, thinking, considering...but he would offer them the chance to call it off anyway.

"Are you sure, Ryan? Meredith? It's all right if you say no."

Max's words caught Diana by surprise. If the Americans backed out, she and her husband would have to get rid of the car...and they had been over and over this...but Max was right giving them one last chance to bail out.

"We're going, Max."

Meredith had said it. She very much liked having the ten thousand euros. She would not part with that much free money.

Max studied Ryan's face.

"We're going to do it, Max. Don't worry about us."

"Okay, good—-you should be in Bari in two days. Once you are there, park the car on a back street, take the keys and lock the car and walk away. Leave Bari. And do not forget to plug in the device."

"Leave Bari?"

Meredith had asked the question and Max would answer it.

"You must not linger in Bari. You must not be there if and when Pontius arrives. Plus, the longer you stay the greater the chance the police could connect you with the car...you must find a back street...well...I won't say more...I don't want to lecture...we've already discussed most of this...except for leaving Bari."

"We'll do it just like you say, Max. We'll park the car and get on a train or an airplane and leave Bari," Ryan said it with emphasis. He agreed with Max. It would be unwise to remain in Bari.

Ryan glanced at Meredith. She didn't seem pleased with the idea. But Max was right.

Ryan turned and pressed the remote to open the trunk. He leaned into it and fished out Max's and Diana's two small black duffels and handed them to them. Now the car *truly belonged* to Ryan—-he loved being the *new owner* of this BMW 650i Coupe, even if it would be for only two days. He liked this car; he loved it.

"So, Max and Diana. It has been a pleasure."

"Buon viaggio." Max pronounced the two Italian words as a kind of benediction.

Diana had to say one last thing.

"He's not really human...the things we told you...are true...read the prophets...something is going on...something more evil than anything that has ever happened...this is why you must leave Bari immediately...he has some kind of bizarre power...his helpers are..." Diana could not bring herself to say it.

Max spoke to the Americans one last time.

"You must forget about us...it must be as if we'd never met..."

"Understood," Ryan said. "We've never met...and we leave Bari immediately."

Max looked up and down the street. It was a quiet winter morning in Torino. There was no traffic here. There were no pedestrians here. There was only the four of them.

Ryan and Meredith pulled away and did not wave good bye.

CHAPTER 44

Bari, Italy...3 days later.

"No, I said...no, absolutely not!"

"Ryannn..."

"No. And stop begging."

Meredith let go of Ryan's right forearm and turned herself ninety degrees to the right, pinning her back to her car seat. She stared straight ahead in a huff. She did not want to leave Bari without exploring the place, especially now that they had hit a jackpot of ten thousand euros. It was enough to pay for this European dream vacation and then some. Max and Diana were fools to make such a deal. But, thought Meredith, they had indeed made such a foolish deal, and Meredith was not about to waste this good fortune, this windfall of cash. She needed to explore this city and do some shopping too. She loved to shop and she needed a nice Italian-made leather handbag and a pair or two of nice Italian shoes...a pair of pumps and maybe a couple pairs of slip-ons. And Ryan needed to understand his wife's needs.

They sat in silence for five minutes. They were exhausted from the long ride from Torino even though they had stopped for an extra night to sleep in another quaint and lovely Italian hotel and arrived a day late in Bari. And, after all, stopping an extra night had been Ryan's idea. So why should he protest staying in Bari for two or three days to rest, hang out, and take a look around? When would they ever return to *Bari, Italia*? Plus the weather was gorgeous. The temperature had to be around seventy Fahrenheit when it should be closer to fifty or forty this time of year.

"Ryannn..."

"Meredith...you know what they told us...plus they paid us ten thousand euros, Me-re-dith. They trusted us."

"And you believe them? You believe all that stuff about the prophets and all that gloom and doom? And please do not say my name like that, Ry-an."

"I believe they trusted us, Meredith."

"Ryan, my dear silly boy, what could it hurt to hang out here for three days? That bad man...that Pontius...he is not coming here in three days...he is not coming in four...and maybe he's not coming at all...maybe he doesn't even exist...besides, we could wait a while before plugging in the device. That would make sure he didn't see this car on his 'radar.'"

Meredith sounded like she was mocking him now...which she was.

"No! We gave our word."

"Okay, okay...you don't have to get mad."

"I'm not mad, Meredith. But we gave our word."

"You're right. We gave our word. So what's next? What do we do this moment? I'm exhausted, Ryan. And so are you. And it's already 3 p.m. Can't we get a hotel room? Staying the night won't make any difference. C'mon, let's get our gear from the trunk and look for a hotel. All right?"

Now she sounded conciliatory. Meredith had changed her tactics.

Ryan let out a long exhale and stared at the dashboard clock. He had to admit that Meredith had a point. It was already late. The day was almost shot. And getting on a train or a plane, at this moment, did not sound good. It sounded horrible in fact. And he needed a shower.

"All right but I'm still going to plug it in."

"Fine... go ahead and plug it in...let that evil man see where his car is..."

Meredith started laughing and Ryan joined in and gave her a hug at the same time. Everything was okay again.

Ryan pulled the tracking device from underneath his seat, popped open the trunk, and exited the BMW. Meredith exited from her side.

"You be the lookout while I do the job."

"Of course, Ryan...isn't this fun? It's so exciting...it's like we're in a spy novel."

Meredith's tone irritated Ryan but he held back. He didn't reply on purpose as he lifted their gear from the trunk, set it on the sidewalk, and hooked up the little black box as he thought how much his wife controlled him. But he had his faults too.

The indicator light said it was up and running.

"All right, it's on, it's working. Let's go."

They hoisted their backpacks onto their backs and walked away. It seemed everything was good, nobody had seen them. This was just another quiet, little back street in Italy. There must millions of quiet, little streets in Italy, in Europe.

They spotted a sign with an arrow pointing to the city center.

"Oh, Ryan. This is so much funnn...let's get as close to the waterfront as possible." Meredith had exchanged her semi-mocking tone for giddiness. She could be such a little brat albeit a nice one most of the time.

Twenty minutes later they spotted a Bed and Breakfast called *Il Sole D'Oriente* ...The Eastern Sun...it was beautiful, the room looked like one of those rooms in a luxury hotel in Dubai. The bath was all marble, the fixtures were all gold, the bed was perfect, the view of the Adriatic was perfect. Meredith was loving it.

"We leave tomorrow, okay Meredith?"

"Sure, Ryan, sure...of course...for now let's shower and take a nap. We'll go out later and find a nice place to eat. We'll ask the owner. He'll know where the best local cuisine is. I want some seafood, and some linguini, and some dry Italian white wine. It will be perfect, Ryan."

She was playing him and he knew it...but he didn't mind too much. And a shower, nap, and a great dinner would be just the thing. It doesn't get any better than that.

CHAPTER 45

The sun's rays made Ryan's face burn. The air was too warm, too hot, too hot for his face and too hot for Bari, Italy in winter. It frightened him a little. He was beginning to think global warming was real. He hated thinking about things like that. He hated liberals and global warming people and tree-huggers, all of them, he hated all of them.

He diddled with the BMW's keys, tapping the ignition key against the top of the table in the outdoor cafe', drumming out a sort of Morse Code as he watched his wife sip the last of a latte' and take the last bite of a *crespelle*, the Italian equivalent of a French crepe. She smiled at him. He did not return the smile as she set down the latte' and wiped her fingers with the napkin.

"Cheer up, Ryan."

"Cheer up?"

"Yeah, cheer up," Meredith smiled out the words.

"Meredith..."

"No, Ryan, don't start in again. We have it all planned. We are leaving tomorrow. Don't spoil the rest of today and tonight with your complaining. I'm sick of it."

"It's been five days, Meredith."

"So what? I've had fun. And I know you have too, even if you don't think so. You should get more in touch with your feelings...maybe see a counselor?" Meredith's eyes were sizing him up.

He ignored her sarcastic expression and her foolish remark and declared, "And all those shoes and that handbag and the other *stupid* knick-knacks you bought! Maybe it's you who needs therapy."

"Stupid knick-knacks?"

Ryan looked down and stared at the keys which he'd laid on the table because he was tired of diddling with them. He was tired of this stupid little exchange. He grabbed up the keys and stuffed them into his right pocket. They didn't go all the way in but he didn't care. He would fix the problem later.

"Sorry...I didn't mean it."

"And I didn't mean it either. And like I told you, silly boy, I'm going to ship everything home. I'm not going to lug them around Europe or make you help me carry them. We'll send them off tomorrow on the way to the train station."

"And the car?"

The question came out of nowhere and startled Meredith.

"The car? What about the car?"

"Maybe we should go back and see if it's still there."

"Why, Ryan?"

"I don't know...I'm curious I guess...I wonder if the police noticed it and had it towed or something. Or maybe somebody stole it or broke into it or..."

"But you have the keys, Ryan."

"That doesn't stop car thieves...they know how to hot wire any car out there. Anyway, we've seen most of this town, shopped most of the shops, eaten most of the food..."

"Okay, Ryan, my detective husband, let's go there now, right this minute. Let's find out the fate of the car, our infamous car."

Ryan didn't like her sarcasm but he managed to form his mouth into a half smile anyway, knowing it bugged her.

He waved to the waiter and asked for the check. He paid with a crisp 50-euro bill. They had gone through too many crispy euros the last five days. It was time to move on. Contrary to Meredith's views about staying this long, Ryan felt guilty. They had given their word and not kept it.

He couldn't wait until tomorrow and getting on the train and heading to Rome and leaving Bari, Italia for good.

CHAPTER 46

Ryan grabbed his wife's forearm and pulled her with him into a shadowy doorway.

"Ouch! Why'd you do that?"

He pulled her to his chest.

"Ssshhh..."

"Wha...?"

He covered her mouth with his hand. "Quiet!" He said it through clenched teeth. He didn't like covering Meredith's mouth like this but she could be so naive and stupid at times.

Ryan nodded towards the car, the beautiful silver BMW which lay less than fifty meters ahead of them on the other side of the street.

Now Meredith saw the reason for Ryan acting crazy like this. A man dressed in a black tunic, black trousers, and black shoes had his face pressed into the driver's window. He was peering inside, studying the interior. He was a young man, not older than thirty or thirty-five, with jet black hair slicked straight back and held in place with plenty of shiny gel.

Ryan took his hand away, gently, slowly.

"Don't say a word. We'll wait and see what he does."

Meredith nodded *yes*. They had to stay perfectly still and watch the young man in black. From this darkened doorway across the street they had a perfect angle for watching the car and the man without being spotted...if they could remain quiet and motionless. Ryan prayed there wouldn't be anyone else around to ask them what they were doing hunkered down in a doorway in Bari. Ryan slid his smart phone from his pocket and began taking a video of the man in black.

The man put his cell phone to his ear and said: "It's here, in Bari." He waited for a response as he paced back and forth on the concrete. Pontius was furious.

Yes, Pontius was furious alright. The BMW had not been moved. It had been parked there deliberately, the tracking device turned on five days ago; the car had been left for the police to discover or for thieves to hot wire it and steal it.

"Find them!" Pontius spat out the two words through his clenched, perfect white teeth.

"They cannot be touched."

"Find them anyway! That's an order!" Pontius nearly crushed his cell phone with his hand that was seven times stronger than any human's. But he calmed himself and sat down in his chair and swung around to view the valley below the Watzmann where Berchtesgaden lay draped in fog. Outside the villa it was snowing hard. The world was a brilliant white. The snow was sticking to the birches and firs and the pantheon of Greco-Roman statues lining the long driveway.

"And the car, sir?"

"Destroy it. At least we can take that away." Pontius needed revenge however he could get it. "After you destroy the car, look around the city. Maybe they're still there. Report back to me if you spot them."

"Yes sir."

The man in black put his cell phone in his pocket and did a slow three-sixty, panning around like a surveillance camera, recording everything...as Ryan recorded him with his phone...

Although Ryan couldn't hear what the man had said, he sensed in his gut it was about something extremely serious or extremely evil. He pulled Meredith even closer and wished they could simply melt into the gray stucco wall inside the shadowy doorway. They must not let this man see them. Ryan had a bad, bad feeling about this man in black. He certainly wasn't a police officer and didn't appear to be a car thief either. And he didn't look normal. But Ryan kept making a video anyway...

The man in black slowly waved his right hand over the car as if pronouncing a kind of spell.

The car vanished.

Meredith and Ryan saw it together. Ryan's phone saw it too. The car had disappeared into the air. It was gone.

"Ryannn..."she whispered.

"Ssshhh...don't talk." He put the phone in his pocket. He was finished making videos...for now.

"What should we do?" she whispered again.

"Stay...stay right here...to wait and see where he goes..." Ryan's mouth was dry and pasty. It was hard to whisper with a mouth so dry.

The man in black was walking toward them on the opposite side of the street; Ryan could hear his shoes grating against the concrete. In a few seconds, he would be directly across from them. If he stopped there, they would be completely exposed.

The man in black did stop there, directly across from them. He panned his head back and forth, again resembling a human form of a surveillance camera. He stopped turning and fixated his gaze on the doorway.

Ryan grabbed Meredith's right hand and pulled her to the right and onto the sidewalk and said, "Run!" As he said it the BMW's keys dropped out of his pocket and clanged against the coarse concrete. He let go of his wife and spun around. The keys lay two meters back. The man was crossing the street. He'd spotted them alright. And he must have heard the keys hit the sidewalk. He'd seen and heard everything. Ryan uttered an oath and grabbed Meredith's arm once more. There was no time to get to the keys and put them away safely inside his pocket. The man was picking up his pace. He was coming for them!

"Run, Meredith, run!"

They ran six blocks and finally had to stop. They were drenched in sweat and getting too close to the city center. There were more people now and a pair of police officers were ahead, standing on a corner and watching.

Neither Ryan nor Meredith had turned around to see if the man in black was following them. Their adrenaline glands had kept pumping and pumping as they had kept running and running like a couple of marathoners making a last dash to the finish line. But where was the finish line? How would they get out of this? Ryan knew they were now being punished for violating their promise. They had given their word to leave Bari immediately and they had not done so. They had stayed for five more days so Meredith could go shopping.

They sat down on one of the two wrought iron benches at the foot of a high wall made of stones glued together with mortar that had begun to crumble and fall. The air roasted them as they sat there, holding hands and gasping for more oxygen. They should look for a shady place to cool down. They needed to cool down, they needed to talk, they needed to figure out what they'd seen back there when the man made the car vanish. Ryan was furious at Meredith for getting them into this jam. Why had he let her get away with it?! The wall behind him showed how he felt. They'd promised to leave the city right away and now things were crumbling around them.

Ryan lifted his head and looked to his left toward the other bench five meters away. There was the young man in black, sitting there calmly and dangling the keys to the BMW in front of his swarthy face. The man wasn't sweating at all, he wasn't breathing hard at all, his clothes were perfectly pressed, not rumpled at all. The man turned toward Ryan now and focused his dark eyes on him as if they were twin laser beams.

"Did you lose something?"

Meredith, too, turned and looked at the man in black and his mesmerizing, laser eyes.

The man vanished.

"Did you lose something?"

The man was standing squarely in front of them and staring down at them as they huddled together on the bench.

Ryan's face was ashen. Meredith's face was white.

"Where are they?" The man in black's eyes were glowing red hot. He repeated the question, "Where are the chauffeur and his wife?"

Ryan drummed up enough valor to reply, "We don't know." He almost choked on his pasty, dry words.

It was true, though. Neither he nor Meredith had any idea where Max and Diana would be now.

"How did you get the car?"

"They asked us to drive it here...and leave it...here...in Bari...that's all we know..."

"Did they pay you?"

"No."

Except for the rising and falling of his Adam's apple, Ryan showed no emotion as he lied. Meredith was proud of him. She had not realized her husband could be this brave.

"Did you see what I did to the car?"

"Yes." This time Ryan did not lie.

"I can do the same to you."

It was Meredith's turn to talk.

"We did nothing wrong. They wanted the car driven here. They said they'd come later by plane. We don't know why."

Ryan was amazed how coolly Meredith had told the lie about Max and Diana coming to Bari by plane.

The man lifted his hand and...

Meredith gasped and took hold of Ryan's forearm, clutching it, squeezing it so hard she could hear bones popping. She sealed her eyes closed. Ryan threw his arms around her shoulders and shut his eyes too, waiting to get zapped, waiting to die.

The two police officers they'd seen a couple minutes ago walked up to them and asked a question in Italian. Receiving no response, they repeated the question.

Ryan was the first to open his eyes. The man in black was gone, disappeared, vanished; poof!

Ryan had not replied to the police officer's question so the officer asked it a third time, in English.

"Are you Americans?"

"Yes," said Ryan.

Meredith open her eyes. Her husband was still clutching her to him as if she were a child in imminent danger. The two cops were watching their body position, their body language. They must look ridiculous to these cops. Meredith pulled away a little, disentangling herself from Ryan.

"Are you all right?" one of the officer asked.

"Yes...yes, we're okay...thank you."

The police officers didn't seem to believe Ryan. But he insisted, once again, that everything was okay.

"All right. We will leave you then. Call if you need to report something."

Ryan and Meredith both nodded their head and said, "thank you" in unison.

They sat there, in a stupor, glued to the metal bench, neither one able to speak for fifteen minutes or more.

"Ryan?"

"Yeah?"

"I want to go home."

"Home?"

"Michigan."

"But we still haven't been to Spain or Portugal or the U.K."

"I don't care, Ryan...I want to go home...I..."

"Ssshhh...it's all right...I want to go home too...let's get our things and head for the airport..."

Meredith began to tremble and weep. Ryan held her hands in his, kissed her forehead, and tried to comfort her.

PART THREE

Cowards die many times before their deaths;
the valiant never taste of death but once.

-William Shakespeare

Give me my robe, put on my crown;
I have Immortal longings in me.

-William Shakespeare

War is the trade of Kings.

-John Dryden

CHAPTER 47

Quito, Ecuador
August 2017

Diana was feeling great. Finally, she could say the high altitude didn't affect her at all. It had taken a couple of years but now it will be all right. Everything will be all right. *Todo sera' bien.*

She poured two cups of delicious, dark coffee and placed a few sugar cookies on a square, terracotta plate and managed to carry everything out to the small patio off the small kitchen of their modest, split-level South American house which somehow clung to the sheer mountainside five hundred meters above the city.

It was a miracle she could breathe so well now at more than thirty-three hundred meters above sea level. It had taken Max less time to get used to it but he, too, had had his days, both good and bad. Now the constant dizziness was gone. Now they could think clearly one hundred percent of the time. Now their new life seemed to make more and more sense.

And Diana was glad it was Saturday and tomorrow was Sunday. She loved the weekends and the time away from the school. She needed the free time, and the rest, even though she'd come to love her job, teaching German to Ecuadoran high school students. And it was a private school, no less—-a school for the children of the elites. It was another miracle—-that she'd been hired as a language teacher there, that they paid her so well, that they didn't ask too many questions. On the other hand, this was Latino America and money could buy a lot of privacy. With enough money one could get about anything through customs. And one could obtain a new ID for another thousand euros apiece.

They'd done just that. They'd gotten new IDs, new passports in Rio. They didn't want to enter Ecuador using their real names in case Diana's family tried to find them. Diana had called them a few times from Pamplona, reassuring them that Max and she were all right...that they'd had to leave Berchtesgaden and Germany and Austria for a time...but they'd be back after more time passed and would explain what had happened.

Yes, perhaps later they would also explain why they'd obtained the new IDs and that Max had become George Richter and Diana had become Maria Lehmann Richter. They would explain why they'd gone to South America and why they didn't want to be found. On the other hand, Diana doubted they would ever return to the EU, to Austria and home. Too much had happened. They'd traveled too far. They'd seen too much. And, Pontius would be there, in his villa, high upon the Watzmann, high above Berchtesgaden, watching, waiting like an eagle waits to spot a fish.

Max loved sitting out here on the patio in the early morning, watching the sun rising over the Andes. He loved to look at the six thousand meter volcano, *Nevado Cayembe*, with its snow-covered cone. The volcano was magnificent—-ice blue in the morning, glittering white during the day, and sparkling gold in the evening. And Max loved his black and white and blue plaid, Alpaca wool blanket draped over his shoulders and wrapped around the rest of him. He looked like a larger version of a cocoon. Diana had the same plaid blanket only hers was maroon and black and white. They were cocoons which had become butterflies. They'd been reborn in Ecuador. The metaphor fit.

Almost every Saturday and Sunday morning they would sit on the terrace like this, snug in their blankets, cozy in the chilly air. The blankets protected them from the cold metallic chairs which would otherwise leave their backside quite numb. The blankets were another sort of metaphor...they symbolized security against the mind-numbing fear they'd felt in Berchtesgaden during those last desperate days when they'd truly grasped how bad, how evil was Pontius and how dangerous their life had turned out to be.

Between them was a small round, metal table; the table came with an umbrella, in case it rained or the sun was too hot during the times Max studied the Bible outdoors. For now the umbrella lay at the edge of the patio beneath a low wall of pink-gray stucco.

The knee-high wall wasn't really high enough to keep someone from falling straight down the mountain but it would do for now...besides, neither of them had any plans of getting close enough to the edge to run that risk.

Max planned to have the wall replaced with a higher one later in the year. He'd already spoken with a handyman and his son willing to take on the project for a fraction of what it would cost in Europe. Life in Ecuador, in the year 2017, was good.

Diana set the two mugs of coffee and the plate with cookies on the table.

"*Gracias,*" Max said, and smiled. Saying thank you in Spanish was one of the few words or phrases he knew despite living in South America for this long.

"*De nada, mi amor.*" Diana smiled too.

Diana worried about Max. He spent too much time alone. When he wasn't home he was out walking alone, climbing the mountain, stopping from time to time, taking in the view, looking at the volcano, and turning and planting his walking stick and walking up the path again until he would come to the top of the ridge high above their cozy dwelling place of off-white stucco and orange tile roof.

From their bedroom window on the opposite side of the house, Diana had watched him doing that so many times. He'd told her he did it while she was working, too. He needed the exercise. He was almost sixty years old now and needed to stay as fit as possible, he had said several times.

Diana wished Max could find a friend. On other hand, she understood why he had not. It was hard to break the language barrier. And, the hard truth was, Max didn't want friends. He didn't want anyone asking why he and his wife lived in Ecuador or how they'd arrived there, two years ago.

And she worried about the times he'd assembled and disassembled the rifle, again and again and again. Each time he would check the scope, make adjustments, and recheck it. He would check the ammunition too. Those pointy bullets looked like miniature rockets to Diana. Max had told her he could take out a fly on a cow's snout from more than three hundred meters without the cow knowing it. She believed him.

But there were good things too. Max read the scriptures every day. He said grace before every meal. He was good to her.

And Max didn't just read the scriptures—-he devoured them. He'd underlined and highlighted most of his rather beaten-up, well-worn Bible. He'd stuffed it with little post-it notes, little scraps of paper; he'd filled the margins with notes, sketches, doodles that meant something although Diana couldn't always tell what. She felt a bit guilty about paging through his Bible while he was out walking alone. She shouldn't do that. She should just ask him what some of those little sketches meant.

Max took a bite from the cookie and remarked how good it was. And the South American coffee was so good too, he said.

"We've done well, Max."

Max did not reply. He was staring at the volcano again, his eyes had that faraway look again. It seemed to Diana that maybe he stared at the volcano and the mountain range running north and south of the volcano, and tried to go back in his mind to Austria, back to his youth when his father took him to the Flughafen in Linz and the puffy clouds graced the high snowfields of the Alps. Diana knew Max well but he still had his mysteries.

After purchasing an old jeep in Zurich they had gone to Spain. They had crossed southern France and the Pyrenees in a week and settled in the City of Pamplona, finding a small flat that cost next to nothing in monthly rent. And they had lived there more than four years, sparingly. Cautiously, they had spent each euro, eating mostly rice and beans and a few vegetables, and small portions of meat only twice per week, hoping and praying to make the money last, and not knowing what to do next, where to go next. Until one evening, sitting at the kitchen table, Max declared he couldn't take it anymore, they had to do something, they had to go, anywhere, anywhere but here, anywhere but Spain.

"You can speak their language, Diana, I cannot. We have to get out of Pamplona, I don't care if Ernest Hemmingway was here," he'd said, and laughed. But his laugh was a bitter one. Max was dying inside, in Pamplona, in the EU, and Diana knew it. One evening, after food shopping, she'd come home to find him drunk, his head slumped on the kitchen table. She'd gotten him cleaned up and walked him to the bed as he mumbled about his fears and how much he hated Europe.

"Would you like more coffee, Max?"

"Yes...and it's my turn to fetch it."

"Gracias, mi amor."

"De nada, mi amor." Saying "you're welcome my love" was another phrase Max had perfected.

A week after finding Max drunk, they'd packed the jeep, paid any rent owed, and left Pamplona. They'd gone to Barcelona and purchased two one-way tickets on a container ship headed for Rio De Janeiro. The crossing took fifteen days and cost two thousand euros. They'd had to abandon the jeep in Barcelona on a backstreet near the docks. And, as painful as it was, they'd also left half their belongings inside the jeep. Max hoped someone needed that jeep and their stuff, all of it available at no cost. Perhaps someone could use the jeep for scrap metal.

They'd remained in Rio, in a cheap hotel, for a week before flying to Quito with even less stuff. Max and Diana were almost as glad to get out of Rio as Pamplona and wondered if they'd feel the same about Quito after time had passed.

All of it seemed so far away now, the EU, living in Pamplona, sailing the Atlantic, flying to Quito, finding another hotel, finding this house, and finding Diana the job, the position as a teacher of German at such a prestigious school.

He poured two more mugs of coffee, brought them out to the patio, and sat down once again. He didn't need the alpaca blanket anymore. The sun in South America becomes hot very quickly once it rises high enough above the Andes.

"Oh, Max, I haven't told you," the school is putting on a lecture series."

Max took a long sip of coffee and kept his eyes on the mountains and the volcano.

"It's to have an assortment of themes...history, film, theater, philosophy, theology, scientific themes ...the first lecture is this Friday evening. Would you like to go?"

Diana bit her lip and prayed a short prayer. It would do Max good to be around others, especially her colleagues and the parents of her students. Max needed to get out more often. And the teachers and parents, most of them anyway, spoke enough English...Max spoke English...they could communicate that way.

"The first lecture is by a Doctor Martin Barrios Rafael from Mexico...it's about genetics...eugenics...cloning...I think..."

Max blinked...and blinked a few more times, processing Diana's words. A huge cloud had moved in, casting a huge shadow over the valley below the house. The shadow moved up the mountain side and covered their house and the patio and them. The air went from tepid to chilly in an instant. Max gathered the blanket around his shoulders once more. He held the coffee mug with both hands in order to warm them.

"The lecture, by Doctor Barrios Rafael, will be in English?" Of course Max knew it would not be in English. A Mexican doctor does not give a lecture for Ecuadorans in English.

"No, Max, but I can interpret for you in German."

Max could see the eyes in the rearview mirror, the hardened eyes, the expressionless face, the grim mouth. He could hear the passenger's voice, his perfect Austrian accent. He could hear *Moonlight Sonata*. He could see the passenger directing the music as if he were Toscanini...his rising and falling hands and fingers keeping time. Max pictured Beethoven composing the piece even though he was deaf.

"All right. I will go. We will go together...and you will tell me what he says."

CHAPTER 48

Diana made everything look fabulous—-her black silk dress and her black high heels and her pale yellow, loosely-woven shawl with long fringes. She'd kept her hair blond to match her passport photo. And Max looked good too, for a sixtyish man. He'd kept his short hair and short beard like Diana had kept her new hair color. He'd not put on any weight at all; his charcoal gray, Hugo Boss suit had not needed alterations. He still had the physique of a thirty year old. Max wished he could be thirty again. He would always have that wish, he supposed. It's because humans desire immortality.

Max opened the driver's side door for her. He didn't like driving in Quito; these days he didn't care for driving much at all even though he had been a chauffeur. Besides, Diana was better at negotiating the South American traffic. She knew her way around the city better than he did, driving every day to the school and back to their house. She would drive to go food shopping and drive on the occasions they would take a day trip into the mountains, exploring some valley or canyon east, west, north, and south of Quito.

She put the key in the ignition of the silver 2014 Toyota Camry and said, "Here we go then...*aqui vamos entonces.*" Max was glad they could afford this comparatively new car. It was because of Diana's job.

Max repeated the Spanish words..."*aqui vamos entonces...*" One of these days, before he was too old maybe, he would make more of an effort to learn Spanish.

After twenty minutes, they came to the quiet residential neighborhood of *Bella Vista*, a combination of low-rise, luxury apartment buildings and upscale, terraced houses of stucco with red tile roofs—-in the shaded, secluded driveways most of the cars were BMWs, Mercedes Benz, SUVs, and an occasional Porsche, Lamborghini or Ferrari. This was how the elites of Ecuador lived...government officials, the professional class and wealthy foreign residents. Here Diana taught German to their children. Here Diana was loved for her grace and charm and intelligence. Here Max had only gone a couple times before...to attend exactly two boring graduation ceremonies and two equally boring receptions.

They arrived early to grab a couple of seats in the back of the mini auditorium, a place where Diana could whisper her translation for Max, a place where they wouldn't disturb anyone.

Max sat and waited, fidgeting with the glossy program flier which he couldn't read anyway. Diana had gone to the Ladies Room, to where the sign above the door said *Damas*, to make sure her make-up was perfect and whatnot.

Suddenly, a man in a very well-tailored gray suit, white shirt, and red tie entered the stage, a man of perhaps fifty or so with dark hair streaked with some gray, a trim physique, and a confident stride. He was behind the podium now, placing some papers, files; he pulled out a laser pointer from his lapel pocket and tested it on the big screen to his right. He must be the geneticist, the doctor, the one to talk about cloning this evening.

The doctor rotated and faced the dark auditorium and its rows of comfortable, high-back seats. He had not turned off the laser. Unaware he was being observed he made the crimson ray of light do a playful dance, resting here and there on one seat and then another...until the beam stopped squarely and uncomfortably on Max's face, hitting him in the left eye, and blinding him a bit.

"Ah! Perdoname. Pensaba que estaba solo! Perdonnn!!!"

With that he clicked off the laser beam as Max said, "It's all right...you didn't know...it's dark in here."

"Ah...American?"

"No...Austrian."

It was soundless in the gloomy auditorium, this dark cavern, quiet enough to hear another man's thoughts.

It was the doctor's turn to speak inside this gloomy cave: *"Vielleicht können wir nach dem Vortrag treffen."*

The man had suggested meeting after the lecture and he'd said it in perfect German.

"Ja, sicher...yes, sure," Max agreed. They would meet after the lecture. It would be nice to speak German with someone besides Diana, Max figured.

Max wondered how a Mexican doctor could speak perfect German...he must have lived there...or studied there for a long time.

Doctor Martin Barrios Rafael had spoken for more than an hour as two hundred people sat there, listening, watching him point the laser at this photo and that photo and this graph and that graph, this chart and that chart. They even watched a seven minute video about the topic. And the doctor had spoken about Eugenics, Medical Ethics, the Rule of Law, Natural law, and about Genocide. He'd spoken about different theologies, different views of the world, the cosmos...as Diana had done her best to translate such intricate concepts and ideas into German for her husband, Max.

The audience had applauded, politely, too politely it seemed to Max. They ought to be as adamant as the doctor, as anti-cloning as he, as Max, as anyone would be after hearing what this doctor had to say about it. But they weren't adamant, they weren't upset; they were complacent. Their inane, empty-of- meaning questions during the Q and A session showed how apathetic they were. Max could tell how frustrated the doctor was...the people just didn't get it...or just didn't care at all.

Max sipped his glass of Chilean chardonnay in the corner of the reception hall. Diana was a few steps away, chatting with an Ecuadoran couple. They must be the parents of one of her students. Beyond Diana a seam opened up in the crowd like a miniature parting of the Red Sea. Instead of water it was people forming a wall on the right and left.

At the end of the seam, on the other *shore*, was the doctor. And nobody was talking to him. He was alone. It would appear nobody had any more questions. It would appear the doctor could use some company. Max would offer it to him.

They shook hands. And for a long moment didn't know what to say.

Max spoke first, introducing himself, in German. He didn't give the doctor his new name, George. He gave him is real name, Max. For a long second or two Max wondered if that was a good idea. But another part of him said the doctor could be trusted. And what difference would it make? Soon the doctor would leave Ecuador and Max would not see him again.

"Es ist eine Freude, dich zu treffen."

And the doctor replied, in perfect German of his own, that it was indeed a pleasure...to meet Max, to meet someone who spoke German, and then he apologized again for shining the laser beam on Max's face.

Max said it was nothing and went on to tell the doctor how much he'd appreciated the lecture. Cloning was indeed a difficult subject, one which required much more thought and consideration. It was...

The doctor stared into Max's eyes. He was examining Max's soul, he was doing psychoanalysis of Max's mind. The conversations of the guests in the reception hall became a sort of muted echo. Only the doctor and Max were here now. The other guests might as well be mannequins.

The doctor's piercing look halted Max's thoughts. He was frozen in place for a few seconds. He didn't know what to say, he couldn't latch onto the correct words.

Max stammered out something as his memories gushed in, flooding his mind like Noah's flood had flooded every corner of earth. Max's mind was once again a kaleidoscope, a black and white film montage...of father and his photos, of going with father to the Flughafen and watching airplanes landing and taking off, and of going home afterwards to mother and her sadness...his mind was full of images from that winter day, and the dry, blowing snow, and the patches of barren ground, and father's coffin being let down by the grave diggers' ropes.

Max centered himself, again trying to let go of the memories that had plagued him so long. Again he resolved not to be tortured by certain terrible thoughts, things that were not his fault.

Maybe the doctor had his own bad memories. Everyone has a few and some have more than others.

The long minute of silence continued as the two men sized up one another. Max took another sip of wine...the wine didn't taste good anymore.

Diana had joined them, breaking the stillness, speaking some pleasant words of greeting in Spanish as she introduced herself...as Diana...and not her fake name. It caused Max to do a double take. She, too, must have felt she could trust this man.

The doctor returned the pleasantries with words in Spanish of his own. Max tried to understand but, as usual, found himself lagging behind by three or four words and then ten words and more. Diana could see Max's frustration and so could the doctor.

She switched to German, telling the doctor how good the lecture was, how informative and that she'd managed to translate most of it for her husband.

Max agreed with his wife, that the lecture was indeed good, very good.

"*Ja, es war sehr gut, Arzt Barrios...*Yes, it was very good, Doctor Barrios."

"Please, Max...call me Martin...and you too, Diana."

Max spoke next: "How long will you be in Ecuador?"

Diana was pleased. At last, Max seemed to be making a friend. She uttered a mental prayer to heaven...please, Lord, let Max make a friend...Max needs friends.

Martin was speaking: "I have a few weeks until my next lecture, in Los Angeles. I need some down time, you know. I have to force myself to take a vacation. It's how I am. Anyway, I plan to explore the mountains a bit...I want to have a look inside the volcano."

"You want to climb *Cayembe*?" Diana's eyebrows were halfway to the top of her forehead. Max blinked his own eyes and took another sip of wine he didn't like. The top of *Cayembe* was four thousand six hundred and ninety meters above sea level.

"No. I'm going to fly there...in my plane...I'm a pilot...I have a Learjet 85...customized...it's very nice..."

Max knew how nice that jet was...

"Would you like to join me?"

"Join?" Max asked.

"Tomorrow...if the weather is okay...and it should be...the latest forecast says clear skies across Ecuador..."

"Yes, we do...don't we, Max?"

"You own a Learjet 85, doctor?"

Max couldn't believe it. A customized Learjet 85 would cost twenty million euros.

"Yes. I own one...I have other airplanes in Mexico, in Merida—-a King Air, a Cessna 182, and a De Havilland Beaver with Tundra tires. The runway on my ranch is just a cleared strip in the jungle and it's kind of rough. The De Havilland is painted in camouflage to blend in with the jungle. I want to hide it as much as possible from aerial surveillance...the cartels regularly use the Yucatan airspace and I want no contact with them."

Now Max was even more curious—-Martin had a ranch in the Yucatan jungle? He'd never met anyone who owned a ranch let alone one in the Yucatan jungle. And he had a De Havilland painted in camouflage to hide it from the drug cartels? Max liked this guy more and more.

"You own a ranch?"

"I have a ranch in the Yucatan jungle...I like to go there and play cowboy...it's another way to relax...I use the De Havilland to get to my ranch."

"Doctor...ah, Martin...you are a lucky man. You have a Learjet, a King Air, a Cessna, and Beaver De Havilland? And a working ranch in the Yucatan?"

"My mother's family *was* very wealthy...she left me a lot of money."

"Was?"

For a moment Martin's eyes had sadness in them. Max wanted to say something but couldn't find the words. He had to fight back sad thoughts of his own.

Diana came to the rescue—-this was no time for sadness. Martin was going to fly them to the top of *Cayembe* tomorrow. Fantastic!

"I'll meet you at the airport at the general aviation gate at 09:00, Martin said. "I'll inform security that you are my guests."

Max locked eyes with Martin once again. Martin knew some things. He knew a lot of things. Max was very good at reading a man's face, his eyes, his gestures, even his twitches and blinks, if he blinked at all, and the way a man shaped his words or the way a man kept quiet.

CHAPTER 49

The next morning Max got up earlier than usual, after not sleeping well, and wrapped himself in his Alpaca blanket. He took hold of his mug of coffee, and went outside to the patio to take in his first breaths of fresh morning air. He needed the cold air like he'd needed the cold water on his face and neck a few minutes ago to wash away the grogginess and the bad dreams he'd had but couldn't remember. Diana was still asleep.

He stared into the valley below but didn't really focus on anything as the last nightlights of Quito still twinkled in the shadow of the Andes; day always comes later down there. Max was glad they lived so high up on the mountain ridge. Max was glad to have this house, this terrace, this eagle's nest. He was glad for some things and unhappy about others. It had always been like this for Max the cocoon turned into a butterfly...for Max who'd once been a sniper...who'd once been a chauffeur...and had been lost but now was found like that famous hymn said.

To the northeast masses of clouds, their tops turned to gold by the rising sun, draped the mountains. The lower halves of the clouds were icy blue with long, dangling, wispy strands that graced the base of the mountains over there. In a few minutes all the colors would change as the sun burned away the clouds and heated the air. The beautiful watercolor painting would be gone, replaced by another South American day.

Max should have slept well—-the idea of flying to the top of *Cayembe* in a customized Learjet 85 should have made him sleep like a baby, should have given him the sweetest dreams. But troubling thoughts creeping along the edge of his mind had kept him awake most of the night.

Max shook his head and scolded himself—-although he was sixtyish now he didn't feel a day over forty or thirty—-and he should live in the moment and be thankful for today, he should be grateful for each new day, and he ought not worry about getting older. He should be happy, he should put away all his bad thoughts forever. He should be thankful, as he took another sip of coffee, as he took every new sip of morning coffee each new day. And if he had to remain here in Quito, Ecuador for the rest of his time on earth it would be all right...he was happy or at least happier than before. His wife was happy. They had had enough difficulties...escaping that monster, that devil Pontius.

To have escaped that fiend was no small thing...that devil that relished the chase, and then the capture, and then torture and death. That man, that demon or whatever he was, that *sadist*. Max shivered...thinking these thoughts always made him shiver. He would always wonder when and if that devil might show up, suddenly, without warning. Max should have killed him. He should have killed the passenger too. They should have been two painted targets the moment before he let out his breath and squeezed the trigger as the army had taught him.

Diana joined Max with a mug of coffee of her own. Not saying a word, they stood side by side for a few minutes, letting the sun warm their face and their muscles and bones. Max wouldn't tell her about the thoughts he'd just had. Diana was happy and not sad at all—-she'd told him many times how happy she was—-how she was overjoyed about her job, about their freedom. She'd told him she thought less and less about finding that letter from that other chauffeur and his wife. She thought less and less about finding their wedding rings and whatnot. Sometimes she'd say that it all seemed so long ago...but sometimes she'd say it seemed like it had happened last week.

Diana, too, had been given a second chance, a new lease on life as they say. Diana, too, had escaped Pontius. And, even if they might think about him from time to time, they hardly spoke out loud about him anymore, and that was a good thing. Every second, minute, hour, day, week, month and year away from Pontius was a gift. Still, Max should have killed him and killed the passenger.

"Max. Can you believe it? We are going to the top of the volcano today?!"

Max took another sip and let a smile crease the side of his face. The smile rippled along the side of his downturned mouth and almost made him look glad. Then the smile was gone.

"What is it, Max?"

"I don't know...I have a feeling..."

"A feeling?"

"The doctor...Martin...he knows..."

"Knows? Knows what?"

"I feel like something big is going to happen...something beyond imagination...in the world, I mean...and to us..."

"Max."

"Yes?"

"We don't have to think about that now. Let's enjoy the day. Let's think about having fun. And you know what?"

"What?"

"I am going to ask Martin to dine with us tonight. I'm going to make Wiener Schnitzel. And we'll have Linzer Torte for dessert....and with the Wiener Schnitzel one of those Riesling wines from Chile—-they are as good as German Riesling. Max, we haven't had Austrian food for a long time."

"I can't wait..."

"Can't wait for what, Max? Having dinner with Martin or my Austrian cuisine or flying to the top of the volcano?"

"All three—-of course." Max was almost smiling again.

Diana liked having light, bantering conversations with Max. She wished they could have more of them. At least things were better than five years ago...and she would always tell herself this...that things indeed were better now...although she could hear in Max's voice that she was too optimistic, maybe. She could tell by the half smiles that came and went on his face.

Martin met them at the security gate accompanied by the airport security guard. It seemed they knew one another, Martin and the Ecuadoran. Martin must have flown into Quito before. It made sense. Any man that can afford a customized Learjet 85 had to have flown around the world many times, Max figured.

Martin was wearing a light khaki jumpsuit. The outfit made Max think about fighter pilots and World War 2 or maybe about one of the latest wars in the Middle East...wars that would last a few days or weeks until another cease fire would be called and another round of useless talks would begin.

"Do you like my flight suit?"

"Very nice," Max said.

"I know...I am still a kid when it comes to planes and things...planes are my escape, my fantasy...planes and my ranch in Mexico..."

"We all need *escapes*, Martin."

Diana had said it and caught the look of Max's self-imposed blank expression and raised eyebrows.

Martin was studying both of them now, trying to read thoughts, perhaps? Martin was smart in addition to being brilliant. Max knew he was right about Martin knowing *some things*. He knew more *things* than just cloning and eugenics.

"Martin...Diana and I would like you to have dinner with us this evening. Can it be arranged?"

The question obviously had caught Martin by surprise.

"Ahh...yes...yes...I would like that...I would enjoy that very much...I had planned to return to Mexico this evening, though...but...it's all right...I can wait until tomorrow. And where will we be going to dinner?"

"Our house. Wiener Schnitzel and Linzer Torte for dessert." Diana proudly sounded out the delicious words and then said, "Here is our address." She handed Martin a small piece of paper. "I'm afraid you'll have to take a taxi. I'll be making dinner and Max doesn't drive much..."

Martin grinned and said, "No problem...marvelous...I haven't dined like that in a very long time. Now, come, the plane is ready." He motioned with his head as well as his arms, directing them toward the shiny silver jet with royal blue markings on the tail. It was one gorgeous airplane. And it was going to be one gorgeous day to fly...

The serial numbers painted onto the jet's flanks were in black: XB17061900.

The numbers, the letters carried Max back to Salzburg...back to the airport...in an instant he was there once again...it was night...it was the month of June so many years ago.

Max could see the cold blue eyes of the passenger in the rearview mirror...those eyes...sifting him...testing him...analyzing him...mocking him?

At first Martin did not see Max staring at the serial number; he was distracted, helping Diana onto the retractable stairs coming down from the jet's door.

"Max?"

Max didn't hear.

"Max? We are ready."

"Ach...okay...sorry..."

Ten minutes later the control tower of Mariscal Sucre International Airport gave takeoff clearance to the Learjet 85 and Martin pushed forward on the throttles. A rush of adrenaline put Max into a state of ecstasy, as he sat in the right seat, acting like he was the co-pilot. Father could only have dreamed of such a thing! If only father could see him! All Max's bad thoughts converted to good ones now.

At one thousand meters above ground level Martin banked the airplane to the right, flying directly above the city center. Diana was in the passenger cabin, sitting in a custom leather seat. She'd taken out her camera to have it ready for taking photos of the volcano and the other peaks, ridges and valleys of the Ecuadoran Andes. Max turned around and looked at her. She was smiling back at him. Diana was having as much fun as her husband. If only the world could be like this always, if only life could be like this...

Max was tempted to take hold of the controls, just to see how it felt to have so much power in one's hands and fingers.

"Max. Do you want to fly the airplane?"

Martin had read Max's mind.

"Yes." Max nodded.

Max couldn't believe it...in a second or two he would be flying a Learjet!

"All right...just take hold, right and left, like this...and keep the nose about 5 degrees above the horizon....like this..."

Max did as told.

"Okay Max, now turn left 10 degrees...yes...like that...excellent...and now...turn to the right 10 degrees."

Max brought the wings back to level flight and Martin reduced power a bit. A Learjet 85 can accelerate to three hundred knots in a few seconds and Martin had planned to fly much slower, with the flaps lowered into first position, as he circled *Cayembe*. And he wanted to get within two hundred meters of the snowcapped cone-shaped peak. Diana would get a lot of great shots from so close up. And the day could not be better—-the air was crystal clear and there was scarcely any wind at all.

"All right Max, now turn the plane 10 degrees to the right and aim for the right side of the volcano...and pull back just a bit on the controls...to increase the rate of climb."

Fifteen minutes later they were above the right flank of *Cayembe* with its shimmering sunlit snowfields that could blind a man if he looked at them too long.

"I'll take the controls again...if you don't mind."

Martin could see how much fun Max was having.

"Sure..." Max let go but wished he could have flown the jet a little longer.

Martin pulled back a bit on the throttles and brought the airspeed to one hundred fifty knots. He lowered the flaps to position 1. He banked left to begin the first circle around the mountain. They were flying at an altitude of five thousand five hundred meters. The volcano looked close enough to touch. Max could see Martin was an excellent pilot, perfectly in sync with his airplane. Max wished he could have had the opportunity to become a pilot as he recalled Martin saying his mother's family had once been rich.

Max stopped thinking these thoughts...at least he would stop thinking them for now...but maybe later, during dinner, he could get Martin to tell more about his life...if Martin didn't mind telling.

Every man has a story...

CHAPTER 50

It was 22:00 hours. Max's favorite CD of German and Austrian composers was softly playing the classical guitar rendition of Beethoven's *Moonlight Sonata.*

Diana sat down once again after cleaning up the table and washing the dishes and Max poured the second bottle of Chilean Riesling into their three wine glasses and Martin toasted:

"To peace in the world...*paz en el mundo...Frieden in der Welt."*

"To peace..." said Diana.

Max didn't say anything. He was *transported* back to Munich, back to that night in the hotel bar. Pontius had used the same phrase—-*Frieden in der Welt*—-as a toast...a false toast...a mocking toast.

"Peace, Martin?"

"I know...it's not likely is it, Max?"

"One day there will be peace." Max declared.

"You believe that, Max?"

"Yes, we believe that, Martin." Diana said it.

"How will it happen, my friends? Iran has nukes now. Japan has them. Japan gave nukes to South Korea and Taiwan. China is *not happy*...not happy at all...but what can they do about it, say about it? They, like their neighbors, have experienced the threat of Islam...school bombings...that container ship blown up in Shanghai. Two airliners hijacked. Two railway stations bombed. The North Koreans are the only power in Asia hostile to the West but they are paralyzed; they know South Korea will nuke them if they make too much trouble. And the Germans are rearming...along with Poland...Ukraine is still boiling...there is talk of some kind of future alliance between the EU, Eastern Europe, and Russia...and even talk about *all the major Western Powers aligning themselves militarily* with China, Japan, South Korea, India, Southern and Western Africa...and...now that America has been brought to heel she too sees the wisdom of this."

Martin continued his analysis of *geopolitics* and *military applications* for another five minutes until Max interrupted.

"Martin. Your German is flawless."

"I grew up speaking it, Max. My father..." Martin took a long sip of wine. "My father was from Germany. And I lived there for five years...in Frankfurt...I earned a doctorate in German history...1840s-1940s...with *specialization* on the Third Reich—-the Holocaust...the *Vernichtungslager...*"

"The war ruined my father, Martin...and Diana's father lost..."

"Don't go there, Max." Diana turned to Martin. "My father was horribly wounded...you are a doctor...you can imagine..."

It was quiet in the living room of the South American house high above Quito, Ecuador. A cool night breeze blew in from the top of the ridge high above the house and lifted the white lacy curtains covering the bay window on the opposite side of the room. The world was letting out a long sigh and taking in a deep breath. The curtains settled in place once more.

"The numbers on the jet, Martin. What do they mean? I know the letters mean the jet is from Mexico but the numbers? 17061900? "

Max's question made the room quieter still. Diana was amazed at her husband, Max. Nobody asks questions like this but Max just did. Martin glanced at the clock on the wall to the left of the lacy curtains.

"I should call a taxi before it's too late."

"It's already too late," Max said.

"You'll spend the night, Martin." Diana smiled.

"Are you sure?"

"Of course. The guestroom is very comfortable. I'll go freshen up everything...it'll only take a few minutes..."

Diana came to her feet and headed for the other side of the house where the extra bedroom lay. She didn't want to tell Martin that he would be the first guest they'd ever had and that the sheets, pillows, and blankets were brand new. No one had slept in them. No one had used the bathroom or the shower either. She needed to make the bed. She needed to dust a bit. She needed to make sure the shower was perfectly clean and that nothing smelled of mold or mildew. She needed to leave the living room for a bit; she couldn't believe Max had asked that question.

As she tidied up everything she thought once again about Max's sketches in the margins of the Bible or the sketches and doodles on the scraps of paper tucked here and there—-the weird-looking animals, beasts, dragons, bears, leopards, a lion or two, horns on the beasts. It was therapeutic for Max to draw apocalyptic images, Diana supposed. One of these days she would ask her husband the precise meaning of them. Some of the doodles and sketches were of Max's rifle and scope and there were some mathematical equations. Diana had a sick feeling about the meaning of those but couldn't quite figure them out...she couldn't be sure...and she'd never said anything...Max needed to study, make sketches, doodles...he needed to relieve his anxiety.

Diana returned to the living room and sat down in her easy chair. Max was still sitting in his and Martin was still sitting in the exact same spot on the sofa facing them. It would appear they'd not moved nor spoken the entire time she was in the guest bedroom. The lacy curtains were still rising and falling in the night breeze.

"Max, before I tell you the meaning of the numbers let me tell you more about me...let me *cut to the chase* as they say in English."

Max nodded his approval. Yes, let the doctor tell his story. Nothing the man could say would surprise Max or Diana. Anyone that had had dealings with a devil like Pontius wouldn't be surprised by anything. Max and Diana had seen it all; they'd seen too much; they knew too much; they knew things they wished they didn't.

Martin sat erect on the edge of the sofa. He clasped his hands and looked intensely into Max's eyes and Diana's eyes, too. He was readying them for what he was about to say.

"My father kept a diary. It was bound in a black leather cover and this thick." Martin illustrated how thick it was, using his right index finger and thumb. "It is the size of Tolstoy's novel *War and Peace*. The diary covered the war years...World War 2...then the Cold War...and the *network* was involved in the Kennedy assassination...and they had Oswald murdered...the *network* managed the KGB...and they were behind 911...it's all there in the diary...Max, my father wrote about 911 several years before it happened...and he wrote about his childhood...his love of horses...his life before..." Martin stopped and took a mouthful of cool night air. "His life before the Reich...and there are things in the diary about the prophecies, about the Prophet Daniel, about the Revelation...they believe they can win... they believe they can defeat God...they believe they are gods, or God."

Martin was pouring out words like water from a pitcher, like water from a waterfall, words he'd kept stored away for a very, very long time.

Max and Diana were frozen by the words, frozen like two blocks of ice.

"The Reich?" Max asked.

Diana was still frozen.

"*Das Reich*, Max."

"Who...who are you, Martin..." Max couldn't finish his words.

"My father was Martin Bormann."

Diana thawed out and gasped....it was a short, quick gasp like she might be choking.

Max was a block of ice again...he was a sniper again, cold and calculating, looking through the scope, his trigger finger moving into position...the laser dot was on the target, painting it...

"But they found his remains, Martin...the West German government issued an official statement... more than forty years ago...in 1972." Diana said it. She had to say it. It had to be true, it must be true.

"It wasn't true, Diana, they didn't find his bones, they didn't find the right skeleton, the right remains....the DNA test was falsified. My father escaped to Italy...to Torino...then south to Bari...he paid a lot of money, most of it in gold, and secured passage on a freighter to South America...he went to Paraguay...Brazil...Argentina...then to Mexico...it's all in the diary...there are details no one else would know...about *the Reich...about him...*"

"About him? About who, Martin?" Max asked the question and waited for the answer...but he already knew what the answer would be.

"Hitler."

Diana came to her feet and went to the wall and turned off the ceiling light. It was too bright in the room for sitting and chatting this late. She dimmed the lights in the two lamps and said, "That's better."

Better? Ha! How could anything be better now, at this moment after hearing this? The doctor claimed he was the son of Martin Bormann? Diana thought about her mother and father and how her mother had taken care of her father. Diana thought about her father's broken body, his war wounds that made him look like a freak. The Nazis had done that to her father, Nazis like Martin Bormann. And now she was supposed to believe Bormann's son was here, tonight, in her house?

"Go on, Martin." Max said it like he wasn't completely sure if he wanted the doctor to go on or not.

Martin could sense Max's uncertainty.

"Max, do you really want me to continue?"

"Yes. Please. Go on..."

Max sounded a bit more certain.

"The numbers on my airplane are my father's date of birth...17 June 1900. But I didn't have the numbers put there to celebrate him...they are there as an act of contempt. I hated him. I still hate him. He ruined my mother...he stole money and other property from her... he used her money to help himself and his friends in the *network*...if I hadn't intervened I would have been left with nothing...he was a despicable man...a murderer...Nazi to the end...the numbers remind me of my mission...I must tell the world about genocide, eugenics...cloning..."

"And the diary?"

"I have it, Max. My father gave it to me before he died in 2008. He told me I would *enjoy* reading it...that it would make everything very clear...that it would be a help to me and my research on cloning...and then he laughed...he said no one would believe me if I showed them what was in the diary...he said I would be a laughingstock...he was a horrible man, Max...horrible."

Max wanted to ask Martin where the diary was hidden but he would wait. Martin would tell him when Martin was ready.

"Continue, Martin." Now Max was sure he wanted Martin to go on. The point of no return had been reached.

"*The Odessa File*...was named by my father in the diary...the file was real, Max...it existed...my father was part of the *network*...the *network* helped him get to Mexico...from Paraguay, Brazil and Argentina...they'd helped him get out of Europe in 1945."

No one said a word for a long two minutes until Max said: "XB 20041889."

It was Martin's turn to be frozen. He was ice. His face looked frosted. He shivered a bit.

"Max. I have seen those numbers. They are on the Gulfstream V..."

"Where, Martin...where have you seen the numbers...where is the Gulfstream V?"

"It's parked in a camouflaged shelter at the side of the airstrip...once in a while they fly it...the airstrip is about 50 kilometers north of my ranch...I've seen the jet landing...I've seen the numbers... the first time I saw them I was flying the Learjet at a lower altitude...I saw the runway in the jungle, the villa...the villa is huge...has high walls...and then the jet came in for a landing and I saw the numbers...20041889...and I have seen the numbers on that jet a number of times while flying near the villa in my De Havilland...and I have seen *him*...it seems he goes to the rooftop of the villa in the evenings...it must be his habit...I have seen him there every time I've made a pass over the villa in the late afternoon...he is always alone..." Martin paused and then asked: "Max...how do you know those numbers?"

Martin's voice was thin and dry. He looked suddenly tired, like he'd not slept well for days, weeks, months or years.

"I was a chauffeur. I picked him up at the airport...I took him back to the airport...in Salzburg...I saw the numbers on the Gulfstream V...the *silver* Gulfstream V...I have seen his eyes, his face. It's him."

"When, Max? When did you see his face?"

"2008."

"Nine years ago?"

"Nine years." Max said it as if these nine years could be a hundred.

"Max and Diana. You are hiding here? In Quito? In Ecuador? In South America?" Martin tilted his head slightly to one side as he asked.

Martin had it figured out. At least he had *some* of it figured out.

"Yes," Diana said. "And we are happy...aren't we, Max?"

"Yes...happy..." Max said it but wasn't as sure as his wife about being happy here in Quito, Ecuador.

"I wish I could show you the diary but it is in Mexico. I would like you to read it. My father was an *aficionado* of the prophecies. He wrote about a vision the Fuehrer had had...about himself...about the blood...he wrote about the world being divided into..."

Max interrupted Martin."Into ten kingdoms...and there would be four beasts...the lion, the bear, the leopard with four heads...and the..."

Now it was Martin's turn to finish Max's sentence for him "...and the fourth beast with ten horns would be different from the others and would crush them. How do you know this, Max?"

"I am an *aficionado*."

It was perfectly silent again until Diana spoke.

"What Max means, Martin, is we are believers...we are Christians...we believe the prophets."

"Ah." Martin didn't know what to say so he just said "ah."

"And you, Martin? Do you believe?"

Another soft night breeze came through the window, making the curtains lift and lightly brush the sill and wall on either side. The curtains settled into place. The breeze was gone. The room was calm except for their beating hearts.

"I wish I could...but I don't...I mean I don't know...and then sometimes I think I know too much...I guess I am an educated cynic...but I believe this much...I believe I am alive because they have decided not to kill me...at least not to kill me yet...my father ended the diary with these words: *Lassen Sie mein Sohn Leben.*"

"Deja que mi hijo viva." Diana translated it into Spanish and then said it in English, *"let my son live."*

"Martin, what do you want me to do?"

The doctor come to his feet and declared: "I...I need...I need some kind of...I need an end...a solution...resolution...in the diary it says he would come back...and they would take over the world...conquer it...he is there, in the villa, in his fortress, Max."

Martin stepped to the window and stared into it. He was tortured. He'd been this way for a long time.

"Martin, what do you want me to do?"

Martin seemed not to notice the question again.

Diana was shaking. She'd noticed the question. She knew what Max was asking.

"What do you want me to do, Martin?"

Martin started talking again, still lost in his tortured thoughts. "They brought him back...my father brought him back with the blood...they are going to destroy the world...he..."

Martin stopped talking and turned to Max and asked, "What do you mean?"

Finally Martin had noticed Max's question.

Diana was still shaking and regretting ever having invited the doctor for dinner.

"I can take him out." Max's tone was icy, it was sure, it was focused, it was a laser dot on a target.

"You? You can...take him out?"

"I will kill him...I will kill the passenger."

"How would you do that, Max?"

"I was a sniper in the army. I was as good as America's Navy Seals or any of their Special Ops people. I'm still good."

Martin remained standing, still lost in his tortured thoughts until at last he recited the numbers: "20041889."

"The year the passenger was born—-20 April 1889," Max said.

"They cloned him, Max...they cloned him!"

"I know..."

It was Diana's turn to speak.

"Max, the prophecies...they cannot be changed...it's all prewritten."

"Billions are going to die...war is coming soon...unless I..." As Max said it he avoided eye contact with his wife.

"Unless you what, Max? Do you think if you kill him it would change anything? It is all pre-writ-ten. Diana trisected the word as slowly as possible.

Martin sat down once more. Now it was his turn to ask the same question Max had asked three times before.

"What do you want me to do, Max?"

"Fly me to Mexico...to Merida...fly me to your ranch in the De Havilland, the one with the big tires...then fly me closer to the villa...we could find a clearing somewhere...I could walk in from there."

"Max, the jungle...it's very bad...snakes...spiders...bugs..."

Max ignored the warning about the jungle and said, "And once it's done, once he's dead, I will get back to you as fast as I can and you will fly me back to Ecuador." It all sounded quite simple the way Max said it.

Max looked at Diana. But she wasn't looking at him. She was looking at Martin, pleading with her eyes not to take her husband on a suicide mission to the Yucatan. They had been happy here in Ecuador. They had been kept safe by the Almighty. They were alive. If they took matters into their own hands they would lose His protection. Diana was sure of it.

Max reached for her hand and took it gently into his.

"Diana, he is pure evil like Pontius...I know the prophecies cannot be changed...but this may not be the time...this could be something entirely different...we don't really know."

As Max said it he knew he was wrong. But a part of him thought he could be right. And if he was right, killing the passenger was the only option.

Diana was weeping.

Martin was embarrassed now and said, "Max, you don't have to do this."

Through her tears Diana managed to blurt out, "Max...the one hundred eighty photos and the dream?! Do you think that was a coincidence now? Do you think escaping the EU and coming here was a coincidence? My job, is that a coincidence? Being safe here? Is that a coincidence? And how many times have we said we would lose our protection if we acted against the prophecies?"

Martin didn't quite understand what Diana was saying but didn't ask for an explanation either. It was clear his new friends had suffered as much as he, perhaps they'd suffered more.

"And do you think it is a coincidence that we met Martin? Is it a coincidence he has seen the passenger's jet and knows the numbers? I have to do it, Diana." Max turned toward Martin and said, "Martin, can you come back for me in two weeks? I'll have everything ready by then."

"Yes...I can. Two weeks. "

It was almost 02:00 hours. Diana had gone to bed fifteen minutes ago after explaining to Martin a few things about the guestroom and bath. Martin had gone to bed as well. But Max knew he wouldn't sleep so he wrapped up in his blanket, went to the patio and stared at the stars, and wished he could go to the Flughafen one more time with his father.

CHAPTER 51

Max read the twenty-third Psalm flawlessly until he came to the words "the valley of the shadow of death" and Diana began to cry. She'd not cried since that night two weeks ago when Max had made the final decision to kill the passenger.

He reached across the small kitchen table and took her hand as she looked up with tears that were leaving wet streaks running down her cheeks.

"Diana...please..."

"No, Max, I cannot agree with this."

Max returned to reading the Psalm and finished it. He closed the Bible and set it to one side.

He got up from the table and stepped to the small foyer by front door of the house. He picked up the larger duffle bag, the khaki-toned one, lying on the tile floor there. He picked up the smaller duffle, the black one, and slung it over his right shoulder. The smaller duffle held the Glock 9 mm in its holster and the rifle now broken down into several pieces. There were more items, a couple of towels, some underwear and socks, inside the black duffle to "fill it up" and make it look "normal." Max was dressed in tan dress slacks, a long sleeve, open collar, loose-fitting off-white shirt, a light-weight tweed sports jacket, and black slip-on dress shoes. He looked innocent enough. Nobody would know he was really a mercenary. Nobody would know he was about to do an assassination. His larger duffle held his camouflage trousers, long-sleeve camouflage shirt, olive drab baseball cap and a pair of jungle army boots he'd picked up for next to nothing in a Quito flea market.

"It's time..." he said.

Diana slipped into a light-weight black windbreaker, picked up the car keys from the table and walked ahead of Max through the door and to the car. Max stayed back to lock the front door and put the keys in his pocket.

If all went according to plan he would return in four or five days, a week at most.

Martin had assured Max he could get the rifle onto the jet because the security in General Aviation parking was lax. Plus the supervising guard there was friendly, and even more friendly after getting a *bonus* of a thousand dollars from Martin. Martin was on friendly terms with all the security at the airports where he landed...in *Latino America*. They *liked* his gratuities. They *appreciated* their dear friend.

Max and Diana didn't exchange one word as she drove the Camry to the airport as she stared straight ahead or glanced in the mirror from time to time to watch the other traffic. Max glanced at her face a couple of times and looked away again.

They came to the security gate and halted. Diana reached down to her left and pulled on the floor latch to pop open the trunk. Max got out of the car and went to the trunk to retrieve his gear. He looked toward the security gate and fence once again.

Martin was over there, walking toward them, the Learjet 85 lay thirty meters behind him, all shimmering in the morning sun. That bird would take them to Mexico in less than four hours at a cruising speed of 459 knots/.80 mach.

Max came to Diana's window but it was closed. She was staring down at her hands and shaking her head. Max wanted to say good bye, he wanted to tell her how much he...

The window scrolled down, making a soft whirring sound.

She looked up at him.

"Diana..."

"I love you, Max...I will always love you..."

Martin was waving to them now, waving but not smiling. Martin must have sensed how distraught Diana was. He knew.

"And I will always love you..."

Max turned toward the gate and Diana backed away in the car and turned toward the streets of Quito and the road which would take her to their house. It was Saturday and tomorrow was Sunday and she had no particular plans. She looked toward the security gate one last time but Max was no longer there. They'd already boarded the plane.

CHAPTER 52

The Yucatan Jungle lay beneath them, sprawling out for hundreds of kilometers until vanishing into a misty, milky white horizon where land and sky met and mingled. The jungle was a gigantic carpet, a huge tapestry woven with hundreds of strands of emerald and darker greens and green-reds, green-browns, chalky grays and specks of sandy yellow dappled with more tones of gray. Most of the jungle was still intact but swaths of it had been cut down and chopped up into squares, ovals and rectangles. Some of it had been cleared into larger tracts and turned into cattle ranches or hardscrabble farms managed by the local Mayan people. And all of the Yucatan, forested or cleared, was home for snakes, scorpions, spiders and other crawly creatures watching and waiting in the thick, dark forest or the sun-scorched scrublands of the clearings.

Martin turned his head to the left and peered through the side window of the cockpit. He was trying to spot something out there in the vastness. Now he reached for his aviator glasses and slipped them on, once again scouring the jungle, trying to find whatever it was he was looking for.

"Max, can you hand me the binoculars? They are in the compartment to your right."

Max fished out the binoculars and slipped them from the brown leather case.

"Gracias."

Max could tell from the cockpit flight data displays that they were cruising at an altitude of five thousand meters and an indicated airspeed of three hundred fifty knots. They would have to slow down and fly lower if they expected to see anything. Martin's next movements confirmed Max's thoughts.

Martin leaned forward and turned a dial to change the jet's course from 360 to 45 degrees...due north to northeast. The jet turned itself to the right and leveled out after a few seconds. He lowered the altitude to three thousand meters and reduced throttle a little. The Learjet's nose came down as the computer automatically adjusted the rate of descent to 400 meters per minute.

Martin had placed the binoculars to his eyes and now was looking over the instrument panel, again trying to spot something.

"There...there it is...the villa...here, Max, take the binoculars...the villa is about five degrees to the right of our current heading...we're going down to three thousand meters to make a couple of passes around it...but I'm going to stay as far from it as I can...I don't want to *upset* anyone...you should still be able to see enough with the binoculars. I have a camera too." Martin produced a beautiful Nikon with telephoto lens. "I'm going to get a few shots."

Max peered into the binoculars, moving them side to side, trying to find the villa, trying to find the place where the passenger lived, the place where the passenger would soon die and go to hell. And Max had to do this—-for the world, for humanity—-and truth be told he had to this for himself...truth be told he'd not felt this alive, ever. A man must find his purpose, his *raison d'etre,* his reason for existence, his destiny. And Max would find his destiny via slaying this monster, this dragon. Max was King David hunting Goliath but Max's slingshot was a sniper's rifle, a British L115A3 AWM with a fine scope, a Zeiss Victory Diarange 2.5-10x50 Rapid Z 800. The rifle had an effective range of fourteen hundred meters but he would try to get within a thousand meters of the villa, if possible. A few days prior to leaving for Mexico, Max had spray painted the rifle in greens, browns, and grays...

Max could see Diana's face and her tears flowing down her cheeks. He could see her now...she was sitting outside on the patio, reading the Bible maybe, praying for her husband. Diana was the best wife a man could ever wish for....she was a trooper...she was tough, intelligent, smart, brave, practical...she was beautiful...she had a beautiful figure...and a beautiful soul...it had been far too long since they'd made love. Once this was over, they would make love again...they would make love often, again...it would be like it was before...they would be thirty again.

Max spotted the villa.

"I see it, Martin."

"Okay. Good. I am going to fly to the left of the villa and then turn right to make a couple of circles around it. You can take some photos from your side. Then I am going to reverse course and take some from my side. We'll upload them later and figure out..."

"And figure out the best spot for me to wait for him." Max said the words without any emotion at all.

"Max. After landing we'll take the De Havilland to my ranch. Tomorrow we will fly closer to the villa...low and slow...we'll try to find a clearing...I think I can recall one now... the clearing will be your drop off point...we'll go in early, day after tomorrow, while it's still dark...to cut down on noise, I'll do a dead stick landing, engine out, glider-style, Max...I'll wait for you there, in the clearing...you call me *when it's done...* and call me again when you are fifteen minutes out, so I can start the engine and be ready to go... and we'll fly back to the ranch, lay low for a day or two...then fly back to Merida...and continue on to Quito in this plane..."

They'd already devised most of this plan as they flew from Ecuador but Martin wanted to go over it again...and they'd likely go over it a few more times before the day after tomorrow arrived.

"When it's done," said Max, quoting Martin. And then he said, "Get me within five kilometers and I'll be all right."

CHAPTER 53

2 days later...03:30 hours.

Martin reached across the polished-oak kitchen table and placed four extra clips of 9 mm ammunition in front of Max.

"Take these, Max...you might need extras...one never knows."

Martin now reached behind him and pulled a Colt .45 from its holster at the center of his lower back. It was shiny black with a few scratches on the barrel. It was beautifully aged. It held eight rounds. The Glock held seventeen.

Max took a sip of hot, black coffee, set down the blue mug and said, "Thanks. I doubt if I'll need it but you are right...one never knows."

"Are you hungry, Max? Would you like *huevos rancheros*? With a couple of tortillas perhaps?"

"No. I'm still full from last night's dinner—-you grill beautiful *fajitas*...all that beef made me dream in color...it always does. And I can't eat anyway...not until this is over, not until it's done."

"Your dreams, Max, were they good?"

"No."

"Neither were mine." Martin paused for a second to consider his dreams and said, "I am sorry the clearing is so close to the villa...three kilometers is too close, Max...and the other clearing is too far...ten kilometers is too far...or, maybe it's not, Max...maybe it would be best to be so far away...it would make it more difficult for anyone chasing you...but it would make it more difficult for you as well...there is no easy way, Max."

"I'll be all right. I can easily walk three kilometers in thirty minutes...if the jungle isn't too dense."

"You know, he might not be there...he might not appear...he might..."

"Martin. We've come too far. This must be done. And if he's not there, there is nothing we can do...except...except come back here and wait until tomorrow...or wait several days, a week...and try again...we can keep trying until we get him...if you have the time, that is."

Martin ran his left index finger along the barrel of the .45, mulling over Max's words.

"Sorry, Max. You are right. But what if he *is* there and what if...?"

Max cocked his head at Martin's question.

"What if?"

"What if something goes wrong? What if you miss?"

"Martin. It's too late. It has to be done. You showed me the diary. You are right, there are things in it no one could know unless they were there. The diary is true. The *network* is real. Their *plans* are real. Your father was Martin Bormann. And I am sorry you had to suffer...I am sorry for what he did to your mother...it is time for justice...the passenger must die...he must be stopped. And if I miss..."

Max hesitated for a few moments, searching for the words.

"Tell me, Max."

"If I miss I will take it as a sign from God. And I will get back to you as fast as I can and we will forget the whole thing...it will be like it never happened."

Martin looked at his watch and announced the hour:

"03:40."

Max made sure his watch was in sync and said:

"Let's go to the plane."

CHAPTER 54

The flight to the jungle clearing only took fifteen minutes which seemed to Max like an hour as Martin flew the De Havilland at tree-top level. A couple of times, Max thought he could hear the belly of the aircraft brushing against leaves and branches but it was only the rush of wind. Of course Martin wouldn't allow the plane to touch the trees and Max put away the silly notion. Martin was too good a pilot to allow something like that. Still Max wondered exactly how close they got to the tree tops...it couldn't have been more than three or four meters. There was just enough moonlight to see just enough to scare the daylights out of Max.

"Okay. Here comes the clearing—-and...engine is out. We're going in, Max." Max could sense the propeller stopping as the engine noise ceased.

It was so quiet inside the airplane and outside the airplane...now become a glider. A dead stick landing from this height would only allow one opportunity...one chance to do it right.

At two meters above the ground Martin flared the plane, pulling back on the controls and lifting the nose to break the rate of descent and slow the airspeed so the De Havilland could land inside the clearing and stay there. It would be disastrous if the plane ended up stuck inside the trees at the far side of the clearing . It could be impossible to free it and their only way of escape back to the ranch would be on foot...40-50 kilometers on foot in the Yucatan jungle.

The big fat tires bounced and bounced again before the entire flying machine settled down and coasted to a beautiful stop.

"You see, Max? Piece of cake...no problem...no problem at all. Now, let's unload and get this bird turned around so she's ready for takeoff."

Neither man spoke as they did exactly what Martin had ordered—-unloading Max's rifle and small rucksack where he carried a bag of mixed nuts and some dried fruit and a four bottles of water. He would force himself to eat to keep up his blood sugar. But right now, he had no appetite.

He was traveling light this morning. It seemed he'd been traveling light for a long time already, since leaving Berchtesgaden. Max knew he'd be traveling light from now on...until his time came to depart this world. It's better that way...to travel light.

"Martin. If I don't make it I want you to tell Diana to go back to her family." Max stopped his words and took a deep breath. "Or..."

Martin waited for Max to finish.

"Or perhaps she and you...you and Diana..."

"Max."

"No. I mean it...she might be too afraid to go back... and then she would have nowhere to go except remain in Quito, alone."

"I am honored, Max. But it won't come to that. No matter what happens...you will make it..."

"It could happen...could be I won't make it..."

Martin waited to answer, to reply, to say something that would make Max feel better. This was a moment of life or death. This was a moment of finality.

"All right, Max. I will look after Diana. I promise."

"Thank you, my friend."

Martin glanced at his watch and announced coolly:

"It's 04:15. First light will be around 05:00."

"Yes," said Max. "05:00. I can get there by 05:30. I'll have most of the day to look around once I'm close...plenty of time for the best possible shot."

Max took one of the bottles of water from the rucksack, twisted off the cap, and toasted: "*Salud, Martin. Y gracias, mi amigo. Gracias por cuidar a Diana.*"

"Max. Your Spanish. It's good. You said it perfectly."

Max took another sip of *agua* and recapped the bottle.

Neither man spoke for forty minutes as each man leaned his back against the fuselage of the De Havilland, each man lost in a thousand thoughts, each man wondering how it had come to this, each man taking his place now on the world stage, waiting for the curtain to rise...waiting for first light and for the rising sun to follow.

"05:00...I'm going in."

"All right, Max."

Max slung the rucksack over his shoulders and tightened the straps. He slung the rifle over his upper body with the strap resting diagonally across his chest.

"Max. *El machete.*" Martin handed it to him now.

"Yes, of course...*por supuesto...gracias amigo.*"

Max hefted the machete. It had good balance...it was a good machete.

Max vanished into the trees and vines at the edge of the clearing and Martin said a prayer and could not recall if he'd ever prayed before.

CHAPTER 55

The first two kilometers had been fairly easy walking. The jungle had been thin there and Max had been happy about that. But the last kilometer, the last thousand meters were covered in randomly woven swaths of dried, tangled-up vines and knotted, waist-high trees underneath the vines. The gnarled, contorted trees were holding up the tangled vines, creating a secondary canopy of jungle which rose to Max's chest. Hacking a thousand meter pathway through that part of the Yucatan took three hours of miserable chopping and slicing and pulling away branches and vines with the machete and with his gloved hands as he worried about snakes and spiders or biting and stinging insects like fire ants or hornets—-all such critters had to be there, down below him, in the murky semi darkness beneath the crispy vines. This expending of physical and mental energy could be a bad sign, a bad omen, a very bad omen, a very bad sign. Max had not planned for this.

At least the hacked-down path would be easy to see and easy to use after he'd done the deed, after he'd killed the passenger.

After killing the monster he would run as fast as possible back to Martin and the clearing and the waiting airplane with its engine all revved up, ready to airlift them to safety.

But these three hours of whacking and hacking had exhausted him and it was only 08:00. He would try to recover some of that lost energy as he rested and waited for the target to appear in the afternoon.

Max threw himself to the ground.

There was the villa, there via a break in the thick brown and green shoulder-high undergrowth he could see a section of the villa and its walls. The edge of the jungle lay barely fifty meters in front of him. That edge had been impossible to see until this split second. He clutched a clump of damp, decaying jungle floor and blinked his eyes. He spat away some leaves that had got into his mouth.

He should have been more careful. He should have known how close he was.

He looked at his hand, the one grabbing at the clump of leaves and greasy mud. The wrist above the hand was pretty scratched up. Some of the scratches would qualify as cuts and qualify for first aid. His other wrist was no better. Blood seeped from both wrists. He could not afford to be injured like this. He needed every part of him working in sync, functioning perfectly for taking the shot. And he was certain he would only get one shot.

Sweat flowed down his forehead, soaking the bandana tied around his head. He fished out the other bandana from his shirt pocket. He tore it in two and wrapped each wrist as best he could. The raw, sliced skin on both wrists was burning. Everything in his body was burning—-it was so steamy and so hot and it was only 08:00. Later it would be even hotter and steamier.

A snake slithered by a meter to his left and turned right, crossing in front of him. It was a pit viper—-Martin had shown him a bunch of photos of Yucatan snakes and had specifically told Max to avoid this one.

Max stayed frozen...in spite of the heat he turned himself into ice...do not move, do not move, do not move. The snake coiled up and lifted its head. Could it sense Max's body heat from a meter away? Max readied the machete but the snake moved off, turning left and vanishing into the bush.

He picked himself up and moved to his right. The rooftop terrace would be on that side of the villa, he was sure about it. Martin had briefed him well, pointing to all the photos he'd taken and enlarged, using some special software. Martin would have made an excellent intelligence officer.

Max crouched low and dropped the rifle and rucksack at his side. He reached into the rucksack and slid out the binoculars. He placed them to his eyes and panned back and forth. The villa was a fortress more than it was a villa—-a fortress with a low profile, a long rectangular affair with a stucco wall of chalky gray covering two-thirds of the villa's height. Only the rooftop terrace and the tile roof showed above the top of the wall. There was razor wire running atop the entire length of the wall...razor wire and metal antennae and discs and other kinds of sensors.

He took a long drink of water and prayed his water supply would last long enough to do the job and get back to Martin and the airplane. The water had to last. There was no alternative. There were no springs or wells. The water had to last, that's all.

Max crept and crawled more and more to his right, moving perhaps two hundred meters from the point where he'd first spotted the villa. If he kept going he'd be squarely abreast of the rooftop terrace, the place where the passenger was first seen by Martin.

But Max had seen the passenger long before his friend, Martin—-he'd seen him at the airport in Salzburg, in the rearview mirror of the Mercedes...the reflection of those unblinking eyes and that perverse little smile laughing at him in the mirror..and Max had seen that ridiculous little jig the passenger had danced in the driveway as Pontius looked on...Max would kill the passenger soon; it would be a pleasure to remove this beast from planet earth and send him back to hell.

Five meters to his right was a tree split into two separate trunks making a perfect v-shape. The v-shaped tree lay about three meters inside the edge of the jungle. If Max could make a place to sit three or four meters up in the tree it would be a perfect firing position—-high enough visually to clear the top of the razor wire atop the perimeter fence, high enough to get a good shot and far enough inside the jungle to remain undetected. Plus, if he could slide down one of the tree trunks for a meter or two, he could safely jump down the remaining distance. He had to minimize the chance of injuring a leg or foot or ankle. He could not imagine having a broken or sprained ankle and having to run three kilometers through the jungle.

A wave of negative thoughts washed over him like someone dousing him with a bucket of ice cold water. Max wished this dirty business was over. He wished he was in the De Havilland with Martin, flying back to the ranch, and later flying back to Ecuador in the Learjet 85. Max wished he'd listened to his precious wife and stayed home. This was madness.

But he was here now. He had a job to do now. He had to make a seat, a place to sit and wait in the v-shaped tree. He had to focus on the mission. Nobody else would do it for him. Nobody else, in the entire world, except Martin and Diana even knew he was here. Nobody else among the masses of humanity could know what they knew

Max unloaded his gear, carefully setting down the rifle next to the tree. He set down the rucksack next to the rifle. Once the deed was done he would get down from his perch, pick up the rucksack, slide it onto his back, grab up the rifle and be off.

He cut thirty to forty branches into meter-long sticks and laid them in a row and tied them together with some string and lifted them up and placed them inside the v. This would be the base of his tree-chair. Next he tied a few more branches together and created a back for the chair. Next he used even more string to bind the chair to the two trunks of the tree. Next he climbed up and tested the chair to see if it would hold.

It held him quite nicely as be bounced his weight a bit, up and down, up and down. The branches were moist and springy. The tree-chair was good. Very good.

Next he found a longer branch but did not remove the foliage. This branch would be in front of him like a curtain and support his rifle's barrel since there was no solid place for the bi-pod. He tied the leafy branch with more string, making sure it was tightly in place and could hold the weight of the rifle. Next he retrieved the rifle and got into his chair and placed the weapon's barrel across the top of the branch and aimed at the villa and terrace.

It was 09:35.

He put a round in the chamber.

Max was ready.

He took another drink of water. The first bottle of four was now empty. He had the second and third next to him in the chair. The fourth lay inside the rucksack, as a reserve for the trip back to the clearing.

Max crumpled the plastic bottle and stuffed it into a pocket. He didn't want to leave any DNA behind. It was bad enough his wrists had been bleeding but blood would be harder to find. DNA evidence left on a water bottle would be easy.

It was 09:40.

He whispered a prayer, for Diana, for Martin, for himself, and closed his eyes and fell asleep in two minutes.

CHAPTER 56

He woke up to some bugs crawling down his neck, trying to get inside his sweat-filled camouflage shirt. At first his grogginess kept him from realizing he was being invaded by spiders...as one of the arachnids took a detour, deciding to investigate the hair atop Max's head. Another had decided to check out his left eye. A third made the mistake of trying to get inside Max's mouth.

"Ppppffffffuuuuaaaggghhhhh....!!!"

Max spat and spat and sputtered and smacked himself in the face and smacked the top of his head and reached inside his shirt and dug out the hairy black creatures and cast them away into the air and to the ground below. He jumped to the jungle floor and tore open his shirt as he kept spitting and sputtering and using both hands and all ten fingers now to brush the short hair on his head. He had to get the little monsters out of there. He should have put on the army green baseball cap. He would in a minute, when this battle with the spiders was over.

He pulled off the shirt and opened his trousers, making sure no spider had gone in there. None had.

He quieted down and scolded himself for letting this happen. He'd made too much noise. He could have been spotted, he could have been heard. And he could have broken his leg jumping all the way down like that.

He was lucky. He'd not been bitten. The spiders were only doing what spiders do—-they'd sensed his body heat and sweat and had gone hunting there. He shivered despite the heat. Spiders had always struck fear in him spiders and snakes and scorpions. Max shivered again and thanked God he'd not been bitten and not broken a leg or ankle.

What time was it?

He slid back the shirt sleeve and looked at his watch.

15:00 hours.

15:03 hours to be exact.

He'd been asleep for more than five hours!

His bladder was full so he emptied it as he watched the villa and noted where the sun was now and how the shadows had grown longer and how the air was a bit cooler and a breeze had come up and there was thunder rolling somewhere in the distance. It might be raining soon. He retrieved the baseball cap from the rucksack and snugged it down tightly onto his head. If it rained the cap's visor would keep the water out of his eyes.

Max climbed the tree once again and sat down in the seat and once more placed the rifle in a firing position. He put his right eye to the scope and panned side to side a few times, scanning the entire scene. He ran the crosshairs along the top of the wall where the terrace lay...and...

Max stopped breathing.

His heart stopped beating.

His mouth and tongue went dry.

His throat went dry.

Adrenaline filled his body, his face, his throat, his head, his arms and hands and legs. He felt all ten toes in his feet. He felt his hands and fingers like he'd never felt them before. His thoughts raced about inside his brain.

He breathed. His heart started to beat again. He reached over and grabbed the water bottle, uncapped it, and took a sip, and recapped it, and set it down all the while keeping his right eye on...

The passenger.

There he was.

Max had not expected him so soon. A part of Max had not expected him at all.

But there he was, staring back at him. There he was, the passenger.

Barking...

What?!

There were dogs barking.

Max panned downward with the scope.

A pack of dogs looking like a crossbred combination of Doberman and Irish Wolfhound was trotting toward Max across the scrubland of the clearing surrounding the villa. There had to be at least fifteen or twenty of the canine beasts with grayish-black wiry hair and pointed, slender snouts.

Max panned upward to the top of the wall where the passenger had just been. The passenger had not moved.

He panned downward again. The dogs were a bit closer now. He panned upward again. There he was again, the passenger. Max took the rifle off safety and took a deep breath.

The dogs were letting out throaty howls. Max had to see what they were doing. One last time be panned downward. The dogs were sniffing all around, trying to pick up a scent, a trail—- and it would be Max's scent and Max's trail, once he'd jumped down and run off with his rucksack and rifle after killing the passenger.

He panned upward.

The passenger was staring into the space between them. And he was smiling that wicked smile.

Lightning split the air and rain fell like a pent up wall of water from behind a giant dam.

Max had to pull the trigger now. He had the passenger in the crosshairs. He had him painted.

Thunder crashed as the rifle spoke. But the passenger had vanished before the round left the barrel. Max knew it.

He scanned right and left, trying to spot him, trying to get another shot, another chance.

But there would not be a second shot, a second chance.

He panned downward once more to spot that pack of dogs.

There they were, still sniffing about. A couple of them were sticking their long snouts into the rain-filled air. One of them let out a long yelp and bolted toward the fence and the jungle. The rest turned and did the same. Some kind of panels or gates were opening in the perimeter fence...to let out the dogs.

And *the dogs of war* were coming for Max.

CHAPTER 57

Max jumped to the jungle floor, clutching the rifle in his hand. He'd landed well. He'd not injured his legs or ankles or feet. Another miracle...it had to be.

He picked up the rucksack, slung it over his back, synched it tight, and slung the strap on the rifle crossways on his chest.

The water bottle!

He'd left it in the seat in the tree. He had to retrieve it. He could not leave behind so much DNA.

Max climbed up the tree and grabbed the bottle. He slid down the tree trunk a bit, sorry for having to waste precious seconds, and jumped the rest of the way. But this was no time for remorse. He had to go, now!

He tucked the water bottle into one of his cargo pockets on his camouflage trousers. He took one more look across the open land just outside the edge of the jungle. The dogs were coming for him...all of them were coming for him now, as they followed the lead dog, the first one to catch Max's scent. Or maybe that dog had heard him returning up the tree to get the bottle of water.

It didn't matter now. The dogs were coming. The dogs of war had been released and Max was their enemy. Max had to be destroyed. That's why the passenger had been smiling. The passenger had let slip these dogs of war.

Max spun around and ran into the jungle. Now he was happy about the suffering he'd gone through to create the hacked-down path through the knotty little trees and bushes and vines. The dogs would be forced to run down this narrow path too. Even dogs could not get through the impenetrable, matted foliage on either side of the path. Even dogs as strong as a Doberman-Wolfhound combination could not do it.

Max ran about five hundred meters and slowed his pace because there was no way he could keep running so hard for the entire three kilometers. He tried his best to pick up the sound of the dogs.

And he heard them once again. And they had not stopped.

To his right, a couple of meters off the path, he spotted a huge, twisted tree branch, 3 meters long and 2 meters in thickness, leaning against the trunk of a tree. It appeared to be unattached. If he could get to it maybe he could drag it back to the path and create a barricade. It might thwart the dogs. It might slow them down long enough for Max to put more distance between them and their prey.

Carefully, he stepped off the path. Carefully, he stepped down on the matted vines between him and the branch. Carefully, he reached for it.

He grabbed it and pulled. It was indeed unattached. And it didn't weigh too much. He held it in both hands and, with a shot of adrenaline flowing into his body, hefted it above his head so it would not get tangled up in the vines. He tried to step back to the path using the same places he'd just stepped. He must not fall. The vines were bad enough to trap him, like a housefly in a spider's web, if he fell the wrong way. He wished he wasn't carrying the rucksack and rifle.

Max dropped the branch behind him, blocking the path. He grabbed at some vines, pulled them to him, and strung them out atop the big branch barricade. The big branch barricade topped with tangled vines looked pretty good. It might work.

Once again he ran as fast as he could as he listened as best he could to hear the dogs.

They were still coming. They had not let up. They were howling and barking and yelping. They were in a frenzy. The dogs were ferocious, vengeful, trained killers.

Max could imagine how bad it would be to be torn apart and eaten by a pack of vicious, murderous dogs. It couldn't be much different than being eaten by a pack of timber wolves or a pride of lions.

Run, Max! Run! You must get back to the clearing. You must get back to Martin and the airplane. You must get away from the dogs.

He had to call Martin so Martin could start the De Havilland's engine in time.

The plane had to be ready because Max would come bursting out of the jungle and running full force. There would be absolutely no extra time, not even a second.

He slowed a bit and fished the cell phone from his pocket and auto dialed Martin's number and placed the phone to his ear.

"Max?!"

"Martin! No time to talk! I'm about one-point-five kilometers out. Start the engine in ten minutes...dogs...ten minutes...dogs..."

"Dogs, Max?"

"Dogs—-a pack of them. They have my trail..."

Martin closed his eyes and squeezed every muscle in his forehead. A pack of dogs was chasing Max. They were chasing Martin's only true friend in this world besides Diana.

"Okay, Max. Engine start in ten minutes. Max? Are you there?"

Max wasn't on the phone anymore.

CHAPTER 58

It had quit raining a few hundred meters back. The unpredictable tropical thundershower had decided to go elsewhere. Max was sorry about that. A wet path would make it more difficult for the dogs to stay on his trail. Rain would dilute his scent. But now it was cork dry. The path was crispy and crinkly and crunchy. But at least the jungle was quite thin here and it would stay thin all the way back to the clearing and the plane and his friend...his only friend in the world besides Diana.

The barking and howling filled the air. The dogs had found their way around the barricade back there in that wet part of the jungle.

Five minutes had passed since Max had called Martin. Max prayed Martin had understood him about the engine and all. He prayed Martin had understood about the pack of angry, hungry, mean, vicious and nasty dogs. Max prayed Martin would start the plane's motor in five minutes, no more.

Max could not keep running like this. He had to slow down again and catch his breath.

He looked behind him. Two of the dogs were coming at him full speed from two hundred meters away. Max jerked the Glock from its holster and cocked it and waited five seconds and fired. He fired again and one of the dogs rolled multiple times as the weight of its dead carcass kept its momentum going. Max fired at the other one and its head came apart.

Three more dogs appeared, leaping and lunging over the dead bodies of the first two.

Max fired three times and made three more kills.

Martin heard the shots and calculated the distance. Max could not be more than five hundred meters from the clearing.

Martin jumped into the left seat of the airplane and started the engine. He didn't do a check list. He didn't need to do one. Plus there was no time for doing one anyway.

He reached to his right and pushed open the door. It had to be open so Max could hop in.

In spite of the engine noise, Martin thought he heard several more shots.

He took out his Colt .45 now. He might have to shoot some dogs...if he'd understood Max correctly, Max was being chased by dogs.

Martin wondered if Max had killed the passenger.

He would know soon enough...unless...

Unless dogs killed Max.

CHAPTER 59

What happened next could not be more horrible:

Max literally fell out of the jungle onto the edge of the clearing. He pulled himself up and stumbled, falling onto his knees and getting up again and spinning around and firing the Glock—-pop, pop, pop...as at least five dogs lunged at him...as at least five more leaped from the jungle...as Max kept firing, and firing, and firing as he ejected an empty clip and reloaded...as one dog after another yelped, and lunged, was struck by a bullet, and lay wounded or dead.

Martin set the parking brake on the plane and got out, Colt .45 in hand. He dashed to Max and the dogs and the big ball of reddish dust that covered all of them, man and beasts. He started firing, emptying the clip, and killing a couple of dogs. He reloaded and repeated.

This could be Martin's and Max's last stand in the Battle of the Yucatan Jungle. This could be it. And if the dogs won, who would know? Who would find them? How would Diana ever find out what had happened to her beloved husband, Max?

Now Martin was next to Max as both men fired and fired and fired and fired their pistols...until there were only four dogs left.

The dogs retreated to the tree line, fifty meters from the two men. They milled about, growling their throaty growls, and pawing the dirt like bulls in the ring, and watching their prey—-the two men they'd not yet killed and eaten.

"They are going to come at us again, Martin! We have to get inside the plane! I will count to three. On three, we run for it."

"Okay!" As he shouted okay, Martin caught a glimpse of Max's left leg. The camouflage trousers there were soaked in blood. Max had been bitten back there in the jungle. How much blood had he lost?

"One...two...three!"

The two men turned and ran and the dogs ran at them and Martin jumped up into the plane and plopped himself down in the left seat and Max tried to get into the plane too but could not. The rucksack had somehow snagged the door handle and the rifle's barrel was hitting against the side of the plane adding to this terrible, deadly predicament.

Martin had a knife in his right hand...a knife he'd pulled from thin air like a magician pulls a bird from his hat. Martin cut the straps of the rucksack in one second. The knife was sharper than a scalpel.

Miraculously, despite the rifle strap across his chest, Max got out of the rucksack and hurled it at the dogs. It distracted a couple of them.

But the rucksack didn't distract the other two—-as Max somehow fired the Glock again, emptying another clip again, and killing one of the two dogs charging at him.

Max got the rifle off him and handed it to Martin who managed to get set it down on the back seat. Max tried to pull the rest of himself up and into the right front seat.

"Aaaaahhh!!!"

The delay had given the other dog a chance to clamp its jaws onto Max's right foot, trying to tear off the boot, trying to get to flesh and bone and blood.

Martin revved up the engine and the De Havilland began to rollout for takeoff as Max kept screaming and shaking his right leg, trying with everything in him to shake off the dog, trying to dislodge its death grip on the boot and foot.

"Max! Here!"

Max grabbed the Colt .45 from Martin and drew a bead on the beast. He must not, not, not, not shoot himself in the right calf or foot or knee or thigh. He was bleeding badly enough from his left leg.

Max fired pointblank at the head and the horrific, murderous dog dropped to the ground with a thud...as the other two, the ones that had been sidetracked by the rucksack, bolted toward the airplane.

But it was too late for the dogs—-Martin had gone to full throttle and Max had closed the door and the De Havilland's tundra tires had left the ground...and Max closed his eyes and fought back his tears.

CHAPTER 60

Quito, Ecuador
August 2018

Max sat in his patio chair, wrapped like always in his plaid alpaca blanket. Diana sat opposite him, in her chair, wrapped in her alpaca blanket, as well. Neither spoke for a long ten minutes as the morning sun warmed the air. It was another Saturday, another weekend day of rest. Another South American day...as day after day after day passed, ad infinitum...

"We should drink our coffee, Max, before it gets cold."

Max's sadness wouldn't leave him. Diana knew it wouldn't leave him. And Max seemed to tire so easily these days. She'd tried to convince him to see a doctor but he'd said no, every time, until she'd stopped suggesting it.

"I'll get more coffee," Max said.

"No, Max. I will. You stay here."

"No."

Max tightened his grip on his cane with his left hand. With his right hand he held onto the edge of the table to steady him as he pushed his weight upward until he was once again in a standing position. He'd never imagined ending his time on earth as a disabled man but that's what he was now.

He turned to the house and the kitchen to fetch more coffee as his sandals made an unpleasant grating sound as he wheeled about. He planted the cane into the patio floor and began the short trek—-but every trek, every distance short or long, was difficult these days with a bad left leg, the leg that dog had nearly destroyed by ripping into the hamstring muscles and veins.

The dog had almost got the femur under the muscles and veins...the muscles and veins Doctor Martin had repaired as best he could that night in the ranch house in the Yucatan Jungle...that day they'd almost been killed. At least the dog hadn't severed the femoral artery. Max could have bled to death.

Martin had told Max to see a specialist in Quito, he'd said a specialist could do a better job of fixing things. But Max had refused. And, he was sixty-one years old now and could get through the rest of his earthly life with a cane and nobody could change his mind. But he was grateful Martin had repaired the leg well enough to walk, albeit with a cane and a limp, and had given him enough morphine and tetanus vaccine and antibiotics and that after a month he'd flown him back to Quito.

Max would never forget Martin standing next to the Learjet 85, waving *adios* to his friends, Max and Diana. And Max and Diana knew they'd never see Martin again. Indeed, they had decided it best never to meet again. Too much had happened and they would have to go on now, hoping and praying the authorities never figured out what Max and Martin were doing that day in the Yucatan. So far, nothing had happened. There had been no reports in the media—-radio, TV, internet. It would appear nobody had found Max's rucksack. It would appear nobody had checked the air traffic patterns, the radars, from that day. It would appear that flying the airplane so close to the treetops had made them invisible that terrible day.

Part of Max wanted the authorities to find out. Part of him rebelled against vanishing into history like a nobody, a non-person. After all, he, Max, he, Maximilian had tried to kill the second Adolf Hitler. He, Max, was the second Colonel Claus von Stauffenberg. He, Max, had gone to the second Wolf's Lair and tried to kill the wolf.

The last thought almost made him laugh out loud. Who would believe him? No one.

No one except Diana and Martin.

Max returned to the patio table and set down the two coffee mugs. He sat once more in his chair and hooked the curved handle of the cane onto the edge of the table. It was a very nice cane Diana had found for him in the Quito outdoor market place. It was the color of redwood and shiny with varnish. It had good balance and could be used as a weapon if Max ever got into a tight spot if he ever went into the city again.

"Max! I must tell you. The school has informed me that if I work until age sixty-five they will completely indemnify me. They are offering us a pension, Max!"

Diana studied his face, his eyes. Max was far away...he was with his father at the Flughafen near Linz, in Austria...and it was a warm, sunny day in the early spring...and later his father would buy a waffle pastry for his son and an extra for his wife.

Diana leaned over, kissed Max's cheek, and squeezed his hand.

Max turned to admire the patio wall the man and his son had built a few months ago. It was a nice wall, a good wall made of stones and stucco. It would keep Max and Diana from ever falling from their small South American terrace.

Max wished he could plant some flowering vines to decorate the wall. But the cliff beneath the wall was far too steep and the earth much too shallow.

COLD RAIN

Ethan opened the drapes in the family room and peered into the cold, dark, rainy night. It wasn't like Elizabeth to be this late. It was nearly 10 p.m.

And it was indeed a cold rain falling—-it was late November and the rain in late November, in Kalamazoo, in Southwest Michigan was always cold. Cold rain made a man or woman imagine what he or she would do if there was no house, no shelter, no warm clothes, no raincoat, no foul weather gear, no water, food, and medicines.

Ethan closed the drapes and returned to the kitchen and checked the slow cooker. He'd made some chili for this cold, rainy night. But he'd held back a little on the spices. Too many always made him have weird dreams. Elizabeth could always add spices of her own. Spices didn't give her weird dreams at all. And Elizabeth could sleep like a baby anywhere, no matter what she'd eaten for supper. Elizabeth could sleep on top of a rock or on a cold sheet of galvanized steel. Well, she could if she had proper bedding. She always slept better than he when they went camping, too.

Thinking of sleeping atop cold metal made him think about the coal bin in the basement of the farmhouse they'd rented. He wondered if the day, or night, would come when they would need to go there, escape there.

Ethan lifted the lid and stirred the chili with a long-handle spoon. He sampled his recipe. It was good. His chili was the best. Besides, there was no one here to argue about it. His chili was the best because he said so. And it tasted even better when Elizabeth and he had gone camping out west, especially all those years ago when the kids were young and they'd camped in the Bitterroots of Idaho and Montana. That was a trip to remember—-except for those three days and nights of cold rain. They'd made it down off those mountains without anyone getting hurt. It was one of those things that can happen in the wilderness.

That was the last time Ethan and Elizabeth had camped in cold rain. But it could happen again. Oh yes, it could happen again. At least the kids wouldn't be there. They were all grown up now and living on their own with kids of their own. Their son had just entered medical school. It was 2021 already.

Anno Domini 2021. November. Cold rain. 10 p.m.

Ethan opened the drapes in the family room once more. He'd heard a car's engine. He closed the drapes quickly, hoping she'd not noticed they were open. But of course she had. Elizabeth didn't miss anything he did. And sometimes she'd tell him he worried too much.

Elizabeth was just pulling into the driveway from the street lined with giant barren trees—-oaks and maples that must have been planted more than a hundred years ago. He listened for the garage door. It would be confirmation that it was her...of course it was her.

Ethan returned to the kitchen again and waited for Elizabeth to enter the mudroom off the garage, hang up her raincoat, take off her boots, and put on her slippers. He counted the seconds, although he already knew exactly how long it would be until she came into the kitchen to see what he'd made for supper—-and if he was the late one, she would do the same as she waited from him. Whoever got home first made the supper. That was their arrangement. Ethan liked it, he liked their little rituals, their habits. And he liked a Crockpot full of mouth-watering chili on a cold rainy night.

And he was glad they'd begun to prepare. The world was coming undone. They knew it. And they knew they had to get ready. They had to stockpile supplies somewhere. Out west maybe? Somewhere in the Rockies, somewhere nobody would think to look. Somewhere they could take their kids and grandkids—-but would their kids go along with it? Would they believe their parents? Would they? These were difficult questions for such a night filled with cold rain and worries.

"Sorryyy...I should have called...I..."

"It's all right, Elizabeth. Look."

Ethan lifted the lid to the slow cooker and the delicious vapor rose almost to the ceiling.

"Mmmm..."

"And it's the best..."

"Of course it is, Ethan. Everyone knows that."

"Cold rain, Elizabeth."

"Yeah...cold rain."

They sat quietly at the bistro table in the breakfast nook off the kitchen and sipped the steaming hot chili from their over-size soup spoons until Elizabeth finally spoke.

"One of my patients, a woman in her late thirties named Meredith, came in for her twenty-week check up. Afterwards she wanted to talk. She wanted to tell me about a trip to Europe she and her husband had taken years ago. She was my last patient of the day so I let her talk. I thought it was kind of strange—-she's a strange woman, I've never quite figured her out—-anyway, like I said, I thought it was weird and kind of intriguing why she would want to tell me about a trip to Europe in 2010. That's already eleven years ago, Ethan."

"Eleven years..." Ethan dipped his soup spoon into the chili and said it again. "Eleven years..."

"She told me about this couple from Germany or maybe it was Austria. They'd met the man on the train and then met his wife a few days later in Zurich, at their hotel, and they had dinner and wine and..."

Elizabeth shivered. The cold rain seemed to have gotten into her bones.

"And?"

"And the Austrian or German couple told Meredith and her husband, Ryan, about this guy...this madman...this horrible monstrous fiend...this crazy man living in a villa in the Alps. The crazy man was trying to kill them..."

"Who was trying to kill whom?"

"The crazy madman was trying to kill the European couple. He was looking for them. They'd stolen his car. The wife had driven the car to Zurich and met her husband there but the husband had been on the same train as my patient and her husband."

"Elizabeth? Why does this matter on a cold rainy night in 2021 in Michigan?"

"The European guy, the man they'd met on the train, told them it was all in the prophecies—-it was all prewritten."

Elizabeth knew that would help explain, perhaps, why this mattered. Anything to do with the prophecies always mattered to Ethan. He had been studying the prophets for many years. And she and her husband had had long discussions about what they would do if they were alive when the Apocalypse began. They'd discussed how they would explain it to their children. That was the hardest part of learning so much, of studying so much, of knowing too much, perhaps. How does a man, a woman, a father, a mother tell their children, their family, their friends that he or she thinks the Apocalypse has begun?

The cold rain was beating hard against the roof. It was beating hard against the windows too, and making a spattering-clattering sound. Elizabeth shivered again, and again was glad they had a warm house—-a lovely house in a nice, secure neighborhood in Kalamazoo in Michigan. Ethan and she had worked so hard to become doctors, to become specialists. They'd gone deep into debt to finance their undergrad degrees and later they gone deeper yet to finance medical school. But now, everything was paid off—-their education, the kids' education, the house...they had two beautiful Mercedes, a silver one for Ethan, and a silver one for Elizabeth. They could afford nice vacations, they could afford another airplane...if they ever decided to purchase one again. Life was pretty good despite all the problems in the world.

They thanked God they had a life that was better than most. And, at the same time, they felt sorry for the less fortunate that had to suffer, going without things because of inflation and unemployment and an array of other reasons...some people just make bad choices in life.

But this life of Doctors Ethan and Elizabeth in Kalamazoo was pretty good on this cold, rainy night. Ethan would wonder, often, how long things could continue like this.

"Go on..." Ethan said it and waited.

"The European couple paid Meredith and Ryan to take the car to Italy...to Bari. They paid them a lot of money. Meredith said it was enough to pay for their whole trip with money to spare."

"How much money?"

"Ten thousand euros."

"To drive a car to some Italian city?"

"Yes. To take a nice BMW 650i Coupe to Bari, Italy and abandon it on a back street and walk away. The European guy was insistent. He made them promise to walk away immediately...to leave Bari immediately. "

"Okay...a BMW 650i was a beautiful car...and ten thousand euros would have been about thirteen or fourteen thousand dollars back then...and they were told just to leave it? Just to abandon the car?"

"Yes. But they didn't leave Bari, immediately, like their European friend had insisted. Meredith said it was her fault. She talked her husband into staying in Bari for several days to sightsee and shop."

"What was her fault? Hanging out in an Italian city to see the sights and shop, eat Italian food, with lots of free money in their pocket? That sounds pretty good to me."

"Things went wrong, Ethan. Very wrong...if..." Elizabeth was struggling for the right words.

"If?"

"If I...if we are to believe what she said next."

"What did she say next?"

"Before I tell you, let's wash these dishes and then get comfortable in the family room. I'll finish the story there."

They cleaned up everything, changed into their pajamas, and sat down on the big couch in the family room as the cold rain kept falling and falling as the wind began to blow harder and harder. Snow was forecast for tomorrow. The cold rain would change into snow. Ethan hoped there wouldn't be a big snowstorm. He wished the rain would stay rain. He wished a lot of things these days. He sent an arrow prayer up to heaven, a prayer for the children and any grandchildren they would have.

"So they stayed in Bari..."

"Yes. And Ryan became more upset every day. And they were having an argument in a cafe' and Ryan suddenly said that they should go back to the car to check on it once more. Meredith said he suggested it so they'd stop arguing...so they'd have something else to think about for a while...and they go to the car and there's this guy dressed in black looking into the car window..."

"The madman?"

"No...I mean, I'm not sure...anyway, they hid inside a doorway across the street...to watch...and the man in black waved his arm over the car and the car disappeared."

"Elizabeth..."

"I already know what you're thinking, Ethan. She's a strange woman, she's crazy, maybe. She hallucinates...maybe..."

"Finish the story...I want to catch the news before bed..."

"They freaked out, Ethan...and then the guy in black looks up and down the street...and he looks straight at them and Ryan grabs his wife and they take off running but he lost the car keys...they dropped out of his pocket...he'd not left them with the car...and they kept running and running back to the center of the city...they had to rest...they sat on a bench...and the guy appeared out of thin air on another bench a few feet away...and the guy was dangling the lost keys...and then the guy reappeared right in front of them...and told them he can make them disappear like the car...but there were a couple of police officers nearby so the man or ghost or whatever disappeared again... and that was the last time

they saw him...they left Bari right after this happened...they left Italy, they left Europe...they flew home to Michigan...they were frightened out of their mind...Meredith never told anyone until today..."

Ethan was speechless. He didn't know what to say to such a wild, crazy story like this.

"Ethan. Ryan made a video. Meredith showed it to me...the car disappeared...Ryan made a copy...Meredith gave it to me...I have it...on a disc...it's in my handbag."

"What?"

"I have a copy of the video Ryan made of the guy dressed in black waving his arm and making the BMW vanish. Ryan made the video with his smart phone."

"Okay...let's watch it."

Elizabeth went to retrieve her handbag and Ethan looked at the clock on the opposite wall. The news had already started.

The video was rather blurry but not blurry enough to ruin the scene of a backstreet in Italy. Ethan thought he could hear a muffled voice or two...and there...there was a man in black standing next to a silver BMW...the man was looking around and looking inside the car...and...

The man waved his arm.

The BMW was gone.

The video ended.

Ethan played it again...and again...and again. He played it four times.

He played it a fifth time.

"Trick."

"Yeah? Like a magic trick, Ethan?"

"I could have it analyzed professionally."

"No..."

"Why not?"

"She made me promise not to show it to anyone except you."

He replayed the video. The car vanished again.

"It looks...real...convincing...but it can't be...real. Nobody can do that."

"No human can."

"You don't think he's human?"

Elizabeth shrugged.

Ethan picked up the TV remote and pressed the button. The news was still on.

There was a man in a really nice dark blue suit, dark red tie and white shirt giving a speech or a press conference maybe. He was in his late 40s, maybe. He was saying something about the Israelis and Iranians and Russia and the United States and China and India...and geopolitics and global something or other.

"Elizabeth. Look at this guy. Look at his face, his hair, eyes...watch how he moves his hands and arms..."

It was a little difficult for Elizabeth to change subjects so quickly—-going from a video of a man in black and a car vanishing to another video of a man in a blue suit giving a speech.

"Ethan, what am I supposed to see?"

Ethan didn't answer right away as the cold rain beat on the roof and against the windows and on the world.

"I've seen him before..."

Elizabeth leaned forward and stared at the man on television.

"You probably have. We all have. These politicians and diplomats and talking heads are all over the media. They're like Hollywood people...always craving attention."

Now the TV was showing a complete head to toe image of the man standing at the podium. The man seemed to be looking directly at Elizabeth. It was creepy. Really, really creepy...those eyes...

Ethan turned off the TV. They'd seen enough for tonight. They'd seen enough for many nights and days and nights. And it was time for bed.

An hour later Elizabeth asked: "Do you think we'll be here when it happens?"

A minute later Ethan answered: "I don't know...we don't know...but we must be ready..."

Ethan went to the bedroom window and parted the curtains. The cold rain had stopped and it was beginning to snow.

CPSIA information can be obtained
at www.ICGtesting.com
Printed in the USA
LVOW12s0425191217
560227LV00003B/272/P

9 781457 531729